I'M FINE...THANKS

JAHQUEL J.

JAHQUEL J'S CATALOG:

Series:

In Love With The King Of Harlem 1-5
To All The Thugs I loved That Didn't Love Me Back 1-4
Never Wanted To Be Wifey 1-2
Crack Money With Cocaine Dreams 1-2
All The Dope Boys Gon Feel Her 1-2
Good Girls Love Hustlas 1-3
I Got Nothing But Love For My Hitta 1-2
She Ain't Never Met A N*gga Like Me 1-3
A Staten Island Love Letter 1-5
Married To A Brownsville Bully 1-3
BAE: Before Anyone Else 1-3
Ghetto Love Birds
Homies, Lovers + Friends 1-5
Confessions Of A Hustla's Housekeeper 1-3
Thugs Need Love 1-3
A Staten Island Love Story 1-2
What A Wicked Way To Treat The Woman That Loves You 1-2
A Staten Island Love Story 1-3

Spin-offs:

In Love With An East Coast Maniac 1-3
A Staten Island Love Affair 1-3
A Brownsville, Harlem + Staten Island Holiday Affair
Rose In Harlem: Harlem King's Princess
Confessions Of A Hustla's Daughter 1-2

<u>Standalones:</u>
I Can't Be The One You Love
I'm Riding With You Forever
Forever, I'm Ready
Emotionless
It's Always Been You, Baby Girl
Homies, Lovers + Wives: A Homies, Lovers + Friends Spinoff.
I'm Fine... Thanks.

KEEP UP WITH ME:

Join my mailing list here + check out my website for
autographed paperbacks:
JOIN HERE!
www.Jahquel.com
Join my official reading group
Jahquel J's we reading or nah group?
Be sure to bless my page with a LIKE!
Subscribe To My YouTube Channel:
Subscribe to my YouTube Channel
(I promise new content is coming on there.)
CONNECT WITH ME ON SOCIAL MEDIA:
http://www.instagram.com/_Jahquel
http://www.twitter.com/Author_Jahquel
https://www.tiktok.com/@_iamjah
Join my text message gang by texting me:
917-809-4238
When writing my books, I run off coffee, anxiety + overthinking.
Like to contribute to my coffee habit? You can purchase me a
coffee hereeee!

SYNOPSIS:

I wasn't supposed to take on any new clients.

All my current couples were already a handful.

A marriage therapist with a failing marriage.

If only they knew.

That is until Kami Lynn walked into my office *without* her husband.

I only treated couples.

I was supposed to help save her marriage. Instead, I was the main reason for its destruction.

I did everything the way I was supposed to.

I graduated college.

Went straight into my career.

Got married and had a few crotch goblins and even accepted an outside baby for that man.

Then why am I sitting on my couch with a bottle of wine, bills scattered all over the kitchen table and divorce papers that I have been prolonging on giving my husband?

So, no... I don't need any help. I'm fine... thanks.

*Lennox Hills, New Jersey, is a fictional town.

Every woman deserves princess treatment.
Everyone woman deserves to be filled the same way she pours into others.
Everyone woman deserves to be the priority.
You're the prize. The blueprint. Always remember that.
Xo, Jah

ONE
DR. ASTORIA JACOBS

WHEN MELANIE FIONA WROTE THE SONG 4AM, SHE MUST HAVE been thinking about me and my husband. I mean, she had to have this scene that I was currently living in her brain when she jotted those words down in that studio. I sat up in my king-sized bed with my arms folded while waiting for my husband to disarm the security alarm and come trailing his no-good ass into our bedroom. I could usually excuse it if he was out on his usual Thursday night out with the boys.

Except today was Wednesday, and this man had been gone all day without a single phone call. I tried calling him a few times in between my clients, but he never answered. All I got was some vague ass text message about going out after work. The problem wasn't that he was going out after work; it was *who* he was going out with after work.

Me and Jace had done this whole song and dance our entire relationship, and my hips were sore from doing the same tired ass two step within this relationship. I could always tell when he was sniffing behind some new pussy. This man had a whole routine of shit that he did, so I always knew what he was up to.

Keeping up with his hair cuts.

Buying new clothes and suddenly using colognes during the week.

When the AmEx notification pinged onto my phone, letting me know he had eaten at Mr. Chow's, I nearly lost my mind. This man hated anytime I picked Mr. Chow's as an option for date night, so for him to willingly want to go there, I knew something was up. Instead of calling his ass to curse him out or pulling up to the restaurant like I usually would have, I practiced what I usually drilled into my client's mind. *A hot head will have cold actions.*

In this very moment, as I lay in our bed with my laptop opened, waiting for his ass to climb those stairs to our master suite, my words were frozen on the top of my tongue. I wanted to jump out this bed screaming and put hands on this husband of mine. I had been cheated on plenty of times to know when he was up to something, and there was something in my gut that was telling me he was up to the same shit.

When we decided to give our relationship a fighting chance, I let everything go. There was no need to go into this new chapter with the old shit I had been feeling. We had two daughters who deserved to witness happy parents.

We deserved to be happy parents.

Jace had gotten in good with the union on his construction job, so everything was good. When he suggested that we move to Lennox Hills, New Jersey, I was hesitant about it. It was a new upcoming town, and I wasn't sure that I wanted to leave the fast-paced life that we lived in New York City. Even though I complained often about the city, I loved my city and couldn't envision living anywhere else. Jace told me that it was a great opportunity and that we could finally buy a house and get married.

When he mentioned marriage, I was all ears.

All I had ever wanted to do was be married. I birthed two kids for this man without a ring, so I needed that ring. I wanted to prove both my mother and sister wrong about my relationship. For so long, Jace had me out here looking like a damn fool to them. They didn't understand why I was putting myself in this situation when I didn't have to be.

At the time, I was in my last year of college with an internship with a very well-known practice, so I could have left him and probably would have been better off.

I stayed.

I wanted to believe that we were building something bigger, and truthfully, I wanted to give Jace a chance. He was so used to people counting him out that I wanted to show him that I believed in him.

I wasn't counting him out.

I believed in him so much that I stopped believing in myself in the process. The hold this man had on me was stronger than the woman that had Gorilla Glue stuck in her hair. Every time I tried to break free of him, I felt like my heart yearned for him more, so I held onto him tighter.

Here it was fifteen years later, and I was waiting up for him like I would when we were in our twenties. A man that doesn't mean you any good doesn't change his patterns; he just changes his location.

We weren't kids anymore trying to raise babies. Our lives were combined, and we had a mortgage, car notes, insurance and all the shit that came with married folks. I was so deep in my irritation that I hadn't noticed my client sent me an email.

Just as I opened the email and was about to hit reply, one of the double doors to our room opened. Jace staggered into the room, shocked to see me still up and working. I usually went to bed around nine so I could wake up early enough to work out and have a little time for myself.

As a mother, you needed that time to yourself. With two teenage girls, I was in desperate need of some peace and quiet before the two of them woke up and started bickering with each other.

"What you doing up?" He asked while crossing in front of

the TV to get to our bathroom. The clothes he had left with this morning weren't the clothes he was walking across our bedroom in.

"Had a few things to tie up before going to bed."

"Oh. Everything alright?"

Whenever Jace started asking if everything was alright, he knew that it wasn't. Nothing was ever right in our home or marriage, and he was the reason.

"I don't know… is it?"

Jace huffed as he took a seat on the ottoman in front of our bed. "We about to start that arguing shit, Astoria?"

"I'm asking a simple question. I didn't raise my voice, so why does it have to turn into an argument?"

"You stay trying to do that damn mind shit you do with your clients. I'm not one of your clients, Astoria." He raised his voice, stood up and went into the bathroom.

I shook my head because he was forever making something out of nothing. The guilt oozed off his body, telling me that he had been up to no good.

I quickly responded to my client and logged out of my computer. There was no need to sit and argue with my husband tonight. He was always going to toss the blame back onto me.

It was always my fault.

I didn't try hard enough, or I was always too consumed with work. At one point, he blamed me because I spent too much time with the girls. What kind of father became jealous over the amount of time I was spending with our girls? There was never an exact reason for why he felt some way or why he decided to step outside of our marriage.

All I knew is that the last time he did, he brought a son home to me. Back then, I should have left when I found out he had got another woman pregnant. Enzo, our youngest daughter, was only a few months old when I found the picture of the little boy in that infamous hospital blanket.

Jace hid that bitch's pregnancy from me for the entire nine

months. Enzo and his son were only a couple months apart. I told myself that I was going to leave. I tried to convince myself that I could do it without him. Jace brought more problems than joy to my life, and with two daughters under two, I didn't need the drama.

Instead of leaving and choosing myself, I refused to leave and let her have him. I didn't want to give her the satisfaction of saying that she took my man away from me and our daughters. So, like a fool, I went with him to meet his son and talk about how things would work between the three of us.

I hated myself for it.

Why did I allow this man to have such a hold over my heart the way he did? Fifteen years later, and I'm still that weak, insecure, and naive nineteen-year-old who hung onto every word that fell from his lips.

I wanted to leave my husband. I truly did. Neither one of us was happy and was just pretending for the sake of our daughters. Date nights were far and few, and we stopped having fun with each other.

Every time I worked up the nerve and courage to leave, it was like he got an alert on his phone, and that was when he tried harder. I would come home to flowers and dinner already made. Or we would go out of town and have the time of our lives.

It never lasted though.

As quick as it started was when it ended. Jace knew he was like my drug, and I couldn't be without him for long. I had never had to be without him, so I didn't even know what the feeling felt like. Our love was compared to crack cocaine. I knew it was bad for me and had me looking all strung out and stupid, but the high just felt so good that I didn't want to come down from it.

I used to pride myself on us never breaking up or being on and off during our relationship. As an adult, I wished we had done the on and off thing. Then I would have known what it would feel like to be without him. It wouldn't be so hard to break ties with this man.

He was like a leech sucking the life out of me. No matter how many times I made up my mind to leave, I was still sitting up in this bed waiting for him to finish his shower so he could come to bed. Jace had a few drinks, so I knew he would sweet talk himself between my legs, and I would allow him.

I was such a fool for him.

His smell, swagger, and voice used to make me weak to my knees. It was his rich brown complexion, hazel bedroom eyes, thick pillow lips and full beard that made me so weak. As much as I wanted to get off this toxic rollercoaster, he was all I had known since I was seventeen years old.

Our daughters were always at the forefront of all my decisions. Would they forgive me for leaving their father?

As much as they were mommy's girls, they did love their father. All they knew was us being together. As teenagers, how would they react to going through a divorce?

One week with their father.

The next week with me.

This wasn't as easy as signing the papers and being done with each other. There were so many other things that needed to be worked out in a divorce, the important thing being our kids.

All day I sat and listened to couples go on about their relationships and even helped some discover that divorce was the better option for their unions. Yet, I couldn't even convince myself to do the same thing. I couldn't tell myself that I deserved to be happy and fulfilled than continue on in this marriage. It had been so long since I had been happy or fulfilled.

The shower turned off, and I heard him drying himself off while humming. It wasn't long before he came out wearing his favorite pajamas shorts.

"Turn the TV off. You know I hate sleeping with that shit on," he demanded as he climbed into our bed.

Switching the TV off, I turned onto my side and pulled the covers over me. Like I knew, Jace pulled me over toward his side, while wrapping his arms around me.

"Is there someone else, Jace?" I whispered.

"Huh? What? Stori, you always thinking it's someone else... I went out to eat with Messiah," he lied.

Messiah was married to my best friend, Ember.

Well, at least he used to be.

It wasn't like I could call Ember and ask her if Messiah went out with Jace tonight. He knew that, which is why he was so comfortable with using him as his alibi.

"Okay."

He kissed me on the cheek. "I love you, Stori. Stop letting that big ass brain of yours get in the way of that."

As women, we knew better. God literally gave us this special gift that told us when something wasn't right. Why, as women, did we choose to ignore that and believe the person who was causing that feeling in the first place? I had this feeling deep down in the pit of my stomach that Jace was back to his shenanigans again. Just because I couldn't prove it, didn't mean that it wasn't happening.

I took a deep breath and closed my eyes. "You alright?"

"I'm fine... thanks," I replied as I got as comfortable as I was going to get tonight. My stomach was in knots, my spirit was disturbed, and the only time that happened was when something was wrong.

I MARRIED this man because it was what felt right at the time. My mother had never been married, so I wanted different for myself and my girls. Marriage was a sense of stability to me.

Though I loved Jace Mitchell, I should have never gotten married, and damn sure shouldn't have spit out not one, but two kids for him to turn around and cheat on me. Like a fool, I stuck around while helping him raise a baby that came out of another woman. He did all the usual apologies, sobs and begging me not to leave him. And like a fool, I was putty in his hands.

We didn't just have one daughter now, we had two, and they needed him. Truth be told, I needed him too, and I refused to let that other woman win, so I pulled up my big girl panties and decided to get married to him. Even with me knowing this man didn't deserve any part of me.

No sooner than we got back together, I fell pregnant with our third child, which resulted in a miscarriage. I was so torn and broken about losing our baby. However, now that I had some years to reflect, it was a blessing disguised as a tragedy.

As I watched him guzzle down his coffee – black – and grab his work boots, I hated how we had become in this marriage. This marriage had ended the moment that he decided to cheat on me. The only reason this marriage was still alive was because I didn't have the courage to end it. We had both become too comfortable with the life we built to end it. I mean, why would he end this marriage?

He was allowed to do whatever he wanted without ever having to take responsibility for it. Jace fucked whoever he wanted and then came home to climb between my legs. And I always allowed it. The cracks in our marriage were starting to show, and I was so busy trying to plaster them up instead of allowing them to crumble.

What was the purpose of saving this?

Last night I should have told him what was on my mind. Instead, I allowed him to talk his way out of it like he usually did. When he pulled me into his arms, I should have resisted until he told me the truth.

I folded.

Like I always did.

This morning, he was so chipper. Like all was great in the world. "Our anniversary is next month... I was thinking we should get out of town," Jace's voice jolted me from my thoughts.

Our anniversary had been something that had been lingering over my head for the past few months. When my mother offered to come over to stay with the girls, I wanted to scream *no*. I wasn't in the mood to celebrate another year of unhappiness with this man. Another year of gaslighting and lies.

"Sounds fun," I replied, not really knowing how to respond to the offer.

It wasn't often that me and Jace did anything together. Our date nights had faded away quickly, and whenever we did have time away from the kids, it wasn't like we spent it together. Jace was quick to take a shower and head out with his boys, and I usually threw myself into my work or a quick dinner with my sister and best friend. Our conversations didn't flow the way that they used to. There used to be a time when I never wanted to be away from my man, but those days had faded away the moment he continued to betray my trust and play in my face about it.

"Damn, Astoria, you could act excited. We are going to be celebrating fourteen years, and you're acting like it's another damn day."

I wanted to tell him that our anniversary was just a regular day for us. It wasn't like we celebrated one another often, so why pretend like this one day was so important? Only for him to go back to acting like he normally acted.

I emptied my cup of coffee into the sink and drew a breath. "What do you want me to do? Jump up and down and celebrate something that's a month away?"

I didn't mean to snap, but I was tired of him always expecting me to be excited about shit that he was supposed to do or know. I wasn't excited for our anniversary, and it hadn't crossed my mind until he mentioned it this morning.

"Man, it's always something," he complained as he stood up to fix his clothes. "I'm gonna be late tonight... don't wait up."

It was Thursday, and Jace never came straight home after work on Thursdays. That was the day he went out with the guys to let loose. He worked hard, so I never complained about him having that one day to spend time with his friends.

"Another night out? Didn't you and Messiah see one another last night?"

According to my husband, he went out with Messiah last night. Why was there a need to go out on Thursday when the two of them linked the night before? This is what I meant about his lies. He was so sloppy with them, and he never cared to clean them up.

"Is Messiah my only friend?" He snapped. "You're acting like I don't have other friends that I hang out with."

What bothered me was how he only looked forward to Thursdays. It was like he watched the calendar just for Thursday to come. In between those days, he never made time for me or the girls. It was always about work and how tired he was. Miraculously, on Thursdays, he always mustered enough energy to hang out until the early hours of the morning. I asked him to carve out a day for us to have date nights consistently.

He never did.

Jace would climb into the bed smelling like liquor and weed and soon fall asleep without so much as a conversation. I used to look forward to his guy nights when he would climb into the bed high with a hint of liquor on his tongue, then slide between my legs while making me feel like the most beautiful woman in the world. It was hard to leave Jace because when he was on, he was on. He had a way of making me feel like no other bitch could fuck with me. Like, he picked me out of all the women that he could have wife'd.

It sounded stupid and made sense to me at the same time. That was when I looked forward to his Thursday nights with his boys.

Now, it was much more of a headache. By morning, he would be too hungover to get up early to help carpool the girls to school. The mornings when he was able to get them out the door were the best for me. I lived for a silent morning when I could hear my thoughts without the sounds of the girls bickering with each other. With Jace taking the girls to school, it freed up time so I could grab a cup of coffee and actually have time to consume it before it became cold.

It was always something between the two of them, and I ended up having to get in between so we could make it to the school drop-off in time. Jace never intervened or gave a shit to make them stop.

Instead of replying to him, I decided to focus on getting our daughters out the door. "Girls, come on. I want to make it before the carpool line gets crazy."

Jace headed toward the side kitchen door. "Alright, I'm gone... see you tonight," he called over his shoulder and closed the door behind him.

After promising the girls that I would take them to Starbucks for a week, I was finally at the office and ready to welcome in my first client of the day. With the morning I was having, I needed to sit on my own couch and have someone analyze my own relationship problems.

A marriage therapist with a failing marriage, if only my clients knew.

"Good morning, Stori... one of those mornings?" Kyle, my colleague, asked as I grabbed a fresh mug from the cabinet.

With all that I had to do and promise to get out the door in time, I didn't even have time to snag me a coffee or latte from Starbucks. "It's always one of those mornings," I groaned and waited for the Keurig to spit coffee into my mug.

`Kyle sat at the small break table and crossed his legs. "Are you and Jace going through it again?"

"When aren't we going through it? He brought up our anniversary and then got upset because I wasn't all that excited about it."

Kyle took a sip of his coffee. "All you ever tell me is how you want your marriage to work. Why aren't you excited about your anniversary? Those are events that are supposed to bring you joy."

Kyle may have started out as my colleague, however, he

quickly turned into a great friend too. He was always down to sit and chat about my life whenever I needed it, and I did the same for him.

Today, I wasn't in the mood to discuss the demise of my marriage.

I didn't need to be put in my place because I was truly drained with my marriage and my husband. Our anniversary wasn't something that I became excited about anymore. It was just another day and another reminder that we made it another year without killing each other.

"Not in the mood today, Kyle," I warned him as I tossed a few sugar cubes into my coffee and then breezed out of the break room.

Kyle never took no for an answer, so he was right behind me as I headed down the hall. We rounded the corner, and my client, was already seated and waiting for me. "You're so lucky," he mumbled as he spun on his heels and headed back to the break room.

Bethany, my assistant, turned to face me. "Your nine-thirty is here, Dr. Jacobs."

"Good morning, Grace. Give me a few seconds, and I'll call you in," I spoke directly to my client.

From her disheveled hair and the trench coat she wore, I could tell the dinner with her soon to be ex-husband didn't turn out the way that she hoped that it would have.

"Can I get you some coffee or water?" I heard Bethany ask Grace as I closed my office door behind me.

I sat my coffee at my desk and started to refresh my office before welcoming Grace in. When I saw her appointment had been added to my schedule last night, I knew something went wrong with her dinner.

"Bethany, you can send Grace in," I said over the intercom, and took my seat in the plush leather chair that was situated by the window.

I loved this position because I was able to see my clients

perfectly without them looking at whatever I was jotting down, which was mostly nothing anyway. The window gave me the perfect view of my car and the perfect autumn trees that were starting to lose their leaves.

Bethany opened the door, allowing Grace to file in behind her. "Have a great session," Bethany replied before closing the door behind her.

Grace whipped off her trench coat, tossed it on the couch and bounced right next to it. She ran her hand through her greasy blonde hair before resting her arms on her knees while staring at me.

"We're not due to see one another until next week. What changed?"

Grace was antsy.

She was always like that though, so that wasn't something out of the norm for her. What was out of the norm was the way she showed up dressed. Grace wasn't the type that threw on yoga pants and was good with her outfit choice. Ever since she had been referred to me, I had always seen her dressed to the nines without a hair out of place.

"The dinner was pointless. He still wants to continue with the divorce... I thought the dinner would solve everything."

Grace was married to a man that only wanted her youth. The minute, and not a second before, she started popping out his children and actually started to age, that was when her husband lost interest in her.

Grayson, her husband, was used to the fun side of her. The side that he could bring on a boring business trip, and she would make a boring weekend fun with her long blonde hair and tanned slim body.

He wasn't used to the woman she became after their twin sons. Gray wanted the youthful woman who only cared about shopping and pleasing him. Grace had been so consumed with being a wife and a mother to their boys that she looked up one day and realized that her husband had fell out of love with her.

The monetary support was still there; however, he had emotionally checked out of their marriage. Grayson sat across from me many times, and I could tell that his wife didn't do it for him anymore. He loved his sons because they were his children. I could tell that if he had a voice in the decision to keep those boys, he wouldn't have kept them.

"The dinner was a suggestion, Grace. You knew that Grayson wanted the divorce before showing up to the dinner."

I kept it real with my clients, which is why they kept me around to help them work through their problems. Grace leaned back on the couch and crossed her legs.

"I guess there was some part of me that thought he would change his mind." She started to chew on her unkept manicure.

"Oh, God… what if there's another woman? Grayson's eyes always wander. I don't want to be the ex-wife with his kids. I want to be his wife!" Tears streamed down her face.

I wished as women, we realized that we were the prize and we shouldn't allow men to play in our faces the way that they normally did. Grayson for sure had another woman he was entertaining. He revealed it to me during our private session, and because what he said was privileged information, I couldn't tell Grace about this new woman.

This was the reason I spent our sessions trying to get her to see her worth. Although Grayson saw the blonde hair and big boobs, she was more than that. Grace was a successful real estate agent before she quit to become *his* wife. She had lived a life before this man, and she had accomplished it without him.

I wanted her to realize that she could do it again without him. The only difference is she would receive spousal support and child support, which would make it easier than the first time.

"Why do you want a man that doesn't want you?"

She paused and looked at me. "Grayson told you that he doesn't want me?"

I sighed. "No. All his actions toward you are telling me that he doesn't want you, Grace. He doesn't come home some nights, stopped attending our marriage sessions, and has basically told you out his own mouth that he doesn't want to be married anymore."

Grayson had done everything that I should have been doing with my own husband. He was honest with his wife, even if it hurt, and Grace refused to acknowledge it. She thought by being the perfect wife and mother it would change his mind.

"I don't want a failed marriage. Are you married, Astoria?"

"Dr. Jacobs," I corrected her. "And this isn't about me."

I made a rule a long time ago that I would never involve my personal life into my career. When you came into my office, it was minimally designed with my degrees hanging on the wall. I didn't have any pictures of my family because I wanted to keep that private. Every time Grace came into her sessions, she tried to get me to relate to her or pull some information out of me.

"How would you feel if you gave ten years of your life to a man, and he turns around, and wants a divorce?"

It was better than giving fifteen to a man who turned around and cheated on you whenever he felt like it. I knew I couldn't say that, so I took a sip of my coffee.

It was my turn to lean forward. "Men suck, Grace. We've discussed this and some of the things that you've gone through with Grayson. Do you truly want your sons to grow and see their mother unhappy?"

"I don't want them to see their parents unhappy."

"We're not discussing Grayson... it's about you. For so long you've worried about a man that hasn't worried about you. Shall I remind you of when the twins were six months old?"

Her hands covered her face as she sobbed into them.

I hated bringing up the past because I could tell it was painful for her. She needed to see that she was better off without her husband, and since he wanted the divorce, she could use it to her advantage.

When their twins were six months old, he made a comment

about Grace's weight at the twin's christening. She was six months postpartum from having his twin sons, and he was worried about how big she had gotten.

Their twins were now six years old, and that was something that still haunted her. Grayson was a bastard, and because he was well off, she had ignored all the red flags.

"God, I hate to even think of that."

"I'm sorry," I apologized before leaning back in the chair. "Grace, tell me a happy memory that you have with Grayson, outside of your children."

She remained quiet while racking her thoughts. "Um, we went to the Kentucky Derby when we first started dating. Grayson was so excited to introduce me to his friends that he picked my outfit out. He even had someone come do my makeup the way he wanted. All his friends couldn't stop complimenting how beautiful I..." her words trailed off.

"Why did you stop?"

"I've been a Barbie for this man. Someone he could dress up, fuck, and show off whenever he wanted to."

The only thing real about the marriage was their boys, and if Grayson had anything to do with it, they wouldn't have existed. "He wants to put you back on the shelf and find him something new with sparkle. You deserve better than that."

"I do," she whimpered.

Me and Grace spent another twenty minutes discussing what she would do, and how she would stop running whenever Grayson called her. I could tell that she would continue to run to that man whenever he called, but who was I to judge?

I was married to a man that I had fell out of love with and was still holding on because he was all I knew. Love was a messy thing, and because women loved so hard, we ended up being the person who became the messiest in the situation.

No sooner than I scheduled Grace's next session, Kyle came and peeked into my office. "She sure looks better than when she came."

"Means I'm doing my job."

Kyle took a seat on the couch. "I'm worried about you, Stori."

"Why? I'm great," I lied, walking behind my desk.

I was used to lying and saying I was fine. It was something that I had done since a child. Nobody truly cared enough to make sure that was the actual truth.

"You're not great, Honey." He crossed his legs.

"Kyle, I'm not in the mood to discuss what's going on. I'm really tired." I plopped down in my chair.

"You do need to take some time off. Stori, you hardly ever take any time for you. When's the last time you took a vacation?" I started to speak, and he held his hand up. "That doesn't include the time you take off when the girls are out of school."

He had me there. The only time I really took off was when the girls had vacation time off from school. I remember sitting in the house as a child during my Christmas and spring break, so I didn't want the same for my girls. I always rearranged my schedule with their school vacations and holidays so we could spend time together and get out the house.

"You're making it seem like I don't take any time for myself."

"I'm making it seem like that, or is that the case?" Kyle smirked and then looked down at his pinging phone. "Look, my next client is here... you need to do something for you that doesn't include the girls or Jace."

"Noted, Boss." I smiled as he let himself out of my office.

My next client wasn't for another hour, so I quickly grabbed my keys and decided to treat myself to the most expensive drink at Starbucks.

That was doing something for myself.

TWO
DR. ASTORIA JACOBS

"He always does this and then likes to pretend like he does nothing wrong," my client, complained about her husband.

I observed as he sat on the other end of the couch and allowed her to say everything she needed to get out. Not once did he speak out of turn, and he allowed her to speak her peace. When the Mirandas first sat on my couch, I could tell Mrs. Miranda was the problem in their marriage. She constantly spoke over her husband and only listened to respond.

"Taj, do you think you purposely push your wife's buttons?"

He fixed his tie, leaned up and then started to speak, but his wife cut him off again. "Of course, he's not going to say he purposely pushes my buttons."

"You've had your turn to speak, and Taj has allowed you the space to do it. Give your husband the same respect and allow him to speak. This doesn't work unless you're both given the chance and space during your time to speak." I stared Mrs. Miranda in the eyes.

Kia folded her arms and rolled her eyes. "Psst. Peace where?"

Taj ignored his wife and then prepared himself to speak again. "Kia thinks everything I do is pushing her buttons." Kia was bursting at the seams to respond, but one look at me, and she simmered down. "I go to work, come home, and help with the kids. Three times a week, I cook dinner so she can have girl time with her friends. All I want is peace in my house. I'm tired of arguing with you, baby." He turned toward her when he said those words.

I wished my own husband did all of what Taj had described. Jace barely cleaned a dish after he finished using it.

"Hmph, you do all those things because you want me to forget that you cheated on me." It was only a matter of time before she brought up the affair her husband had over three years ago.

"Kia, the moment that you chose to forgive Taj and work on your marriage, we agreed that couldn't be used in arguments. It's not fair or has any standing on the current issues we're dealing with."

I can't pick the kids up. Can you grab them? Jace's text message popped across the screen on my iPad, which I was using to take notes.

I made it a point to look at my watch, signaling that their time was almost up. "It still hurts. Why can't I continue to bring it up?"

"If it hurts, then you should leave." Taj looked like he wanted to rough me up. This was the most emotion he had shown since we started our sessions last year. "Don't stay in something that is physically and emotionally causing you to become a different person."

As their therapist, it wasn't my job to sugarcoat and try to save a marriage that wasn't meant to be saved. I could tell the moment they sat on that couch last year that Kia was trying to hold onto her marriage for the sake of saying she tried to make it work. Sis had been tired and over her husband long before he decided to step outside their marriage.

Kia dabbed her eyes and violently shook her crossed legs. "O...Our children," she stammered.

"Having children together isn't a reason to stay married.

During our session next week, we'll dive more into that... Kia, I'll see you Friday."

I met with both Taj and Kia together and then separately. It was best for me to get to know them separately so I could help them together. Kia was always early to her solo sessions, while Taj was almost always late. His excuse was that he had to drive across town to make it to my office, and he just couldn't make it on time for his appointment.

It was his money that he was wasting, not mine. If he showed up late, I was still compensated for the time we were supposed to spend together.

"Thank you, Dr. Jacobs." Kia collected herself and headed out the door with Taj trailing behind her.

The moment they were gone, I quickly sanitized my couch, grabbed my purse, and breezed by my assistant. "Please move all my appointments to tomorrow."

Bethany quickly stood up in concern. "Is there something wrong?"

"I have to pick my daughter up from dance," I replied and continued out the door to make it to her in time.

Demi hated whenever we were late to pick her up from dance.

If this was a once in a blue moon situation, then I could excuse it. Except, Jace did this almost every other week when it was his turn to pick the kids up from school or their afterschool programs. The Mirandas were still in the parking lot when I came rushing out of the building. I could tell from the swaying of Kia's neck that she was probably getting into her husband's ass for speaking during their therapy session.

Inside Kia's home, it was her world, and everyone else had to deal with it. She couldn't take her husband having an opinion of his own. She wanted him to sit back, be quiet and allow her to have all the feelings.

I'd never say it to her face, but I knew exactly why Taj cheated. When he spoke about his affair, there was a happiness that he just didn't have with his wife. I sat in our solo sessions and listened to how this man spoke on this mistress, and how she listened to him. I wanted to encourage him to leave his wife so that he could have that happiness with the woman that made him smile.

It wasn't my place to suggest something like that.

They were paying me to help make their marriage work, so that was my job and task while having clients like the Mirandas.

Kia didn't want any suggestions on what she should do with her marriage. I was convinced that she made her husband pay my hefty fee just to hear herself talk.

As a child, she didn't have much of a voice. Nobody asked her opinions, and she couldn't voice them either. When she got married to Taj, it was the same way. Kia was a stay-at-home mom that had to deal with whatever was tossed her way. Her husband worked long hours, leaving her with the children all day. When he did come home, it wasn't like they shared deep conversations with each other.

The minute Taj decided to step outside their marriage was all the grounds Kia had for finding that voice. Now that she had it, she refused to quiet it, even if that meant slowly losing her husband in the process. I watched them continue to bicker by Taj's car before pulling away.

They both knew I had a rule that nothing was to be discussed outside of therapy. It was a rule that I implemented to keep couples from going upside each other's heads the moment they stepped outside of my office.

It was clear Kia didn't listen.

Jace's name popped across my car's screen, and I rolled my eyes. Hitting the green phone icon, I drew a breath, and prepared for the excuses he already rehearsed.

"Hey."

"What's up, Babe? Did you receive my text message?"

"Yep."

"You heading there now?"

"Uh huh."

"What's with the dry ass responses, Stori?"

It always killed me how he had the nerve to have an attitude when he was in the wrong. It was like he never wanted me to feel any way about his inconsistencies.

"This is the second time this month, Jace. I can't keep pushing off my clients to pick up the kids whenever you can't get them," I sighed.

"I need to stay behind to write an accident report from today. I just wanted to make sure you received my text because I can't make it over there in time."

"Yeah."

What more did I have to say? I knew I should have been used to it because this always happened. I guess I just wanted him to come through for me this one time.

"What's that about, Astoria?"

He always used my whole name whenever he was becoming irritated. Jace always expected me to just roll with the punches he delivered. As if I was never supposed to be disappointed in him because something had come up. Things always came up in my life and career, and I still managed to be a wife and mother.

"I'm heading to pick her up now. There's no need to get into how I feel."

I was still in my feelings about the other night and had been avoiding talking about it. Jace had this way about him that forced me not to confront him. Every time I confronted him, he turned it around on me.

"See, this that shit I'm talking about," he huffed, annoyed that I decided that I wanted to feel a way about my husband constantly never coming through for me or our daughters.

"Jace, I'm not going to get into it with you. Demi will be picked up, like I always do," I stated.

"The fuck—"

He didn't get the chance to finish his sentence because I had already ended the call. I was tired of him always getting into his feelings when he was the one to blame.

I was always expected to toss my shit to the side because he couldn't come through for me. It was always about Jace and what he had going on. His shit had always taken priority over my stuff. Even when I was in college, it was more important for Jace to make it to work than for me to study for a test.

Then he had the nerve to act like he was the victim in all of this. Demi had been taking dance for the past few years, and her schedule had been pretty consistent. The dance studio was pretty good about announcing any changes to their schedule ahead of time. I marked it down on the shared family calendar and made sure to send a quick text reminding him after he left out the door this morning. He assured me that he would be able to pick her up. Now he was singing a different tune.

I was so over having to do everything myself like I was a single mother. Demi's dance studio was over thirty minutes away from my office. Jace literally had to pass her studio on his way home from work.

No sooner than I ended the call, my best friend's name flashed across the screen of my car. "Shit... I'm sorry, Ember," I answered the phone apologizing.

"See, now I have to pay Harlym money because she knew you would stand us up." She sucked her teeth into the phone.

"It's not my fault. Jace can't pick up Demi, so now I'm racing to pick her up to bring her home. I had to cancel the rest of my clients today."

"Is she still at the dance studio off Rhode Avenue?"

"Yep. Which is at least thirty minutes away from me."

"I will pick up my God daughter... you just meet us for dinner... on time," she made sure to add.

My shoulders relaxed as I leaned my head back while the traffic light was red. "Em, I don't know what I would do without you."

"Good thing you never have to find out... I will see you soon," she replied and ended the call.

I had only gotten about ten minutes away from the office and was glad that I could quickly turn around. I cancelled my other clients for the day to rush and pick Demi up, and now I regretted it.

Instead of climbing into my bed after a few shared drinks with my sister and best friend, I was going to be up trying to rearrange everyone back onto my schedule.

"I thought you had to pick up your daughter?" Bethany leaned forward when she saw me walk back inside the office.

"Ember is going to pick her up."

"I reached out to everyone so we can work late to rearrange everyone on the schedule for tomorrow."

"No, ma'am. You're going to log out so you can get home to your son on time. I will figure everything out tonight when I get home."

Bethany smiled. "Thanks, Astoria."

My assistant was always down to work and do whatever needed to be done. I never had a problem with Bethany ever being late or not doing her job. She was in college while being a single mother, so whatever way I could make things easier for her, I often did it. It wasn't her fault that my husband fucked up the schedule, so why should she stay late to help fix it.

"No problem. Is Kyle still here?"

"Yep. In his office. His last client of the day just left," she replied.

There was three of us that shared this office space. Each office had its own reception area and office, then down the hall was where all the offices connected with the break room. Between Bethany and Kyle's assistant, they kept each up informed on our schedules. Kyle was notorious for accessing my office from the hall to come and sit and chat with me, so today was my turn.

I tapped on his opened door. "Hey, you busy?"

"Hey, you. I would have thought you were still with clients."

He took a quick bite of his sandwich and got comfortable in his chair.

"I had to cancel because Jace couldn't pick up Demi from dance."

Kyle looked at me confused. "Then why are you standing in my office?"

I sat down in one of his comfortable armchairs. "Ember told me she would pick her up and drop her home."

"How does that make you feel?" He questioned while continuing to eat his sandwich.

"We're not about to pretend like I'm one of your clients, Kyle." I rolled my eyes at him while he smirked at me.

"Okay, okay," he laughed. "Seriously, how are you feeling right now?"

"Annoyed. It's one thing that he couldn't make it to pick her up, but he always acts like he's the victim in this. Like my career isn't as important as what he's doing. I had to cancel clients last minute because he sprung this on me."

"I get we need buildings and stuff, but he's a construction worker… his job isn't all that serious," Kyle winched.

I laughed. "You're an asshole."

The only reason Jace became a construction worker was because his father put him on to it. He was busy fucking anything that had legs and neglecting me and Demi in the process. I was the one who was buying diapers and formula because he was never anywhere to be found. It was when his father got him hired at his job that the money started to come in, and he started to come around more.

Being a construction worker was the one job that he had managed to hold down. Every time Jace got a job, he was always fired or quit the next month. He was never at a job long enough to get a damn pay stub. When things were good between us, he would come home so excited to tell me everything that he was doing that day. College was never his thing, it was mine, so I supported him. The money was pretty consistent and more than either of us was used to. With two daughters and me in college, we needed whatever money that we could take.

"All I'm saying is he needs to put some respect on your career too. What you do isn't easy, and if he keeps making you cancel, you're going to lose clients."

"I know," I groaned.

This wasn't the first time that I had to cancel with clients because of my husband's inconsistent ass. I was grateful that all the clients I had were so understanding and willing to work with me when it came to rescheduling them.

"Why do you stick around when you know there's better out there for you?"

It was a question that I often asked myself. Why did I stick around with this man when I knew there was better out there for me?

"Guess that's something that I need to figure out." I stood up, preparing myself to head out of Kyle's office.

"Seems like you need to figure it out quickly. Stori, you deserve to be happy and in love, and if your husband isn't doing that for you, then you need to call it quits. It's not fair to you or him."

"You think I care what's fair to him?" I snapped.

Kyle leaned back in his chair. "If you don't care what's fair to him, then start caring about what is fair to *you*."

"I don't even know what that is anymore." I headed toward the door. "See you tomorrow."

"Later... See you tomorrow," he replied, probably too tired to go back and forth with me.

Whenever I got like this, Kyle knew not to press on and leave me alone. I was so drained and tired from having the same conversations. There were times when I wanted to fight for my marriage, but I was also so damn tired.

Whenever me and Kyle got into heated conversations, it was usually because he was trying to get me to see that I was being foolish. No matter how annoyed I was with him, he was one of my closest friends and one of the only people I allowed to put me in my place about my behavior.

"IF YOU THINK he's fucking another woman, then he probably is." Ember shrugged as she took a sip of her second drink of the night.

"Well, damn," Harlym muttered.

"Way to make me feel better, Em." I rolled my eyes at her.

Ember was outspoken and would tell you about yourself in a quick second. She never sugarcoated anything. That was the reason we've been friends since high school.

Sometimes, I hated how honest she was because her honesty could hurt at times. I knew she meant well, and she was always on my side through whatever I went through. "I'm sorry, Stori. How many times are you going to put up with the same shit from him? When is it going to be enough?"

"Chill, Em," Harlym jumped in.

Even though Harlym was my baby sister, she was always super protective of me and her nieces. She didn't care how stupid I had been over my husband; she was going to always stand beside my stupid ass.

She would just tell me I was being stupid later.

"I just want better for you." She looked over at Harlym. "We all do, even if she doesn't want to admit it right now."

I knew both Harlym and Ember were tired of hearing the same shit from me, and I was honestly so tired of having to tell them. I was always complaining about my marriage. Then I turned right around and allowed this man to continue to do the same shit to me.

Harlym had turned her attention back to her phone. "Who are you texting?" Since I had arrived, she had her face planted into her phone.

"Cam." She blushed.

I rolled my eyes.

"Don't do that. I don't get on your man, so don't do it to me."

Cam was Harlym's on-again/off-again boyfriend who was locked up. One week, she was so in love with him, like today. Then the next week, she would block the prison's number and make subliminal posts so the blogs could chat about their relationship.

"At least her man is home and can give her some dick. Your man is rocking an orange onesie."

"And where's your man?" Harlym quickly replied.

Ember became quiet. "You real cold for that."

"Am I? Me and Cam are together through thick and thin."

"Five years though? Harm, you're twenty-five and have your entire life ahead of you. Waiting five years for Cam is crazy."

"To you. I love Cam and was with him when he was out making money, so I'm going to be with him through his sentence."

"On which day? Because you're forever switching if you wanna be with him or not." Em finally had her come back.

Harlym cut her eyes at Ember before returning her gaze to me. "Anyway, this week, I'm with my man and sticking beside him."

Cam was an underground rapper who had been discovered and signed to a label. But once he was signed to a label; he couldn't leave the streets alone. He was rapping about the stuff he was still out there actively doing. Since he was too new of an artist under the label, his label didn't go to war behind him. He had no other choice but to take a five year plea deal.

I wanted better for my sister because she deserved that. Putting your life on hold for a man that put himself behind bars was crazy. She didn't have a ring, and they didn't have any children, so it didn't make sense why she wanted to wait for him. By the time Cam touched soil on the freedom side, nobody would be worried or asking about his ass. Harlym was so focused on his career and the clout that came with messing with him that she didn't realize she was pausing her life to wait for a man I wasn't sure was even worthy of her loyalty.

"You'll be around our age when he gets out of prison. Girl, do you know how hard it is to get pregnant at my age?" Ember told her.

Ember wanted kids more than anything, and that was one of the many reasons she and Messiah's marriage didn't work out. They had been trying to get pregnant since they had gotten married. After a few miscarriages, I think their signals got crossed, and it meant more to Ember than it did to Messiah. I sat on Em's bathroom floor consoling her after every loss. I wanted my friend to experience motherhood badly, because no matter how stressful it was, it was the most beautiful experience and bond I had ever had.

"At any age. Waiting around for a man who might come home and want someone else sounds ridiculous."

"And being married to one who does whatever the fuck he wants is equally ridiculous," she muttered.

I couldn't even be mad because what she said was true. Jace did whatever he wanted, and I sat there and accepted it because I was so stuck to this man.

"Not fair, Harm," Em butted into the disagreement. "Your sister has nearly fifteen years in with this man... you and Cam don't even compare."

"And what does she have to show for it?"

I already knew where this was going, and I was too drained to go back and forth with Harlym about my relationship with Jace. Every time I tried to step in and be the big sister with advice, she got defensive and would lash out about my situation.

Did she not know that I already knew how fucked up my marriage was? That was why I was trying to save her from making the same mistakes that I did. Jace hadn't been locked up, but I had spent my good years chasing behind a man who clearly didn't want to be chased.

At the end of the day, the only reason he married me was

because he knew I was going to leave after finding out about his son. Jace knew I was fed up. He could feel his hold loosening up, so he tossed marriage in to sweeten the deal and make sure I didn't leave him.

"I just want to have an enjoyable night out... no beef." I took a sip of my wine while silently reminding myself of all I had to do the moment I made it home.

"Sorry," Harlym apologized.

"It's fine," I assured her.

I could tell from the way Ember was staring at me from across the table that we would save this conversation for a time when it was just the two of us.

"So, um, I forgot to mention that I can't push back the dates any further for our trip," Harlym blurted.

Em choked on her cocktail. "What you mean? We spent a lot of money on that expensive ass resort."

"Exactly. I'm not about to lose out on any money."

Harlym leaned back in her chair. "You were going through your divorce, and you were too busy with the kids. How many times did you both expect them to keep accommodating us? After speaking to the resort manager and emailing back and forth, he was able to accommodate us, but this is the last time we can push out the date, or we're going to forfeit the deposit we put down."

"How soon is this, Harlym? You know I have work and need to make sure the girls are settled."

"Um, next month. That was the latest he would allow, and it happens to be during their single's week, so yeah." She brushed a piece of her curly hair behind her ear.

"That's fine with me... I need to find me a new man." Em sipped her drink, all too thrilled to be in paradise surrounded by fine single men.

"I'm not single but looking around won't hurt."

"Hell, how does Cam expect me to sit around and wait for him for five years without no dick?"

"But she just—"

"Em, drop it," I told her.

My sister was confused about what she wanted. I knew she wasn't going to last the entire five years with Cam, so she needed to quit this whole façade she had going on. Harlym was young, beautiful and a successful influencer. Unlike me, she wasn't interested in listening to my mother's spiel about college.

My mother was on me hard about going to college and getting a career. She worked as a cleaner in the airport, so she wanted better for both me and Harlym. However, Harlym wasn't with the whole college thing, and she decided she wanted to do the social media thing.

I wish I thought that way because she was just listed on Forbes top fifty successful influencers on social media. The nice condo she had in the posh neighborhood of Lennox Fox wasn't too bad either.

Harlym was the rich auntie in every sense of the word. Anytime I told Demi no, she would shoot her aunt a text, and Harlym would make it happen for her almost instantly.

"We all could use some time away. I can work some things within my schedule to make sure we don't lose out on the deposits."

Nearly two years ago, we all made plans to spend a week in the Maldives with our men. We each put down a very hefty deposit on our over water bungalows. This was going to be an early birthday gift to Jace, and we could use the time away from the kids. Life happened, and then Ember was going through a divorce. It didn't help that me and Jace weren't on the same page and were sleeping in separate rooms. When Cam got locked up, that's when the trip stopped being a priority for any of us.

"That's the spirit, Stori." Harlym held up her half-filled glass, and we all said cheers together while talking about the details of our trip.

Me and Ember walked to our cars after saying bye to Harlym, who was heading to an event in the city.

"What is she even doing with that man? Harm could have any man she wants, and she wants a man that has a bedtime."

"We didn't even know what we were doing at that age. I had two kids and was chasing behind Jace with his bullshit. You and Messiah were trying to figure out your relationship. None of us had our shit together at twenty-five."

"I don't know about you, but I had my shit together," Em joked around.

"Girl, please. You were too busy in the passenger seat while we followed and spied on Jace's ass."

We both broke out into laughter. "I don't know how you're a therapist because you have more than a couple screws loose."

"That's why I'm the best person for the job," we stood by Ember's jeep. "Anyway, how is everything with you? I feel like I haven't been able to check in with you."

"I'm trying to keep busy. It's lonely going home to an empty house every night." She sighed and leaned on her jeep.

"You know I have the guest bedroom whenever you're feeling lonely. Me and the girls would love to snuggle with you in that big bed."

"I know. Just don't want to impose on you and your family."

I nudged her. "You're family, Em. I want to be here for you because I know the divorce hasn't been easy."

"It's definitely not easy, but it was needed. Neither of us were happy, and we were both so angry with one another. I wanted to be able to have my friend back... eventually."

"You will find happiness again, and you will have that rainbow baby. I can feel it, Em."

"From your mouth to God's ears. Right now, all I'm focused on is work and trying to keep my mind busy, so I don't call Messiah and beg him to come home."

"Well, me and the girls are due for a cleaning soon, so we're def going to keep you busy," I joked a bit to lighten the mood. I could tell from the expression on her smooth chestnut skin that she was inside of her head - again.

"Only if Enzo promises not to cut up." She smirked as she hit the locks to her Jeep and opened the door.

Ember was a dentist and owned her own practice in Lennox Square in town. My best friend was so damn smart and gifted at what she did. She had everything she could ever ask for except a baby.

She had the husband.

House.

Career.

She was just missing the baby, and because of that, it caused the destruction of her marriage. "Well, I'm not going to keep you long. Thanks for tonight, I needed a night out with the both of you."

She smiled. "I always know when you need a little escape. Text me when you get home."

"Always."

I watched as Ember pulled out of her spot before getting into my car. Demi sent me a few text messages letting me know she and Enzo ordered pizza. I replied, letting her know I was heading home and pulled out my spot to head home.

THREE
DR. ASTORIA JACOBS

THE CONSTANT BICKERING BETWEEN MY CHILDREN WAS LIKE NAILS on a chalkboard. Both my daughters were whining, yelling, and trying to get their points across. I could tell neither of them was listening to what the other was saying. I never got involved because let's be real, the mornings without a cup of coffee was too early to play mediator between both of them. The fights were always so juvenile and never lasted more than ten minutes.

"You took too long in the bathroom this morning. I didn't get to wash my hair," Enzo complained to her older sister, who couldn't be bothered to give her eye contact.

Demi was too busy in her cellphone, while Enzo was trying to express what was bothering her. I was proud of her for standing her ground and making Demi aware that she had done something to bother her this morning.

Enzo hated confrontation, and she struggled with voicing her problems. So, as much as I wasn't in the mood to hear their argument, I was silently cheering her on.

"It takes time to get ready. You'll understand when boys start paying you attention," Demi shot back, unbothered by what her actions caused.

"Would you like it if I did that to you?" Enzo was far from done with the conversation her sister had already written off.

"You could never," Demi chuckled. "Why do you think I wake up so early? I enjoy taking my time before you rush into the bathroom. Wake up earlier if you want to wash your hair."

Enzo was angry.

From her balled-up fist to the way her ears had turned a bright beet red, her body language told me that she was holding in anger that she desperately wanted to unleash on her sister. Demi was fifteen, but you would have sworn she was seventeen with her constant mood swings and attitudes.

My husband stalked down the steps, holding his construction hat and boots. "Morning, babe," he kissed me on the cheek on his way to put his things down. "Demi, you need to stop using up all the hot water in the morning. There was barely enough for me to use this morning," he scolded Demi.

"Why is everyone on my case this morning? Just because I like to be put together, I'm the bad guy?" She screeched.

Demi was the villain in this morning's story, and she couldn't deal with it. I loved my daughter more than life, and even I could admit that she was selfish when it came to others. Demi would always put herself first.

Maybe that was something I could learn from her.

"Oh yeah. Can you swing by to pick Tyler up and take him to school?" Jace asked as if it was some small favor he was asking.

"Why isn't his mother taking him to school this morning?"

He filled his stainless-steel tumbler I had got him for Christmas up with coffee. "Tonya's car is in the shop. She asked if I could pick him up and take him, but I can't because I'm running late."

"And you don't think I'm going to be running late? Enzo and Demi both have to be dropped off at two different schools, and you want me to add a third kid to the rotation?"

Tyler, Jace's son, didn't even live in the same city as we did.

We lived in Lennox Hill, and he lived in Essex Village, which was a twenty-minute ride past the girl's school.

Jace did a subtle groan while staring at me. "Can you just do me a favor without complaining how much it's going to inconvenience you? How many times have I stopped what I was doing to do something for you?"

It was always tit for tat when it came to this man. He could never do anything for me without tossing it back into my face that he had done it. "You need to figure something out with his mother. I have a client at nine, and I'm already going to be running late for that."

"You make your own schedule, Astoria. I don't have that flexibility, and we don't need me losing this job." He shoved his feet into his boots, grabbed his keys and tumbler before heading toward the door.

"Have a good day at school, Daddy," Enzo called behind him.

"And you have a great day at work, Enzo," he replied back. It had been their game since she was younger.

Enzo always cried when it came to being dropped off at school, so Jace made up a game where he called work school, and she called school work.

"Um, hello?"

"Just do this solid for me. Damn, Astoria," he griped and then headed out the door without even confirming if I could do this solid for him.

I tried hard to keep a neutral face, but my girls knew when I was pissed. "Seems like we're always picking Tyler up when his mom can't," Demi muttered before hopping off the stool.

"Go get your things so we can head over to pick Tyler up," I called behind both girls.

Demi and Enzo were Irish twins. I thought my world was complete with just one child, and then God put another one right inside me - again. My pregnancy with Enzo was hard because of my relationship with Jace. It was already a struggle with Demi, and even back then I wasn't sure we would make it. Then I found out I was pregnant with Enzo and felt like we had no other choice but to make it work.

It never works out when you have that mindset.

Now, here I was all these years later and unhappy. I felt like I was starving in this marriage, and all Jace could do was toss out some scraps whenever he felt like it. I wished we could use the excuse that the kids took over our lives, so the romance faded. The truth was that the romance had faded way before our children became toddlers, and the affairs that he had added to the lack of trust.

Hence Tyler.

Tyler was a few months younger than Enzo, and I've had to deal with that every day since I found that picture in his phone. Even knowing that she had a baby with my man, Tonya still refused to come to me as a woman. In her mind, she was going to let Jace handle that while being able to walk around and brag that she had his baby.

It hurt like hell to watch this little boy grow up under my roof, sharing the same face of my husband. Tyler was my husband's twin, and Tonya took complete joy in knowing that she produced Jace's only son.

Apparently, he got Tonya pregnant during his guy's trip to Chicago with his friends. He never planned on telling me that she even went on the trip with them, and that they shared a hotel room that weekend. Tonya was that chick everyone in the hood had, and Jace just had to be one of the men that had her. Every time I brought her up, he always made excuses and said she was like a sister to him.

While I was walking around trying to find somebody to watch our daughter so I could take finals, he was in another state, laid up with Tonya, while ignoring me and his daughter

I should have left.

The moment he showed me that he didn't give a fuck should have been my reason to leave. Instead, I stayed because I thought I could change this man and make him into the man I needed him to be.

Word of advice, ladies. You can't change a man that doesn't have the desire to change. It's not our job to change a grown man into what we want them to be. That was their mama's job, and if she failed, it damn sure isn't our job to take on the challenge of raising up a grown man.

It was a lesson that I was learning now.

Tyler had been a part of our family since the first time I sat down with Tonya. She held that baby in her arms with this smirk on her face that I would never forget. It felt like she was letting me know she would always be a part of our lives, and there wasn't a damn thing that I could do about it.

When we moved to Lennox Hill, that following year he moved to Tonya and Tyler to the neighboring city, Essex Hills. He happily paid for Tyler's private school but gave me shit about wanting to put both our daughters in separate private schools.

Demi loved dance, so I felt it was fitting for her to attend a private performing arts school that would give her more opportunities when she graduated from high school. It was a three-day argument because I decided to put down the down payment for her tuition.

Meanwhile, Tyler played football, and he had no problem paying for him to go to football camp and all the shit that his mother barely wanted to help with. Tonya was a flight attendant, so at any given time, she would have to work, and Tyler would stay with us.

When we bought this house, I gave up my office so he could have his own bedroom and we could still have a guest room for family when they visited. At the time, I was doing everything because I wanted Tyler to feel comfortable and for our lives to be normal. We had experienced so much change over the years that I just wanted my girls to have some type of normalcy.

It was Jace that decided to stick his dick into another woman, which caused this shift in our lives. I felt like I was the one making all the sacrifices for Tyler while Jace continued to push on like everything was peachy.

Me and Tonya didn't get along at all.

I felt like she didn't respect my role as Tyler's stepmother or Jace's wife. In her eyes, I was just another baby mama, and she didn't need to have any respect for me. We kept it cordial around the kids, but we both couldn't stand each other.

"Why do we have to drive all the way to Essex Hills when neither of us attend school there?" Demi groaned.

"What's with the stupid questions this morning? You know why we're going to Essex Hills, and it's to pick your brother up."

She folded her arms and rolled her eyes. "Couldn't you drop me off first?"

If I decided to drop the girls off, then I would have to drive all the way across town to make it to Essex Hills to pick up Tyler. It was better to pick Tyler up, drop him to school and then continue to drop the girls off before going to work.

"I'm not arguing with you this morning, Demi," I warned her.

"I don't know why she's complaining... she has perfectly clean hair." Enzo continued on about the hair-washing debacle.

Between the two of them, I just wanted silence on the ride to Tyler's house. I turned up the morning radio while Demi popped in her Air Pods and ignored the rest of us.

I loved being a mother more than life, and I was so grateful for my girls. They were both conceived during a time when my life was challenging, and I believed they saved me. Both of them gave me something to look forward to and helped push me toward my goals.

Walking across the stage during graduation while holding both girls in my arms was a dream to me. It showed me that no matter what came my way I would always be able to accomplish it. Jace was no help while I was in college because he was too busy being selfish. If it wasn't for my aunt, I probably wouldn't have graduated with honors while having two kids a year apart.

I took a deep breath as we pulled up to Tyler's house. His mother's Nissan was parked right in the driveway. "Go and get your brother." I nudged Demi.

"Why do I always have to go ring the doorbell?" she complained as she got out the car.

Demi knew when to mess around with me and when I wasn't playing with her. This new attitude tour she was taking us all on was getting old - quick.

"Mom, I could go ring the doorbell next time," Enzo offered.

I reached in the back and pinched her cheek. "My sweet baby. What am I going to do when you start acting like your sister?"

It wasn't that long ago that Demi used to be my sweet baby. She had her moments, but lately, all we did was argue over the most mundane things. I just wanted my little girl back without all the sassy behavior that came with her these days.

Demi skipped back to the car when Tonya swung open the screen door. She waved out the door, and Tyler pushed by his mother behind Demi.

"She had the nerve to mention we're late," Demi said the minute she got into the car.

Although we kept it cordial in front of the kids, my daughters knew how much I disliked Tonya, and I didn't hide it. Hell, Tyler probably knew how much I disliked his mama too.

I never took my feelings out on Tyler. Was it hard to raise a child that was conceived behind your back?

Absolutely.

It was even more hard when your husband constantly played favorites. He gave me shit about the girls wanting to do different hobbies, yet he shelled out all the money in the world to make sure his boy stayed involved in football.

I couldn't lie and say that I wasn't jealous.

All I had given Jace was two beautiful, smart, and sassy little girls. I never gave him a boy, and even if that baby I miscarried was a boy, Tyler was still his first-born son.

The only reason he wasn't named Jace Jr. was because Tonya was being petty when she named him. Something that still bothered Jace to this day.

"Hey, Ty." I smiled when Tyler climbed into the car.

"Hey, Stori."

I always cringed when he called me Stori. Did I expect him to call me mama?

No.

Maybe something close to mom, or something that showed that I had been actively in his life since he was a couple months old. I had changed his diapers, made his bottles, and took him to the emergency room whenever he was sick.

Tonya's schedule was always up in the air, so I spent a lot of time caring for that boy like I had birthed him my damn self, and he turned around and called me *Stori*.

"Your dad had to go into work early today, so he couldn't come pick you up."

"He texted me."

"How's everything with school?" I was trying hard to make conversation, but he wasn't the least bit bothered.

Like most teenagers, his head was in his brand-new iPhone that I knew his mama didn't buy him. "The iPhone 14 pro max? I still have the eleven," Enzo groaned.

"Dad bought it for me." Tyler shrugged like it wasn't nothing.

My knuckles were nearly white from how hard I was gripping the steering wheel. Out the corner of my eye, I saw how hurt Demi looked when Tyler nonchalantly told us that his father, her father, and my husband bought him a brand-new cellphone.

By the time I dropped the kids to school, I was almost a half an hour late for work. Thankfully, my client had texted and told me she was running late too. I was so angry that I didn't even stop to grab coffee because I had been in deep thought since dropping Demi off at school last.

Even she knew the mood was off, so she reached over and kissed me on the cheek - something she never did. Something as small as a kiss on the cheek from my oldest did make me feel slightly better.

"Morning, Dr. Jacobs! Um, your appointment at nine cancelled. Something with her childcare and husband."

"I guess husbands all over the world are pissing their wives off," I sighed and took a seat in one of the waiting chairs.

"Men," she scoffed.

I made it my business not to know too much about my assistant's life. All I knew was things that were on a need-to-know basis, like her son. She never spoke about having a boyfriend or girlfriend if that was what she was into.

"Tell me about it. Who is on the schedule today?"

"Not much… you do have an introductory session with a new client. Kyle referred her to you."

"What?"

"Yeah, he gave me the files this morning." She held the files up, and I snatched them out her hand and marched over to Kyle's office.

"Where are you stomping off to?" He caught me as I was storming past the break room.

"Looking for you. What is this?" I waved the folder in his face.

He chuckled. "I told Bethany to hide that damn folder at the bottom of today's files."

"As if I wasn't going to notice a new client? What is going on, and why are you giving me clients?" I tossed the folder onto the table and sat down across from him.

"My workload is too much. I currently have about twelve clients that I'm trying to juggle, and I can't take on anymore. They come highly recommended from a good friend of mine in New York."

"They?"

"It's a married couple. She hasn't convinced her husband to attend therapy, so she's going to start with the hopes he will join her."

"You know that's not how I operate, Kyle."

"They are very high profile and the money they are willing to pay to keep things discreet is amazing. If I wasn't so stretched thin, I would have kept them for myself."

"Why are they paying more for me to be discreet? That's included in therapy even if you're homeless."

"Take on the appointment and feel her out. If you don't want to take her on as a client, then I will give it to Claire."

Claire was the other therapist in the office; however, we weren't close with her. She kept the door to her side closed, so we couldn't even access her office unless we walked around front. Other than our forced holiday parties, we didn't mingle with her often. Claire was there to get the bag and return home; she wasn't here to make friends, and I respected it.

Snatching the folder, I leaned back in the chair and flipped through the questionnaire and paperwork she had filled out previously. "Married for five years... hmm."

"They're very interesting and *paid*." Kyle made sure to add again like I cared.

My clientele was very diverse, and they came from all different walks of life. I had clients who were old money rich and some who were new. Hell, I had couples like the Mirandas that were regular middle-class families trying to make their marriage and life work.

"Wait, Kami Lynn!" I blurted and put my hand over my mouth as if there was anyone else in this office.

"Yep."

"She's married? When the fuck did that happen?"

Kami Lynn was a radio personality with her own morning show. The girl was so private that everyone wondered what her life looked like off the air. Other than the staged photos that her management probably made her post on social media, there wasn't much to know about her.

"Girl, she's been married for quite some time too. Both she and her husband moved to Lennox Hill, over in the Lennox Fox neighborhood."

"I didn't hear anything."

"How would you? Kami has always been quiet. Don't even know where she lived before moving here."

"Why did she move here?"

"All in the paperwork." Kyle smiled as he stood up. "Lunch today? I have a client in ten minutes."

"Sounds good. Tell Bethany, please."

I crossed my legs and read all of Kami's information that she provided. She had been married for five years, and they didn't have any children. She and her husband moved to Lennox Hills from New York City to get away from the busy city.

Everyone that ended up here usually moved to get away from the city. We had the best of both worlds. We were away from the city and could still access it whenever we needed with an hour car ride. When I moved to Lennox Hills, I thought I would miss the city too much.

I closed the file and headed to my office to prepare for this introductory appointment. If I had to choose my favorite part of therapy, it would be getting to know my clients.

Once they became comfortable, they opened up more and gave me more insight on the kind of person they were. Reading people had always been easy for me, so when I decided to become a therapist, it was the perfect match. Jace always thought he was getting over on me when, in reality, I knew what he was up to before he got into it.

I didn't know if that made me smart or stupid. It was something I was still trying to figure out nearly fifteen years later. Just the thought of Jace right now was pissing me off. Seeing Tyler with that new phone ignited something inside of me.

Jace was against upgrading the girl's phones because he

claimed they were spoiled. He always gave me shit about the way I parented because I was a gentle parent with conditions.

I wasn't going to batter my child to get a point across to them. When I approached them calmly and levelheaded, I got more accomplished, and they were much more willing to come to me when they needed something. Me and Harlym grew up completely different from how Enzo and Demi were being raised. If we wanted something, then we had to work for it.

Our mother wasn't running around spoiling us because she had to pay bills and put food on the table. Demi and Enzo were both old enough to get a little after school job, but neither of them wanted to work, so I didn't force them.

The reason I went to college and accomplished all that I did was so my kids could have a choice. I had to work if I wanted the things that I did, and I didn't have a problem with that.

My kids didn't.

On any given day of the week, Demi was always begging to go to Ulta or Sephora with her friends, and I allowed her to. My daughters drank Starbucks, shopped, and lived a soft life.

Jace hated it.

When he saw the credit card statements come through, he complained about how much money I allowed them to spend to shop. He even refused to contribute to that part of the credit card bills because he felt so strongly about it.

When it came to *my girls*, he complained about them being spoiled and not being appreciative, which wasn't true. When Tyler was mentioned, he would go to the end of the earth to make sure his precious boy had whatever he wanted - including a new phone.

I wasn't upset that Jace took care of his responsibilities and played an active role in his son's life. During our entire marriage, I had encouraged him to be that kind of father. What bothered me was the fact that he played favorites. If Tonya bought the iPhone, it wouldn't have been a problem because that's her son, and she's allowed to do what she wanted. It was Jace who bought the phone after refusing to do the same for our children. Our girls got all the grief while his son was able to happily exist because he was the only boy.

It seemed like the girls got the short end of the stick when it came to Jace's parenting. Almost every weekend, he was riding out to Essex Hills to watch Tyler play football or hang out with him.

I never saw him offer to bring the girls so they could support their brother. Demi liked to hang with her friends, so I understood why he never extended the invitation to her. Enzo was always home with her head in a book, but she loved hanging out with her father. With the way I was gripping my phone, I realized I needed to calm down and put the situation out my mind until we were able to talk later tonight.

"Hey, Dr. Jacobs, your client is here. Let me know when you're ready for me to send her in."

I stood up, straightened out the blazer I wore and grabbed my iPad. "You can send her in."

Within seconds, the door gently opened, and Bethany stepped through. Kami Lynn came in behind her. "Hi, Kami. It's so nice to finally meet you." I reached out and shook her hand.

"Thank you, Bethany," I dismissed her.

She quietly closed the door behind her, leaving me and Kami alone. "Thank you so much for meeting me. You come highly recommended, Dr. Jacobs."

"Have a seat," I gestured to the couch and got comfortable in my armchair. "How was the drive in?"

"Perfect. I've gotten so used to the traffic and the anxiety that comes with having to drive in it that this was the complete opposite."

"Lennox Hills is pretty peaceful. Traffic usually gets thick around school dismissal and five."

I crossed my legs and fired up my iPad, ready to take notes. "I've noticed. I'm usually stuck in it coming from the station."

"Hmm." I was creating a new client file for Kami, which I should have done before she arrived.

My mind had been so stuck on my husband and his unfair treatment of his children that I wasn't focused.

"So, how does this work?"

"What work?"

"Therapy."

"Is this your first time ever coming to therapy?"

"Yes."

I smiled. "It works however you want it to work. You can share how much or how little you want. I do advise my clients that even if you decide to sit quiet for the entire session, I will still be compensated."

She snickered. "I hear that... get your money."

I wanted to agree but decided not to break my professional persona. "Kami, tell me about you. Why did you seek out therapy... specifically a marriage therapist."

The other side of me wanted to toss this iPad to the side and kick back while she spilled all her tea out to me. Hell, I had my own set of questions for her.

"Wow. There's so many reasons." She played with her hands.

A sign that she was nervous.

"Let's start with the main reason."

She looked up and had a nervous smile. "I had an affair on my husband."

THE GIRLS WERE DOING their homework, dinner was complete, and I had popped a bottle of wine on the back porch. I sat cuddled up on my wicker egg chair. Everyone in the house knew it was my favorite chair, and if you didn't find me in my bedroom, you could find me in the backyard with a bottle of wine - like tonight.

Jace had sent a text stating that he was on his way home from Tyler's football practice. He failed to let me know that he was going to his practice after work. I wish I could say that this favorites thing just started, but that would have been a lie.

He had always played favorites. Demi could count on one hand how many times her father showed up to one of her recitals or dance weekends. He always sent his love or had me buy flowers and say it was from him. He was never interested in what she did like he had been with Tyler.

Demi never told me it bothered her, so I always pushed it out my head. As long as I showed up, I felt that was all that mattered. It didn't matter what I had going on, I always showed up and moved mountains to be one of the smiling faces she recognized in the audience.

I took a sip of wine and looked out at our beautiful back-yard. The string lights added the perfect touch to the small yard. We had a fire pit toward the left side of the yard and a full dining table that we used during the summer months. With fall here, the entire yard was filled with beautiful auburn-colored leaves that would turn into a crunchy mess in a few days.

"Hey." Jace came out to join me with a plate in his hand. "Broccoli is good as shit."

"Thanks." I took less of a sip and more of a gulp.

"How was practice?"

"Good. Ty just needs to increase his speed and stop second guessing the plays. He always does that shit and it drives me crazy."

"Hmm."

"Yeah. I was looking into this football camp that's in Atlanta. They have actual NFL players that coach the kids."

"Sounds expensive."

"Shit, it is. I think it would be worth it, though. All of this is an investment… when he goes pro—"

"What if Ty decides he doesn't want to play football, Jace?"

He had all these plans for his son and never considered what he wanted.

Tyler played football because it was something he and his father bonded over. It was all he knew since Jace had signed him up when he was a toddler.

"Football is life for Ty. He's always going to want to play. I was talking to the coach on the high school team at his school, and he says that Ty has a chance to make varsity." I wanted to be as excited as my husband was for Tyler.

This man never showed any kind of excitement like this for nothing. I didn't even see him this excited when I graduated college after birthing two babies and putting up with his bullshit.

"Make sure this is something that he wants, Jace," I warned.

"Why the fuck are you being so negative?"

"How? Because I want you to consider your son's feelings. He has played football because *you* have always pushed him. He's in high school now. Maybe he might want to do something else. That's all I'm saying."

His mood was already spoiled. "If he didn't want to play football, he would have told me. The whole reason we got him into that private school was because of their varsity football team. There's a few NFL players that attended that school."

The tuition for that school was forty thousand dollars a year - more than the girl's private school.

Since I wanted the girls in different private schools, I paid for their tuition - alone.

It was up to me to cut the check each semester for the girl's school, and he didn't even act like he wanted to help me. When Demi was accepted into her performing arts school, I knew I had to find a way to make it work. My girl has always loved dancing, singing, and acting. Anything with her being the center of attention, and Demi was all down for it.

Enzo was the complete opposite of her sister. She hated having the spotlight on her and would prefer to sit in a corner to read. She was a freshman and already reading college-level books. My girl loved reading and engineering, so I encouraged her like I did with Demi. The school she attended was a regular private school that specialized in all the things Enzo was interested in.

"I just think you need to consider how much money we're spending on Tyler. You have two other kids that need things too."

Tonya didn't offer to pay for shit when it came to Tyler's school or football. She left all of that in Jace's hands, which is why he worked so much, so he could afford all of it. At one time, his credit cards were maxed because he was trying to keep up with it all.

"I'm not supposed to support my son's dreams now?"

"What about your daughter's dreams? Does she not matter to you, Jace?" I snapped.

"The fuck is that supposed to mean?"

"You don't pay for her dance classes or her school tuition. She asked you about going away to dance camp this past summer, and because it cost over two grand, you refused to send her."

"Two thousand dollars so she could prance around a fucking camp is crazy, Stori. Even you said the price was steep."

"Yes, it was steep," I agreed.

"Then why the fuck is it a problem when I say it?"

"Because you don't contribute shit to her dancing dreams. I'm the one writing the checks to the school and dance studio. Meanwhile, you over here researching football camps and willing to spend the money."

"When he's in the NFL, I bet none of you will be complaining about all I've been doing."

I chuckled. "Is that what you're banking on? You want to sit beside him when he puts that team's hat on his head?"

"Yo, you really be on some shit."

"Why does Tyler have a new phone?"

He ran his hands across his beautiful face. My husband was handsome, and I think that was the reason I allowed him to get away with so much. Staring at him had me about to forget that we were in the middle of an argument. "His other phone broke, and Tonya said he needed a new one."

"And she couldn't get him a new phone?"

"I'd rather not hear her mouth about it."

I leaned forward with my half-empty glass of wine in my hand. "You basically handle everything when it comes to Tyler. You mean to tell me that you would rather not hear her mouth, but hear mine?"

"That's not what I'm saying, Stori. You know how she gets with that arguing shit, and I would rather not deal with it."

"You told both Enzo and Demi that they didn't need new phones, and then went to get him the newest damn phone out."

"Is this because he has something better than them for once?" He screwed his face up.

"What? No, and you know that's not what this is about... don't even try to switch this to something that it's not."

"The girls get everything they want. Tyler barely asks for shit, and when he does, I want to come through for him. Demi and Enzo are being raised in a two-parent household... Ty don't have that."

Did he just....

I was trying to collect my thoughts before I spoke out of term. "So, the girls have to go without things because their father decided to fuck a slut that produced their brother? Please tell me if I got this correct, Jace."

"Why the fuck you always gotta go there with it?"

"Why should they suffer because you decided to have a baby outside of our relationship?"

"*Suffer?*" he scoffed and chuckled. "Those girls don't know shit about suffering. They both have their own rooms and share their own bathroom. Ty has a room because you gave up your office. He has to use the guest bathroom like this isn't his home.

And you mad because I bought my son a phone that he wanted... get the fuck over yourself, Stori."

He stood up and went back into the house. God knew I was trying hard to make things work with this man, and he refused to ever see things from my view. I didn't have a problem with him doing for his son. I just wanted things to be fair.

When the girls both asked for Air pods for Christmas, I bought each kid their own. Tyler was going to be spending the holidays with us, and I didn't want him to feel left out because his sisters' received headphones as their gifts.

Jace made it seem like I only thought about our daughters and not Ty. If I didn't care about him, then I wouldn't have risked a client to take him all the way to school along with my own kids. He never appreciated the efforts I made when it came to dealing with his son. I went above and beyond and did more than some women would have if they were in my position.

I didn't need him to sing my praises for all I did, but it would have been nice if he saw things from my side every once in a while. He made me feel like I was the wicked stepmother who didn't want Ty to have anything. Our kids were the most important thing to us, and I wanted to support each of them in everything that they wanted to accomplish.

We also needed to be smart and support within reason. Demi couldn't go to that dance camp because it was overpriced, and I didn't think it was a smart financial decision to make at the time. Although she was bummed that she couldn't attend, she understood and decided to do more dance lessons during the summer.

The dance camp was something that she actually wanted to do.

Jace took the time to actually look this football camp, and he would more than likely force him into being excited over it. Then it was the fact of how we were going to afford to pay for this football camp. Jace never thought of things like that. He just promised Ty things that he damn near killed himself to afford.

· · ·

"NIGHT, DEMI AND ENZO," I called to the girls as I walked down their hallway to our bedroom. Jace had gone up to bed over an hour ago. He was either watching sports in bed or pretending to be asleep to avoid talking to me.

He acted like I was going to fall over and die because he didn't want to stay downstairs with me. I welcomed the peace and quiet away from him, and I knew the girls did too. When he was up in the room, we didn't have to hear him complain about imaginary crumbs on the counter or sweeping after every little thing that fell.

Jace was OCD, and it drove me crazy at times. How could a man be so anal about cleanliness and not about breaking a woman's heart? I saw him give a shit about the wrinkled sheets on our bed more than what I was currently feeling.

Like I expected, he was laid back with his arms behind his head watching ESPN peacefully. I walked past the TV to head into the bathroom to do my skincare routine. There wasn't a need to continue with the conversation we were having downstairs. The minute he walked away, he shut down the conversation, so I wasn't going to bring it up anymore. I hated having the same conversation with him about Tyler and Tonya. I sounded like a broken record because he didn't give a damn about anything I had to say.

He disregarded that his daughters asked for the same phone, and he shut them down. The moment Tyler asked for it, he went out his way to get the phone that he wanted. The treatment was unfair, and I was tired of trying to get Jace to understand how unfair he was being when it came to his kids.

As I was using my cleanser, Harlym's name popped up on my screen. "Hey Harm, you're on speaker," I made sure to inform her.

Jace was nosey, and I knew he would be watching the game and trying to listen in to my conversation at the same time. "What you doing?"

"My skincare... you?"

"Trying to figure out these flights. What's the point of having a group chat when you never respond to none of the messages in there?"

"Today has been a day," I exhaled as I removed my makeup from my face. If she only knew all the shit I went through today, she would have extended me some grace.

"Everything alright?"

"It will be... eventually. What did the message say since I have you on the phone now?"

"Trying to figure out these flights. Let me know how we coming before I go spending a bunch on business class."

"Well, I planned to fly business class. I have a bunch of points with the airline, so I plan to cash in on those to fly comfortably."

"And what about Ember?"

"She's the miles queen, so I'm sure she's going to do the same thing too." I chuckled.

"Guess I need to spend some money on my flight because I used my miles last week when I went to Aruba."

Harlym had the life that I would have wanted when I was her age. She didn't have to worry about anybody else except herself. She was free to travel and be selfish whenever she wanted. That was my only wish for my daughters.

I never wanted them to end up married to a man that was as selfish as their father. If I was stronger, I would have left a long time ago and went on to live my life without him. I allowed this man to trap me with two kids and gaslight the fuck out of me every step of the way.

"You big balling, so I know you got it," I joked with her.

"Cam has it. You know he left me in charge of all of his accounts," she bragged.

"Give them accounts to his mama and move on from that, Harlym," I tried to convince her again.

Having access to Cam's accounts was the last thing that she needed to have. That was one more thing keeping her tied to this man that she didn't need to be tied to. I had nothing against

Cam, and in a perfect world, the two of them would have been together. This wasn't a perfect world, and I wanted my baby sister to have the love that she deserved, not wasting five years waiting on a man that may or may not be ready to settle down when he comes home.

"Here you go with this again. Why is it so hard for you to understand that me and Cam are serious, and I'm holding him down?"

"Because it's a joke, Harlym. Waiting five years for a man you're always off and on with is crazy. What are you trying to prove to everyone? That you can hold him down?"

"I don't care about proving anything to anybody. Our relationship is ours; I don't need validation from the outside world."

She was saying this to me now, and then she would be going on a rant via social media about the different chicks that claimed to still be messing around with Cam while he was locked up. I had been there and done that, and I knew that man was talking to other women while he was with Harlym. She was too young and naïve to believe that he wasn't out here doing her wrong. A nigga behind bars didn't have loyalty to anybody.

Harlym was young and successful; she didn't need Cam or his money. He was probably scared, so he was keeping his options open with other women who would stick around and wait for him.

"It's your life, and you are a grown woman," I replied.

She was grown, and I wasn't her mother, so I couldn't tell her what she could or couldn't do. I knew if I wanted to continue to have a relationship with my sister, I needed to butt out her life.

"Thank you for remembering that... I have to go. I'm going out to dinner with the girls tonight."

"Be careful and I love you."

"Love you more. Go and get some sleep, you sound drained," she told me, and I let out a soft chuckle.

The truth was that I was drained.

Sick and tired of feeling like I was grasping at straws in my marriage. Had I been my own client, I would've suggested divorce to myself. I knew there wasn't much that I was holding onto in this marriage with Jace.

"You weren't going to mention you're going out of town." Jace didn't wait for me to climb into bed before he got on my case.

"I planned to talk to you about it tonight. You are the one who walked back inside the house," I reminded him.

"A trip right now, Astoria.... seriously?"

"What does that mean?"

"We have a lot going on with the girls and Ty. How am I supposed to handle getting them to school and being on time to work?"

"The same way that I do it every morning, Jace. You get up earlier and make it happen."

Every morning I was up before him and downstairs making sure the girls had breakfast before we headed out the door. I never complained or forced him to help out with the morning drop-offs because I knew he had to get to work himself. I always sacrificed my own schedule to make it easier on my husband.

"I wish you would have asked me before making these plans."

"*Asked*? I'm a grown ass woman who works hard and raises her children. I don't have to *ask* you a damn thing. As my husband and their father, you should be encouraging me to take some time for myself."

I wasn't going to mention that this was the trip that we were supposed to go on together. There was a reason we never made it on that trip together, and I was determined to leave his ass here.

"Come on, let's go to bed." He tried to scoop me into his arms, and I resisted.

"I don't want to be touched tonight," I snapped and pulled the covers over my body.

I could tell he was staring at the back of my head for a while before he rolled over and turned the light and TV off. Instead of getting the much-needed sleep I required, I stared at the family picture on my nightstand while I listened to his soft snores.

We were never truly happy with each other. Jace found a woman that would put up with his shit, and I found a man that I could make a *home* with. I watched my mother date man after man, and none of them ever made a commitment to her.

She had two daughters from two different men, and none of them wanted to marry her. As a kid, I used to think there was something wrong with my mother. Why didn't a man want to make her his wife? Was she not worthy of marriage from her Prince Charming?

Now, as an adult, I realized that it was her choice not to get married. Why get married to a man that would suck the life out of you? Jace sucked the life out of me before I even accepted his half ass proposal, and because I wanted to prove that I was worthy of being someone's wife, I allowed that to push me further into a relationship that I should have been running away from.

My eyes grew heavy as I adjusted my alarm clock. Peeking over at Jace, he was asleep like all was great in his world.

Who was I kidding? All *was* great in his world.

FOUR
BRAY WILLSHIRE

"THE FUCK YOU MEAN I NEED TO CLEAN UP MY IMAGE? I'M AS clean as this cheap ass Dollar Tree soap that's on this counter," My younger brother, Ashton, went off on our publicist.

She looked at the bottle of dish soap and then back at me and Laurent, my other brother, before she spoke. "He slapped a stripper in the mouth with money because her breath smelled like," she cleared her throat as she read from the paper. "And I quote. Like she's been eating ass and chewing on tires."

Me and Laurent both stifled our laughs. "And it did. She was all in my face acting like she was about to be my next baby's mother or something. I slapped her in the mouth with the money so she could get the fuck out my face."

"Next baby mother?" Sammie looked at both me and Laurent for clarification.

"He doesn't even have one baby mama," Laurent clarified.

Sammie nodded her head. "You are Ashton Willshire. You can't walk around acting like some regular person. Your name means more than others, and you are putting a bad taste in the media's mouth."

"What does any of that shit have to do with me? I already

made it clear that I don't want to have nothing to do with the family business. I'm a photographer."

Ashton had made it very clear since he was old enough to understand that he wanted nothing to do with the family business. His passion was photography, and that was what he wanted to do for the rest of his life. We all accepted and supported that he didn't want to follow in the footsteps of our father.

He was the youngest, so it wasn't really expected of him to carry the torch. It was expected of me. And I carried it, no matter how heavy it felt at times.

"All we want is for you to conduct yourself a certain way. Even with you not wanting to be directly part of the Willshire hotel chain, you are still a Willshire. Slapping money into a stripper's face isn't the best image for you or your brand, let alone Willshire Hotels and Resorts." Sammie stood her ground.

Ashton was used to running every publicist we had out of here with tears in their eyes. She stood firm as she stared my brother in the eyes while holding the folders that were tucked into her arms.

"Man, fuck you and the hotel." He stared into her eyes.

Sammie smirked, stood up and adjusted the pencil skirt she wore. "Ashton, you need to grow up. That stripper chipped a tooth, and she was going to sue until I talked her out of it. You might want to be a bit nicer before you start having to pay legal fees and lawsuits without the Willshire money. Laurent and Bray... a pleasure seeing both of you."

"Let me walk you out," Laurent offered and followed behind her.

I leaned back in my seat and looked at my troublesome younger brother. "You need to get your shit together, Ash."

"Don't tell me you about to give me a lecture too."

"Nah. I don't need to give you one because you're old enough to get shit together without me having to give you one.

After Pops died, you told me that you didn't want to follow in the family's footsteps, and I respected that. Hit you with some bread, and allowed you to do your own thing, which you did. AMW photography is a force to be reckoned with, and I respect it. You prayed and put in the work for the dream to come true, now it's time to pray for some discipline."

Ashton avoided eye contact with me. He knew that he was wrong for whatever went down in that strip club. I never read the media and tried not to get involved in any of my brothers' business. They were both grown and capable of handling things without having to get me involved. When Sammie hit me up and told me that we needed to meet to discuss my brother's recent behavior, I knew that it was serious.

"I hear you."

I stood up. "I hope you do. Your actions fuck with the company, and I don't want to have to come sit and have a conference like you some little ass boy."

"I got it," Ash assured me.

Since he was a teen, he had been giving us a run for our money. Ashton was used to doing whatever he wanted without having any consequences. It was my fault because I allowed him to run around like a maniac with a camera for far too long. He was now twenty-seven and needed to get his shit together.

"Why you had to come at my Dollar Tree soap?" Laurent lightened the mood when he came back from walking Sammie out.

You could always count on Laurent to lighten the mood whenever shit was becoming too tense. Me and Ashton were always butting heads over the silly shit he was always doing, and I was tired of the shit.

"He better clean his fucking act up like this soap or he's cut the fuck off."

"You acting like I can't support myself without my cut of the Willshire money. Did you forget that I'm a in demand photographer?"

"You forget that I have the power to stop those connections? Stop playing on my head like I'm not about that pressure, Ash," I reminded him who the fuck I was.

If I wanted Ashton in a fucking three-piece suit in the board-room nearly every day, he knew I could make it happen. He had his career because I *allowed* him to have this career.

"Fuck you, Bray," he spat.

"Chill the fuck out with all of that. Luna is asleep in her room, and after the morning we had, I don't need her being disturbed," Laurent stepped in.

"She good?"

"Yeah, her teacher said she was stimming this morning."

"She usually does though," Ash joined in on my concern.

"Not when it comes to school. I think her spending the weekend with her mom is fucking with her. I noticed this morning she was more irritable than normal. Should have kept her home, but I was in a rush to get to the office."

My niece, Luna, was on the autism spectrum, and it had been a challenge for my brother and his soon to be ex-wife. We all knew Luna was different, but she was *our* Luna. What kid didn't have their own quirks about them? It wasn't until Laurent pushed the issue with her doctor that we got the official diagno-sis. It meant more work, and that meant that my brother and his wife had to roll their sleeves up and advocate for their daughter.

That's when Alice rolled down her sleeves and left. She claimed it was too much for her and overwhelming, which was understandable. But to abandon your husband and daughter, then flee to another country to chill and lay back, was crazy to me.

What made it crazier was because of who my brother was and what his last name was, he was obligated to still take care of her while having to become a single father.

"You gotta stop letting Alice pop in and out, bro," I told him. "Luna is used to a routine, so seeing her mother is throwing that shit out of whack."

Laurent had the same routine with Luna for as long as I could remember. Wednesdays were my days that we did our uncle and niece days out. We would grab her noise-canceling headphones and enjoy the entire day together. It was in my schedule, so everybody knew not to bother me on Luna days. She was used to it, and it was something that she looked forward to.

Whenever she saw me come into the condo, she tossed her arms up and did a little dance that was only for me. My niece was my heart, and I would do whatever I had to so I could support both Luna and Laurent.

"It's hard, yo." He plopped down on his couch. "She's my wife."

"*Ex*-wife," I corrected.

"Not yet. Neither of us signed the papers."

"Then how the hell is she getting spousal support?" Ash questioned.

Laurent leaned his head back and closed his eyes. "I agreed to pay her support while we figure this out."

Shaking my head, I shoved my hands into my pockets. "Shit, L."

"Is it wrong for me to make my marriage work?"

"Not when the bitch is in another country getting dicked down by some niggas playing in a mariachi band," Ash said exactly what I was thinking.

"We sat down this past weekend and talked. She said she isn't dating anybody."

"And you believe that shit?"

"She's my wife." He repeated like that meant something.

Alice was down for the fun life that came with being married to a Willshire. She loved the traveling and money that came with being among black wealth. The Willshire money was old money, not that new shit that Ashton was trying to collect. We came from a long line of black men who paved the way for us to live the life that we were privileged enough to live.

It was fun for her while she was shopping, traveling and having wild sex in different hotels and resorts that we owned. The minute a baby was made from all that wild sex and she was diagnosed with Autism, that became too real for her. Laurent was optimistic that he could save a marriage that wasn't meant to be saved.

"I want whatever is best for you, Laurent. If you think fixing your marriage with Alice is what needs to be done, then I'm here for you."

I didn't believe he should fix his marriage because it wasn't worth fixing. Marriage was through sickness and health, and she abandoned him during an important time in their lives.

There was no coming back from that.

"Appreciate it."

"Sammie was telling me about the Maldives resort. She said nobody has been by to visit since it opened three years ago."

"We all been busy. With Pops passing, it wasn't a concern. I sent the right people to oversee it, and they did a splendid job."

"Splendid? You hear this man?" Ashton snickered to himself. "When's the last time you went on a vacation?"

"Me and Kam—"

"I don't want to hear about your honeymoon either." He cut me off.

"It's been a minute," I confessed.

Work was the center of my life and all that I busied myself with. I was determined not to toss everything my father had worked for down the drain. Yeah, we had other family members that were involved within Willshire Hotels and Resorts, but I was the person at the head of the conference table and the person whose name was on everybody's check. It was up to me to put in as much work as everybody else, and that was exactly what I did.

"All you do is work and try to tell me what the fuck to do," Ash interrupted me.

"We should go and get away. My mom can watch Luna while I'm gone. I could use some time out the office."

Laurent was my half-brother. We didn't share the same mother, but we shared the same father. "And I need to steer clear of the media anyway. Ducking off to the Maldives doesn't sound like a bad idea."

"Fuck it... we ball," I agreed.

There wasn't anything holding me back, so going away with my brothers sounded like a plan. The only reason I was going was because of Laurent. He worked hard and was a single father so he could use the time away from Luna to recenter himself and decompress.

"That's what the fuck I'm talking about. We taking the jet or flying commercial?"

"Jet... the fuck this look like?" Laurent chuckled. "You could use some time away after making that big move to Lennox Hill."

"Yeah. The house is always so damn busy with movers and organizers putting shit away and together."

Ash stood up and went onto the balcony to take a call.

Laurent got more comfortable in the chair. "How is Kam doing with the move? She adjusting?"

"It was her idea, so she better be adjusting."

"Why there?"

"Guess she felt like it was even more private."

"She should just become a damn turtle with how secretive she is with her life. The fact that you both have never came forward with your marriage is wild."

I shrugged. "It's what she wanted."

"Then maybe I should ask how you are adjusting there?"

"It's alright. I like the area and it's laid back. The only thing we both have to worry about is the commute into the city every morning."

"I mean, she has to worry about that... not you."

"I like coming to the office in the mornings. It's been my routine since Pops passed."

"And routines are meant to be switched around. Sit your ass home some days, or work from your home office. We don't need you sniffling around the office all the damn time."

"Damn, it's like that?"

"Hell yeah. Seriously, I think we all could use this trip. When's the last time we took a trip with just the three of us since Pops passed?"

"It's been a while. I think the last one was when you revealed you and Alice were going to get married."

"Even more reason for us to get away and enjoy the fruits of our labor. Who else owns hotels and resorts and can just vacation there for free?"

"Chill out. You don't have to continue to rub it in. I said I was going to go," I chuckled and headed toward the door. "I'm gone… gotta meet with Uncle Simon and Woody."

"Tell Woody I said what's up," Laurent called behind me.

"Love y'all."

"For life," he called back.

KAMI WAS SITTING on the kitchen counter eating an apple with peanut butter. I just knew she was on some wild ass diet, and that was probably all she could eat.

When I tossed my keys onto the counter, she looked up at me with a weak smile. "Hey. How was your day?"

"Busy."

"Are you going to ask about mine?"

"If you would have given me a minute to take my jacket off," I snapped. "How was your day?"

"I had my second session with my therapist. She's really good, Bray. We should both see her to fix this mess in our marriage."

"You mean the mess that you created?"

"I deserve that."

"I need to shower before my conference call with our Japan team," I replied and headed upstairs to the guest bedroom.

The day I walked into Kami's condo and saw her getting fucked on her kitchen counter by some loser ass rapper named Cam was the day I checked out of our marriage. The image of her face in complete ecstasy was forever etched in my mental.

Our marriage wasn't the normal kind of marriage, and that was why I respected it. She wanted to do things different, and because I had always witnessed shit the old school way, I was down to experience marriage in a different way.

We never moved in together and kept our own separate spaces. Kami claimed that she liked having her own space and I liked having mine. We rotated on whose house we were going to sleep at. With both of our crazy schedules, we had to make time for one another or else we wouldn't see each other.

Despite living apart, I was still locked into my marriage and wanted to show her she married a semi-romantic kind of guy. The day I caught her fucking on her counter was the day I was letting myself in to surprise her with dinner. The chef was supposed to come in an hour, and I wanted to put some rose petals in the bedroom and run a bubble bath for when she got home. The shit I walked into was something I wouldn't wish on my worst enemy.

My wife with her face planted into the marble countertop while this nigga shoved his dick inside of her. Kami nearly passed out when she realized I was standing there. What could she say to excuse her actions in that moment? There wasn't a damn thing that she could say to change what I had witnessed from her.

Then to insult not only herself, but me with some low-level fucking rapper was a low blow. I could never look at her the same after witnessing that shit nearly two years ago. How could you betray somebody that was down for you? I had bitches throwing themselves at me on a daily, and I never paid any of them attention.

I wore that ring on my finger because I was a married man, and I respected my vows. When we decided to sneak away and get married, I was serious about being the kind of husband my parents would be proud of. My parents were married up until my father passed away, and he made my mother happy every day.

They had their fair share of problems, hence why Laurent was born, and even with all of that, they were able to reconnect and fix their marriage. That was the *only* reason I hadn't served Kami with divorce papers. There was this small piece of me that felt like I *had* to make my marriage work with her. We couldn't just toss five years of marriage down the drain.

Whenever I stared at my wife, I used to get fucking butter-flies, and now all I became was disgusted. Sex with her wasn't the same. I just fucked so I could bust my nut and keep it push-ing. When she rode my dick and moaned, all my mind went back to was when she was letting that little nigga fuck up all inside of her like a slut back in high school.

It was Kami's idea to move to Lennox Hills. She was the one who suggested we sell our condos and try living under one roof. She was convinced that it would make us stronger as a couple, but I didn't agree with shit she was saying.

How the fuck was this going to make us stronger when we had never lived together. Spending a few weeks at each other's condos wasn't living together. I didn't even know how she took her coffee in the morning or what her favorite breakfast food was.

Kami wanted our marriage out the media because she didn't want her personal life to overshadow her career. I agreed because her morning show was at the top of the charts, and she was considered the voice of New York. Before meeting Kami, I knew she was private, and there wasn't much to be known about her.

Her real name wasn't even Kami, which is why the media never found the marriage certificate. Her personal life was strictly off limits and I respected that. I didn't want my name to overshadow everything she had worked for in the music industry, so I agreed to keep things quiet.

The only people that knew that we were married was family, and we had kept it that way the entire marriage. It did get lonely showing up to events without my wife on my arm or coming home to an empty bed because she decided she wanted to stay at her place for the night. The type of marriage we had wasn't for everybody, which is why I worked hard to make it work.

When I found her on that counter, I stopped putting in the work. Honestly, I didn't understand why I was still sitting here trying to make it work. The move here wasn't going to fix the problems that we had within our marriage.

Kami thought moving here, and therapy was going to fix everything that we had been going through these past few years. I appreciated her for being there for me when my father died, but I didn't want to be with her.

I didn't trust my wife.

She allowed one moment of weakness to ruin all that we had built together. How could I trust her not to do it again? She was surrounded by rappers all day long. She let a little ass rapper get the panties. What could I expect when a bigger rapper came along?

Our family thought shit was sweet between us because we kept our marital problems inside of our home - or homes. Kami wasn't the type to run her mouth to her friends, and I didn't involve my brothers. Like I gave them the respect to live their lives without my input, they did the same for me.

I was constantly torn between trying to do what I knew my mother would have wanted me to do. She wanted more grandchildren, and she loved Kami. Since Alice had taken off, Kami had moved up to the favorite daughter-in-law. I often questioned how my mother would have felt if she knew the truth about Kami.

She had been cheated on, and that produced a child out of it.

How was she able to forgive my father and continue to have a happy marriage after? I was against bringing my problems to my mother's front steps, so these were internal thoughts that I was always silently battling alone.

"I ordered sushi for dinner. I figured we could have dinner together before your meeting," Kami offered while I dried off.

Looking down at my phone, I had an hour to spare before my meeting. "I could eat."

Kami licked her lips as she looked down at my towel wrapped around my waist. "I could too."

I watched as she lowered herself onto the floor and pulled at the towel. My dick sprang from the towel and touched her lip while she caressed it. "Kam, you got my shit all excited... you gonna deep throat this shit or what?" I didn't have time for her to sit there admiring the shit.

Without warning, she took all of me into her mouth while holding onto the shaft. The sounds of her gargling and gagging filled the guest bathroom. I held onto the back of her head and the counter while shoving every inch of me inside of her mouth.

When she pulled my dick out the back of her throat, all of the saliva fell onto my dick. She looked up at me with red, watery eyes. "You like that, baby?"

"Yeah." I pushed her head back down and allowed her to get me right. We had been so busy with the move and work that I hadn't been able to bust cheeks in a minute.

This head was needed in this moment. With all the stress of this move, work and trying to coexist in the same space as Kami, I needed to release this shit that had been building inside of me.

"Fuck... Kam... Damn," I grunted.

She popped my shit out of her mouth and licked the nut that was oozing out the tip before covering it with her mouth again. My body jerked as I busted into her mouth.

She swallowed it all down before giving my dick a kiss on the tip and standing up. "I want some dick, Daddy," she cooed.

"Not now." I turned her down.

Kami wanted to argue and then decided against it. I could see the resistance in her, but she decided to let it rock. "I'm going to clean myself up and then plate our food."

"Bet."

She slowly walked out the bathroom like she wanted me to stop her. Everything inside of me prevented me from doing that. Kami had always been top notch at head, and she knew how to get me off when I always needed it.

My mind always sauntered to how many other niggas she was gagging and slobbering on? I refused to believe that fucking that nigga Cam was the first time she decided to step outside of our marriage.

Kami sat on the other end of the obnoxiously large dining table. I ate my sushi while checking my emails. Dinner used to be filled with us laughing and catching each other up about our day. Now, there wasn't much to discuss unless it was going to end up in an argument.

Which it almost always did.

"You know what I would really like?"

"What's that?" I asked without picking my head up from an email I was responding to.

"You coming back into our bedroom."

"Can't come back into something I never came into." When we moved into this house a month ago, I had the movers put my shit into the guest room. Kam thought by pitching this idea of us moving in together, that it would force us to have to share a room.

"You know what I mean, Bray. I want you in the room with me... I miss you." She looked down as she pushed her sushi around with the chopstick.

"You wanted us under one roof, you got that. Don't push something I'm not ready for."

"When the fuck are you going to get ready? We've been having this same fight for the past two years, and we're nowhere close to figuring it out."

"If you found me shoving this big dick in another woman, would you feel the same way?"

"Just forge—"

"Nah, you wanted to talk, so let's talk. Imagine walking in on me shoving my dick inside another chick while wearing my wedding band. How the fuck would that make you feel? You want me to move on because what? That nigga in jail now? Is that supposed to make me feel better that you can't fuck him no more?"

"It happened one time, and I regretted it the moment it happened."

"You regret that you were caught, Kam. That look on your face was far from regret. Damn, if I'm not working this big muthafucka right, tell me... don't go fuck some young ass nigga."

"Bray, it wasn't about that."

"Then what the fuck was it about?"

"I don't know," she sighed. "We were both working so much and not making enough time for each other, and I needed to release something."

"Why the fuck didn't you come to my office? I could have dropped something off in your draws and sent you on your way. If you needed me to fuck you more, then communicate that shit to me!" I slammed my hands on the dining table, causing Kami to jump. "You don't go fuck another nigga and use that as an excuse. You think you gave the best head when we met? I taught you how to suck this shit, you forget? I didn't go get head from one of my hoes in the past... I communicated what I needed from you and went the extra mile to teach you the shit too."

I was done with the conversation. "Come to therapy, Bray. Please," she pleaded.

"Why the fuck am I coming to therapy? I wasn't the broken one who fucked up our marriage. You wanted me to move here to see if we could make this work, and I did that shit. Stop asking for therapy because the shit ain't going to happen." I snatched my phone up and went into my office, slamming the door behind me.

FIVE
DR. ASTORIA JACOBS

W<small>HEN</small> J<small>ACE</small> <small>CALLED</small> <small>ME</small> <small>WHILE</small> I <small>WAS</small> <small>AT</small> <small>WORK</small> <small>AND</small> <small>TOLD</small> <small>ME</small> <small>TO</small> meet him home, I should have known it was going to be some bullshit. I should have just hung up the phone and ignored his ass. Instead, I took my lunch to drive home to see what he wanted.

What was he doing home in the middle of the day in the first place? I was expecting the worst as I pulled into the driveway slowly. His truck was parked in the driveway and not in the garage like it usually was when he was home. There was a small part of me that had a little excitement that my husband was doing something sweet for me.

He called off this morning and had even taken the girls to school so I could sleep in. If that hadn't completely shocked me, I probably would have utilized that extra hour of sleep instead of analyzing my husband's actions. Now he was calling me in the middle of the day to come home like it was an emergency.

I killed the engine and sat in the car for a minute before going into the house. "Jace?"

"In the garage, Babe," he called back.

I sat my keys and purse on the kitchen counter and headed into the garage. Jace was sitting on a motorcycle with the biggest smile on his face. He was so damn excited that he could barely contain himself.

"Who's motorcycle is that?"

"Mine. I went to pick it up today." He beamed with such pride that I wanted to be excited for him.

Jace had always been into motorcycles. A few years ago, he totaled his motorcycle and walked away without a scratch. We both decided that he was going to put a pause on motorcycles and focus on something else. I could always tell that he missed the action from riding with his friends.

I'm sure if you were to go through his Google searches, it was filled with different pictures and listings of motorcycles. I felt bad asking him to give up his passion because I knew how much he enjoyed his motorcycle. But, after that accident, I had to think of his three kids and myself. We didn't want to bury Jace because he got into a bad accident or ended up paralyzed because of it.

"Um, I thought we spoke about this?"

"Stori, I missed having a motorcycle. The only reason I got that truck was because you convinced me it was best with the girls and Ty."

"And it was."

"For whom? You? Because you're the only one who seemed satisfied with the arrangement. That accident was years ago; I'm ready to get back on the bike."

"How did you pay for this?" I folded my arms.

"Took money out of our savings... I been contributing to it too."

All the air was knocked out my lungs when he mentioned our savings. That was our funds for a rainy day, so we never had to worry about money. Jace had *just* started contributing to our savings.

I was the one who saved all the money I earned into that account. "Please tell me you didn't pull money out of *my* savings account."

"Stori, stop acting like I'm some stranger pulling money from the accounts." He downplayed it like I didn't have a reason to be frantic in this moment.

My hands shook as I opened up my bank app and went to the savings tab. "Twenty thousand dollars? Jace, why the fuck would you take this out our savings account!" I screeched.

I slowly held onto the wall and made my way back into the kitchen. My vision was starting to go blurry, and I felt like I couldn't breathe. The measly six thousand dollars that was left in the account felt like a slap in the face. It was me who saved up all that money and made sure to put it away for us. How dare he go into that account and take money that didn't belong to him.

Then to buy a fucking motorcycle that wasn't needed. He could have been killed the last time he was on a motorcycle, and he wanted to get back onto one again and have the same fate?

I heard the garage door close and Jace's footsteps. "Calm down, Stori."

"Don't fucking tell me to calm down. Please don't tell me to fucking calm down when you took money out of our account without even having a conversation with me."

"That's why I told you to come home."

"After you fucking purchased the bike! Twenty thousand dollars, Jace? You have to take that bike back."

"It's a Ducati, Stori. That was the best price I saw on eBay and decided to jump on it. I couldn't sit and wait to have a discussion with it. You didn't have a discussion when you came in here with those designer shoes last month."

I laughed and ran my hands through my perfectly curled hair. "I should have known."

"Known what."

"I should have fucking known something was up." The reason I was able to have perfectly curled hair was because Jace decided to take the girls to school. My hair was usually brushed back into a bun instead of in its natural loose curl pattern.

"What are you talking about? Stand still... you pacing and making me nervous."

"Ha, you have a reason to be nervous? You just emptied out our account because you wanted to buy a damn bike."

Whenever Jace was being nice, I should have known. He was never nice or helpful unless he wanted something. In this case, he knew he was going to withdraw money out of our savings account and thought by picking up the slack this morning that it would go over smoother when he dropped this bomb on me.

"Why can't we never discuss shit without you being sarcastic?"

"Do you not see why I would be upset? You took money I had been putting away for our future and spent it on a fucking bike. How did you expect me to react?"

It truly fucked my head up that this man couldn't understand why I would be upset. He went behind my back to buy a motorcycle that I was sure he had researched and planned to buy. This wasn't a spur-of-the-moment purchase like the pair of shoes I bought last month.

He was comparing apples to oranges, and it was pissing me off. Jace always acted like I was over the top or dramatic for my feelings. It was like he hadn't done some off the wall shit throughout our marriage.

"I honestly thought you would be happy. The charge for that resort went through on the American Express, and I didn't see you consult me about it."

"Are you fucking serious right now? You knew about the trip."

"Yeah, I knew about the trip. Not the three thousand dollars that came with it."

I paced around the counter and tried to control my breathing. Every time I looked over at the knife block, sticking that steak knife into his neck didn't seem like a bad idea. "I work hard and make sure everything is always paid. You contribute; however, I make more. If I want to take myself on a trip to get away from being a mom and a wife, that's my right. I earned that money, and I pay that credit card bill every month."

Originally, we had three separate bungalows since we were all going with our men. With us making it a girl's trip, the resort allowed us to put our deposits toward a bigger villa that we could share. All that was left was the three thousand dollars that was charged onto the credit card, which was being split among the three of us. Both Harlym and Ember had Zelle'd me the money for the remaining balance.

Jace wanted to monitor the charges on the bill, but never the bill that came in the mailbox at the end of the month. He didn't pay shit on the balance of our shared card, but he was forever charging something onto it.

I never complained.

That had been my problem our entire marriage. Maybe I should have complained more and voiced my frustrations with him. He was a construction worker in the union with mediocre credit, and I was the one who helped him by adding him onto my credit cards.

"The bike needs to go back, Jace. I don't care how or what you do... you need to take that damn bike back now."

"I can't return the bike, Astoria. Stop throwing a tantrum, and let's discuss shit like adults."

I nearly snapped my neck, turning to stare him in the face. "Adults sit down and have conversations with their wives, not go behind their backs and buy a fucking motorcycle."

Your client just confirmed she will be to the office in ten minutes. The pinging from my phone caused me to pause.

"I'm trying to have the conversation with you right now."

"I can't even have this conversation because I have to go back to work. Thanks, Jace. I appreciate you throwing this on me in the middle of my work day."

I was so angry that I wanted to spit in his face and that was something I swore I would never do.

I hated this man.

The way he stood there like he hadn't done anything wrong kept replaying in my head as I backed out of the driveway. That had always been the problem within our marriage, and I continued to allow it because I chalked it up to it being Jace's personality.

He was manipulative and knew how to play the game of Astoria. Throughout the years, he studied how to play this game better, and I just sat there and allowed him to do it to me. My mother warned me that I should have had a separate savings account, and I didn't want to listen to her. This was my husband, and he was welcomed to anything that I had or was working toward – within reason.

Had Jace had a conversation with me about the bike, we could have come up with a different solution. Instead, he went behind my back because he knew touching our savings was off limits. I wanted to hurt him so bad, and that wasn't even my nature.

I was the person who tried to figure out shit before resorting to violence. Not only did he take the day off to go deceive me, but he stood there like I was making a big deal out of nothing. As if I was crazy for reacting the way that I did. He had no right to go into our account and take money out. When I bought my shoes, I bought them with my credit card, and it was paid off before the month was over.

I had always been a responsible spender, so it was rare that I would spend money on something big without sitting on it for a few months. Those shoes and this vacation had been the exception to the rule.

The shoes caught my eye and I felt like I deserved a pick me up at that moment. It didn't help that the girls were on my neck about it and cheering me on to buy them. This vacation was something that was being forced because none of us wanted to lose out on the money we had already paid. Even with us feeling forced, it was a well-deserved and needed vacation that I was paying for myself.

Not once did I pull money out of our savings for it.

Bethany handed me a coffee when I walked back into the office. "Grabbed some coffee for the office on lunch."

"Thanks, Beth. I needed this."

"Good thing I added an extra shot of expresso. Kami should be coming in any minute."

I nodded and headed into my office to get ready.

This was me and Kami's third session together, and I felt like today was the time to get deep. She mentioned surface-level things like cheating on her husband but never got into why. She paused more than I cared for and always seemed like she had somewhere better to be. From the moment her ass hit the chair, she checked her Rolex watch frequently as if I asked her to sit here with me. Every time she checked her watch, I made a mental note to choke Kyle for referring her to me.

"Dr. Jacobs, Kami Lynn is here for your scheduled appointment." Bethany's voice came over the intercom.

"You can send her in." I walked over to my seat and tried to clear my head for this session.

Jace calling me home to drop that bomb on me truly shifted my mental space for the day. While I needed to be here to earn a living and listen to my clients, I needed to be home to fix this mess that he has made.

Kami walked into the office *alone* and took a seat on the couch. Like expected, she took a quick look at her watch before she shook her coat from her shoulders. Her blonde curly tresses were freshly washed and fluffed.

Her fair skin was plastered with makeup, and the hazel eyes that she kept hidden behind her favorite Celine sunglasses were now visible. I guess she wanted to stop putting up a façade and get deep into conversation today.

Kami Lynn was one of those girls who never had to worry about anything. She was beautiful, so men naturally gravitated to her, and opportunities perfectly fell into her lap. I went through high school and college with girls like Kami. The type that said they were fat, knowing damn well they weren't.

Then there was me, who was actually fat from giving birth to two eight-pound babies. My job wasn't to judge her, but to help guide her through whatever problems she had going on. Clearing my throat, I decided to stop messing around in my thoughts and get this session started.

"Sorry about that. I was just reading up on an email I received," I lied, knowing I had zoned out, but my iPad sitting on my lap gave the perfect excuse.

"You're fine." She smiled. "How are you today?"

"I'm great. And you?"

"Confused."

"About?"

"Life."

Kami could either thank or hate Jace for my forwardness. "Kami, this is our third session, and you haven't opened up about anything. We spend our hour talking in circles about surface-level things. You're upset with a co-worker, or the traffic made you extra mad, and you can't figure out the source of the anger. Today, we need to dig deeper, or you're just wasting both of our time."

I was already being pretty understanding that her husband refused to do the sessions. I was a marriage therapist, not someone who treated singles. I could, but that wasn't what I did, and she knew that when Kyle referred her over to me.

By the third session, I was already welcoming in her husband into the sessions because I had a clear idea of who she was. I had no clue who Kami was, and I was tired of digging and not getting anywhere with her.

"I'm sorry. It's weird to open up to someone I never met. I don't even open up to my husband or family in that way."

"You're used to being private... I got that." I crossed my legs and stared at her fidgeting with her hands again. "You mentioned that you cheated on your husband and never elaborated on that."

She mentioned she cheated on her husband and then never

followed up with any more information. "It was stupidity, not even that important."

"Every detail is important in therapy. That is the main reason that you're sitting on the couch across from me."

"I cheated because I was feeling neglected by my husband. All day I'm surrounded by men in the entertainment industry, and they literally drool over me. When I'm with my husband, I don't ever get that same energy from him."

"What energy do you get from him?"

She sighed. "He calls me pretty and kisses all over me, but he's always in his phone. His work takes priority over me, and I feel like he forgets about me at times."

"Do you tell him how you feel?"

"He's not the type that sits and just expresses his emotions. You see that side of that couch is quite empty."

"Just because he doesn't express his emotions doesn't mean that you can't tell him how you feel."

"We just moved into our first place together in the Lennox Fox neighborhood." The Lennox Fox neighborhood was comparable to Calabasas Hills. It was an upskill neighborhood in Lennox Hills where the homes in that area started at a million dollars or more.

"First place together? Were you not living together before you moved here to Lennox Hills?"

"No. We decided that we should continue to live separately. I love having my own space, and I wasn't ready to move into his space."

"But you were ready for marriage?"

"Yes."

"Why couldn't he move into your place? You didn't have to move into his place once you were married."

She giggled. "My husband giving up his penthouse with views of Central Park to move into my two thousand square foot condo with a view of the emergency side of Cornell hospital."

My next question was why she didn't want to give up that

condo and move right in with her husband. "Marriage is about combining two people who are in love into a life they can build together. Right away, neither of you was receptive to that by keeping your own places."

"Couples live apart all the time. My best friend and her husband lived apart for six months before she moved to California to be with him."

"You are missing the key point. She moved to be with him after a certain time. You and your husband." I took a minute to read through my scattered notes on Kami. "For five years. You've never lived with each other once during those five years, correct?"

"I mean, I spent weeks over at his place, and he's done the same."

"Weeks don't equate to living with someone. I've had family come visit for weeks, it doesn't mean that they live with me."

"It worked for us." She tried to defend their decision.

"Who was the one that proposed this?"

"Me. I enjoy having my space and worked hard to afford a condo in my building. I didn't want to just toss all that away because I married a man with money."

"You don't have to toss anything away. When you decided to marry your husband, you decided that you wanted to have *one* life with that person, not separate lives. You both lived in the same city but not under the same roof."

"We're living together now."

"And how is that going?"

"He sleeps in the guest bedroom, and I sleep in our bedroom. I tried to talk to him about coming into the room with me, but he refuses."

Kami should have come into therapy the first day telling me everything she had told me in the last fifteen minutes. Being married and living in your own apartment away from your husband wasn't out the norm. There were plenty of couples that lived apart, but at some point, they used to live together. Kami and her husband had never lived together.

"Hmm. Does he know that you cheated on him?"

"Yes."

"How much does he know?"

"What kind of question is that?"

"A lot of people omit a lot when it comes to being honest with their spouse. Either to cover themselves or spare their partner's feelings. Which one are you?"

Kami groaned and put her face into her hands then started to rock. "He thinks it happened the one time he caught us, but it was a full affair for an entire year."

"And why did you choose to keep that piece out?"

"He would leave me if he knew what I did. The day he caught us having sex was almost two years ago, and we haven't recovered. Do you know what he would do if he found out it was more than that one time?"

"Why did you cheat? I know you mentioned that you wanted more attention from your husband, but there has to be a reason you had an affair for a year."

Kami was around Harlym's age, maybe even a few years older than her. She was definitely younger than me. I could tell from a lot of her responses that she had so much growing to do.

"Cam made me feel young again. My husband is ten years older than me, so we don't have the same likes and interests." She toyed with a piece of her hair as she reminisced about her affair. "I was twenty-one when we decided to get married, and it was the most spontaneous thing I had ever done. I wanted to be adventurous and have fun. Somewhere along the line, we stopped having fun, and things became routine, even with us having separate homes."

"Marriage isn't fun all the time. Sometimes you have to roll up your sleeves and fight, and those are the times when it matters the most. It sounded like you expected your marriage to be a fantasy every day, and it could be, but that's not ideal.

People change, and shit does get real when you exchange those vows."

"Yeah. I'm starting to see that now."

Marriage was hard.

Every day, you had to wake up and choose that person, no matter their flaws. It didn't matter how much I disliked my husband in those moments and how unhappy I was in our marriage, every morning when I climbed out of our bed, I chose him. Kami seemed like she wanted her marriage to be butterflies and rainbows every day, and that wasn't the case when it came to marriage. The fact that her husband was older than her proved that they were on two different levels with what was wanted and required out of marriage.

"What about children?"

"We don't have any and I don't want any."

"And your husband feels the same?" She checked her watch, which pissed me off. We were finally getting somewhere, and she was more concerned about the time.

"I don't know. He tells me that he's fine either way. A small part of me feels like he does want children and he's not being honest with me. I guess that's why it was so easy to get caught up with Cam

Once again, she mentioned the name Cam, but she never elaborated on it. It was like she expected me to know who she was discussing. "This is the second time you mentioned Cam. What is he like?"

She waved it off. "He just some rapper that I used to date when I was younger. We had a daughter together and gave her up for adoption when we were teens."

This was the part of the job that I hated. I couldn't go and tell my sister what I had just heard because that would be breaking not only my client's trust, but it would be unethical, and I could lose my license behind something like that.

There weren't many Cams running around in the music

industry, so I knew she was talking about the Camron that Harlym was obsessed with and willing to wait five years for.

"So, you have a child already?"

"Had," she quickly corrected.

"Do you see your daughter?"

I could see she was becoming uncomfortable and annoyed by my questions. It was my turn to look at my watch, and I saw we had a little over ten minutes left in our session. "She's not my daughter. We gave her up for adoption when I was a teenager, and it was a closed adoption. She could be anywhere from here to fucking Egypt. When I signed those papers, I wrote her out of my life."

Kami seemed like she rewrote a lot of her life when it didn't fit the mold of the life she was trying to live. "Does your husband know?"

"No, thank God. Me and Cam share a special bond that nobody understands. It doesn't matter where we end up in life, we are always drawn to each other like magnets."

I wanted to tell her to stop quoting the movie Hancock but decided against it. "So, this can happen again?"

"No. He's in prison, and from what I heard it's a lengthy sentence that I'm not going to sit around and wait on."

At least she had more sense than my sister.

I wondered if Harlym knew about Cam's daughter he had given up for adoption or the fact that he and Kami Lynn had this soul mate lover thing going on. Harlym didn't tell me everything about what she and Cam went through because she didn't want me to judge her. For all I knew, this wasn't news to her, and she had already been put onto the chronicles of Cam and Kami.

"Don't you think your husband should know about your past? This a man that you're building a future with, and he doesn't know anything about you."

"He knows plenty."

Flipping the case to my iPad closed, I knew it was time to end the session here. "I want you to journal. You spend a lot of time trying to fit into this mold that you sold to the world, and you're not honest with yourself or those around you."

"So, the solution is to journal?" She replied, skeptical.

"Yes. Be open about everything inside of this journal. Nobody will ever read this but you, so be as raw and open as you can."

"Not even you?"

"Not even me," I repeated. "If you want to discuss anything in the journal, we can do that, but as far as reading, I won't be doing that."

"Okay."

After Kami left the office, I leaned back in the chair and closed my eyes. No sooner than my eyes closed, I heard the door to my office open, and Kyle appeared.

"I know I can't ask what is going on within the sessions, but just wanted to ask if she's a good fit for you."

"I mean, her husband won't even attend the sessions so we're just doing solo sessions with her for now."

"She seems happier when she leaves the office than when she comes. Like she's unloading a lot that needs to be unloaded."

"Yeah." I sighed and closed my eyes back.

Kyle took that as his sign to close the door and sit on the couch Kami had just been sitting. "What's going on?"

"Jace took money out of our savings and bought a new motorcycle." I could tell from Kyle's calm demeanor that he was used to treating clients with these problems. Usually, I hated to be treated like one of his clients. However, today, I needed to unload everything I was feeling and didn't care if he sent me a bill after we were done.

"Did he even have a discussion with you about it?"

"No. He took off from work and got a motorcycle without telling me anything, then turned it onto me like I'm some unhappy bitch that can't celebrate something that makes him happy."

"I want to be the voice of reason in this situation, Astoria, but

I really can't. That is going too far, and the fact that he didn't talk to you about it before doing it is a red flag."

Jace was a walking red flag, and I knew it when we got together. Back then, it was cute to date a boy that was on the wild side. As a mother and now his wife, that shit was nowhere near cute, and I wished I could turn back the hands of time.

So many wasted years, tears, and energy for someone who wasn't worth it.

Kyle crossed his legs and took a deep breath. "I am always down for a couple making their marriage work for them and then the kids. As your friend, I want to see my friend happy. You help all these other couples realize what is right in their face. Why is it so hard for you to do the same thing?"

Damn.

It was right in my face and instead of facing the fact that my husband wasn't the right one for me, I had been pushing past it and ignoring the truth because it hurt too much to think about ending our marriage.

*$187.65 Mr. Chow's restaurant * Lennox Hill, New Jersey*

I looked down at the app notification from my AmEx app. It was just charged now, and I was sitting in this office losing my mind over my husband's bullshit, and he was out to eat spending nearly two hundred dollars on one meal.

"He's at Mr. Chow's again," I whispered, now holding my phone in my hand.

Kyle gave me that look that I was all too familiar with. "You know what needs to be done, and you are dragging your feet because you're scared."

"I'm not scared."

"Babe, it's fine that you are. Shit, it's normal that you're scared. You've been with Jace since you were a teen and more than half of your adult life. You've raised children with this man and experienced all your first with him. Moving on from someone who is familiar and comfortable is scary and that's a normal emotion to feel."

I wiped the tears that slid down my cheeks away. "This is why they pay you the big bucks."

We both paused and broke out into laughter. It was needed because I was feeling some heavy emotions in this moment. "And better be glad you don't get a bill slipped under your door."

"I will always be grateful."

"You can't change or teach a man something that he doesn't want to do. If Jace wanted to salvage his marriage, he would have started to do the work already."

Kyle stood up and walked over to me. He pulled me out the chair and gave me the biggest hug. "I love you."

"Love you more, babe. You have to stop pretending to be fine and actually be fine, and that doesn't happen until you start cleaning house. Go ahead and finish your work so you can get out of here and enjoy your trip. I am too jealous."

"You could always join us."

"We will have our time to have a trip... you enjoy your sister and bestie."

"Thanks, Kyle," I called behind him.

"Anytime." He winked and closed the door behind him.

I quickly wiped my face and prepared myself for my next client of the day. There were so many emotions that I was feeling, and I didn't expect for them to just come up while randomly venting to Kyle.

Me and Bethany locked up my office together and walked to our cars. It was the end of September, so it was a breezy night. I was cursing myself because I had forgotten my favorite cardigan that I loved to wear.

"Please, please, please enjoy your trip, Dr. Jacobs," she pleaded with me.

Everyone around me knew how much I needed this trip. "I will. Enjoy your time off and do lots of fun things with your son. Pumpkin patch, apple picking and all of that. Once they become teens, they act all funny."

"My son isn't even a teen, and he acts funny all the time," she rolled her eyes. "I be ready to snatch him up."

"Tell me about it."

Demi and Enzo hated doing anything as a family like we used to do. I would dress them in matching outfits, and we would go pick apples or find the perfect pumpkin for our front porch. Now all they wanted to do was hang out with their friends at the mall or have their heads in their phones.

After saying my goodbyes to Bethany, I headed to my hair appointment before I had to go home to the mess that I ran out from earlier today. Jace wasn't going to see where I was coming from, and tonight wasn't the time to try to make him see that.

When I stepped into the house, I could hear talking and laughter coming from the dining room. Rounding the corner, I saw Enzo, Demi, Tyler and Jace sitting at the dining table laughing. He took a bite of his food and looked up to see me standing there.

"I scooped Tyler up on the way from Mr. Chow's and decided to have a family dinner... wash your hands, and I'll make you a plate."

"Mom, come sit next to me." Enzo pulled the chair out beside her.

Anytime my baby girl wanted me to sit close to her, I was game. I sat my purse down on the hall table and went into the kitchen to wash my hands. "Red or white wine?" Jace asked while I washed my hands.

"Red."

I was still angry with him. He had all the kids gathered for a family dinner, so he didn't have to deal with the fact that he bought a damn motorcycle today. "Mom, I got invited to a Halloween party today," Demi revealed.

"You only want to go because Connor is going to be there," Enzo blew her sister up. "It's not even October yet, who is throwing a party this early?"

Tyler remained quiet while shoving food into his mouth. "Is

this a boy you like?" I smiled, happy to be getting any small amount of tea.

"No, we're just cool. I help him in math class, and he helps me in science."

"You better not be thinking about no boys. We don't pay that high ass school tuition for you to be focused on boys," Jace interrupted the conversation while pointing his fork at Demi.

I could see the annoyance on my baby's face when her father scolded her. Jace couldn't, or maybe he didn't want to understand that his daughters were growing up. Demi was into boys and all things dance. I didn't mind because she was a good kid, and what teen girl wasn't into boys at her age?

"I just said that we're just cool. Why do you have to make everything into something?" She tossed her napkin onto her plate and excused herself from the table.

"You just had to run your mouth," I mumbled.

Enzo and Tyler were too into their food to care what was going on. "She's boy crazy. You don't hear the little conversations she has with boys that be calling her phone."

"She's fifteen and allowed to have friends, no matter the gender. I'm not going to be strict on her when it comes to dating."

"Maybe we should. You want to be her friend instead of her damn mother."

I paused.

There was so much that I wanted to say to him, and I stopped myself because the kids were here. "Enzo and Tyler, how was your day?"

"Good. I had football practice, and then dad took me to buy new sneakers."

"Yeah, the newest Jordans," Enzo muttered under her breath, but I heard her clearly. He must have used his own money for that because I didn't see a charge on the card from a sneaker store.

"Ryan got a pair, and I wanted them, so dad surprised me

with a trip to the mall." Tyler popped a piece of bourbon chicken into his mouth.

"A new iPhone and sneakers... cool."

Jace cut his eyes at me.

I didn't doubt that my husband loved our daughters. He just had a funny way of showing it whenever it came to them. When they were younger, he used to be more involved with them, and they were daddy's girls. Enzo kept up their little game with each other because that was all she had with him. Now that they were older, it was like he didn't know how to connect with them, and their relationship was dwindling away. His relationship with Demi had gone downhill over the past few years. Other than the occasional banter during dinner or in passing, she and Jace didn't speak or spend time together.

I was curious to know how things would go down while I was on vacation. Demi didn't have me to relay the message to her father, and she couldn't come to me instead of him. For an entire week, she would have to depend on her father, and I knew that would be hard for her.

I assumed Tyler was staying the night over, and Jace would end up driving him and the girls to school in the morning since he was off from work again. I wanted to know why he had so many days off, like he didn't have a motorcycle sitting in the garage.

"I think I'm going to keep Tyler over while you're out of town," Jace broke the silence in our bedroom.

I moisturized my hands while staring into my vanity mirror. "Wouldn't that be a commute for you? His school is way across town and the opposite direction from the girl's school and your job."

"Tyler has fall break, and his football team is having extra practices during their week off. I only have to get the girls to school, which shouldn't be a problem."

"You have paid time to do that?"

"I had a couple of days that I needed to use, and I'll take the loss on the other days." He was trying to get to me to blow up.

"Why in the hell would you take time off when you just bought a motorcycle? If anything, you need to be working to put that money back."

"You acting like we were using that money for something. It was just sitting in the account... I will put money back slowly but surely."

"It's a fucking savings account for emergencies... what part don't you understand about that? You took that money without asking me, then went on to spend nearly two hundred dollars for dinner. Why are you determined to dig us into a financial hole?"

"You bitch when I don't do nothing, and when I finally grab dinner and have a family night, you on my case about that too."

"A family dinner could be pizza, cheap Chinese food, or fast food. It didn't need to be fucking Mr. Chow's on a random ass Tuesday."

I was down for indulging in something that made you feel better. Mr. Chow's was my favorite spot, and I loved to eat there occasionally. Jace had never been a fan of the place and always said it was overpriced. He had eaten there twice already, and both times were without me, besides what he brought home for us to eat.

"After our fight, I thought this would cheer you up because you always talking about their potstickers. My bad for trying to do something nice for my wife."

"Oh please, Jace. Don't try to turn this onto me. You did it because you know I'm pissed about that damn motorcycle. You need to try and sell it because it's not staying here."

"This my house too. Stop talking like you the only one that pay bills in this bitch."

"Barely," I mumbled.

I wasn't the kind of woman that expected a man to pay for everything. This was our home, and I was more than happy to help share the cost it took to run this house together. There had been times when I covered the mortgage alone because his check wasn't what he was expecting it to be. I never complained because that was what you did in a marriage. It had become tiring when my husband never took it upon himself to cover something, so I didn't have to come out of pocket for it. The only thing he could claim he did was physically paying the mortgage and cell phone bill. I moved the money into our shared credit union account and allowed him to feel like a man. I thought by letting him have the responsibility of the bills that it would force him to want to actually make the payments out his own damn account.

"What you said?"

"Nothing."

I could always set my clock to when I was going to receive that text from Jace to pay the mortgage. He paid the mortgage, and I sent my half while I paid all the other smaller bills since he couldn't be so bothered to pay those.

He never thought of surprising me by covering the mortgage once in a while, so I could use the saved money for us to go out and do something together. He expected me to send that money as soon as he was emailed the billing notification.

"I told Messiah I would come to the bar and kick it with him for a few hours."

"Be careful," I choked out, upset that he didn't see anything wrong with the shit he was doing to me. He had time and money to hang out at the bar, but not to make shit right between us. He didn't even mention anything about my new hairstyle, and that hurt more than I thought it would. I was truly invisible to my husband, and that was what hurt the most.

"Always am." I jumped when he slammed the bedroom door behind him.

Wiping my tears, I looked into the mirror. Where did things go so wrong for us? Had he never cared about me in the way that I cared about him? I felt like I had taken my blinders off and was seeing my husband in his true light for the first time.

It was a shitty sight to witness.

I RUMMAGED through my purse to make sure I had my passport and everything I needed before leaving the house. It never mattered that I knew I had my passport and had checked at least twenty times, I always had to double check to make sure that it was still there. This was my first vacation without my daughters or my husband, and I had all intentions of enjoying every part of it. I wanted to let loose and forget all the bullshit that would be waiting for me when I arrived back home next week.

This was the girl's trip that had finally made it out the group chat, and I couldn't wait to board the plane, order a drink and kick back with Ember and Harlym. As women, we put our all into our careers, and this was the chance for us not to worry about anything for an entire week.

"The car is outside, Mom," Demi called from the foyer.

I held my passport briefly before shoving it into the back pocket of my purse. "Good. At least he's on time," I muttered as I quickly headed into the kitchen to find Jace.

He was sitting at the counter with his face planted into his phone with his coffee sitting beside him. "Alright now, y'all need to hurry up so we can get out the door before traffic gets too bad."

He was so into his phone that he didn't look up once. Demi was already waiting by the steps, and Enzo was in the dining room with her book.

"Hey. My ride is here... I will shoot you a text when I get to the airport and before I take off. Don't forget that Enzo has her engineering workshop later this afternoon that she can't miss. The money for the dues are in the—"

"Damn, Stori. I know how to take care of my kids, and you went over everything for the past week. Go and have fun with your friends... we're going to be fine." He finally looked up from his phone.

Things between us were still tense, and there was still a lot that we hadn't talked about. We were basically tiptoeing around the fact that we had serious problems. I was doing everything in my power not to get into it with him because I didn't want to start my trip on a bad note.

"I want to make sure that everything runs smoothly while I'm gone," I replied, annoyed that he wasn't taking my instructions seriously.

"I'm their father... you don't think I can do a good enough job while you're gone for the week? Come the fuck on," he raised his voice.

Tossing my hands up, I left the kitchen and went to retrieve my purse and suitcase. Demi was still sitting on the stairs in the foyer when I came out the kitchen. "Mom, have the best time." She smiled.

I hated that my daughter had to witness all the strife me and my husband went through. She wasn't a stranger to the arguments that we had on a daily basis. When she was younger, we had been able to hide so much from the girls, but now that they were older, I was sure they heard our fights no matter how much I tried to shield them from it. Plus, the five-bedroom old craftsman house didn't have the thickest walls.

"I will, baby. Please make sure to remind your father that Enzo has her workshop today. Make sure to light some fire under him." I smiled, pinching her cheeks.

"Got you, Mom," she replied.

I placed my purse on top of my suitcase and hesitated for a bit. Enzo was preoccupied with her book, so I quickly kissed and squeezed her cheeks before leaving.

"See you next week, baby."

"Love you, Mom. Turn up and stop being so boring... enjoy yourself," my youngest told me and I shook my head.

"When did you become so big?" Both of my daughters wanted me to have the best time and didn't seem worried that I was leaving them for a week.

Maybe that meant that I should have a great time and let my hair loose for once. "I'm not a little kid anymore. Whole teenager here." She closed her book and packed it into her backpack.

Tyler jogged down the steps with his football gear and bag in his hand. "Later, Stori. Have a safe flight."

"Thanks, Ty. Have a good practice."

I could tell they were all ready for me to leave. It would probably be the most peaceful week the two of them had with me out the house. Anytime me or Jace traveled, I knew they looked forward to it. They were usually able to get over on the other parent when one was away.

It had been a while since I had gone on a girl's trip or traveled anywhere since the girls were younger. Other than dinner out with my Harlym or Ember every so often, I didn't get out much. Jace, on the other hand, had no problem making plans with his friends every week or whenever they planned a boy's trip out of town. I was always skeptical of these boy's trips because that was how Tyler was conceived. It was the source of many arguments that we were always getting into. Whenever Jace went out with his boys, he never called to check in on me or the girls.

When he went out of town, he acted like he didn't have a wife or daughters at home. I wouldn't hear from him unless he was boarding his flight and returning back home. That was something that bothered me the most about Jace.

"I love you," I reached down and kissed Demi on the cheek. "Make sure homework gets completed... both of you."

"Mom, please go before you miss your flight, even though you're like four hours early," She took some time to poke fun at me.

"You say early, and I say more drinks at the lounge... okay, please text me when you both get out of school."

"Okay." She ushered me out the door and watched as the driver took my suitcase and held the door open for me.

I couldn't believe that I was on my way to the airport, and we were finally going on this trip. After the past few years we all had, this trip was much deserved for all three of us. I prayed that I could convince my sister to leave Cam alone and live her life. The deposits had been paid, so it was meant for us to go on this trip.

"Yes, Harlym?" I answered as soon as I climbed into the back of the black navigator. "I just got into the truck, and we're on our way to the airport."

"Good. I texted Demi to make sure too."

I scoffed. "Seriously? Using my kid to spy on me?"

"She's my niece... I was checking on her, and if I so happen to ask if her mother left the house yet, that's not a crime."

"Whatever." I fixed my freshly braided hair and pulled my shades over my eyes.

I was so convinced that I would be able to pack, shower and read a few chapters of my book last night, and ended up packing until three this morning. With only a few hours of sleep and no coffee, I was dead to the world and ready to sit in the lounge and decompress before this flight.

"Me and Ember know exactly how you are... you never want to leave the girls."

"Life has been so bus—"

"Save it, Astoria. All of our lives have been busy, and we deserve some time away. Especially you and Ember... I know you both are overwhelmed with everything you both have going on. Being wives isn't easy."

"Well, you know Ember isn't a wife anymore... so you need to make sure that you correct yourself before we all get together."

"Shit," Harlym cursed. "I keep messing that up. Anyway,

have a safe drive, and I will see you in a little bit… make sure to flirt with the driver. Ember already texted and told me that hers was cute."

Harlym had slipped up during our dinner a few weeks ago, and Ember got upset. I ignored her comment about flirting with the driver and put my headphones on to enjoy the ride to JFK airport. It was rare that I had a moment to sit and enjoy the scenery whenever I was in a car. My drives were usually filled with me in the driver's seat, arguing with the traffic that I was stuck in. Today, I was able to watch the beautiful sun come up as we drove on the highway headed into New York.

It was Ember's idea to hire a limousine service to chauffeur us to the airport. When she told me, I turned it down because it was expensive and definitely a splurge. She reminded me how we didn't do this often, and we needed to go all out, so I threw caution into the wind and decided to hire one. It took us an hour to make it to the airport. By the time I checked my bag and headed through security, I was desperately searching for the lounge to grab a glass of champagne that was much needed.

"Astoria!" I whipped my head around and saw Ember rushing toward me with a huge beach hat and her luggage trailing behind her. "Girl, I was calling you since gate three… we are now at gate twelve."

I hadn't noticed she was calling me because I had my headphones in while trying to send a text to Jace to let him know that I had arrived at the airport. I was annoyed that he read my message and never responded.

"My bad, Em… I was trying to get a hold of Jace. Do you know he left me on read and still hav—"

Ember held up her hand. "We're not doing this for the entire week. Whenever Jace goes out of town, I know he doesn't even mention you or the girls to his friends. How do I know? Because Messiah says none of them do."

I heaved a sigh and looked at her dramatic hat. "They didn't have anything bigger?"

She popped the hat onto her head and smiled. "I saw a woman on Instagram take a picture with a big hat like this, so I'm trying to recreate the picture. I'm in my single divorced era… gotta get new pictures for the dating app."

We found the lounge and checked in before finding seats near the alcohol. "Do you think you are finally ready to get out there?"

"Me and Messiah have been divorced for six months and separated for almost two years… It's time for me to move on." She sat her purse down and plopped down into her seat.

"I mean… starting to date just sounds so…" I allowed my words to trail off. "Soon."

"Ain't nothing soon about getting back out there. I'm tired of using those toys… I want the real thing."

The server in the lounge came over to assist us. We both ordered champagne and an expresso to give us the boost we both needed this morning. "Shit, I want the same thing too. Me and Jace haven't had sex in almost a month."

"Which is even more of a reason you need to stop trying to force something that isn't there." Ember raised her brows at me.

"We've been married for years… we're just going through a rough patch." I tried to convince myself when I knew better.

We had been going through a rough patch since we first met. I had grown used to the struggle in our relationship that it became normal to me. Each time I tried to make an effort, I was met with so much resistance that eventually, I grew tired and gave up. That wasn't any way to live, and I could admit, it wasn't fair to either of us.

One of us had to make that call.

A call that was easier said than done because we had built so much together, and it wasn't just a typical boyfriend and girlfriend relationship anymore. We were in our thirties, grown and married with children. Our kids were who we had to consider. They were the most important in all of this.

"I loved Messiah; the lord knew I did. Stori, the minute I

stopped worrying about the time we put in and started thinking about my happiness, that's when I started to have those conversations with him. We had gone through so much with the infertility that it drained the both of us. Just like I was unhappy, he was too, and he was just waiting on me to come to him."

Messiah and Ember had been married for as long as me and Jace. They got married a few years after us. I was Ember's maid of honor, while Jace was Messiah's best man. All throughout the wedding, everyone kept referring to me and Jace as the blueprint. It felt nice that our marriage was being recognized, but we were far from that. In fact, we were struggling hard with our marriage and pretending like everything was perfect.

Typical for us.

"How about we make a pact right now. We don't talk about my marriage or anything that pertains to it for the next week."

"Or lack thereof," Harlym came and tossed her Gucci tote in the empty seat beside me. "I need me a big ass drink because the way my driver tried me this morning." She sucked her teeth and crossed her arms.

"My drive to the airport was so soothing... I could hear myself think for the hour we were driving. Traffic wasn't that bad either." Ember said exactly what I was thinking.

I couldn't remember the last time I experienced a silent car ride that I wasn't the one doing the driving. "Same here."

"My driver was on the phone arguing with his baby mama about working all night. Then he tosses his phone to me so I could lie and tell her that he was my driver all night."

"And what did you do?" I questioned, knowing my sister, and knowing how she got down. Harlym was the loudest out of all of us.

She also had the biggest heart to match that mouth.

"I'm a girl's girl... I told her the truth. If he thought he was going to use me as an alibi, he got me fucked up." She plopped down right beside her bag. "Anyway, I don't want to hear about

Jace or Messiah's whack asses. The goal is to get you laid and maybe even get you laid too."

"I am married, Harlym," I reminded her.

"Barely," she quickly shot back.

I ignored Harlym and accepted the drink from the server. Soon as she had handed both me and Ember our drinks, my sister pulled her over to let her know all the drinks she needed prior to us boarding our flight.

"One week in the Maldives… I cannot wait." Ember clinked glasses with me and downed her champagne in one gulp.

"It only took us damn near two years to make this happen. The hotel receptionist started to give me attitude before I told her I was calling to lock in our dates." Harlym cut her eyes at me.

"What matters is we're here now, and we're going to have the best time. I'm so happy we decided to fly business class because whew," Ember diffused the situation quickly.

Harlym was stuck on the wrong things. What mattered was that I was sitting in this lounge next to her, and we would be spending the next week together.

As much as I loved Harlym, she had a way that stepped on my nerves often. She didn't care who she offended with her words and because of that, we often bumped heads about it. Harlym didn't understand the sacrifices you took as a mother because she didn't have any children or a free man. She was so hell bent on waiting on Cam, that I feared that she would never know of the sacrifices I've had to make being a mother, because she was putting her life on hold for him. Even if she decided to step outside her relationship, she would never make a commitment, and wouldn't settle down. Fear forced Harlym from looking for someone better, which is what she deserved. The timeline on when Kami was discovered fucking her ex-boyfriend lined up with the exact time that Harlym and Cam were together.

Which meant he cheated on her.

I wanted to tell my sister so bad but knew I couldn't utter a word that Kami had told me in therapy. Harlym deserved so much better, and I desperately wanted that for her. It was one thing to be a fool behind my husband, but it wasn't alright for my sister to be one behind a man that had a damn bedtime.

When I thought about what I wanted for my daughters, they didn't have a great example from none of the women in our family.

"I don't think neither of us would have lasted in coach. We are not those youngins anymore that could book cheap flights and not worry about seating."

"Tuh, speak for yourself. I'm not as old as you heifers," Harlym disagreed.

"Oh, shut up." Ember rolled her eyes.

"You lucky my man is calling me." Harlym held up her phone and then skipped away from our seating area.

"When the hell is she going to be over him? I've literally been watching her social media pages to see when he's going to piss her off."

"You just want to win that bet you both have going on. Harlym isn't going to leave his ass alone until she has a reason, which sucks."

"Let her live her life. You can't fix everybody. She needs her sister the most, not a therapist," Ember reminded me.

Me and Harlym have had many fights in the past because I felt like I needed to dig into her personal life. It was the reason she barely told me things now, and I hated myself for being the overprotective therapist sister that she didn't need. All she wanted was her big sister to agree with her no matter if she was wrong or not.

"I know."

"He has some damn nerve. Got mad at me because I'm going on vacation and won't be able to take his damn call until we get to our layover in Dubai." Harlym slumped down in the chair again.

"He'll get over it." Ember pushed another glass of champagne over her way.

"Drown my sorrows in champagne," Harlym downed the champagne and closed her eyes briefly. "Sometimes trying to hold him down is draining."

"He's probably just insecure because he's in there and you're out here," I said, trying hard not to dig deep and tell her to leave him alone.

"Probably."

They ended up calling our flights to board, so we downed a few more drinks and headed downstairs to the gate to board. I couldn't wait to strip out these clothes and toss on a bathing suit. The amount of weight I had gained throughout the years usually bothered me, but not on this trip. I promised myself that I would love myself and show every inch of this body. With the amount of revealing clothes I packed, there was no going back, even if I wanted to.

This week, I was just Astoria. I wasn't Demi and Enzo's mama, or Jace's wife. I was going to channel that fun, flirty and adventurous woman I always wanted to be.

The flight attendant took our drink orders as we stored our carry-on luggage away, and I plopped down in my seat. "To a week we're never going to forget." Ember smiled.

"A week that will bring us closer and change our lives," Harlym added.

"To a week of new beginnings," I concluded.

SIX
BRAY WILLSHIRE

"MAN, WHY THE HELL ARE YOU SITTING HERE IN YOUR VILLA WHEN there's a party at the beach club?" Ashton came busting through my villa into the back where I was sitting. "They having a greeting party for all the new guest tonight." He proceeded to sit on the empty chair beside me and kick his feet up on the small wooden chair that separated us.

Pushing his feet down, I continued going over the emails I had received while traveling. "They scheduled a tour for me and Laurent tomorrow morning. I'm not trying to be out all night getting drunk."

Ashton screwed his face up. "What happened to the Bray telling us fuck it, we ball? Now you wanna be sitting here with your specs on doing work. We're not here for none of that... we supposed to be bonding as brothers. You always asking why I don't want to be part of the family business, and this is the reason. I see you and Laurent giving your all like Pops did, and I refuse to go out like that."

I paused and looked at my baby brother. Whenever I asked Ashton why he didn't want any parts of the family business, he could never give me a solid answer. It was always filled with bullshit about wanting to be free or not wanting the responsibility. He had never told me that he didn't want to end up like me or Laurent. Part of me felt bad that my brother looked at me as a workaholic that didn't have an off button.

He sounded like Kami whenever we argued about work. She loved her career just as much as I loved mine, but she complained whenever I had to work or travel for work. I used to feel bad about leaving her because she was my wife and wanted to spend time with me. Now, I couldn't wait to be away from her. When she asked about our trip, I told her we were going out the country and didn't offer any more information. Staring into her eyes, I could tell that she wanted to ask more questions.

Was I punishing her?

Yeah.

I wanted her to pay for the shit she did, and I didn't want to talk about it either. Whenever I saw her break down about us not getting anywhere with fixing our marriage, the shit made me feel good. Seeing her hurt made me feel better because now she knew exactly how I felt. Now she could feel the pain I felt seeing my wife in that compromising position with another man.

"You right. We came here to enjoy the resort and kick back, so I won't work during the day," I compromised.

I'd be a liar if I said I wouldn't work at all. I couldn't go an entire week and a half without at least touching base and making sure things were running smoothly. My cousin Woody was holding down the fort while I was away, so I felt a little bit better about letting loose.

"You dead ass? All I had to do was mention Pops, and you ready to turn up? Well, shit, I kind of want a Rolls Royce for my birthday—"

"Chill, kid." I laughed and closed my laptop. "Where's Laurent?"

"In his villa on facetime with Luna. You both get me tight, acting all soft like y'all don't remember how to turn up and have fun."

"Chill the fuck out... I said I'll come to the party on the

beach." I headed back inside my villa, and put my laptop on the desk in the kitchen area. "I'm married; you act like I'm out at clubs all the time."

"Yeah, married.... Not dead."

My marriage was dead. It had been dead for the past few years, and I was just holding onto it to play with Kami's head. It was too fucked up to admit out loud, so I kept it quiet from my brothers. They looked to me and Kami as the blueprint to marriage, and I didn't want to feel like I was letting them down.

Despite not being the biggest fan of my wife these days, I wanted to save her image in front of them. Having them know she liked to fuck on the kitchen counter with low budget rappers wasn't something I'm sure she was proud of.

Especially Ashton.

"You right. Give me a few to get my shit together."

Ashton nodded. "If you not ready within twenty minutes, I'm kicking the door in... and I can because my name on this bitch," he threatened as he headed out the door.

I shook my head as I walked into the room to check my messages. Like I expected, Kami's name was the most called. Pressing her name, I looked across the room at all my clothes unpacked. The butler that came with my villa unpacked and prepared everything for me. I didn't have to lift a finger if I didn't want to.

"Hey, Bray. I've been calling you all day."

"Yeah, I noticed that."

The line grew silent.

"If you knew I've been calling you all day, why didn't you answer the phone?" She replied.

I could hear in her tone that she was annoyed because I hadn't answered the phone for her today. In my defense, I hadn't answered the phone for nobody. My assistant had been hitting me all morning and I ignored her calls too. It wasn't often that I got to sleep in or wake up to a view of just the water. With the way each villa was set up, you didn't see your neighbors. Soon as the curtains opened, all you saw were miles and miles of water and the occasional fishing boat.

When Kami's name popped across my screen this morning, nothing inside of me pushed me to grab my phone to answer. That was a sign that my marriage was over. When I didn't even get excited about hearing from my wife. That never used to be us. When Kami's name used to come across my screen, I stopped everything to answer it for her. I didn't care if she called in the middle of a meeting, I was pausing that shit to answer the phone for wifey. She was a priority to me, and I made sure she knew that. Our lives were so hectic because of the careers we'd chosen, but I tried my hardest to make shit work with her.

When I had feelings for someone, especially being in love, I made sure to apply pressure behind that person. Kami used to be the one that I wanted to apply pressure behind, and now I didn't even want to come home some nights. I didn't feel the same about her, and I thought the feeling would eventually fade. All the articles I read about marriage infidelities told me that you could get through it together.

I didn't think that was true for me and Kami. Every time I stared at her, I couldn't help but to think about that face she had while fucking Cam. The only reason I stuck around was because Kami wanted this badly. I always told myself that as long as we fought, that this marriage would be worth it for me. She was the only one fighting for this marriage because I had mentally tapped out that day in her kitchen.

I felt less than a man.

My wife had to go to another man to get what she felt she couldn't get from me. Kami liked to make the excuse that I worked too much and never made her a priority, and that may have been only half true. I did work too much, but I *always* made her a priority. Kami had more ways to get in touch with me than my mother.

"Kam, I was unplugging... damn."

"Unplugging? If I had done something like that, you would have been pissed," she countered.

"Nah, you can feel free to unplug all you want... I won't be mad."

"Bray, why?"

"Why what?"

"You giving me this attitude... I feel like I don't know you anymore," she confessed. "I'm trying so hard to fix my mistakes, and I feel like you just keep punishing me."

"Just because you want to fix the pain you caused doesn't mean I'm open to that."

"Then why the fuck are we still married?"

"Shit, Kam... I've been wondering the same thing."

Rod said this shit the best, I used to look at Kam and feel butterflies, and now my stomach turned at the sight of her. I listened to her soft sniffles on the other end of the line, and the fucked up side of me enjoyed it. Knowing that she was hurt was something that I had found comfort in, and that wasn't even me.

She turned me into a man that my mother wouldn't have been proud of, and I didn't like that shit. "I do love you, Bray. I didn't get married to be divorced."

"I didn't get married to have my wife fucking other niggas."

"Instead of fucking punishing me, why don't you just come to therapy? We've tried to fix this ourselves. Now it's time for us to get a professional's help. Therapy has been a blessing to me."

She wanted to sit on the phone and have a conversation about our fucked-up marriage, and I wasn't in the mood for that shit. "I'm 'bout to take a shower and meet my brothers down on the beach. I'll call you tomorrow."

I didn't plan on calling her tomorrow. If she had something to look forward to, then I considered myself doing a good deed. "Please, Bray," she pleaded.

"I gotta go." I ended the phone, tossed it onto the bed and went to get ready. Kami wanted to sit and have a conversation that we had been having for the past two years.

I was tired.

It was time for me to get off this rollercoaster and live life without feeling angry all the time. I could be having a good day, and then she would call, and my day would go to shit real quick. That wasn't any way to live, especially not with someone that was supposed to be your wife.

"About time this nigga made it down here. I was getting my ass kicking foot ready to kick that damn door in." Ashton took a shot and pushed over the bottle of white Hennessy they were taking shots from.

The beach club was real chill and relaxed with the DJ playing Afro beats. Everyone inside was dancing while those sitting at the sections on the beach were chilled out, smoking hookah or drinking. I grabbed the bottle, poured some into a glass, and took it back.

"Damn, bro... that wasn't even a shot," Laurent choked on his smoke.

"I had one of those days," I vaguely responded, and got comfortable in the chair. "This shit is a little vibe."

"Right?" Ashton countered. "I been watching that one right there... what are the odds we at the same resort?"

Me and Laurent turned to see what Ashton was chatting about. My eyes landed on the thick beauty that was swiping her braids out of her face. It was her olive complexion, almond-shaped eyes and sandy brown braids that did it for me. If I had been closer, I would have been able to tell what color her eyes were. When I looked over her body, I almost wanted to run over there and grab her for myself.

She was thick.

In all the right places too.

She wore a coral two-piece skirt set that exposed a little bit of her stomach. The skirt had a deep split that showed me exactly why my member was starting to rise.

Down boy. I spoke to myself because baby was fine, and I

could tell she knew it. She twisted her hips, held her drink as she grinded along to the songs that were playing.

Plus size women were my weakness. A queen like her could get whatever she wanted out of me, and I would never complain. I watched as she tossed her head around and those braids hit that round ass of hers while she giggled with her friends.

"You wanna go over there? Damn... you fucking drooling," Ashton snapped me out of the trance she had put me in.

"Matter fact, I do."

"What?" Ashton nearly freaked out.

"You were just talking all this shit about shorty... go and talk to her."

"Yeah, that was *talk*. She one of those influencer types. She not about to have me in her get ready with me videos and shit," Ashton took another shot of liquid courage. "Fuck it, come on."

"This nigga is as confused as Luna on ice cream day." Laurent chuckled. "We heading over there or what?"

I stood, making the first move. My brothers stood and followed behind me as we maneuvered through all the party-goers. When we made it to their section, the woman Ashton had been eyeing was the first to notice. The other two women were too busy drinking and dancing on one another to notice us.

"Ashton Willshire." She stood with this smirk on her face. Shorty resembled the other woman - my woman.

The other two stopped dancing and noticed us standing there. Ashton not only invited himself into their section, but he made himself comfortable by taking a seat and propping his feet up on the small table. "Harlym J."

"You know each other?" My beauty spoke first, clearly confused.

"We know *of* one another...he has worked and fucked a lot of my friends." She turned her face up at him.

Leave it to Ashton to have his dirt follow him thousands of

miles away. "Chill out. I handled my business with them, that is all."

"Yeah, if that includes taking their pictures, fucking them and then giving them money for a Plan B after."

"Damn," Laurent muttered.

"I wouldn't make you take one though." Ashton touched her chin, and I peeped the small smirk before she slapped his hand away.

"Excuse our brother, Bray Willshire," I introduced myself to both women, making sure I held onto the beauty's hand a little bit longer.

She smiled, exposing a side dimple that was so deep it could probably hold all my billions in it. "Hey, you are good. I'm Stori, and this is my best friend, Ember."

Her name.

It was funny because I never believed in that love at first sight bullshit. As I stared into her light brown eyes, I could see our love story unfold right in front of us.

"I'm rude as shit... Laurent Willshire... It's nice to meet you, beautiful." He kissed the back of Ember's hand.

"It's like you know I'm freshly divorced." She blushed.

Laurent's eyebrows raised. "Oh shit, then this might be my lucky night. Can I buy the section anything?"

"We're fine," Ember politely turned down Laurent's gesture. "We're not against you guys coming to hang in our section with us... we know how to share."

Me and Laurent chuckled. "We didn't mean to offend you. Do you have a section of your own?" Stori questioned.

"Over there," I nodded toward the VIP lounge that we had abandoned to come over here.

Her eyes widened. "Hmm, okay, you actually stunting on us... I'm scared of y'all." She held her hands up in a playful surrender.

Ashton and Harlym were still bickering with each other while Laurent and Ember had taken a seat and were talking.

With the way she was flipping her hair back and forth, I could tell she was feeling him. This was the first time I had seen Laurent even interested in another woman.

"Something like that." I looked down at her, and she met my eye contact and held it.

"I was about to head to the bar to grab another lemon drop... want to walk me over?"

"I think my mama would be mad if I didn't escort a beautiful woman such as yourself." I winked.

She removed the braids from her face again and then headed out of the section.

There were different bars situated around the beach. The sections had their own bar to avoid overwhelming the bartenders and having a bunch of drunken people crowding the bars.

When we designed this resort, we wanted everything to be easy. With the amount of money people were spending to come here, we didn't want them to have to lift a finger to do anything.

"Another lemon drop, please." She smiled at the bartender.

"I told you I make the best," he replied in broken English and then smiled. When he noticed me, he stood up straight. "Er... hi... Mr. Willshire, can I get you something?"

"I'm good, Eugene," I read his name tag. "Get this woman anything she wants and put it on my tab."

The resort wasn't all-inclusive, so I knew she was running up a tab on drinks with her girls. "That isn't necessary," she paused.

"What's wrong?"

"Willshire... y...you're a Willshire?"

"I am." I sat on the bar stool, and she stood between my legs, now eye level with me.

"Wow... Sir, you don't have to do an—"

"Come on, Ma... don't do me like that." I laughed.

She smirked. "Like what?"

"This. Don't treat me differently because my last name

happens to be on the doors of this place." I reached out and touched her cheek.

Eugene slid her drink over to her. "Thank you."

"Those drinks must be hitting."

"Oh God, they are. Totally worth the fourteen-dollar price tag," she rolled her eyes. "What's with that, Mr. Willshire?"

"Damn, you gonna call me out like that?"

"Yes. Why the drinks and food so expensive?"

"It's a seven-star resort... what you expect?"

She slowly took a sip of her drink, leaving the blush pink lip gloss stain on the rim of the glass. "You're right about that. I might have to sell my kidney when I get home."

"What brings you out here? Celebrating or something?"

"It was a trip that was planned two years ago. We couldn't push it back anymore, so we decided to come. We all work hard, so we deserve it."

"Looks like those two finally stopped fighting."

We turned to look at Ashton and Harlym laughing with each other instead of her pointing her finger into his temple. "You and your other brother I can see in the boardrooms... him? I just don't see it." She giggled.

"He's not. Ash don't want nothing to do with the hotel business."

"Seems very lucrative... why?"

"What do you do, Stori?"

I switched the subject, not wanting to discuss my brother's life decisions when I was in the company of this beautiful woman. "I'm a therapist."

"Oh, word?"

"Uh huh. You should actually address me as Dr. Jacobs."

I was impressed. A woman with a degree was a turn-on for me, especially one that could separate her life and have fun. "Oh shit... Dr. Jacobs," I leaned forward and whispered into her ear. "Can I call you doctor when I'm deep in those guts?"

She held onto the bar and her drink at the same time. "Mr.

Willshire," she gained her composure, and looked me in the eyes. "I know you see this wedding ring on my finger."

"I see it." I made her aware that I did see the ring, and I was choosing to ignore it. "I also see the woman who hasn't stopped eye fucking me, like I haven't stopped eye fucking her."

She rested her hand on my thigh and looked me in the eyes. "Are you always this blunt?"

"Only when it's something or *someone* that I want. Tell me that ring means something, and I can be on my best behavior. Tell me something else, and I promise I'll do the opposite."

I wanted her.

This was my first time meeting her tonight and I didn't know her from a hole in the wall, still, I wanted her. On the walk to the beach, so many women were throwing themselves at me, and none of them made me do a second look.

Stori…

She had me doing a second, third and fourth look at her. I didn't want her out of my sight, and I made sure of it as I held her waist and kept her locked between my legs.

She played with the ring while battling her thoughts internally. I could tell she was choosing her words and actions carefully while playing out every possible scenario before she opened her mouth and spoke. I watched as she took the small diamond ring off her finger and slid it into the pocket of her skirt.

"Guess you made your decision… how long you here?"

"A week."

"Stay longer." We were staying for a week and a half, and I wanted her with me the entire time.

"Boy, this week already costs too much. I can't even imagine staying longer."

"Ma, look at me." I held her chin up so she was staring me directly in the eyes. "Nothing about me screams *boy*… I'm a grown man. Lose that word out your vocabulary whenever you're addressing me."

She nodded her head. "Okay."

"I'm about to bust this man in the head with this bottle." Harlym stormed over to us with her phone in her hand. "He just picked up the phone for my man and told him to go back to bed and stop calling from his doo-doo butt phone."

Me and Stori broke out into laughter because only Ashton would say some shit like that. "I'm... I'm sorry, Har," Stori said through tears.

"It was nice meeting you and your other brother... But Ashton can go to hell." She pulled Stori away.

"Sorry." She mouthed as she allowed her sister to pull her off the beach. Ember quickly wrapped up her conversation with Laurent and was right behind them.

I walked back over to the section where Laurent was sitting, pissed. "Leave it to this nigga to fuck something up. Me and Ember were hitting it off."

"Oh, shut up... We're *hitting* it off," Ashton mocked. "Talking like you from High School Musical or something."

"You really fucked up our vibe though, Ash."

"Harlym too damn fine to be fucking with that loser ass nigga," he muttered as he watched them continue to walk off the beach.

I watched the way Stori's ass moved in that skirt and made a mental note to get her villa number from reception. When she twisted that ring off her finger, she let me know she was on the same type of time that I was on.

SEVEN

DR. ASTORIA JACOBS

"I CANNOT BELIEVE HE DID THAT LAST NIGHT." HARLYM WAS STILL going on about what Ashton did while she was on the phone with Cam.

While she paced in front of my beautiful view, me and Ember remained in the bed, trying to recover from all the drinks we had last night. I wasn't drunk, but tipsy was the perfect way to describe us last night. Between the shots and lemon drops, I was ready for anything that Bray wanted to do, and that was horrible.

I was a married woman.

Was it that horrible though? Jace did whatever he wanted within our marriage and didn't take our vows seriously. That didn't make me any better either. Just because he did something didn't mean that I had to do the same thing.

"Girl, shut up." Em had finally heard enough of Harlym's complaining. "Cam was going to find a reason to be mad at you even if Ashton didn't pick up your phone... making all this noise... be quiet." She rolled her over, pulled her blanket over her head and didn't say another word.

Harlym stood there shocked, unsure of what to say or do. "Come out on the pat—"

The doorbell to our villa caused us both to pause. "You expecting someone?"

"No." I was just as confused as Harlym as I grabbed my robe and shuffled to the front door.

If Harlym didn't wake up venting about last night, I probably would have been still asleep. "Good morning, Dr. Jacobs. I have breakfast for the room."

"Um, we didn't order anything."

"Mr. Willshire requested we bring your villa breakfast this morning. He also told me to give you this." He quickly pulled an envelope from his front pocket.

I moved aside and allowed him to push the cart into our villa. "You can set up outside." If Em had to listen to the sounds of plates and silverware, I was sure she would have punched this man in the face.

I slipped the man a twenty-dollar tip on his way out and closed the door behind him. "Breakfast?" Harlym sat Indian style on the lounge chair while taking a bite of bacon.

"This was sweet of them."

"Girl, now who you trying to fool? This wasn't sent by *them*. Bray sent this shit to you."

I ignored my sister and opened the envelope up as she started to dig into the breakfast.

Dr. Jacobs, I refuse to believe that oatmeal didn't play a part in how thick and scrumptious those thighs and that ass is... so I sent extra.

"Why the hell they sent four bowls of oatmeal?" On cue, Harlym asked.

I smiled and tucked the note away. "It's a joke."

"You got jokes with this man already and only met him yesterday... teach me your ways."

"I don't have any ways. Last night, I had too much to drink and flirted when I shouldn't have. I'm married, Har."

Harlym cut her eyes at me. "Does your husband know that?"

"Don't start," I warned.

"Seriously, Stori. You are on an island with a fine ass man

that obviously wants your time. Fuck Jace and do you for once. It's always been about Jace since the both of you were younger; it's time for you to have fun." She looked down at my hand. "And I don't see that wedding ring on your finger anymore."

I ran my hand down my face and sighed. "I took it off right in front of him last night."

"That's what the fuck I'm talking about!" she clapped her hands together.

The door slid opened, and Em came out and sat on the lounge chair next to Harlym. "Can't even get back to sleep."

"Cause you woke up hateful." Harlym pointed the piece of bacon in her face.

Em snatched it out of her hand, took a bite and rolled her eyes. "Whatever, you needed to hear the truth. We ordered breakfast last night?"

"No, Bray sent it to lover girl right here."

Ember smiled widely and clasped her hands together. "Did he really? I could tell you both were feeling each other."

"I could say the same about you and Laurent."

She blushed. "He's married though."

"What?" Me and Harlym both said at the same time.

"Why the hell are you smiling about it?"

"They've been separated for years."

"Hmm, that is what *every* married man says. If they have been separated for years, why hasn't he filed those papers?" Harlym took the words out my mouth.

"I don't know, and I didn't get into all of that. We were talking about our lives, and I mentioned being divorced again, and he was straightforward and told me about his wife and daughter."

"Awe, he has a daughter?" I smiled.

"Yes. She's beautiful." Em gave me a weak smile. Children were her weakness. I couldn't wait for the day that my best friend's womb would be blessed with a child. If anyone deserved to be a mother, it was Ember. "Anyway, you and Bray seemed to hit it off pretty well. The way that man stared at you sent shivers down my spine and into my vagina."

"Easy on Bray now," I jokingly warned.

"Oh shit, look at her getting all defensive over her man." Harlym laughed and made a small plate of food.

"Seriously though, you both look so good together. He's nice and tall, and he swallows your short ass up," Ember complimented.

"I need to remind you both that I am married. Whatever happens this week, is all that happens. It's not going to follow us back home because say it with me... I'm married."

Both Em and Harlym rolled their eyes at me. "Oh, please. Once you get some of what that man has between his legs, you not letting him go. The man owns the damn resort and countless other resorts and hotels around the world."

"You knew?" I looked at Ember.

"Me and Laurent were talking about Singapore, and I said it was on my bucket list, and he mentioned them having a hotel there."

"I love how he can casually mention having a hotel in Singapore. Big fucking flex," Harlym said with a mouth filled with food.

"Right? It was the way that he didn't make a big deal out of it, that made it sexy. He just nonchalantly mentioned it and we continued on with our conversation."

"I didn't put it together until we were at the bar," I admitted.

"You caught his eye, so you better be on your best behavior." Em winked.

"And when we say best behavior, we mean your worst one. It's been a while since you been out on the prowl."

"It seems so wrong though."

"Astoria, please," Harlym waved me off. "Do you think those boy's trips are innocent?"

"Hell no," Em interjected.

Me and Em both knew that those boys' trips that our

husbands took weren't innocent. Anytime Jace headed out of town, he forgot about our vows. I always felt sick whenever he left for one of those trips. It was my body telling me what I already knew.

"Just because Jace was out there doing wrong doesn't mean I have to do the same."

Harlym squinted her eyes at me. "Stop trying to make excuses for you to be a good wife to a shitty husband. Astoria, you already knew your marriage was over when you took that ring off."

My sister always gave out horrible advice that I never agreed with. This was the first time that she said something that I agreed with. When I slipped my ring off in front of Bray, I was telling him that I was ready for whatever, whenever, with him. I wanted him to bend me over, slap my ass and make my pussy leak before he even pushed himself inside of me.

Even as I sat here, my body reacted to the thought of running into him again. Me and Jace didn't have that connection we once shared when we had sex. Sex used to be the one thing we did well, and over time it became routine. There wasn't any passion and half of the time the only time Jace climbed between my legs was when he had a few drinks, and I always obliged.

There wasn't any passion or butterflies I felt when I got around my husband. He was just a constant fixture in my life, and I had become used to it being that way.

"I'm not making any excuses," I defended.

Harlym looked at her watch. "Let loose and have fun, Astoria. You have been responsible and a mother for your entire 20's. When's the last time you let your hair down and didn't sit and try to make sense of everything?"

Never.

I had always been focused on being the mature one out of me and my husband. I had to be because he damn sure wasn't going to be the one. While Jace was allowed to party and have fun with his friends, I was the one who was focused on college and our daughters while he only showed up half the time.

If it wasn't for our aunt, I wouldn't have known what to do with Demi half the time. My mother had her own life, and she wasn't about to miss out on money because Jace couldn't get it together. She always used to give me such strife when Demi was younger, and I was in college. I always put so much faith into this man, and he forever let me down every single time.

"She's right," Ember paused. "As much as I hate to admit, she is right. I know how important marriage is for you, but you've been done. Why waste this beautiful vacation and that beautiful man...do something for you, Astoria."

"The way you both are talking me into cheating on my husband is wild. I do hear you both though. We can see where it goes." I wasn't making any promises when it came to sleeping with Bray.

"We have the boat tour today," Ember reminded us.

"God, please don't let anybody get sick on us. I'm already mad that we have to even be crammed onto a boat with strangers."

"It's not going to be that bad. The excursions' lady told me that there is another family on the boat."

"So, kids?" Harlym shrieked.

"Don't look so horrified, Har." Ember laughed.

"No offense, I came here to be away from kids, not share a boat with them for the next three hours."

"I just want to be in the water." I ignored her dramatics.

"And that is the only reason that I'm even going on this boat." She pushed her plate away and got up to go inside.

"Why is she so dramatic?"

I shrugged. "Blame my mom."

"Anyway, I was serious about what I said."

"Em, do you know how scary this is?"

She screwed her face up at me. "Bitch, I am currently living it right now. I am so scared to date and let someone in, but I'm doing it."

"Me and Jace aren't on the best terms, and I feel so petty to go out and cheat."

"You're allowed about six hall passes with all the shit he's put you through."

We both laughed and slapped hands. "You can say that again. Shit is so tense at home since he bought that fucking motorcycle with our savings."

Ember nearly jumped out her skin. "Bitch, what?"

I had forgotten that I never had the chance to tell Ember about the motorcycle situation. We had both been so busy preparing for this trip that we didn't get the chance to catch up with one another. Plus, I tried hard not to think about the situation because it made me sick when I thought about it.

"Oh yeah. Jace bought a motorcycle with our savings."

"You mean *your* savings," she reminded me.

"We're married, so what's mine is ou—"

"Bullshit, Astoria. You make way more than Jace and have been putting money away for years into that account. He needs to take it back, and you need to make him."

"He acts like nothing happened. As if he didn't spend that money."

Ember's entire body language changed. "I want to choke the shit out of that man. How are you not angry right now?"

"I'm tired, Em."

I was defeated.

My husband had taken every ounce of energy that I used to have from me, so much so that I didn't have any more fight inside of me. As angry as I was about the situation, I didn't have the artillery to fight that fight with him.

She reached across the table and grabbed my hand. "I know when we spoke a few months ago, you agreed not to file those divorce papers because you wanted to give your marriage a fighting chance. Astoria, you have fought harder than any woman I know to keep your marriage afloat. At some point, you have to know when to let go and finally choose yourself."

"I hear you."

I had fought so hard because I didn't want to be a failure. Here I was equipped with all the tools to have a successful marriage and I couldn't even do it. It felt like I was fighting this fight alone, and no matter how much I fought, it felt like this was a fight I wasn't meant to win.

"HEY DEM, I tried calling your father's phone, but he didn't answer. How is everything going there?" I sat in the waiting area of the hotel while we waited for our guide to pick us up.

"Dad said he was going to hang with Uncle Siah. He took his motorcycle too," Demi informed me.

"He did what?"

"Chill out, Mom. He was sulking around anyway and didn't want to do anything after taking Tyler to practice."

I hated how Demi and Jace's relationship had become. When she was younger, you couldn't tell her anything about her father. Now that she was older, she much rather him gone than home.

"Are you and Enzo okay? Where's Tyler?"

"I'm fifteen and know how to watch over my sister. Enzo is taking a shower, and Tyler took his bike and went over his friend's house."

Tyler had a few friends within our neighborhood, so it wasn't out of the ordinary for him to take his bike and go hang with them for hours. "Okay. As long as you both are alright. Please call me if anything."

"How is everything there? Please tell me God mommy and auntie got you turning up."

"Yes, they did. I don't even know if I should be telling you that." I laughed.

"Of course, you should… Mom, I want you to have fun. Let down those braids and shake that fatty of yours."

"Demi!"

"What? I know I would if I had that shape," she snickered, and I shook my head.

"Goodbye, Demi. Call me if you guys need anything."

"Okay. Love you, Mom."

"Love you more, Baby." I ended the call and tucked away my phone inside of my beach bag.

On the boat tour, we were stopping along another island where there was a beach. Mostly cruise ships occupied the island with their passengers. I wasn't all that excited about sharing the beach with more tourists, but I brought my laptop and planned to get some work done while on the beach.

"Dr. Jacobs, your ride to the boat is here." The front desk attendant came over to the lounge to get us.

Harlym was feverishly typing away on her phone while Ember was ready to get on the boat already. This trip was well needed for the both of us. We spent so much time in our careers that we never made time for ourselves. It was rare that I saw Ember outside of her scrubs, especially since the divorce. It seemed like she worked even more since the divorce was finalized.

"Guess he's still in his feelings about another man answering her phone," Em whispered as we walked toward the front.

The attendant held the door open for the black Rolls Royce Cullinan open for us. "Um, I think you have us mixed up with someone e—"

"Shut up, the least we can do is ride to that boat in style." Harlym pinched me and smiled. The attendant held the passenger door open for her.

Me and Ember both looked at one another before proceeding to climb into the back seat. The peanut butter leather interior felt like butter against my skin. Ember messed around with all the buttons and took a bottle of water out of the small cooler that divided our seats.

"Dr. Jacobs, please let us know if there is anything that you need during the ride to the yacht." The driver smiled, closed the door, and walked around to his side.

"Have a great outing, ladies," the attendant said through the cracked window.

"I know I was complaining about this boat, but I'm excited now." Harlym was damn near bursting with excitement in the front seat. "Good thing I brought my tripod too. Def need to get some content getting out, so gonna need you or Em to scoot out the way."

"I know we spent a little change on this excursion, but she never mentioned it came with this." Em was trying to make sense of it just like I was.

"Maybe it's a mistake. Let's enjoy it because I know we're going to be on the shared bus ride on the way back."

"The Mercedes sprinters aren't that bad," Em chuckled.

"Yeah, well, I'm going to enjoy this air conditioning and leg room." I crossed my legs and snagged one of the waters.

The twenty-minute ride to the dock was comfortable. Me and Em talked about everything while Harlym was busy making videos before the service on the boat started to suck – her words. I thought my day would have been ruined after Demi told me her father went to hang out with his motorcycle, but it wasn't. After hearing my baby assure me that she and her sister were fine, I was able to relax and enjoy my trip like she wanted me to. Demi gave me more shit than a little bit, however, I think she just wanted to see me live my best life.

The driver put the car in parked and got out to open the door for Harlym, then he went on both sides to open me and Em's door. "Welcome ladies. My name is Carlos. We're going to board this speed boat to get to the yacht." He pointed at the large mega yacht that was sitting in the middle of the ocean.

I know Harlym wanted us to go with it, but I needed to make

sure this shit wouldn't be charged back to us. "We booked a shared boat tour. I think the resort might have mixed things up."

"Ma'am, everything is correct. This is a shared tour."

"Are you sure?"

"Damn, Astoria. He's sure, now come on," Harlym took off toward the speed boat.

Once we were seated, the driver of the boat told us to hold onto our things as he backed out of the dock. I held onto Em's hand, while Harlym was recording everything. This was her job, so I expected nothing less from her.

The boat ride was a quick ten-minute voyage over the choppy waters. They helped us out the boat onto the yacht, and I still felt like this was wrong. "Sir, I really think something is mixed up. We're supposed to be on a shared boat tour."

"It's shared," I looked up top on the second level and Bray was on the balcony overlooking us. "I wanted some more of your time, so I hope you ladies don't mind that I switched out your boat tour for a day on the yacht."

"Shittt, you won't hear a complaint out of me. Show me where the rooms are so I can switch into my bikini." Harlym didn't give a damn. She was ready to make this yacht her home in few seconds.

"Maury, can you show Harlym to her quarters?"

"As you wish, Mr. Willshire." Maury came and took Harlym's bags while she followed behind him.

I told her to change into her suit before leaving. Me and Em opted to wear our bathing suits and coverups, so we didn't have to fight to look for a bathroom to change. I wore a cream netted maxi dress that stopped at my ankles from Hanifa, my favorite black designer. Underneath, the gold two piece showed every inch of my body that I always kept covered up. I bought this bikini and coverup on a whim. The whim of *I'm going to lose weight by the time I have to wear it.* Now, I was out here just wearing it when I hadn't stepped in the gym in months, and I had been eating like crap. I was fine wearing this around a bunch of strangers from a cruise ship, but now I wasn't so sure having to wear it around Bray.

"Stop fidgeting, you look amazing, Astoria." Em reminded me.

This was why we had been friends all these years. A good friend was one that got inside your head and knew exactly what you were thinking without you having to tell them. "Get out my head."

"You're not the only one that can get inside people's heads," she winked.

"Dr. Jacobs, I think I might have pulled something in the gym this morning. Do you think you can take a look at it?"

I put my hand on my hip while staring up at his sexy smirk. Bray Willshire knew that he was everything and then some. It was his smooth brown skin, piercing dark brown eyes and thick black lips that probably drove the women crazy. His dark Cesar fade was as sharp as his banter. Other than him looking good enough to taste, it was his tattoos that drove me up the wall. I wanted to take oil and rub down his arms butt ass naked while he palmed my ass in the process. The thought alone sent shutters down my body and into my vagina like Em said earlier.

"You do know I'm not that kind of doctor," I reminded him.

He chuckled. "I'm fucking with you... I do want you up here with me though." He nodded for the other attendant.

"Follow me, Ma'am," He took hold of my beach bag and brought me upstairs to where Bray was patiently waiting.

As we walked through the yacht, I couldn't help but to lose my breath at the contemporary modern flare that followed throughout this boat. It felt less like a yacht and more like someone's home with everything that was inside. I didn't even want to know how much something like this cost.

The upper deck where Bray was, was considered the owner's suite. It had a bedroom, living room and its private balcony that overlooked the rest of the boat. Maury ran into us halfway to the owner's suite.

"I'll take over," He waved the other attendant away and carefully took hold of my bag. "We are so happy to have you aboard the boat today, Dr. Jacobs."

I wanted to slap Bray for having these people call me Dr. Jacobs. At the same time, I thought it was the cutest thing. "Thank you for having me. I'm sure it will be a relaxing day on the water."

"We will make sure of it." He held open the door, and we stepped out onto the deck.

Bray was leaned against the railing with no shirt and his hands tucked into his short's pockets. I couldn't help but to smile when he looked at me with that look. Em didn't lie when she said that he stared at me a certain way.

One that gave me chills.

"Mr. Willshire, we are preparing lunch on the lower deck. Do you want us to call to let you know when it's ready?"

"Nah, we're going to have lunch up here... just the two of us."

I came on this tour to be with Ember and Harlym so we could spend time and make memories. "We're not going to eat with everyone else?"

Bray walked closer and took my beach bag from Maury. "You heard me, Dr. Jacobs." He licked his lips. "Maury, we're good... I'll hit you if we need something," He quickly dismissed Maury, who nodded and left out the sliding doors.

Once Maury left it was just the two of us. "So, your plan was to hijack my boat trip?" I folded my arms.

He pulled at my arm, causing me to drop them at my side. "Let me get a look at you." It was then that I noticed the peeks of gold inside his mouth.

Goodness, what can't this man do?

"Yeah. I told you I always get what I want," he nonchalantly replied.

"And you want me?"

"Now you're catching on, Doc."

I rolled my eyes. "Is this your boat?"

"Nah... a friend of a friend owed me a favor."

"You must have some friends in high places." I examined the upper deck. There were lounge chairs positioned to catch the perfect amount of sun, a hot tub that was shaded so you could enjoy the view without going blind and a bar off to the side that a bartender would have been working at.

"The highest." He winked and grabbed my hand to bring me inside the living room area. There were views from every angle of the boat.

"Um about last night. I think I had too much to drink when I took my ring off." I had become nervous and started to fiddle with my hands. Bray didn't know it, or maybe he did, but he made me nervous. It had been so long since a man made me feel nervous in his presence. I felt all giddy and silly while being around him.

"You don't have that shit on now, do you?"

"I left it in—"

"Doc Thickems, if this is something you don't want, let me know. We can kick it and keep it platonic. It ain't no sweat off my back. I'm not the type of nigga that's going to get mad because you don't want to go there with me."

"Doc Thickems?" I snorted.

He licked his lips and smirked. "What is it going to be?"

Why was I so hesitant when it came to this man? I shouldn't have been worried about Jace because he damn sure wasn't worried about me. It wasn't like he had called to check in with me or ask me how the trip was going. Other than him liking a few pictures I posted on Instagram, he didn't give a damn about what I was doing.

"I took the ring off... didn't I?"

"Oh shit, you being cocky now." He put my bag down on the marble table and walked over toward me. "See, it was never about sticking my tongue inside of you until I could taste your sweetness. I needed to see if you were on the same type of time that I was on." He reached down and palmed my ass with both of his hands.

It was that kind of sexy shit that flew out his mouth that turned me on. How could I not throw caution and my ass into the wind and have a fling with him while being on vacation? "I'm standing here with you, so I guess that means we're on the same page." I stared up at him.

In one swift motion, Bray scooped me up while holding a handful of my ass. I searched his eyes for any signs of struggle and couldn't find one. We stood in the middle of the living room, staring into each other's eyes.

"Fuck, I can't do this," he said, and I looked away, avoiding eye contact with him. It was awkward because he was still holding me up in the air. "Aye, look at me."

Our eyes met, and I couldn't ignore the jolt of electricity that sent shocks waves throughout my body. "It's fine... You don't need to make me feel better about it, I'm a big girl."

He hiked me up further, walked over to the couch, and sat down. I was straddling his lap, staring into his face. "If I thought less of you, I would have fucked the shit out of you on this boat. You're the wifey type, so I don't even want to do you like that."

"You just met me last night; how do you know what type I am? I'm a married woman who was about to throw this ass on you, so how?" I folded my arms.

"I'm good at reading people. There's a reason you're on this trip with girls and not your husband."

He was right about that one.

"So, what now?"

"I wanna get to know you."

"Um, do you know how flings work?"

He grabbed two handfuls of my ass and then adjusted himself on the couch. I could feel his stiffness through his shorts. I desperately wanted to pull this bathing suit to the side and slide down his pole. My pussy leaked at how good his sex would be, but that was something I wouldn't find out because he thought I was too *good*.

"This not a fling though."

"What do you call this?" I tried to move off his lap, and he held me in place.

"I call this getting to know my future."

"Bray, I can't fall for false dreams... especially not now."

I stared into his eyes and could see forever with this man. We had only met last night, and I could picture having a life of good sex, traveling the world, and feeling secure within his arms. This was our second time together, and I noticed that he had a particular hip that he liked to hold onto, like a baby having a favorite corner on their favorite blanket.

He felt like security, and it went beyond the financial aspect. I had always been able to take care of myself and my girls without the help of a man. Bray's security was different. He felt familiar, safe, and that was something I had been searching for my entire relationship with my husband.

It was less about his money and more about him. Even if he wasn't the owner of one of the successful black hotel chains, and worked a regular job, this shit would still be in him. He was a natural born leader.

"Kiss me," he demanded.

Without hesitation, I kissed his lips and then went in for a second. "This attention is going to go straight to my head."

I haven't had attention like the kind Bray was giving me in so long. Truthfully, Jace had stopped trying long before I did, and I tried to convince myself that we needed to fight for us. There was never any real effort on his part to make me feel beautiful, desired, and needed. A woman needed those things from her partner every once in a while, and a good partner was going to make sure that they did those things. Bray didn't just look at me. His eyes slowly sauntered over my body as he tucked his bottom lip and bit down on it. Each time he looked at me, it was like he wanted to devour me right then and there.

"A woman like you should be getting this attention on the daily."

"If only that was true."

"Why isn't it true?"

"Me and my husband grew apart, I guess."

He touched my chin. "No guessing... you know why you and your husband have friction."

I felt like one of my clients when I put them on the spot. "He hasn't exactly been all that faithful or fully in when it comes to our marriage. That alone has caused more problems than a few, I'm sure."

"When he got *this* at home?" He continued to grip every inch of my body. "Man sounds like a bozo."

I looked out at the beautiful turquoise water behind us. "I'm not like this when I'm home. I can nag and get on his ner—"

"We're not about to give him excuses for betraying your trust. Nag all you want; real men like that because it means you fucking care. No real man wants a perfect woman... I like the imperfections more."

"Why are you single? You always seem to know the right things to say."

"I'm not single... I'm newly separated."

My eyes widened. "Separated by what terms?"

"Like I'm going to sign the papers the minute I'm home," he clarified. "Got them on my laptop waiting."

I giggled. "I do too."

It was his turn to kiss me on the lips, then pull back. "You're so fucking beautiful, Doc."

I loved the way he called me Doc, like he had known me my entire life. He wrapped his arms around me and pulled me closer to him, then started to suck on my neck, leaving passion marks that I would spend time trying to cover up with makeup.

"Have dinner with me tonight."

"Okay."

EIGHT
BRAY WILLSHIRE

THE DAY ON THE YACHT WAS FILLED WITH FOOD, LAUGHTER AND getting to know one another. I couldn't keep my hands off Stori's body. I wasn't even the type to like another person in my immediate space, and with her, I couldn't get enough of her being in my space. I could live with my nose in the crook of her neck forever and never get tired of her essence. It had been a while since this woman had been touched in all the right ways. Shit made me sad because if she was my woman, I would never let her out of my sight.

It made me want to continue to show her that a real man, one that was obsessed with his woman, showed that shit through physical touch.

Two Rolls Royce's pulled up to the docks after we got off the speed boat. I held onto Stori's hand as I walked her to the one she would be riding in.

"I enjoyed spending the day with you, Doc."

She stared up into my eyes. "I did too. Thank you for inviting us out, it was well needed." She looked over toward Harlym, who was so Zen, not even Ashton could fuck with her vibe right now.

"I'm going to see you tonight, right?"

"That's if you still want to see me. I mean, we spent the entire day together. It's okay if you want to spend the night alone or with your brothers."

"Stop playing… I'll be by your villa to pick you up." I opened the door for her, and she climbed inside.

I resisted the urge to grab her ass. "Thanks again for the yacht day, guys," Ember thanked us as Laurent held the door open for her.

"Guess I'm gonna open the door for myself," Harlym muttered before Laurent opened her door.

"She not sucking my dick, so I'm not about to open doors for her." Ashton remained seated on the dock poles.

"Asshole." She flipped him the bird and rolled the window up.

"Precious cargo. Make sure she gets to the resort safe and sound," I told the driver.

"Of course, Mr. Willshire."

"Oh, so fuck me and Ember, huh?" Harlym laughed.

"Make sure they all get there," I corrected myself and watched as the car slowly pulled away with my future wife in the backseat.

Our Rolls Royce pulled up and we piled inside. "She got you opened, Bray." Laurent was the first to speak.

I was waiting for Ashton to say something slick from the front seat, but he remained quiet. "What's good with him?"

"He wanna a little bit of Harlym and her ass turned him down." Laurent laughed.

"Laurent, how 'bout you talk about sucking Ember's pussy? Yeah, I heard y'all on my way to the other bathroom." Ashton blew Laurent's spot up.

"Damn, you had your ear to the fucking door or something?"

"She wasn't exactly fucking quiet."

Laurent shrugged and rubbed his hands through his beard. "I mean, I'm always down for a good meal."

"Seafood on the yacht, huh?" Ashton teased.

"Ain't nothing fishy about what that doctor has between her legs."

"She a doctor too?" I questioned.

"Yeah... Dentist."

"Hmm."

When we arrived back to the resort, we each broke off to our own villas to decompress. After spending the day on the boat with limited cell service, I knew Laurent was going to call and check on Luna while Ashton was going to check in on whatever chick of the week that had his interest. I made a call to the concierge and then went to take a quick shower.

I wanted to bend Stori over a few times and fill her with everything I had inside of me. The thought haunted me a few times when she was on my lap. Stori was confused about me not wanting to have sex with her. She deserved better from me, and I wanted to make sure that she got that. Women like her didn't come around often, and I had to show her that I wasn't *that* kind of guy. Pussy came a dime a dozen, but someone like her didn't, and I wanted to look back and feel confident that I moved the right way when it came to pursuing her.

Any woman could lie about their husband not doing their job to be on a yacht and get stuffed with dick. When I looked into her eyes, I could tell she told no lies about her marriage. She was tired, worn down and exhausted from being that man's wife. Even when she had every right to have someone show her better, she was still hesitant on betraying her husband.

The concierge called to assure me everything I requested was being set up, and a gift I asked to be picked up in town had been secured. After my shower, I laid my clothes on the bed and then went out back to sit and enjoy the view while calling my mother.

"Hey, Bray. I was hoping you would call while you were out of town," she answered.

It didn't matter which one of us called, she would always answer using our name. It was never a hey, hello or hi with mom. She was going to make sure she addressed whichever kid was calling her. "Hey, Ma. What are you doing?"

"Just got back from the country club... I went to gossip with Loretta, you know how she can run her mouth."

I chuckled along with her. "Ms. Loretta sure can talk."

"It wouldn't be Loretta if she didn't. I had a little visitor today."

"Oh yeah, who?"

"Your wife, Bray. We talked over tea, and she was quite emotional. Poor baby has been carrying a lot on her chest and just broke down right on my expensive wooden table."

"What did you tell her?"

"I told her water is water, doesn't matter if it's tears or a drink." She went on about her damn wooden table and not what Kami was crying about.

"Mama, I'm talking about with Kami."

She did a light laughter. "Oh, I told her to tell me what is going on, and I will be able to help her the best that I can."

"And did she?"

"Bray, you know she did. Got tears and saliva all over my damn table. Why didn't you tell me about the affair in the first place? You walk around all tough and worried about everyone else, but never give me the chance to be there for you. I'm your mama... I want to be there for you."

"Did you run to Grams about everything going on in you and Pop's marriage?"

"Well, no, but it was a dif—"

"Exactly. I didn't want to bother you with what we had going on. I don't even know why she bothered you in the first place. Wasn't like she was trying to fix things when...." I stopped myself. "Never mind. I didn't call to talk about me and Kami's situation."

"She is right. You should talk to somebody about it if you're not going to talk to her. She said that she started therapy. Maybe you should join her."

"I'm not about to sit in a therapist's office."

"You know... Me and your father went to therapy shortly after Laurent was born. We were both unsure of what we wanted and needed someone who wasn't biased to talk to. I always say if it wasn't for that woman, our marriage would have ended the moment we got off her couch."

Pops stepped outside his marriage and that produced Laurent. He wasn't the type that made children and never took care of them, so Laurent was always around. Mama and Laurent's mom had beef for a while before he sat them down to squash it. He made the mistake and refused for the children to pay for it. He wanted us to be raised with our brother, and that's exactly how it went. Laurent was three years younger than me, and we had always been best friends.

I never claimed that half-sibling bullshit, and neither did Pops. In his eyes, we were all full-blooded siblings, and that was exactly how he raised us to be. My mom was always open about the affair with Laurent's mom, and let it be known that she stuck beside her husband because she loved him. Pops slipped once and never did that shit again.

"What if I don't want to save my marriage?"

She dramatically gasped. "You love Kami."

"*Loved* her. I fell out of love with Kami a while ago and have been trying to search for it."

"Oh, baby. If you lost it, then I don't think it's coming back," she sighed. "I really hate this. I for sure wanted some grandbabies."

I hated to break my mom's heart, but I wasn't concerned with having kids. If I had kids in the future, that was great. If not, I was cool with never having children of my own. Kami told me early on that she didn't want to have children, and I respected her decision not to have any. The longer we were married, the more I understood her decision. Especially after how everything went down between us, I would have hated creating a toxic household with children in it.

"I just wanted to check in on you. How are you, Ma?"

"Good. I've been missing your father more as of lately. I find myself calling out to him, thinking he's in the next room."

My father passed away from Pancreatic cancer. It spiraled quickly, and before anyone of us knew it, he was on his deathbed. The cancer progressed so fast that it hadn't set in for me until we were lowering him into the ground. My mother and father were soulmates, meant to be together forever. You never saw one without the other, and it pained me to know that she was alone without him.

"Sorry, Ma. I promise I will make more time to come visit you," I promised her.

"Kami offered the guest room at y'all new house. Maybe I do need to get out the city for a bit."

"You know you're always welcomed at the house. When I get back, how about I come pick you up? We can stop at my favorite diner in Lennox Hill too. Spend some good quality mama and Bray time."

"That would be so good, Bray. I love spending time with my biggest baby." She giggled.

"Call me if you need anything, Mama... I love you."

"Love you so much more, Bray."

I ended the call with my mother and then went to get ready for dinner. Although I had Stori's undivided attention all day, there was still more I wanted to know about her. The conversations we had were all small shit, nothing that was too deep. I wanted to get deep into shit, like why her father's side tooth was missing?

I didn't know if it was, but that was how deep I wanted our conversations to be. She was capable of having those conversations because people paid her to have them for a living.

The chairman's golf cart was provided to me for our date. The resort was massive, but accessible with walking. Upon check-in, you were provided with a booklet that let you know where all the shortcut routes were hidden within the resort's grounds.

Dressed down in a matching handmade linen shirt and pants set that the staff had gifted me upon arrival, I paired it with my Hermes Chypre slides. I always questioned men who judged other men for sitting in the nail salon. I had a standing appointment with my lady down on Fulton every other week. Yeah, I could afford to have someone come to my penthouse or office, but I liked parking on the street, using the meter and going into the salon.

I always tipped her generously, so soon as she spotted my Mercedes parking, she rushed to get the seat all the way in the back prepared for me. I could pay an expensive amount of money to some boisterous salon, or I could line the pockets of the everyday hardworking immigrants. I chose the latter.

Turning the golf cart off, I climbed out and pressed the doorbell to her villa. The locks turned, and the door opened. Harlym poked her head out the door.

"She's not ready yet. Give us ten minutes."

"No problem."

She smiled. "Cool points given for being early."

Then she slammed the door while I leaned on the golf cart. I felt at ease waiting for Stori. Her aura and vibe was so laid back and chill. She didn't try to pretend to be somebody that she wasn't, and that was what I liked the most about her.

A few minutes later, Stori opened the door. "You know, I do love a man that pays attention to details." She touched the diamond necklace that I had sent to her room. "How did you know I loved diamonds?" she joked.

"My mama always told they were a woman's best friend."

I took in her body in the outfit she wore. She wore a champagne-colored satin maxi skirt paired with a white button-down shirt that she had tied up, exposing a peek of her stomach and cleavage. Her braids were pulled up in a top bun with a few curly pieces framing her face. Then the heels... I wanted to take them off her and suck her freshly white manicured toes. The fuchsia strappy heels set the outfit off. The colors weren't something that I would have paired together, but Doc had set the shit off.

"Damn." I bit down on my bottom lip and walked closer to her. "I almost don't want to take you out tonight…. Want to keep you to myself."

"If your mama told you that a diamond is a girl's best friend, I know she taught you about sharing."

"Don't mean I always like to."

She reached up and pinched my cheek. "I don't know about you, but I am starving."

"Ah, yacht belly."

"Excuse me?" I extended my hand so she could comfortably climb into the front seat of the golf cart.

"Something me and my brothers joke about. When you've been on the yacht all day eating and chilling but get to land and could eat a horse."

"Ain't that a flex… I probably would have never been able to relate to that until today." She giggled.

"You'll become very familiar with yacht belly." I held onto her thigh as I drove us through the resort.

"This resort is really breathtaking. Everything you could think about, they have provided. Did you have a hand in this, or do you just sign your name and approve everything?"

"A little bit of both. My father was hands-on, and I like to delegate where I feel it's necessary." She nodded her head.

"Hmm, I like that." She took in more scenery as we continued to drive through the resort. "So, is Willshire Hotels and Resorts completely Willshire owned?"

"Hell yeah. There's been some very generous offers over the years, but Pops wanted to keep it in the family."

"I love that for you. So, you and Laurent both runs things?"

"Laurent is a lawyer… he runs legal. I run pretty much

everything else. He's my go-to when I need to run something by him."

"Your voice of reason."

"Yeah, my brothers mean a lot to me. I couldn't do this shit without them, even Ashton's hardheaded ass."

"Younger siblings are always hardheaded. I go back and forth with Harlym all the damn time... they want to live life their way and don't want no advice."

"For real. If I'm giving you advice because I been through the shit, why wouldn't you take it?"

Ashton drove me crazy because he was determined to do shit on his own. He didn't want help from not one, but two older brothers who been through the shit he was probably going through. Instead, he wanted to do his own thing and make mistakes on his own, which irritated me.

"Our mistakes made us into the people that we are, so we have to allow theirs to do the same."

I pulled up to the beach where I had a dinner set up on the sand. The huge blanket was laid out right under where the sun was beginning to set. There were candles sitting up in the sand surrounding the blankets so we would have light when the sun eventually went down. "You right about that."

"We're having dinner here?"

"Yeah."

"I've always wanted to have a beach picnic... this is beautiful, Bray." She complimented me and couldn't take her eyes off the setup.

"Then I'm happy I'm the first person to make your dream a reality."

"Help me with my shoes... I can't wait to get my feet in the sand." Had this been Kami, she would have complained that I planned this and made her dress up nicely.

It was comforting knowing that she didn't pull her phone out once and shove it into my face. My wife made our relationship and marriage private, but she couldn't help but to shove the phone in my face to share with her close friends.

I helped unlace the heels and pulled them off her feet while still holding her perfect ass feet. They fit in the palm of my hands so perfectly that I continued to hold onto them while we stared into each other's eyes.

"You're perfect."

She blushed. "Bray, you're the sweetest." Stori accepted my hand and climbed out the golf cart. I sat both our shoes on the front seat and held her hand as we walked onto the beach.

Still holding her hand, she sat down on the blanket and looked through everything that was prepared. "Bacon, egg and cheese?" she snorted.

I was grateful that she understood my sense of humor. "How many can say they had a bacon, egg and cheese in the Maldives?"

"Now that's the biggest flex." She continued to look over stuff while I turned my phone off in the middle of Kami calling me. "Um, how the hell did you manage to get Arizona's here?"

"Doc, whatever you want, I can make happen... trust."

She smiled and continued to pull out all of New York's staples. I didn't want to have a stuffy dinner where we cut into steak and pretended to have a deep conversation because all eyes were on us. When I told her that I wanted her to myself, I meant that shit, and this was me showing her.

I could have taken her to the finest restaurant on the resort to wine and dine her, and there would be time for that too, however, tonight I wanted to chill on the beach with just her. "I believe you."

"Don't know if you smoke, but I got these too." I went into my pocket and pulled out two rolled blunts."

"Alright, now I need to know how you got that."

"I have my ways."

"I haven't smoked since college... but I am def down."

"Perfect."

We ate our food and she spoke about small shit, and how she didn't realize how much she needed this vacation. I watched and listened to every word that left her mouth. It was small stuff I noticed about her, like how she chewed on one side of her mouth, and used her hands when talking a lot.

"I'm going to try and do more mini solo vacations often. It's hard to get away with my kids," she confessed.

This was the first she mentioned having kids. "Doc, you keeping secrets?"

"No, I'm just used to hiding parts of my life from my clients, not that you're a client." She giggled. "I have two daughters. They're teenagers and don't need me as much, so I don't know why I'm so scared to leave them."

"Because you're a good mother."

"I guess so. My oldest daughter literally had to force me out the door to come on this trip. She wants to see me having fun so badly."

"Then why don't you show her that?"

"Being honest, I don't even know what fun looks like. All I know is survival, and that's all I have been doing most of my life. I was a mama by the time I turned nineteen, and then had another baby right after while still in college. Now that I'm financially secure and can take care of myself, and don't have the fear of bills hanging over my head, I stopped living my life for me. It's all about my girls."

Damn.

I could admit that I never had the fear of worrying about money. My father busted his ass to build Willshire Hotels and Resorts to what it was today. He made sure that me and my brothers never had to ask for handouts like my grandfather and my great-great grandfather did before they were established.

"My grand-father and father came from humble beginnings and built themselves up to what we have today. Before he passed away, it was important that I continued in his footsteps like he did with his own father."

"I'm sorry." She gently rubbed the back of my hand.

It was such a small gesture, but it sent major shocks through my body. "Thank you."

"He has a lot to be proud of, and I know he's looking down at you and your brothers." She continued to rub the back of my hand.

"It's funny because I grew up going to private schools and having golf lessons at the country club during the week, then on the weekends, I hung with cousins that still lived in Bayview projects. My father would pack our asses up and drop us off for the weekend."

"He wanted you to have the best of both worlds."

"Yeah." I smiled thinking about my old man. "He told me that you needed to have both to be a shark in those board meetings."

"Was he right?"

"Hell yeah."

"He sounds like he was a good man."

"The best. I miss sitting in his office soaking up all his wisdom."

She moved closer to me, coming between my legs. I allowed her to take my hands and wrap them around her. "You and your brothers live a very blessed life because of the work that he put in for you boys. He raised three amazing men, and you guys will continue to carry that torch."

"This feels so right."

She turned to look me in the eyes. "I keep telling myself the same thing. In a perfect world, this would be our life... we would have met sooner and not been married to other people."

"I don't live or want to live in a perfect world, Stori. This is the world that I want to live in, one that includes us and the hurt we've endured in our past relationships."

"One week in paradise isn't the same as being back in the real world with real problems. As much as I love this, I know it's not real and cannot last."

I wanted to tell her that it could last. We could make one another happy and get this love shit right for the second and final time. To her, I was just a stranger on vacation that was making her happy in the moment. Soon she would return back to her real life that didn't include me.

Before she could protest, I laid her down onto the blanket and pulled her skirt up over her waist. Pulling the white thong she wore down and tossing it to the side, I shoved my face down between her legs.

"Brayy... omg... people will see," she breathlessly protested.

"This part of the beach and resort is closed off for tonight," I said, purposely speaking into her pussy. The vibrations from my words caused her to arch her back and push my head further.

I placed small kisses on her second pair of lips and took my time with her. Since the yacht, I had been desperate to smell and taste her. Teasing her center, I flicked my tongue over it while she moaned loudly.

"Ummm.... Bray," she continued to moan while holding my head in place.

Stori squirmed and tried to move back, but I pulled her right into my face. "Don't run, Doc... let me have my second meal," I growled as I pulled her closer to me.

Stori's legs opened wider, and I dug right in as the sun began to set on us. I took my time feasting on her goodies as she enjoyed someone making her feel good for once. I held up one of her legs and ran my tongue from her crack to her pussy while kissing the back of her thigh.

"Ohh... shit... ummmm," she moaned. "I'm about to cu..." she tried to speak, but her words were cut off each time I nibbled at her lips.

When her legs started to shake, I knew she was ready for what I had. I quickly came out of my pants, grabbed the condom from my wallet and pushed it onto my dick before getting between her legs.

I was naked from the waist down on this beach and didn't

give a fuck about anybody possibly seeing us. When you owned shit like I did, you could fuck on the beach uninterrupted. "Tell me you want this, Doc."

"I...I want this, Bray," she stammered, inviting me further into her.

I teased her opening with the tip of my dick and then slowly pushed inside of her. The deeper I went inside of her, the more I wanted to moan out just like she was. Stori's pussy was so warm, tight and good that I couldn't focus.

I wanted to bottle this shit up and keep it all for myself.

It was a combination of looking into her beautiful eyes and feeling her at the same time. The shit fucked with my mental because how could someone be so perfectly imperfect. I liked her for everything that she wasn't.

Reaching down, I kissed and sucked on her lips while she held my face. I didn't believe in perfection, but if I did, this moment would have been it. I didn't want to be anywhere but between her legs.

NINE
DR. ASTORIA JACOBS

AFTER CONVINCING BRAY THAT HE DIDN'T NEED TO WALK ME BACK to my villa, I made the walk back to my villa alone. Knowing Em and Harlym, they would make a big deal out of me staying out last night, and I didn't want him to witness me do my little celebratory '*I got dick*' dance. We decided to ditch the golf cart at the beach and walk back to our villas this morning. The walk was filled with laughter and reminiscing about everything that happened the night before. He held my hand and kissed it several times as we tried to navigate his resort.

It felt so nice to laugh and feel free with him. We didn't pretend or try to act like we were something that we weren't. He knew as much as I wanted him to know about my situation. We didn't get deep into our marriages because they were the whole reason we were here, to escape them. I spent way too much time talking about Jace. For the last few days that I had here, I didn't want to think about him at all.

Last night was incredible. Our bodies under the moonlight, knowing what the other was going to do before doing it, felt magical. Bray Willshire was blessed between his legs. I wanted to take it and bottle it up for home. It was like he had known my body his entire life with the way he performed.

I walked into our villa humming and holding my shoes, ready to give them a full recap of last night's festivities. This morning I was paying for the soreness I felt between my legs, but it was well worth it to me.

"Is your phone not working?" Harlym rushed to the foyer of the villa as I sat my clutch down on the wooden table.

"It died. Why?"

"Your bright husband got into a motorcycle accident. Messiah called Ember to tell her because he couldn't get in touch with you."

My hands started to shake as I remembered the last accident and where I was when I got the call. Thankfully that time he walked away without a scratch. "Where's the girls and Tyler?"

"They're fine. Mom is at your house and is going to stay with them until we're back."

"W...what about Jace? Is he alright?"

Ember came into the foyer, fully dressed in a sweatsuit. "He broke his femur and his wrist. Messiah said the bike is totaled, and he's lucky he didn't walk away with worse injuries."

"Breathe, Stori." Harlym had to remind me to take a breath. I don't think I took a full breath since she told me about the accident. "I was able to get into your laptop and rebook all our flights for this afternoon."

"Your stuff is already packed. Last night we called all over the resort looking for you and Bray, and nobody would tell us anything, so we packed and kept busy until you came back."

Their dark circles and weary eyes were signs that they hadn't gotten a lick of sleep all night. I was truly thankful for my best friend and sister. Honestly, I don't know what I would have done if they didn't handle everything for me.

"I fucking told him about that motorcycle. He spent our savings on a fucking motorcycle that almost took his life." I think I went through every emotion possible in that foyer. Now that I knew my daughters and Tyler was safe, I was now furious.

"He did what?" Harlym blurted.

"Not now, Har," Em told her.

All I wanted was a nice vacation away from the day-to-day obligations I had. One week to let my hair down and enjoy the fruits of my labor. My body told me something like this was going to happen, and I ignored it. I wanted Jace to prove me wrong for once. Show me that he cared enough to allow me to have time to myself without having to fix any problems.

It was always on me to handle everything around our home and life. For once, I wanted to be a passenger princess in our life. I didn't want to worry about how the bills were going to get paid, or when our taxes were going to be prepared and filed. Other than paying the mortgage because I put the money in the account, the only thing that Jace was consistent with was paying Tyler's football dues and his school's tuition. If I was lucky, he would pay a few of our smaller bills, along with his car payment.

A husband was supposed to lead and provide, and Jace didn't do any of those things. I just wanted something for me this week, and he couldn't even give me that. I dedicated my life to raising our girls and making our house a home, and this is how he pays me back.

"I'm just so fucking tired," I wailed as I fell to the floor.

Em and Harlym came over and pulled me into their arms. "I'm sorry, Sis," she apologized, even when she didn't do anything wrong. "I love you so much."

"It may seem impossible right now, but I promise there is good on the other side of this. A happier you because you are so deserving of it, Astoria. You deserve to have your cup filled the same way you fill others, and I promise it's coming. I've been praying for it."

I wanted to believe everything Em was saying to me, I really did, but it was so hard to believe that things would become better after this. This felt like a cruel rollercoaster that I was on, and it didn't seem like I could get off it anytime soon, which scared the hell out of me.

"I just want to be happy. Not fake happy for my girls, but really happy that people can see it's not a mask I'm wearing."

I wanted to wake up ready to tackle the day because I was excited about my life. Other than my girls, my life was miserable. I woke up beside a man that clearly didn't want to be married to me and put on this brave face so I could make it through each day.

Every day, I felt like I was seconds from having a mental breakdown, and I couldn't afford to have that. I had to be there for everyone, and I rarely had people that would return the favor, besides Ember.

Anytime I didn't feel like myself she was quick to take a personal day or her lunch to come sit with me. I had to be everything to my husband, daughters, family, and clients. There was no time for me to breakdown.

"Then do it, Stori. You are the author of your own story, and only you can make that decision." Ember hugged me tightly as we sat on the floor of our villa.

If it wasn't for the price of this place and my girls, I probably would have never returned back home. "I feel bad for you both giving up your vacation. I can head home myself; I promise."

"We came together, and we're going to leave together. Plus, my manager sent me an email about a brand trip I've been invited to."

Even with my world feeling like it was crumbling, I was so proud of my baby sister. When she told me she wanted to be a content creator and influencer, I told her she needed to go to college. I didn't see the vision that she had for her life, and even with none of us believing in her, she stayed true to who she was and what she wanted, and now was able to benefit from it. Even with her relationship with Cam. Everybody around her hated that she was dealing with him, but because he made her happy and it was what she wanted, she did what she wanted when it came to her relationship with him.

It didn't matter who she pissed off, it was her life, and she was going to live it on her terms. It was something that I could learn from her.

"THANK YOU SO MUCH. No, I think that's all I have that needed to be picked up today," I thanked the pharmacist in town and prepared to leave.

"Tell Jace we're praying for him to make a full recovery." Mr. Orlando, the old man that owned the *Lennox drug store*, told me.

Nothing ever happened in Lennox Hill, so when Jace got into a big accident right on Mulberry Avenue, the entire town was tuned in and sending well wishes to us along with casseroles. We had so many flowers, gift cards and food being sent to our home that I could barely make it through the door without a balloon slapping me in the face.

A few of Demi's friends had recorded the accident, and Jace was lucky to escape with his life. He could have lost his life, and I don't think that fully processed in his brain. God was truly looking over him.

"I will let him know. We appreciate the flowers your wife sent over. Please tell her thank you."

"Don't worry about it." He handed me the bag filled with Jace's medication.

Instead of floating into my office and feeling good after an amazing vacation, I was running around picking up medicine and handling everything that Jace couldn't do because he couldn't walk. He had to sleep downstairs in Tyler's bedroom because he couldn't make it up to our room.

"Have a good day, Mr. Orlando." I waved and quickly exited out the pharmacy to make it to our insurance broker's office.

I needed to talk to her about filing a claim and submitting everything. It was giving me issues online, so I decided to stop by while I was in town. Our insurance broker's office was a quick two-minute walk from the pharmacy.

"Hey Astoria, I wasn't expecting to see you walk through my doors today. How is everything going with Jace?"

I was so tired of hearing about Jace. Since I been home all anybody asked about was Jace and how he was doing. "He's doing better."

Whenever someone asked, I kept it short and sweet. It was hard to feel bad for my husband when I first saw him after the accident because he caused this on himself. If he had been spending time with his kids, he wouldn't have gotten into an accident, and wouldn't have almost lost his life because of it.

"That's good. Come in the office," she ushered me into her private office. "I'm sure your house is overrun by flowers and balloons, so I sent you over an Amazon gift card to your email. To help get anything that he needs."

"You're so sweet, Aria. We do appreciate everyone wrapping their arms around us, especially the food. I can't even begin to get in that kitchen to prepare a meal for the kids."

The girls didn't mind living off takeout or casseroles. "Don't mention it... what can I help you with?"

I dug into my purse to pull out the papers from the motorcycle. "When I tried filing a claim for the motorcycle on the website, it was giving me some trouble. I printed out the pictures of the damages. The mechanic said it's totaled."

She whistled. "He is so dang lucky."

"Don't we all know it."

Aria sat down at her desk and started inputting our information in. I could tell she was having some trouble, then figured out the issue soon after. "Okay, I found the issue."

I leaned forward. "I knew something had to be wrong."

"Jace inquired about adding the motorcycle onto your policy, but he didn't actually add it on." Her finger followed the screen. "The system sent him out a quote four weeks ago, but he never called to add it onto the policy."

If looks could kill, bring you back, and kill you again, Aria would have been faced down on her desk. I knew it wasn't her fault, but I was so angry that I needed someone to blame temporarily.

"So, the motorcycle isn't covered."

"I'm sorry, Astoria. I know this isn't what you need to hear right now."

My heart was speeding so fast that I couldn't stand up right away. I needed to calm my breathing so I could make it out of here without looking crazy. Once I stabilized my breathing, I gathered my purse.

"It's not your fault, Aria. Thanks again for informing me."

The one thing I was banking on was insurance paying us out for the totaled bike. I figured that as soon as they cut the check, I could put it back into the savings account, and we could try to put this behind us. I had already called our bank and removed Jace off the account because he couldn't be trusted.

Now, we had to eat the loss of the money he spent without my permission, and we were losing even more money because he was going to be out of work until he healed. His job was real good about allowing him the time to recover and even sending things to the house. Since Jace used all his paid time off, he wasn't collecting anymore while he recovered. His job didn't offer medical benefits, so we had health market insurance plans, which were crap. All of the surgeries and rehab he would have to undergo would be an out-of-pocket cost or billed to us.

"How was your day, Mom?" Demi asked when she climbed into the passenger seat of my car. Enzo put her instrument on the empty seat in the back and hopped into the back.

"Stressful. How about you guys? I hope you had a better day than I did." I smiled at Enzo through the rearview mirror.

Demi put her phone away, which was rare. I could always count on her having her head down in that damn phone. "What's going on? Let me be your therapist today."

As much as I wanted to load all this stress onto my daughter, I didn't want her to carry my burdens. "How about you tell me about some new boys you met? That would make me feel so much better."

"Boys are so stupid. I like this Kyle boy, and he acts like he doesn't notice me... I'm cute... duh?" Every time Demi spoke, she reminded me so much of Harlym.

I knew I would never have any problems out of her. She was so sure of herself and didn't take any nonsense from anybody. My girl didn't need any snotty boy to feed her compliments because she was already confident.

"Boys are like that," Enzo called from the back.

I pulled away from the dance studio. Enzo's best friends' mom offered to pick Enzo up and drop her to Demi's dance studio. "No, stupid boys are. Good boys notice a beautiful girl and don't pretend not to see them... never settle for a stupid boy that doesn't see the beauty in either of you." I looked at both my girls.

"Yes, Mom." Demi smiled.

"Hear you, Boss," Enzo confirmed.

Growing up, whenever a boy would hit, kick, or punch us, we were told that they did it because they liked us. As girls, we're taught to accept the weird or funky behavior from boys because that was how they showed their feelings toward us. Instead of parents raising emotionally mature boys, they allowed this behavior and that transferred into emotionally damaged men. I wanted my girls to always expect the most from a man, so they never settle like I did with their father.

The minute the cute boy on my block started giving me attention, he had me. I never made him work for it, I was so easy for him to have, and that was why he took me for granted every chance that he got. For the sake of wanting to have that young love, I accepted way too much from a man that did the bare minimum.

The girls got out at the end of the driveway to talk with their friends from across the street. Since the accident, they hadn't been outside or over their friend's house, so I allowed them time to catch up. Grabbing their backpacks and my purse, along with the other bags from my errands, I entered the house.

"Stori, that's you?" Jace called from the back room.

"Yes." I put the bookbags in the mud room and then headed toward the back where Jace was. He was sitting on the bed with the lunch I had given him before I left.

"Did you get the medicine? I'm in so much damn pain and you took your time," he scolded me.

"Excuse me? I had to pick up the girls and handle the insurance stuff for the bike. Which I found out that we're not insured for." I tossed the bag at his bad wrist on purpose.

"Oww. What the fuck, Astoria?" he struggled to reach forward to grab the bag. "I didn't get a chance to do it because the app was acting stupid."

"Bullshit. Aria told me all you did was request a quote. We're out fucking money because you weren't smart enough to insure the damn bike, Jace!" I yelled, not caring that our girls could walk in at any moment.

"I don't need to hear this shit right now."

"Are you serious? You are going to be out of work for God knows how long and don't have any income coming in right now. Our savings could have been used right now, and now we have nothing."

"There's still money in there."

"Not enough to pay half of our bills. Who is going to cover the football fees and Tyler's school tuition?"

"Tonya will just have to cover it until I'm able to get on my feet."

I laughed. "The one who can't keep her car fixed?"

"You act like you can't go half on it with her."

"I'm already paying for both of our daughters to attend private school; I have my office lease and all the other bills it takes to run this damn house. What do you mean I can go half with her?"

I stormed out the room before I punched him in the face next.

Whenever I started to feel violent, I always removed myself before I did something I would probably never regret. The girls were seated at the counter when I entered the kitchen, which meant they heard everything.

"Mom, if I need to quit dance for a few months, it's fine. Me and Whitney could practice in her garage to keep up."

I sighed and walked over to hug my daughter. "No, baby. You're going to continue with dance classes. Me and Daddy just had an argument. Everything will be alright."

Demi snatched away from me. "No, it's not. Dad is going to be out of work for a while, and that means we'll see even less of you because you'll be working more. All because he had to have that stupid motorcycle!" she yelled and ran upstairs.

I didn't know what to say or do. How could I correct or discipline her when she wasn't wrong? Jace was the cause of all of this, and I would end up taking more sessions to make sure we could pay all of our bills.

I worked so hard, so I didn't have to live paycheck to paycheck, and he ruined that for me. He took all the money I had been saving and tossed it down the drain when he decided to make the impulsive decision to buy that motorcycle.

"You better talk some sense into her, Astoria!" Jace yelled from the bedroom. "We're the parents, not her. Demi gets slick out that mouth like she can't get that phone taken away."

"The phone that mom bought?" Enzo muttered.

The urge to high five my youngest was so strong I nearly had to hold my hand down on the counter. "Enzo, go change out your school clothes. How does sushi from your favorite spot sound?"

"Like I'd rather be there than here." She smiled and hugged me before going up to her room.

Since I had been running around like crazy, I needed to quickly wash up and change clothes before we went out. The girls could sense the tension between me and their father, and I was trying hard to avoid that.

All I wanted was to be in Bray's arms on that beach. I could smell his strong cologne if I sat in my thoughts long enough. Things happened so fast that I didn't get the chance to tell him goodbye. Who knows if he was even thinking about me anymore. He probably did this to all the women that frequented his resort. All I did was make it easier for him to ghost me because we didn't exchange numbers. Unlike me, he was pretty easy to contact with a quick Google search. I could probably find an email or office number to get in contact with him. All he had to go off of was Stori. It wasn't like I offered my full name.

Then again, he owned the resort, so that was easy information to come by. Either way, it had been nearly two weeks since I had been back from the Maldives, and I hadn't heard anything from him. Two weeks of having to push clients back because I needed to handle this emergency situation. Jace didn't realize, or maybe he didn't care how much he fucked us up.

"Mom, you ready?" Demi came into my bedroom. I guess Enzo told her we were going out to eat.

I put a little bit of my favorite perfume behind my ear. "Yes. I'm ready." I closed up the bottle and headed out the room with my daughter. A mommy and daughters date was much needed and well deserved.

TEN
BRAY WILLSHIRE

WHEN LAURENT BYPASSED MY ASSISTANT'S DESK AND HEADED straight for my office, I knew it was something important, not that he respected Kimberly's role in the first place. None of my brothers listened to the rules she set in place when she first became my assistant.

"Is there a reason that you haven't signed the new offer for the hotel in Paris yet?" Laurent cut straight to the point.

I looked at my watch and logged out of my computer. Today was a half day because I was picking my mother up and taking her to my house. When we spoke in the Maldives, I promised to spend more time with her, and I always honored my word.

"Because none of us stayed at the original hotel to know if it's a good deal or not."

Laurent screwed his face up while holding his infamous iPad. I was starting to believe that he slept with that damn iPad every night. "What you mean? We sent the team out months ago."

"And I didn't like their response." I shrugged it off.

"Bro, lose the fucking attitude because you can't find her. Just ask Ashton to hit her sister up," he pinpointed exactly what was wrong. "You acting like you can't call the hotel and get her information."

"I'm not like that."

"It would make a cute stalker wedding story when I do the toast."

"Ha. Funny." I stared at him with a blank expression.

"I'm not doing it the new way. I want to do it the way that Pops used to do it. He went and stayed at every hotel before he even considered purchasing it."

"You don't have time to do that shit though. It was you that came up with this new system because you didn't want to be away from Kami for long periods of time. If you want to do it the same way as pops, don't forget about all the birthdays and anniversaries he missed with us and your mom."

The downside to having it all was that you were going to miss things. My pops always made his presence known whenever he couldn't be there for an important event. He could be all the way in the middle east, and it felt like he was standing right next to me blowing out my candles.

"That's not a problem anymore."

Laurent nodded his head. "Bet. I guess you need to get snappy out there to book you a flight to Paris," he snorted, annoyed that I was holding up the signing of our newest property.

"I'm taking the rest of the day off to spend the day with my mom."

"Tell her I send my love," he replied and headed out of my office quicker than he came. I grabbed my coat and breezed past Kimberly.

"Enjoy your day with Mrs. Willshire," Kimberly called behind me.

"Thanks, Kim."

Before my father passed, he and my mother decided to sell our childhood home. They didn't need the extra space, and it was easier to move into a smaller home within the same community. I was pissed that they decided to sell our home. After my father was diagnosed with cancer and then eventually passed, I felt comfort knowing that she wasn't in that big house all alone.

The security guard let me through the gates when he recognized me. I cruised down the perfect tree lined blocks with beautiful brick masonry until I came across my mother's one-story cottage styled home.

Killing the engine, I climbed out of my truck and made my way to the front door. Using my fingerprint to gain access into the house, I sat my keys on the foyer table. "Mama?"

"In here," she called.

I followed her voice into my father's office, where she was sitting his favorite chair. "What you doing in here?"

"Looking for my passport."

"It should be in the safe with all the other important documents."

She snapped her fingers. "You're right... it's in there. Why did I think it was in his desk all this time." I watched as she rested her back in the chair.

"What do you need it for?"

She fixed her glasses. "Do I need to have a reason to want my passport?"

I smirked. My mother was the most beautiful woman in the world. Nobody could light a candle to the beauty, brains, and class she possessed. Maybe Stori was a close second, but Mom was always number one. All my friends back in the high school used to swear my mother resembled Vanessa Williams. I couldn't lie and say that I didn't see the resemblance because mama really did favor that woman.

"Yes."

She knew I was waiting for an answer, and I wouldn't drop the subject until I had one. "I was thinking about doing some traveling. We own all these hotels and I never go anywhere now that your father is gone. I need to get out and see something more than this house and the country club."

When we were younger, my mother didn't travel much with

my father because she was too busy raising us boys and taking care of our home. Once we were all grown, she would slowly travel with Pops, but by then, he wasn't doing much traveling anymore himself. Now that he was gone, all she had was the small reminders of him all over the home they once shared together. I understood why she would want to get out and travel the world. I would distract her from the loss she had experienced.

"How about you come with me to Paris?"

She gasped in excitement. "Paris? Why are you going there?"

"We're in the process of buying an existing hotel there, and I want to check everything out before we sign our names on the deal."

She clapped her hands together. "Just like your father."

"Trying to be."

"Baby, you're on your way. I would love to tag along... it's been a while since I've been to Paris."

I couldn't lie and say I wasn't excited about going on a trip with my mother. The last trip we took together was during my senior trip to Germany. It was a trip that I would cherish for the rest of my life because we made so many memories together. As the oldest, I was always held to a higher standard, and expected to be the strongest one out of all of my brothers, and I played my role pretty well. On that trip, my mother showed me that I was still her baby boy, and I was able to just be Bray, not the oldest Willshire boy.

"I will make sure Kimberly books everything. Is your things packed?"

"Of course."

We grabbed Starbucks before we got on the highway and headed to Lennox Hill. Kami had been out of town covering a festival in Las Vegas, and she was due to fly in tonight. I enjoyed having the house to myself without seeing her whimper because I didn't want to fuck or sleep in the same room as her. She thought she could fix our marriage by sleeping beside one another or having enough sex that I would eventually forgive her.

All I thought about was Stori and what she was doing. When reception told me she had checked out earlier than normal, I thought it was because of the night we shared. Maybe it was too much for her. She did tell me she was married and seemed hesitant, and even with all of that, we still took it a step further on that beach. What if she couldn't face me later on that day and decided to just leave without saying anything.

I could easily make a call and get her information, but I didn't want to come off like a creep. The best way was to go through Ashton, and I had been dragging my feet about it. Since I had returned, I had been in a sour mood because I didn't know where my Doc was.

"Are you going to move forward with the divorce?" My mom broke our silence after being on the highway for a few minutes.

"I am."

"I just really wish there was a way that you both could fix things." She sighed.

Carol was a natural problem solver. If there was a problem, she would want to fix it right away, so I understood why she wanted to fix the problems between me and Kami. This problem wasn't hers to fix, so I couldn't let her stress herself out trying to.

"Mama, I know you want us to fix things, and I wanted to do the same. Sometimes people don't belong together and that's perfectly fine. Me and Kami had a great marriage up until she betrayed me, and that's the memories I want to keep. The good memories."

"And what about this new house?"

"She can keep it. I doubt she'll want to stay in Lennox Hills after the divorce though."

"Why not?"

"Her entire purpose was to move here to make our marriage

work. I think she'll go back to the city because that's where she's the happiest. If she doesn't keep the house, I'll take it."

I put a fight about moving out here and I had to admit that I enjoyed it. It was a slower pace of life, and everyone knew everyone. Whenever I needed that thrill that only New York could provide, I knew I could jump in my car and be there in record timing. I hadn't spent much time in Lennox Hills other than eating at a diner that I couldn't get enough of. I spent most of my time in the city and at my penthouse since I decided not to sell it when Kami suggested it.

"Maybe I'll move here with you."

"Mama, I wouldn't mind that one bit."

"Your brother acted like I was trying to kidnap him when I suggested moving into his loft." She shook her head. "I worry about him sometimes."

"Ma, we all do. Ashton is his own man, and he has to figure out life himself. I'm always here whenever he needs me, but I can't hold his hand."

"Spoken like a true Willshire man. Have you spoken to Woody as of lately?"

Woody was my cousin and operations manager for the hotels. "Not since I been back. I think he took some personal time himself. He did tell me him and his girlfriend were coming to visit soon."

"Oh good. I wanted to meet this new woman that has him smitten."

"Me too."

We pulled into the parking spots located in front of the diner that was in the prime location of Lennox square. It was considered the town's city, but all it reminded me of was a Hallmark movie. I was waiting for some lady to bump into me and fall instantly in love with me.

"It's so cute... the leaves are even still crisps and clean," my mother pointed at the leaves that had fallen onto the cobblestone sidewalk.

We walked into the diner and seated ourselves before a waitress came over. "Welcome to Dale's diner." She finally looked up
from her notepad and smiled. "Well, I haven't seen you in for
some time. Butterscotch pancakes and candied bacon?" She read
off my usual order.

"Not today. Trying to watch my weight."

My mother pursed her lips. "Oh please. With abs like yours,
you can eat everything off this menu and still have them." She
turned to the waitress. "He gets that from his father."

"Meanwhile we have to limit carbs and eat air to just fit into a
dress," the waitress agreed with my mother, and they shared a
laugh together.

"Ain't that the truth?"

"What can I get you, beautiful?" She turned her attention to
my mother, completely ignoring me.

It wasn't my fault that the weight never clung to my body.
Ever since I was a teen, I could put away three full meals and
never gain an ounce of weight. That was the main reason I liked
weight on my women. A thick woman could have me wrapped
around her finger, and that was clear from how sprung I was
over Stori.

Once me and my mother ordered our food, I pulled my
phone out to check a few emails that Kimberly had forwarded
over to me while I was out of the office. My mother was on her
phone, and we were quiet. I loved spending time with my
mother because we didn't always have to be having a conversation. We could sit in silence and still enjoy each other's
company.

The waitress came and put our coffees down on the table and
then disappeared again. "This place is really cute and gives me
that small southern charm feeling without actually being in the
south." Mama finally looked up from her phone.

"I try to come here at least once a week since we moved up
this way. Sometimes I sit in that booth in the back with my
laptop and get some work done." I took a sip of my coffee. "I

believe the owner is from the south, so that explains the southern charm you're feeling."

"Does Kami join you?"

"Nah. She's usually already in the city by the time I'm heading here."

"I guess I thought your marriage would have lasted because you both had your own thing going on."

I groaned. "Ma, come on."

"I'm sorry. You want me to be cheerful because my son is getting a damn divorce. I wasn't happy when Laurent and Alice decided to file for theirs."

"I was." I murmured.

"He and Luna deserve someone that is all in, not halfway in like Alice is." I don't know when the conversation turned from me and Kami to Laurent and Alice, but I welcomed the change.

"I agree."

"We should hook him up with someone. I also think he needs to move out of that condo that they shared together... I need to call him."

"Ma, chill." I laughed.

Despite Laurent being an affair baby, she never treated him any differently than us. If we got in trouble, his ass was getting in trouble right with us. Even when it came down to celebrating his accomplishments. When he graduated law school, I think my mother was the loudest one there. Just because he wasn't her child by blood didn't mean he wasn't her child. Her dislike was for his mother, but that eventually faded, and they were cordial with each other.

"What?" She mixed in three packs of Equal and a splash of almond milk. "I'm just worried about him. Shanny is worried too."

"You spoke to her lately?"

"She called me while you guys were on your brother's trip. Luna left her favorite stuffy at my house when she was over, so we met up to do the exchange."

"I bet Luna liked both of you together."

My mother smiled. "She did. We decided to grab Lu—"

"I don't have time to run across time to pick up the referral from the ortho doctor... the girls are in the car, and I have to bring Demi to dance," I heard a familiar voice and looked up, not hearing a word my mother had said to me.

Before I knew it, I had removed myself from the booth and was walking toward Stori at the takeout counter. She was dressed down in a pair of sweats, a baggy sweatshirt, and sneakers. Her braids were balled up in a messy bun, and she didn't have a lick of makeup on her face, and she was still the most beautiful thing in the world to me.

She grabbed her order and then jumped back when she noticed it was me. "Er... um... Jace, let me call you back." She ended the call before the person on the line could agree.

"Doc, what you doing in Lennox Hills?" I looked down at her while biting my lip, a reaction that only she could pull out of me.

"The question is what are you doing here? I live here." We never discussed where we currently lived, just that we were both from New York.

I watched as she dropped her phone into her purse and looked up at me, clearly happy to see me too. "It so happens that I do, too."

Her car's horn sounded, and her head snapped toward the door. "Bray, I'm so sorry... I'm really pressed for time right now. I wish I could sta—"

"What the hell possessed you to get up in the middle of our conversation?" My mother had made her way over to us.

"I saw an old friend that I wanted to say hi to, Ma."

Stori looked at me and then at my mother. "Mom? Now I know you're lying to me. This has to be your sister or something." She smiled at my mother.

My mother blushed and waved her off. "Awe, stop. You are a beauty yourself."

"It's so nice to meet you, Mrs. Willshire. I wish I could stay to talk, but I have to drop my daughter off to dance class."

"Ma, let me walk her out."

My mother went back over to our booth because our food started to arrive, and I held the door open for Stori. We moved off to the side while she continued to look from me to the car. Her windshield was slightly tinted, so I could only see a figure in the front seat.

"God, I didn't need this today. I have so much that I have going on and I just—"

"Aye, calm down. Take a breath. Go handle what you need to handle, but I need your number. I'm not about to let you disappear on me again."

"It's not that I disappeared, I have so much going on in my life right now." She was near tears as she tried to explain it to me.

Out of respect for her daughter in the car, I refrained from taking her face into my hands and kissing the worry away from her eyes. "No explanation needed. I want to see you today. Make some time for me," I told her.

"Bra—"

"You can't expect me to see you disheveled and stressed and not want to take that away from you. Meet me back here tonight after you handled all your business, okay."

She nodded her head up and down slowly. "K."

"Drive safe, Doc. If it wasn't for your daughter in that car, I would have given you wet nasty ass kiss and grabbed that ass."

This was the first time she smiled since trying to explain her situation to me. "You so nasty."

"The nastiest." I winked and watched as she slowly switched away to her car.

I waited until she pulled off, and then went back into the diner, where my mother had already cut into her French toast. "I don't look at my friends that way."

"Mama, what are you talking about?"

"You damn near floated over to that woman. If I didn't turn

to look myself, I wouldn't have believed it. Our waitress was the first person to point it out. Who is she, and why are you floating over to her?"

"We met in Maldives."

"And she happens to live in Lennox Hills?"

"Apparently so."

"You never discussed where you both lived?"

"Ma, we were more concerned with other things," I vaguely explained. "She left before we could even get that deep."

"Hmm. I just want you to open your eyes. That woman could have found out information on you because of who yo—"

"She's not like that. Clearly, she been living here before me if her kid is enrolled in dance class." I shut her down before she could make her own narrative about Stori.

"Close out your business with Kami before getting involved or getting her involved in your life." She warned and took a bite out of her sausage.

I nodded and cut into my steak and eggs. Had she told me this before I met her, then I would have probably considered her advice. It was too late to handle my business and not get her involved because I craved her.

Just seeing her for those five minutes awoke something inside of me that had been asleep since I been back home. I pulled my phone out and sent a text message to Kimberly. Once she assured me that she would handle my requests, I put my phone away and focused on spending time with my mother.

"HEY, MAMA CAROL," Kami sat her suitcases down by the fridge and hugged my mother. "After all that traveling, it feels good to see the both of you." She smiled at me, then came to get a hug.

I offered a standard side hug and continued eating my yogurt. Once my mother was settled in, I ordered Indian food for her and Kami to eat because I was heading out. "How was the flight?"

"So much turbulence and then I was delayed twice. I am so damn happy to be home and off for the next few days."

Anytime Kami traveled for work she was always given a few days to decompress and unwind from work. Those days used to be spent at my house where we would stay in bed for days and order in.

"You look as beautiful as ever, even with all that you went through with your flight." My mother smiled as she observed the both of us.

She was so busy watching us that her greeting back to Kami was delayed. "Awe, thanks. You got Indian food, my favorite." Kami smiled and hugged me again.

"How about I shower, and we can put a movie on and eat together." She looked from me to my mother.

"I'm going to put on my mud mask and soak in that beautiful garden style tub in the guest suite. You both can enjoy movie time and get reacquainted after your travels."

When I was returning from the Maldives, Kami was heading out to cover that festival, so we hadn't seen each other since I had been back. I wasn't complaining or anything, I enjoyed not having her hovering over me and complaining about what I did or didn't do or say.

"Enjoy, Ma."

She smiled. "Night, guys."

"Night, Mama Carol." Kami replied. She washed her hands and then hopped up on the counter. "I've missed you, Babe."

I didn't miss her.

I wasn't as cold hearted because although our feelings weren't mutual, I didn't want to hurt her feelings. "Me too." That was all I could muster up.

"Movie night in our bedroom? We can eat in the bed, and I won't freak out over the crumbs." She nudged me while giggling.

"Cause we know you get crazy if there's crumbs in the bed."

"You know I'm OCD."

"I can't tonight."

She screwed her face up in confusion. "What do you mean?"

"Got prior plans." I stopped to look at my watch before returning my attention back to her. "Actually, I need to be heading out now."

"Seriously? You knew I was flying in tonight, Bray."

"What the fuck is that supposed to mean? I'm supposed to break plans because you're flying in tonight?"

"Um, duh. I'm your wife. You should have wanted to spend some time with me."

I didn't mean to laugh in her face. "Kam, go unpack and enjoy the food I ordered for you. We not about to do this arguing shit with my mom here."

"I'm not arguing. All I want is some time with my husband, and you've been making it damn near impossible." She jumped off the counter and stormed upstairs.

I had made it a habit to fix things with each other before any of us left the house. Now, I was more concerned with leaving the house and meeting up with Stori. I was ready to stop wasting both our time and get the divorce started so we could move on. Kami may have learned from her mistakes, but I wasn't willing to forgive her for them, and I couldn't move forward in a relationship with her.

Despite our marriage not working, I did want Kami to be happy. I wanted her to find the right man that was going to give her everything she desired from a husband. I could admit that I had checked out of this marriage, while she had been holding on trying to piece it back together.

I sat in the kitchen for a bit before leaving and getting in my truck to meet Stori. All I wanted was to feel her in my arms again while sniffing her neck. It was funny because we had only met on vacation and this woman felt more familiar to me than my own wife of five years. As I drove out of my neighborhood and throughout the town, the town was fast asleep. It was a welcomed change from the hustle and bustle of New York. My penthouse had soundproof windows that didn't allow any sounds in. occasionally I would open up my bedroom window hoping to hear some sounds from the city. I was so high up that all I ever heard were birds, or the sound of the wind.

In Lennox Hills, it was so quiet at night that I found myself watching TV or doing work until I was too tired to fight my sleep. As I turned onto the street where the diner was, I smiled at the Kia Telluride parked in front.

I quickly pulled up beside her and got out the car. She was sitting in the driver's seat occupied with her phone that when I tapped on the window gently, she jumped.

"You're late," she reminded me.

"Or you were early. Couldn't wait to see me again?"

She killed her engine and opened the door, stepping out. I wrapped my arms around her and kissed her on the neck. "I've missed you," she admitted.

"I missed the shit out of you, Doc."

"How long can I keep you out tonight?"

"I need to be back by morning so I can drive the girls to school. Demi, my oldest, is going to keep an eye on her father and sister for me."

I wanted to dig more into what that meant but decided to wait. "Come get in my car." I held the door open for her and helped her climb up.

I jogged around my truck and climbed in. "Where are we going?"

"To my house."

"That you share with your wife?"

"Nah... In the city."

She buckled her seatbelt, ready for the ride. The hesitation I was met with when we were in the Maldives had disappeared. Stori was ready and willing to come with me to the moon and back. Soon as we got on the road, I reached across the arm rest and rubbed her thigh.

"You know, I Googled you and debated on calling your office a few times."

"Why didn't you?"

"I just figured that all that mess was talk, and it was really a fling."

I quickly looked at her before turning my head back to the highway. "You think I say shit like that to every woman I come across?"

She exhaled. "I don't know. Maybe that was easier to believe."

"All the shit I said on vacation I meant that."

"I didn't see you looking for me."

"You don't think I looked up Stori and Doctor on google?"

She broke out into laughter. "My full name is Astoria Jacobs," she revealed. "I'm so used to telling people Stori when I meet them," Stori paused. "Well, you could have called the hotel and got my information."

"So you could think I was some rich creep? Nah, I didn't want to betray your trust or invade your privacy like that. My next course of action was to ask my brother to hit Harlym up."

"She probably would have ignored his message. She really can't stand his ass," we both laughed because it was true.

I licked my lips as I looked over at her. She had changed out what she was wearing earlier and had on a black T-shirt dress, a jean jacket and a pair of sneakers on. "Lift that dress up."

"What?"

"You heard me."

While I drove, she lifted that dress up, exposing those thick ass thighs that I couldn't wait to put my head in between. I reached over and pulled her panty to the side and inserted my fingers inside of her. "Bray..." she moaned.

I kept my eyes between the highway and my baby as her eyes went cross-eyed. When I felt like she had enough, I pulled my fingers out and licked them clean. "Needed a little taste before we get to our destination."

"That is not fair," she accused.

"Be patient for Papa, ight?"

"Yes," she cooed, and wrapped her arm under mine for the remainder of the ride.

I hit my access code, and it took us to the top floor where my penthouse was. The doorman looked a little confused when he noticed the woman with me wasn't Kami. He better get used to seeing Stori because she was going to become a familiar face around here.

"This is fucking sexy," Stori gasped as soon as the elevator doors opened for us. "It screams I'm a bachelor." I watched as she stepped off the elevator and took everything in.

The moment those elevator doors opened, you were greeted with panoramic views of Central Park and the Manhattan skyline. The expensive black zebra wooden floors were the second thing you noticed because they were just that damn beautiful not to. Soon as your eyes adjusted from that million-dollar view, the sunken living room sat right in the middle of the penthouse with a huge black cloud sectional that felt like they were begging you to sit on them. My interior decorator had to convince me on them, and I was glad that she did.

The charcoal coated wallpaper made the place darker, which is something I preferred. The windows made it bright inside at times and adding light furniture and fixtures would have had me sitting in this bitch with sunglasses on every morning. I watched as Stori took everything in with a look of admiration on her face.

"And you moved to Lennox Hills after having this view?"

"Damn, you making it seem like Lennox Hills is a dump," I walked up behind her and wrapped my arms around her. "You're there... so it's special."

"It's a special place, but it's not this." Her eyes hadn't moved from the huge floor to ceiling windows. There wasn't much wall space in this condo, so the little bit of wall space I did have, I got a textured wallpaper that I sourced from Dubai.

I saw it inside of one of our hotels there and made them track it down to install it inside of my home. "Anywhere is special because you're there."

She turned around in my arms. "You make me feel so good, Bray."

"I want to continue to do that too, Doc."

Stori reached up and touched my face. "I know. I would like to return the favor, but I have so much going on right now. I don't think I have the capacity to sneak around."

"Then let's not."

"I do enjoy having you to myself."

I grabbed her hand and took her out onto the patio, where there was rose petals and candles littered onto the floor. Off to the side there was a massage table, robe and oil waiting for her.

"Tonight, I want to be *your* therapist. I'm going to rub your body down while you tell me what's going on."

"N...nobody has ever done something like this for me." She tried to pull away because she was getting emotional, and I pulled her back.

"I'm not just nobody, Doc... I'm that somebody that's going to make sure you're fulfilled mentally, physically, and emotionally."

She wrapped her arms around my neck and kissed me on the lips. "Thank you, Bray."

I grabbed her ass and kissed her on the neck. "Go inside, change into the robe and come on." I slapped her on the ass.

"Um, this place is massive. How the hell will I ever find the bathroom?"

"Go down that hall, and it's two doors on the right."

Stori came back onto the patio in the oversized robe. I helped her take the robe off and get under the blanket. Taking the oil, I put some on my hands before I started at her feet. I've been wanting to rub, suck and do everything to these feet since our date on the beach.

"Tell me what's going on?"

Stori took a deep breath and let me in on all she had been going through and why she left from her trip earlier than usual. I rubbed each part of her body while she let everything out. As I made my way to different body parts, I could tell that this was releasing the tension within her body. Her husband sounded just like I knew he would be – a bozo.

What kind of man would willingly put his woman in a position like this? She was stressed out while still being there for him and their kids, and this man had the nerve to be demanding shit from her.

"So, yeah, this is what has been going on." She leaned her head back down. "Hmm, this feels so damn good," she moaned.

"How much you need for your savings?"

Her head snapped up, and she stared at me. "Absolutely not."

"Why? I can't sit back and watch you struggle."

"You're not sitting back and watching anything because I don't plan on putting it on display. This only works if you don't toss your money at me. I will figure out a way to fix this. I always do." She sighed.

"You shouldn't have to figure this shit out on your own though. Not when you have me that wants to help you."

"I don't want your help, Bray. Those are my kids; I can provide for them. It will be tight for a while, but I will make it work."

"You fucking stubborn," I accused, and pulled the sheet back, exposing her body. Every dimple, stretch mark and blemish was exposed.

She started to cover herself and then eventually gave up because she saw me coming out of my pants. "I just want you… not your money," she whispered as I climbed onto the table and between her legs.

"Let me help you, Doc," I groaned into her ear as I kissed them.

She wrapped her legs around me as I slowly inserted myself into her. "No," she gasped as she tossed her head back.

There were a few surrounding buildings that could probably catch a glimpse of us, but fuck it... I wanted to put on a show.

"Baby... let...me...take... the...stress...from... you," I said in between each kiss I placed on her face.

"Make me feel good, Papa," she cooed, giving me the cue that she was done talking and was ready for some dick.

ELEVEN
DR. ASTORIA JACOBS

"MOM, YOU BEEN SPENDING A LOT OF TIME OUT THE HOUSE?" DEMI narrowed her eyes at me as I packed my overnight back for the weekend.

After work, I planned on getting on the highway and heading straight to Bray's penthouse for an entire weekend filled with relaxation, sex, and a little bit of fun. With Jace's accident and the tension around the house, Bray had been doing an amazing job at keeping the stress to a minimum. I wanted to spend every second with him.

"I just need to get away to keep my mind right. You don't mind, right?" I questioned, because this would be the first weekend I would be spending away from the house since the accident.

Jace had rehab a few times next week, so it was either this weekend or never for me and Bray's weekend getaway. He didn't tell me what we were doing. All he told me to do was pack a bag before leaving to work in the morning.

"No, I like that you come back less stressed and happier. If those quick overnight trips do that, then this weekend should do wonders."

I smiled at my daughter's smart ass remarks but was grateful that she didn't mind me spending the weekend away. Especially after just spending almost a week away on vacation. I had to get it through my skull that my girls were older and didn't need me as much.

"Have you and your father sat down and had that conversation yet?"

"Nope." She quickly shot back.

I had been trying to encourage Demi and Jace to talk, and they both refused. He felt like he shouldn't have to apologize to his teenage daughter, and Demi felt the opposite about it. Although they were opposites, I could agree that Demi got her stubbornness from her father.

Jace did need to apologize to both his daughters because his accident put a monkey wrench in everything. We all had to take turns to make sure that he had food, or things before leaving the house. If it wasn't for our insurance, I would have had to pay for an aide out of pocket. Thankfully, our insurance covered that. The company didn't have the best reviews, but at this point, Jace better had been appreciative.

That had been the only way I was physically able to get back into my office. I knew my clients were tired of being rescheduled or having to do their sessions over video calls. Demi quickly went upstairs to grab her things while I headed to Tyler's room, where Jace was.

"Morning," I greeted and sat the orange juice and medicine that I had prepared a couple minutes prior to rearranging things in my overnight bag.

"Where are you going this weekend?" He didn't bother to greet me back, not that he ever did anyway.

"Here's your medicine for the day. Enzo loaded the mini fridge with a bunch of water and Gatorade." I purposely ignored him. "I'm going away for the weekend to read and decompress," I lied.

He winced as he leaned up in the bed. "You walking around

here complaining about the bills and money, but you can afford to go out of town for the weekend?"

I knew this was going to be the topic of conversation this morning. When I originally told him that I was going out of town, he didn't have any questions and waved me off because he was too consumed with the football game that was on. Now that he remembered I was going out of town, he wanted to bombard me with questions this morning and I wasn't going for it.

"The girls assured me that they can handle themselves this weekend, and your aide is working this weekend, so you'll have someone to help you."

"Why the fuck is that aide still coming? I told you that I don't like her."

Since Jace had been bedridden, all he did was complain. He never uttered a thank you, or offered any other sign that he was thankful. All we ever heard was complaints about his coffee not being hot, or we didn't use the right amount of sugar to cream ratio.

I was tired of his ass.

"I wanted to get out this weekend to see Ty's football game. We supposed to sit in the house all weekend while you *decompress* all weekend," he mocked.

"I don't know what to tell you." I folded my arms. "The girls are going to have their own movie night, and I plan to order them pizza."

If he wanted to make it to Tyler's football games, he should have thought of that before he decided to ride that damn bike over to Messiah's house instead of staying home with his kids. Now he wanted to be concerned about the kids being home all weekend. When in reality, the girls didn't mind spending the weekend at home. Usually, they were busy with their hobbies that the weekend passed by quickly for them.

"This is the shit I be talking about. You don't give a fuck about the shit that I have going on," he complained.

"Jace, I have to do school drop off and get to work. Your aide has the code to the front door... have a good day." I shut him down before he could make this a whole thing.

"My pain meds need to be refilled."

"It's too soon," I replied, and headed out the side door to the driveway.

Enzo was already sitting in the back waiting while Demi was right behind me. "You're not going to say goodbye to your father?" I asked as I placed my work bag in the backseat next to her.

"Mr. Crabs has been on my nerves, so no," she scoffed while looking down at her phone again.

"Enzo, he's your father."

"And I'm allowed to need space from someone who isn't making me feel good."

I wanted to turn around and kiss her beautiful, smooth caramel skin. The real flex with parenting was raising children who had boundaries and weren't afraid to enforce them. As a kid, I would have never been able to tell my mother that. It would have been considered disrespectful in her eyes, and to me, as a therapist and mother, I was beyond proud.

"Okay, baby... when you feel ready make sure to have a conversation with your father." I stared at her through the rear-view mirror.

"Okay."

Demi got in the car and buckled up. "I'm sorry... had to grab my lunch from the fridge."

"Salad again?"

"Yes. I like arugula, and they don't give that at school. Only stupid iceberg." She held up her Betsey Johnson lunch box.

"Brat," Enzo teased her.

"When I'm lean and trim for this dance competition, don't be jealous."

"You are already beautiful," I reminded her as we pulled out of the driveway. I allowed Demi to eat cleaner because it was something that she enjoyed. I had no doubt that my girl would be vegan or something in the future. She had always been obsessed with vegetables since she was a toddler. While other kids wanted chicken nuggets and French fries, she was obsessed with broccoli and zucchini fries.

"Thanks, Mom."

After I dropped the kids to school, I stopped to grab a coffee on the way to the office. While at the light, I smiled when I saw Bray's number come across my car's screen.

"Good morning, Doc."

I was like a child, giddy as ever hearing his deep baritone voice on the other end of the line. "Morning, Bray."

"Oh, I'm Bray this morning?"

"Good morning, Papa," I sang into the phone.

"Damn, Doc... make some time for me to release this tension growing in my pants right now."

"No, Bray... I have a session in a little while. We will see each other later; do you still want me to meet you at your place?"

"I got a meeting in Philly today, so I'm gonna be running behind you. My doorman already knows to let you up into our space."

"*Our?*" I choked out.

"Yeah, it's *our* place," he confirmed it, making me feel all warm and fuzzy on the inside.

I almost wanted to cancel all my meetings today and head straight to his place and wait there for him without any clothes on. Bray made me feel special whenever I was in his presence, something I had never felt before. He took care of me, and I didn't have to make a single decision whenever I was with him.

I earned more money than Jace, and that had never been a problem for me. We both knew that I would eventually earn more than him because of my degrees. What bothered me the most was that he never stepped up and made decisions as a man. If he was taking me out on a date, I could count on him asking me what time I wanted to go, the restaurant and which car we were going to take. Every decision had to be made by me, and it was mentally draining.

As a woman, I wanted to be led instead of having to do the leading at times. Each time I had been with Bray, he made the decisions, and I followed behind him without any hesitation. I had to be in control with my career and in my marriage, and I was tired of it. Spending time with Bray was freeing, and it opened my eyes to a lot of things I never knew I wanted in a man. I was so young and inexperienced when I fell in love with Jace that I wasn't emotionally mature enough to understand the concept of what I required from a man.

All Jace ever did was toss me scraps and expect me to feel loved with whatever he provided. For years, I made use of the scraps provided by him, feeling like I deserved better but never asking for it. With Bray, I didn't even have to ask for it because that was the vibe that he provided from the first moment we first met.

The way he held onto my hip as I stood between his legs, and offered to cover anything I needed while being at the resort made me feel protected and secure. That wasn't something I had never felt before.

"Doc, don't get all quiet on me."

I had gotten so far into my head that I forgot I was on the phone with him, and driving. "I'm not… it was surprising to hear."

"I can't wait to wrap up this meeting and see you later. Do I have you for the whole weekend or do I gotta make sure my boo gets home by morning?" He teased.

"I'm yours for the whole weekend, Papa."

"That's exactly what I want to hear… text me when you get to work. I'm sending lunch to the office for you and your assistant. I don't want to hear about you forgetting to eat."

"Thank you… see you soon."

Soon as I pulled into my parking spot, I had a huge smile on my face as I sipped my coffee. Killing the engine, I grabbed my bag from the backseat and headed into my office. Soon as Bethany saw me, she perked up.

"Good morning, Dr. Jacobs! I sure missed seeing your face around here." Bethany stood up and handed me a cup of coffee from our favorite coffee shop.

I held up the coffee that I had already picked up. "I was actually able to snag a cup this morning because the girls were on time, but I'm never against extra caffeine."

She handed me the cup and walked around the desk with her iPad. "We had clients send flowers and well wishes with flowers and more gift cards for lunch."

"It looks like we're going to be eating well for the next few weeks." I winked and headed into my office to sit my stuff down.

"You have a pretty light day. Kami Lynn is coming in today, and then you have a solo session with Mrs. Miranda."

"Perfect. I have to leave here a little bit earlier because I have plans out of town," I informed her, and placed both my coffees down on my desk. "Is Kyle here?"

"You know I am." Kyle entered my office and dramatically tossed his arms around me, pulling me into a tight hug. "I've missed you around the office."

"I've missed you too."

Bethany took that as her cue and excused herself. She closed my office door behind her while I got comfortable in my armchair, and Kyle sat on the couch. I had at least a half an hour to kill before my first client.

"What has been going on? You've been real vague over our text messages. There was a few times I wanted to come over there and make sure you were trul—"

We were interrupted by a knock at the door. The doorknob turned and Ember stuck her head in. "Hey, I brought your favorite coffee and breakfast sandwich from Muddy's. I know it's your first day back since everything," she quietly closed the door behind her. "Hey, Kyle."

It wasn't unusual for Ember to stop by my office every so often. "Awe, Em... thank you." I stood up and kissed her on the cheek.

"Don't mention it. Are we in here shit talking this early in the morning?" She slid over on the couch and crossed her legs.

"You're right on time because that's exactly what we were about to do." Kyle smirked and hugged her quickly.

Ember looked at her watch. "My first patient isn't for two hours, so I have time to indulge." She got even more comfier in the chair.

Ever since Jace's accident, I hadn't been able to catch up with anybody. All Ember and Harlym knew was that we slept together in the Maldives. I never got the chance to tell her about going to his place and spending the night with him whenever I got the chance. Kyle wasn't clued into any of what was going on since my vacation.

"I was just about to dig into why she been so quiet and vague with me."

"Text message wasn't the right way to clue you into what was going on. Jace's accident really put a lot on my shoulders, and I'm trying to balance my time with work, the girls and Bray," I added in there.

Em clapped her hands together. "So, Bray *is* back into the picture?"

"He is."

Kyle looked from me to Ember, confused. "Who is Bray and when did he first come into the picture?"

I smiled, thinking about my man, my man, my man. Goodness, he made me feel so good that I never wanted to lose that feeling. "He's somebody I met on our trip."

"Um, what? Girl, you went all Stella got her groove back on me... I knew you looked like you had an extra pep in your step on the security cameras this morning."

"You saw me on the cameras this morning and didn't come help open the door for me?" I cut my eyes at him and smiled. "It was just supposed to be a fling, and then it followed me back home. We ran into each other at the din—"

"He was here in Lennox Hills?" Em nearly screamed.

"Apparently, he lives here. The world is so damn small."

"Or its fate," Ember added.

"I agree."

"We're spending the weekend together at his place in the city."

Kyle jumped out of his seat like he had ants in his pants. "Alright, so we're fully going there... let me prepare myself."

"For what?"

"To go with you to file those divorce papers. I know that is the next step in all of this."

"It's long overdue if you ask me," Em muttered.

The thought of divorcing Jace made me both excited and scared at the same time. I knew this was something that I needed to do, and I was still scared to do it. Our lives would change, and it would become messy. Jace was emotional when he felt blindsided and hurt, so I could expect him to be petty and want things he never cared about in the first place.

Who would get the house when we divorced? Or would we be forced to sell because neither of us could come to an agreement? These were the things that worried me and prevented me from filing the papers I've had in my possession for too long.

"He can't work right now, and I'm the main source of income right now. His disability amount is basically pennies, but it will help with some things."

"Not your problem. This is the bed he made when he decided to buy that damn motorcycle. Are you supposed to sit back and stop living your life because of a decision he made?" Em questioned me.

"No, but I'm not heartless either."

"You not being heartless is what got you into this situation in the first place. Stori, you're in a loveless marriage with a man that doesn't value or consider you as a person."

"Ouch," Kyle uttered.

"If Jace gave an inkling of a fuck about you and all you've done for him and y'all family, he would have never bought that motorcycle, or used it while you were out the country. He does whatever he wants and doesn't give a fuck about the outcome because he knows his wife will handle it, which is what you're doing now. I'm sorry but being on vacation was the first time I saw you let loose. You're always so uptight and trying to be the problem solver that you miss out on living your life too."

"I have to say I agree with her. You're usually the first one in the office and the last one to leave. You come in on the weekends when none of us do, and you never take time for you," Kyle paused. "We both chose to be in this career because we wanted to help people, and there's nothing wrong with that. It becomes wrong when we put everyone before ourselves and don't prioritize us."

If I wasn't so mentally drained, I probably would have cried. I understood what both Ember and Kyle were telling me, however, that was easier said than done. My husband was home injured with no work, and it was up to me to carry the weight of our home on my back.

"I love you both and appreciate that you both care so much about me. Just give me time to make these changes because they won't happen overnight."

"Seems like the changes aren't the only thing working overnight." Ember winked and slapped hands with Kyle.

"Byeeee. I need to get ready for my client." I rolled my eyes at them and stood up. The day would have been perfect if we could sit around and shoot the breeze with each other.

Kyle jumped up. "I know when I'm not wanted. I do know that you better have a damn good time this weekend with *him*." He winked.

"And don't worry about the girls. I will pop over there to check in on them. I may even take them shopping since I have nothing planned," Em assured me.

"Love you guys," I called behind him.

Since I hadn't been here, I straightened up my office and made sure to fluff out the pillows on the couch. When I was done with the light clean, I popped a fresh box of tissues on the coffee table and plopped down in my chair to wait for Kami to arrive.

Sending you safe travels to Philly. Being me back a cheesesteak, jk. I sent Bray a quick text.

Thanks, Doc. Can't wait to be done so I can hold you captive the whole weekend. Ordered Sushi for you and your assistant for lunch. I read his text message while smiling before silencing my phone and tucking it beside me in the chair.

"Dr. Jacobs, Kami-Lynn is here," Bethany spoke over the intercom.

"You can send her in," I replied, thankful that I opted for the two-way intercom system that didn't require me to press a button to reply when I wasn't near it.

Kami rushed into my office like a bull in a China cabinet. She tossed her Chloe purse onto the couch and then plopped down right beside it. Her hair was frazzled, and she looked like she had been crying.

"Kami, are you alright?"

"No!" she shouted, then jumped to her feet and started pacing the small space between the couch and coffee table. "My husband had divorce papers served to me minutes after he left for a work trip. The sick fucker planned it out because when I tried calling him, he turned his phone off."

I didn't see this change of events happening. Last we spoke over our video session, she said that they were hoping to work things out, and his mother had come to stay with them to assure that.

"I'm sorry, Kami. You've had to know that this could happen."

"Yes, I should have known. He hasn't touched me in months,

and the last time we were intimate, he looked so out of it, like he was envisioning anyone but me underneath him."

The pain on her face was heartbreaking. I believe Kami regretted stepping outside of her marriage with Cam. You could tell she was just begging for attention from her husband, and now she was getting the wrong attention from him.

"Divorce is usually the last step in a relationship. Of course, he could pull the filing and decide to work on his marriage with you, but men usually never file first."

"My cousin's husband filed for divorce."

"I said usually, I never said it doesn't happen," I corrected her.

I hated to be the person to tell her that her marriage was over. Men usually held onto a marriage longer than a woman did. They would drag a woman to hell and back and never think about the word divorce. Women filed the moment they were fed up, and usually pulled the filing and tried to make the marriage work. Her husband didn't only file for divorce, but he lined it up perfectly for her to be served when he wasn't around her.

Kami needed to move on with her life because it seemed like her husband already did. She was spending time in marriage therapy alone. That man hadn't showed up to one session, and I didn't think he would because he didn't see the need to meet with me.

He was done with the marriage, and she needed to get on board and get on with her life. "I love him so much, Dr. Jacobs. He's all I've known in my adult life." she sat back down and sobbed into her hands.

"If the shoe was on the other foot and he cheated with an ex-partner of his, would you have been so forgiving?"

"I would have given him shit, but I would have wanted to work on my marriage." Kami sniffled.

She answered the question too quickly. If the shoe was on the other foot, she would have been ready to jump ship just like he was. I couldn't be upset with her husband wanting to end the marriage.

It showed that he knew what he was worth, and he wasn't willing to settle for Kami, who didn't respect or appreciate the union of their marriage before she decided to sleep with her ex-boyfriend.

I could learn a lot from this man. When Jace cheated the first time I should have been gone and never accepted his bullshit proposal. It was easy for Kami to tell me that she could forgive her husband had the shoe been on the other foot. That was because the shoe hadn't been on the other foot, and her husband didn't cheat on her.

"I think you can say that now because you weren't cheated on. In fact, you were the one who cheated on your spouse. You have to respect your husband's decision just like if you decided to file for divorce, he would have to respect yours."

"Whose side are you even on?"

I always hated when clients asked this question. They thought because they paid me that they were paying for me to be on their side. I was on the side of what was right so that I could send level-headed clients back into the world.

"You have fought for your marriage and tried to fix what couldn't be repaired. Kami, I think it would be best for you to move on with your life. Keep a friendship, if there is one, and allow each other to have a fresh start."

"It's so much easier for him to walk away because our marriage isn't public. I should have made our relationship public, so he would want to fight for us. That was the one thing he hated,

"Making it public now won't do any good. Divorce privately. Trust me, you're going to want the private healing... both of you."

The only reason I agreed to take on Kami was because she was married. I thought after a few sessions that I would eventually meet the husband and have some shared sessions. We were about five sessions in now, and I didn't even know the man's name. Now that he filed for divorce there was no way he was going to attend a therapy session with his future ex-wife.

It was time for me to refer her back to Kyle. "Making it public might force him to want to fix our marriage."

"Kami, you should focus on healing," I encouraged, making a note to refer her back to Kyle before our next session could be scheduled.

She wasn't in the right mental space to accept that I was assigning her back to Kyle. I listened to her talk about things that she wanted in her marriage, and how she wasn't ready to accept defeat. When our session was done, she had used half the new box of tissues that I just put out.

Since she was my last client of the day, I quickly packed up everything and checked in with Demi before hitting the road. She told me she and Enzo were catching a ride with our neighbor across the street. She was seventeen and had her license and was responsible. I appreciated her getting the girls from school for me because I would have been late heading to Bray's place.

A small part of me wanted to call and check in on Jace to see if he needed anything. I was trying to put space between us and practicing boundaries, so I tossed that thought out my head and headed toward the highway.

TWELVE
BRAY WILLSHIRE

WHEN THE ELEVATOR GOT TO MY FLOOR, I COULD SMELL THE AROMA penetrating my nose through the slits of the elevator door. Soon as the doors opened, I was met with the beautiful view that always took my breath away, and then I looked down and noticed something even more beautiful.

Astoria.

She was standing in the foyer with two glasses of wine in her hand while wearing a black teddy that left little to the imagination. Her hardened gumdrop nipples were protruding through the lace, causing my mouth to water.

"Fuck, Doc... what are you trying to do to me?"

She giggled and walked over to me. "I figured you might have had a stressful day, so I made you a home cooked meal, and opened a bottle of wine. I opened one of the bottles in the wine cellar."

I had converted one of the pantries into a see-through wine cellar. If I had to pick between wine and the hard shit, I usually went with wine. Wine didn't leave me fighting for my life the next morning like a bottle of rum would.

"Definitely had a stressful day." I ignored the glass of wine and put my bag down on the floor.

"Woah…wa…wait, you're gonna spill the wine."

I didn't give a fuck about the wine or the glasses, I grabbed the glasses and put them onto the floor and grabbed Astoria up. She giggled and wrapped her arms around me.

I kissed her sweet lips and stared into her eyes. "I missed you today, Doc."

"Are you admitting that I got you open?"

"Like your legs about to be in a minute." I walked over to the couch and leaned her on the edge.

Stori kissed my lips, neck, and face as I fought to get my Ferragamo buckle open. I wanted her so bad, had dreamed about that shit the whole ride back to the city. When I finally got the buckle undone, I dropped my dress pants and pulled her closer to me.

"Crotchless." She winked.

"Fuck," I groaned and shoved my dick into her wet opening. She moaned as she tossed her head back, while holding onto my shoulders as I pounded into her pussy.

She threw that shit on me as we stared each other in the eyes. We both needed this. I couldn't sit and pretend over dinner when I knew I wanted to fuck the shit out of her. Stori secretly wanted the same thing. Why else would she put that shit on and meet me in the foyer?

The sound of my balls clapping echoed through the living room as she hummed, and her eyes rolled to the back of her head. "Who pussy is this?"

"Y…Yours, Papa… it's yours!" she screamed.

"Tell me again, Doc… tell me who pussy this is?" I reached behind her and grabbed a handful of her braids, pulling her head even further back.

"Harder… fuck…. Papa…. Ah…Ah…" She continued to scream out in pleasure.

Taking my hand, I carefully placed it around her neck, and she lifted her head to stare me in the eyes. When that sly smirk came across her face, I tightened my grip and continued to pound her pussy on the edge of my couch.

"Fuck... Stori.... fuck! You making me about to nut!"

"Do it, Papa... X marks the spot," she cooed, which drove me crazy. I stared into her eyes as I emptied my load into her.

Pulling her closer to me, she licked my lips and opened her mouth wide. I kissed her mouth before I spit inside of her mouth. She licked her lips with a smile on her face, then sucked on my bottom lip.

I kissed her neck, leaving small passion bites on the left side. Grabbing a big handful of her ass, I pulled back to take her in. She seemed like a dream, one that would disappear the minute I opened my eyes.

"You don't feel real at times," I said into her ear.

"I could say the same thing about you... about this." She kissed my lips and wrapped her arms around my neck.

"Doc, I want you. I don't want no bullshit to come between us," I expressed because I was serious about her.

About us.

She looked up into my eyes, and I could tell this was something she had wanted to hear from me. "I'm scared."

"Of what?"

"You," she admitted.

I held her close and kissed her lips a few times. "I'm scared of you."

She sucked her teeth. "Me? Why?"

"Cause I never met somebody that I felt this protective over. Not even my own wife, Doc. With you, I want to protect you from ever being hurt again. When I think about you being hurt in the past, I'm mad at myself because I couldn't be there to shield you from it." I gripped her hip tightly. "If this is too much, I need you to let me know now before I fall even harder for you... I don't want to pull you into something that you're not ready for, not with children. I need to know that you're ready for me."

She kissed me on the lips. "What if I'm too much, Bray? I come with baggage, and a host of trust issues."

"You're never too much for the right man, Doc." I kissed her on the lips, and she wiped away the tear that slipped down her cheek.

"The food is going to get cold."

"Stop deflecting. I don't take our paths crossing lightly. We were supposed to meet, and it didn't matter how that happened, it was supposed to happen. The man above put this into fruition."

"Now you're trying to put God into this?"

"The big guy always give me what I want."

"Is that right?" she sniffled.

"For sure, Doc."

We quickly cleaned up and then went into the kitchen, where Stori was moving around the kitchen like she had been here her entire life. I stood up from the bar stool and came behind her, kissing her on the neck softly.

"Go get in the bed... I'm going to fix the plates. You made the food, so I'm going to serve you."

"Bray, you don't hav—"

"My day isn't the only one that matters, Doc. If I had a stressful day, then I know damn well you had one too. Let me take care of you." She kissed me on the lips and then left out the kitchen.

She must have known I was a pasta man because the shrimp scampi with freshly baked garlic knots had my mouth watering. As I scooped the noodles out the skillet onto a plate, I noticed the small bits of lobster, clams, and scallops.

I could tell the garlic knots were homemade from how wonky they were shaped. She didn't pull these out an oven safe bag, she got down and dirty and baked them herself.

"I'm just going to settle down and enjoy my night with a book," she lied, knowing damn well we was about to be fucking soon as my stomach was filled.

"Okay, Mom... Have fun. You could fix your hair though," her daughter snorted, and Stori quickly went to fix her hair.

"What are you girls doing? Where's your father? He didn't answer my call when I called him earlier."

"Tonya picked him up to take him to Tyler's football practice. He called to check in an hour ago and said he's going to grab something with Ty and Tonya."

"Oh, okay. What are you eating for dinner tonight? I can order some pizza o—"

"Since you're offering... um, can we please have Benihanas? I would kill for their chicken fried rice right now."

I sat our plates down, careful not to get in the view of the camera. While she was on FaceTime talking to her daughter, I grabbed my phone and opened up my UberEATS app. I put a little bit of everything on their menu in the cart and then put my phone down next to Stori. I mouthed for her to put her address in, and she looked confused.

She quickly put her phone on mute and placed it down so her daughter couldn't see her face. "What are you doing?"

"The princess said she wants Benihanas, put your address in." I pushed my phone toward her.

Stori put her address in and handed me back the phone. "Bray, you don't have to do that."

"I know what I don't have to do, Doc." I winked and hit the confirm button.

Stori returned back to the FaceTime with her daughter. "My friend ordered you and your sister Benihana." She nervously told her daughter.

"Friend? Who?"

"Someone you haven't met."

"Yet? Cause um, if they ordering us Benihana, then we need to meet... period." She spoke in the usual teen lingo.

Stori smiled. "Call me when your sister wakes up from her nap. I will be watching the cameras for the delivery guy. Wait until he puts it down before getting it, Demi."

"Mom, I already knew the deal," she groaned. "Call you back."

Astoria ended the call and then looked at me. "Are you trying to spoil them? They're going to be asking for all kinds of stuff whenever I'm out of town."

"Hopefully, next time, you won't be alone." I kissed her on the lips. "Now eat, you gonna need all the energy you can get."

"What are the plans this weekend? Cause you about to have me too tired to drive back home."

"I can arrange for you to get back... and have your car brought to you." I kissed her once more.

I couldn't get enough of kissing her lips. If I could sit back and do it for the rest of my life, I wouldn't even be mad about it.

"You literally want to fix all my problems."

"I plan to." I tasted the pasta.

The spices and taste were on point. I've been to restaurants where the shrimp was overcooked. She cooked this shit like she was hiding a culinary degree. "You can't fix all my problems."

"You're used to being with *that* man who can't. It seems like he's the reason for almost all your problems. With me, I plan to fix all your problems because the only thing I want you stressed about is what color teddy you gonna wear for me. Doc, stress is normal, but having a partner that helps is key. You ain't never had that, so I can see why you're skeptical."

"Filing for divorce could get messy. I know my husband, and I know that it will get messy with him. I'd rather not drag you through something like that. You have your own situation going on."

"If shit gets messy, then I'm right here with a mop ready to clean that shit up. You need a divorce lawyer; I got one on retainer. Stop resisting and let me take care of you."

She finally tasted her food. "It's so hard to let go and trust. I'm sorry... I want to let go and give you control, but I've never done it before, and it's hard. My girls... I can't let go, and this goes wrong."

"The only way this goes wrong is if you're not open to us. I need to know that you got me like I got you. If I know one thing, I know I'm a man of my word."

She moved the plate to the side and crawled over toward me. "I've always been a woman of my word."

"Then kiss me and then toot that ass in the air," I demanded.

Stori kissed me on the lips and then bent her ass off and looked back at me. "Like this, Papa?"

The food was good, but I couldn't even think with her ass on full display, ready for me to slide into it. Pulling my briefs down, I slapped her ass and prepared to shove everything inside of her, but her phone went off.

"Shit... it's the girls." She dived across the bed and grabbed her phone, fixing her hair in the process. "Hey, Dem. What's up?"

"Why you rizzing so hard right now, mom?"

"What?"

"Your eyes all low and seductive... you being flirty with someone?"

"Demi, what did you want?"

"Um, the food came. Tell your friend Bray we said thank you. There's so much food here. I don't even know where to start." She sounded excited.

"Ma, the crunchy sushi rolls are so good! You said you wouldn't pay twenty dollars for them, but Bray did," another voice spoke on the phone.

Her eyes widened. "What you mean by Bray?"

"The name is on the bag... Bray Willshire. Tell him we said thank you."

Stori ran her hand across her face and shook her head. "Girls, enjoy your food. Call me when your dad gets home."

It was clear the girls had dug into the food because they were smacking all in the phone. "Alright, Mom... love you."

"Love you girls more."

She ended the call and folded her arms. "Really? They have enough to host a feast."

I shrugged and pulled her back over to me. "Your girls are part of you, so like I got you... I got them." We shared a kiss. "Now, as we were."

She didn't hesitate to toot that ass up, and I didn't hesitate to slide right up inside of her. "Like this, Papa?"

"Just like this, Doc."

"I FEEL like I could run a marathon, cook Thanksgiving dinner and build a skyscraper," Stori collapsed on the tufted armchair in our spa house at the Willshire hotel in Midtown.

Stori had just finished one of her many spa treatments that I had planned for the day. She was so relaxed that nothing could fuck with her right now, not even me. My dick was so hard watching her in this element. The only thing I wanted to provide for my woman was a soft life, one where this was what she expected whenever she was stressed out. We spent the entire night fucking, tasting one another and being in each other's arms that we were exhausted. I booked one of spa houses for the day, and we had been enjoying the many different treatments that came with booking a full day's stay.

"Speaking of thanksgiving. What is your plan?" It was only a few weeks away, and I didn't want to spend it without her.

If her pasta was any indication of how she got down in the kitchen, I was ready to try her baked macaroni and cheese. "We usually go over to Jace's mama's house. It's tradition, and we never break it."

"Some traditions are meant to be broken, Doc."

"I know, and they will be eventually. This could be our last thanksgiving as a family."

"*Could* be?" I raised my eyebrow.

"You know what I mean, Pa."

Her soft voice mixed with her New York accent made the word *Pa* roll off her tongue. Shit turned me on whenever she called me that. "I'm just trying to make sure our wires ain't crossed, Doc."

She took a deep breath and walked over to me seductively. "I know this may not be easy with the girls, especially with me having to reveal we're getting a divorce. Christmas could look very different for us, so I want to give them this one holiday." She looked off toward the beautiful view of Manhattan.

"Astoria." I gently turned her face back toward me. "I need to know if you're divorcing your husband for me, or because of you."

"For me. Even if I never met you, I was going to divorce Jace. I guess... you just expedited it." She smiled, as she touched my face. "Why did you ask?"

"I want you to divorce your husband because of you, not me. As bad as I want you, I don't want you to ever regret your divorce or feel any ill feelings toward me."

"I could never. This is my decision, and it's something that has been on my mind for a while. You ain't that good, Bray Willshire."

I poked her with my dick. "Want me to remind you how good I am?"

As Stori was about to drop her robe, the staff came into the room. "I am sorry, Mr. Willshire. We have Mr. Willshire on the phone, and he says it's urgent."

"Which one?" Me and Stori both asked.

"Ashton."

I nodded for him to bring the phone forward and pressed the speaker button. "This shit better be good since you tracking me down at the spa."

"Nigga, please. We all know you ain't got no cucumbers on those swollen ass eyes. Check your phone."

"For what?" Stori had climbed off my lap and went into the next room. She came back with both of our phones.

"I got my phone... happy?"

"You ain't gonna be in a bit." Ashton ended the call.

I powered up my phone and waited for the apple sign to disappear. Was it so hard to have a peaceful day with the woman of my dreams?

"Your wife is Kami Lynn?" Astoria shrieked and hopped back off my lap.

"She is."

"Why the fuck wasn't that the first thing you told me when we met?"

"Why would it be?"

She was shaking her head while pacing the floor. I could spot the vein in the side of her neck as she waved her hands in the air. I learned long ago not to meet emotion with emotion. This was her moment to be emotional and freak out, I wasn't going to take that from her. I also wasn't going to downplay her feelings because they were valid.

"How are you so fucking calm now? Oh, God... I could lose my license," she ranted to herself.

"You're Kami's therapist?"

"What? No," She lied.

Stori couldn't even look me in the eyes. I also knew she couldn't confirm or deny if Kami was her patient because of confidentiality. She stormed out onto the terrace and leaned her head on the marble pillar.

Instead of going directly after her, I gave her some space. My phone chimed, alerting me of all the news stories and blogs that were reporting the news. Kami had always wanted to keep our relationship and marriage a secret. I told her there was a difference between being private and a secret. Our marriage was a secret since everyone assumed she was single.

I clenched my jaw when I saw the Instagram post from Kami's page. She shared a picture of our first Halloween together as a married couple. She dressed as a zombie bride, and I was a zombie groom.

The happiest times with you as my husband and by my side. Love you, Bray-Bray.

She did that shit on purpose. Kami had never wanted to claim our marriage or relationship in the media, and the fact that she decided to share this photo confirming we were married after I had divorce papers delivered to her was low, even for her.

I called her phone, and it went directly to voicemail. She had turned that shit off on purpose because she knew what her post would do. Laurent's name came across my screen as I was about to call her back.

"Yo."

"Maybe I'm confused because I thought you served her with divorce papers."

"I did."

"And she pulled this?"

"Exactly. I'm with Stori, and she's flipping the fuck out over it. Apparently, she's the therapist that Kami been seeing."

"Stori told you that?"

"No, but I could put the pieces together and tell from the way she's acting."

"I was about to say," Laurent chuckled. "Do you need me to get Sammie on this? Release a statement or something?"

"I don't even fucking know right now."

"Look, take a minute to figure out what you need and let me know... I got you."

"Appreciate it."

I ended the call with my brother and leaned my head back. Why the fuck would Kami do something like this? "Doc!" I called to Stori, who was pacing back and forth.

"Bray, not righ—"

"What did we promise each other last night?"

"This is dif—"

"What did we promise?"

"To not let anything get in between what we're trying to build."

"And what are you about to do?"

"I just can—"

"I don't ever want to make this a habit with us."

"What?"

"Me constantly cutting you off. I want you to always speak your peace and complete your thoughts." I leaned forward and grabbed her back onto my lap. "But, Doc, you working yourself up. Look at me." I stared her in the eyes.

"Bray, this is so messed up."

"I will handle it. You hear me?"

"I'm going to have to—"

"Let me stop you real quick. Did you hear me? I'm going to handle this. If she is your patient or not, you handle that part. Everything else I got."

I had front row seats to witness a woman let down her guard and submit to me. Her shoulders loosened, and the scowl she wore on her face disappeared. "Okay."

"Give me a kiss." Stori gave me a kiss and then leaned her head on me. "I got you, Doc."

This was where I wanted to be, but I also wanted to wrap my hands around Kami's throat. Why couldn't she just let me go? She was the one who fucked up, so why was she doing petty shit to me?

I wasn't even tripping on her keeping whatever she wanted. All I needed was a clean break to do me, and that was to be with Stori. She wrapped her arms around my neck, and I kissed her forehead. The feelings that I felt for Stori scared the shit out of me. How could you give another woman your last name and five years and never feel the same emotions for her? I wasn't the type to believe in love at first sight, however, Stori had me second guessing my own beliefs.

THIRTEEN
DR. ASTORIA JACOBS

KAMI LYNN WILLSHIRE.

Kyle told me that she wanted someone to be discreet, and I obliged because a lot of high-profile clients wanted those same things. You didn't hear about Beyonce and Jay-Z in marriage therapy, but you could assume they were in therapy after the Lemonade album dropped. Still, you would never hear those words from their mouth. As a professional, I was expected to do the same and keep my client's secrets.

I combed over the files that Kyle had given me, and nowhere on there had I seen the last name Willshire, or Bray's name mentioned anywhere. I've been trying to rack my brain on how I missed the clues.

Bray living in Lennox Hills and just moving here at that.

He never mentioned his wife's name, which I didn't find weird. Only my emotional ass brought up my husband while trying to have an affair. There was so much that I missed that I felt stupid. Kami warned that she would go public with her marriage, and I didn't even piece it together. Even after I told her it wouldn't be wise to do something like that, she still went ahead and did it.

"I know, I know. What the fuck?" Kyle said and pulled me

toward his office. He closed the door and then turned around. "It's everywhere. What are you going to do?"

"The plan was to refer her back to you since all the sessions I've had with her have been solo. He refused to come to any of the sessions, which showed that he was done with the marriage."

"I can quickly accept her back as a client. What about you and Bray?" Kyle questioned. "It's a conflict of interest, Astoria, and you know this."

"Is it really? I didn't know he was her husband, and they are going to be divorced soon. He wasn't actually a client of mine... I don't have any papers with his name on it either."

"You know how this could go down, Stori. Is this man worth your career?"

I sighed, leaning my head back on the door. "He said he would handle it."

"And you trust it? A man that you don't even know."

It was hard to explain to Kyle, who knew me as a control freak, that I trusted this man. I was someone who had to be in control of everything, and I wasn't the least bit worried because I trusted that Bray was going to handle it.

I had no choice but to trust that he would handle the situation. Kami was a woman scorned, and she would do whatever she needed to make sure she hurt Bray and whoever was trying to slide in her spot. My career meant the world to me, and it was something I busted my ass to achieve. I'd be damned if she took it away from me because she was found with her pants down – literally.

"Are you sure you're, okay?"

"I'm fine. When I'm not, I promise I will let you know."

"That's all I ask."

I had more than a few clients today, and I barely focused on any of them. Besides jotting a few things down and asking rhetorical questions, I wasn't in the mood to hear anyone's problems today. Bray was on the West Coast for an opening of another Willshire Hotel, and I wanted to be next to him all the time, and that scared me because I didn't even want to be around my own husband as much and I had been with him since I was younger.

Bethany had a family emergency, so she left early today. I handled my last client of the day and closed down our office. Kyle had one client before he was out the door to start vacation prep. I grabbed my keys and purse then headed out to my car. Soon as I pressed the button to start my car – nothing.

I pressed it again while pushing my foot on the break to see if it triggered something to come on. "Fuck." I pulled my phone out and called Jace.

"What's up, Stori?"

"What is the AAA membership number again? I lost my card, and you were supposed to order me a new one." I huffed into the phone, irritated because I needed to head to the grocery store before picking Demi up from dance class.

"Er, um, we don't have them anymore."

"What do you mean?"

"I stopped paying them because we never used them." I paused, unsure how I was supposed to reply to that ridiculous ass statement he had made. "Hello?"

"Jace, the reason people pay for AAA is because of emergencies. You know… you never know when you're going to need it, so you have it."

"We haven't had the shit in at least a year, Stori. What's going on?"

"My fucking car is having those electrical problems again. I'm at my office stranded."

He whistled. "Damn."

That wasn't what I wanted to hear when my car wasn't working, and I had a ton of other shit to do. "Is that all you can say?"

"What the fuck else you want me to say, Stori? It's not like I can get behind the wheel and come get you."

I wanted a solution. For once, I wanted him to come up with a solution while I played damsel in distress. I didn't want to be the one that had to come up with the plan to get us out of our messes.

"Never mind, Jace. I don't even know why I stayed on the phone with you this long." I ended the call and dialed Ember's number, hoping she didn't have any patients and could scoop me.

Just when I was about to press the call button, Bray's name came across my screen. "Hey." I huffed, not really wanting to take my attitude out on him.

"What's wrong?"

He didn't need to see my face to see that something was clearly wrong with me. "Nothing. I have to call you back, Pa."

"I'm not hanging up, and you not either until you tell me what's wrong."

"My car is dead, and I'm trying to figure out how to fix the situation. I need to pick up Demi and still go food shopping because we barely have food in the house, and I haven't felt like doing it!" I snapped.

It wasn't his fault, and I felt bad that he was on the receiving end of my irritation. "Send me your location."

"Bray, I go—"

"Send me your location, Doc," he told me and ended the call.

I sent him my location and went back inside the office. The last time this happened with my car, I was able to go ahead and handle everything without Jace. He wasn't going to leave work to come help me, so I had no other choice but to get it done without him.

Bray called me back after a few minutes. "Hello?"

"Doc, my guy from Cadillac is bringing your new Escalade so you can pick Demi up from dance. He'll take your current car back to the dealership and wait for further instruction from me."

"*Your*?" I blurted.

"The papers are being sent over to me as we speak to sign for it… it's yours, Doc. Enough space for you and the girls, and all Demi and Enzo's afterschool stuff you said crowds your trunk."

My heart swelled because he actually listened when I vented to him. Some men pretended to listen, Bray actually paid attention, which was hard considering that I was usually naked laying on top of him while I was venting.

"Bray, you didn't have to do that. I can take it back to the dealership and have them fix it like last time."

"I know what I don't have to do," he paused. "It's not considered fixed if you have to send it back to them to do what they were supposed to do in the first place. I'm not trying to have you stranded again… I need you in something reliable."

"My car was reliable," I mumbled.

"Yeah, if you wanna believe that. I also sent takeout to your house, so you don't have to worry about grocery shopping. You already stressed out, and that's one less thing off your plate."

I sighed. "Sorry for snapping on you. Pa, I'm just so annoyed."

"Wish I could be there for you right now."

"I miss you," I admitted.

"Miss you too, Doc. I'll be back in two days, and I'm gonna need you to clear your schedule because I want you at the crib just like before."

"I could really use that, Pa." I leaned my head back and thought about that weekend before all hell broke loose.

"Stori, I'm not going to pretend to know that man's struggle or speak down on him because I'm not that kind of man. I do know my woman isn't going to struggle as long as I have breath in my body. You're not about to be outside stranded because you don't want to call and let me know. Trust that I'm gonna always handle shit on behalf of my queen, and I need you to realize that shit."

"I hear you."

"You in the office or still waiting in the car?"

"In my office."

"He shouldn't be too much longer. I had to call the one in Jersey City because the other two were giving me the runaround."

"Why are you so good to me?"

"Because you're so good to others that it needs to be returned. Call me when he gets there."

"Will do."

The man pressed the doorbell on my office door twenty minutes later. I opened the door to let him in, and he shivered slightly. "Getting colder... ain't it?"

"Yes, it is. Can I offer you a cup of coffee or tea?"

We were in the last week of October, and the cooler weather wasn't waiting around for winter. Around this time, I could usually get away with wearing a light sweater to work. Today, I had on a trench coat, and I was still freezing.

"This is a terrible time for your car to go dead on you." He flipped through some pages on his clipboard. "Those Kia's usually struggle with electric problems. I just need you to sign here, giving us permission to take your car to our dealership. I believe it was your husband I spoke to. He said he'll handle it once he's back in town."

I wished my husband would have handled this situation like Bray did. All he had to offer was attitude with no damn solutions.

I held the keys in my hand and wanted to break down and cry, but I held it together. "Thank you!"

"Do you need a tutorial on how to work the truck? Or are we good here?"

"A small one." I smiled.

"No problem."

The man waited for me to grab my things and then showed me around the truck. I couldn't believe my eyes right now. There were a few moms in both Enzo and Demi's private schools who drove an Escalade, and I always envisioned having one. My car wasn't a hooptie or nothing, but it wasn't this beautiful, majestic machine. I assured the man that I understood, and he hooked my car up to the tow truck. I watched as he climbed into the passenger side of the truck, and they pulled away.

The clock on the dashboard let me know Demi's class was about to get out, so I started the truck and headed across town to pick her up. I knew she would have a bunch of questions, and I didn't have any answers to give her right now. How was I going to explain that a man her mom had been fucking bought her a brand-new truck and wanted to be her everything.

Demi and her father may have not been on good terms, but she was still going to ride for him through whatever. I've done a good job at shielding them from the fuck boy their father was. They didn't know how many times he had cheated one me, or the disrespect I accepted being married to him. In their eyes, they knew he wasn't perfect; but he was still their father.

"Demi, it's me," I called as I rolled the window down so she could see my face.

I was proud of my girl for not moving from the front of the studio. Each time I honked my horn at her, she folded her arms and looked away. She opened the back door and tossed in her dance bag before climbing into the front.

"Mom, did you get a new car?"

"I did. The other car was giving me troubles, so I got a new one."

"An Escalade at that? Oh, we moving on up in the world." She clapped her hands and then started messing with the different features.

Bray had got me the fully loaded version, and I was scared to look up the price on this truck. Just as I was thinking about him, his name came across my screen. Thankfully, I hadn't set up the Bluetooth feature in the truck yet.

"Hey."

"Everything all good?"

"Yes, Demi is in the car right now. I just picked her up."

Demi was less concerned about my conversation and more

interested in messing with all the buttons. "Handle your mommy duties and call me later."

"Okay." I ended the call and headed home since he told me he ordered us dinner. That was one less thing that I had to worry about tonight.

When we made it home, Demi couldn't stop talking about the new truck. Both she and Enzo were all on their phones snapping pictures for their social media accounts. Like promised, Bray had food sent to the house. Jace had the nerve to be taking a nap when we made it home, which annoyed me because I was still stranded as far as he knew, and he didn't give a damn to make sure that I was alright.

Bray sent food from the Italian restaurant in town. After I showered and changed into house clothes, we all sat at the kitchen table with the food. "We sure been having takeout often," Enzo mentioned.

"I'm not complaining, so you shouldn't be," Demi snapped on her.

"Not complaining. I like that mom has more free time to herself."

I cut into my stuffed shells. "Awe, thanks, Enzo." Demi ate her broccolini and smiled at the both of us.

"What's all of this?"

Jace rolled into the kitchen on the one leg scooter he had got in rehab. We were all thankful he was able to move around more, so he didn't keep harassing us for shit.

"Mom ordered food for dinner."

Jace winced as he got comfortable in the seat across from me. I looked up from my food and couldn't stare at him for too long. I hated this man, and I didn't think that was a feeling I would ever feel for him.

"Luciano's? Pretty expensive for a weekday meal, huh?"

Luciano's was expensive and we had both agreed that it was a special occasion place. With Bray, every day was a special occasion, and he didn't give a fuck about the price. It was nice being with someone that went into their pockets before you had to go into yours.

"Good thing you didn't pay for it," I snorted.

"What the fuck is that supposed to mean?" Jace didn't care that the girls were there because his pride was hurt.

"You didn't have to pay for this expensive meal," I clarified, in case he didn't understand what I meant.

He turned his attention to our daughters. "How was school, girls?"

"Good. Um, Mom… I have a dance competition in Orlando at the end of this week," Demi dropped the bomb on me. "I figured we could road trip in the new truck." She nervously laughed.

"New truck?"

"The end of this week? Dem, seriously?"

"What new truck?" Jace asked again.

"Sorry. I wasn't sure I even wanted to go, and then Debra told me I should reconsider," Demi explained the reasons for her last-minute decision.

"We'll make it work." I promised her while trying to figure out how we were going to make it to this competition on such short notice.

"I guess I must be speaking another language. What fucking truck?" Jace slammed his hand on the table.

"There is no need for yelling, cursing and hitting the table," Enzo told her father. "Use your words, Dad."

I could tell he wanted to say something smart and decided against it. "Enzo, watch yourself." He turned his attention back to me. "What truck, Astoria?"

"The Kia kept giving me problems, so I decided to splurge on a new truck," I lied.

With the way he was acting toward us, I wanted to throw what Bray had done for me in his face.

He needed to see that what he refused to do; another man had no problems doing those same things. "It was a problem when I decided to get a motorcycle, but you can decide off a whim that you need a new truck and decide to get one."

Jace wasn't the brightest crayon in the box. Had he been, he wouldn't have brought up the uninsurance motorcycle that we took a major loss on. He would have steered far away from the mention of the word motorcycle. The reason he felt so comfortable bringing it up was because he didn't feel like he did anything wrong, which was sad.

"Did I not call you and tell you I was stranded? This wasn't the first time this happened, and you know it."

"What kind of truck did you get?"

"An Escalade," Demi proudly announced.

"What? How could we even afford that?"

"*I* can afford it."

"Shit doesn't make sense. You were all bent out of shape about having to cover things, yet you can afford this brand-new truck?"

I was tired of him pressing me about what I could or couldn't afford. In reality, I couldn't afford a truck like this, especially with the way Jace had set us back.

"This is a conversation we can have privately, not at the dinner table," I shut the conversation down.

He nodded his head and ate his food. "Mom's kitchen is getting renovated. They found mold in the back wall near the pantry, so she can't host Thanksgiving dinner."

"Is your sister going to host it at her place?"

"No, her apartment is too small. I told her she could host it here since our original plans were to go over to her house anyway."

"Oh, okay."

Jace's mom, Verlonda, hated me more than she hated the summer heat. I don't know what it was about me that caused her to dislike me so much, but Verlonda always made things difficult. Her little snarky comments showed how much displeasure she had for me.

It always felt like Martin's mama and Gina whenever she came around. You would think after being married to her son all these years and having two of her grandchildren that she would have become nicer. Spending Thanksgiving with her only sounded appealing because I knew this was the last holiday I would ever have to spend with both her and Jace's miserable asses.

I cleaned up the dinner dishes while Jace went back into Tyler's room. He was complaining of pain, so he went to take his medicine for the night. I washed the dishes and added them into the dishwasher.

"Mom, are you happy with Dad?" Demi asked as she hopped up on the counter.

A question like this coming from her would have scared me a few months ago. I welcomed the question because I was tired of lying to her. My daughters deserved to witness a happier me, not this fake façade I put on whenever they were in the room.

"No, baby," I answered honestly.

"Why stay married to someone that you're not happy with?"

"Love." I leaned on the counter opposite of hers.

"Love is supposed to make you happy. I'm old enough to know that it isn't always beautiful or sunny... I watch Grey's Anatomy." She winked. "I also know that it's not supposed to drain you."

"You think I'm drained?"

Demi gave me this annoyed look. "Bffr, mom. You try to pretend that you're fine when me and Enzo know that you're not. We know that you and Dad haven't been good for a while."

I did all this pretending, and they could see right through the lies. Demi went from fighting over Barbie dolls to being this mature teenager who wasn't so little anymore.

"Guess I wanted to protect you both. Me and your aunt never had our fathers around, so I wanted to give that to you and your sister."

"By making yourself miserable? Kathy's parents got divorced

last year, and she was the happiest I've seen her. She hated them fighting all the time."

"How would you feel if me and your father divorced?"

"Relieved. I love Dad, but I also know he's selfish, and you give more than he does."

"Where did my little girl go?" I pinched her cheek.

"Not so little anymore. I also know about Bray."

"Wait, what?"

She pulled her phone out and scrolled for a bit then showed me her Google search. "Mom, I'm not stupid, and I would appreciate if you stopped acting like I'm four. Bray isn't just a friend, and I can tell from the way you talk to him when he calls. Why would this man be sending us food and you talking to him almost every day?"

"It is not every day," I defended with my arms folded. "And you listen in on my calls?"

She snorted. "As if. I have my own interesting conversations I be having. Did you forget the back porch is right under my bedroom window? I can hear the way you giggle with him, and act like a teenager."

All I could do was break out into laughter because I thought I was being so discreet, and my nosey ass daughter was right in my business the whole time.

"Little girl, you are truly nosey. I don't know what will happen between me and your father. However, when we know, you girls will be the first to know about it."

She hopped down off the counter. "I just want the both of you happy. Even if I have to have a stank new step-mama."

Had Demi said something like this a few years back, I probably would have been jealous by the statement. If another woman wanted Jace, she could have his ass. I was so over my husband and wanted to put as much space between us as I could.

The only positive thing that came out of waiting all these years was that the girls were older. We didn't need to talk to each other if we didn't have to, and with the way this man had treated me during our marriage, I didn't want to be his friend.

Hell, I barely wanted to be his ex-wife or co-parent with him. Demi gave me a quick kiss on the cheek and skipped upstairs to her bedroom. I continued to clean the kitchen and then went to check in on Jace.

His mouth was wide open with his water mug in one hand and the remote in the other. I gently took the items from his hand and sat them on the nightstand. This remote was the bane of our existence. Every time he dropped it, he would call one of us to come pick it up, and we were tired.

Tonya: Hey, Babe. Did you want to spend the night this weekend again?

Tonya: Hello?

Tonya: I also need money for Tyler's tuition.

Tonya: Jace, you promised you wouldn't ignore me for her... answer me now!

Missed call – Ty

Ty: Mom said to call her.

There came a time in every woman's life when she had been tossed around and down so many times that she didn't have anything else inside to give. Not a tear, sob, or any bit of emotion she may have in her reserve mattered. Jace deserved for me to slam the phone into his face and tear up this room, leaving his ass confused behind my actions.

Why though?

I didn't give a shit that he and Tonya were messing around behind my back. What bothered me was that he didn't have enough respect for me to *not* mess around with her. I know I hadn't been the perfect wife to him, but damn, I was pretty fucking decent. I made sure I held down our home and him at all times.

I showed up every day in our marriage, even when I didn't want to. He didn't deserve the kind of woman I had been for him. When I should have packed me and the girls shit and left, I remained true to him.

Plain stupid!

"I THOUGHT I was going to have to come down to your office and do an office visit." Dr. Kelly, my physician, pursed her lips at me.

"I have had so much going on that I can finally get to my own to-do list."

"I've heard. I pray Jace is doing better. How have the girls been? Did Demi tell you that I saw her at the studio a few weeks ago? That girl is going to be a tough one to mess with."

"Now you know teens don't tell us anything." I purposely ignored the Jace question. He was the last person I wanted to speak about. If I was lucky, he might choke on those damn CBD gummy candies he had been obsessed with lately.

"I know that's right. I nearly have to pry any information out of Riley." She chuckled as she washed her hands.

Dr. Kelly had been my doctor for the past four years. The minute I heard there was a younger black doctor in town, I immediately made an appointment, and she had been stuck with me ever since. I appreciated other black professionals, and that was one of the reasons I loved Lennox Hills.

The amount of black professionals that had moved into the area was amazing. The restaurants, bars and businesses were overflowing with black excellence.

Once she flipped open my chart, her expression turned serious. "Your blood pressure is a concern for me, Astoria."

I should have known something when the medical assistant made a little noise when she took it. I never paid attention to getting my blood pressure taken because it was always within the normal range. The only time it had been elevated was when I was pregnant with Enzo, but since then, it had been normal.

"There's been so much going on. Do you think it could be due to that?"

"Yes, stress is a factor. I don't want to put you on any medication since your pressure is always within normal range. However, I do want you to sit here for an extra hour and relax, and let's see if it comes down. If not, I'm going to put you on some medication until we can get it under control."

"Medicine? Is that even necessary?"

Dr. Kelly closed the file and looked me in the eyes. "More than fifty percent of our people over the age of twenty have hypertension, Astoria. This isn't anything to take lightly. If you want to be here for your daughters, you will remove the stress and eat better. Make better choices when it comes to the food you're consuming."

"Thank you, Dr. Kelly."

"Of course. I'm going to shut the light so you can calm down. Hopefully, your pressure is able to come down, so we don't have to resort to medicine."

I watched as she shut the lights, and then closed the door behind her. The comfortable exam table converted into chair, so I was comfortable enough to sit up for an hour. I scrolled my phone and liked a bunch of Harlym's pictures before Bray's name popped up on my phone's screen.

"Hey, Pa."

I was so afraid of falling deeper for Bray, and then at the same time I wasn't willing to lose this man. He made me feel things that I had never felt for the opposite sex before. My emotions and feelings did the Harlem shake inside my body whenever he was near me.

"Hey, baby… what you doing? I wanna take you out to lunch since you're off today."

I smiled. "Awe, you're so sweet. I'm stuck at my doctor's office for the next hour."

"Everything all good?"

"My blood pressure is high, so she's worried. I still think it's nothing."

"Blood pressure ain't shit to mess with, Doc."

"I'm not saying that it is. I have so much going on with my husband, and now having to leave for Florida tomorrow for the dance competition is a lot. So, yes, my blood pressure might be elevated because I'm trying to wear a bunch of different hats at one time." I took a deep breath.

It wasn't like this was all news to Bray because I told him about everything when he flew back. I spent the night at his place, and he rubbed my feet while I whined to him about everything. It felt nice being able to whine about my problems without having someone act like you were being dramatic. It always bothered my spirit whenever Jace acted like that with me. As if I wasn't allowed to have any problems or complaints.

"Shit... forgot you mentioned that," he mumbled. "Did you get the flights?"

"Demi wants to drive there."

"Yeah, that's not gonna happen. You don't need that added stress on your plate. I'll send a car to pick you and the girls up tomorrow morning."

"Do I even wanna know what you have planned?"

"It's on a need-to-know basis.... I just need to know one thing."

"And that is?"

"Are you comfortable with me meeting your daughters?"

I wasn't expecting him to ask me that question. Demi and Enzo knew about Bray and had been having conversations about it since he sent the food to the house. If Demi showed me anything the other night, she showed me that my girls weren't toddlers anymore and I needed to have a straightforward conversation with them.

Jace had no idea that I had saw the text messages on his phone and I wanted to keep it that way. He had kept me in the dark about so much stuff that I wanted to keep him in the dark for a little bit longer.

"Yes. I'm going to talk to them tonight about everything going on."

"If you're not comfortable with us meeting, I can respect that."

"No, I am comfortable. I just need to have a conversation with them first. They need to hear it from me before meeting you."

"Got you."

"And what about Kami?"

"She's been ignoring me, and hasn't signed the papers yet, which is what I expected."

That following Monday, after I found out about her being Bray's wife, I sent the email I had been planning on sending to her. I explained why she was being referred and let her know it was a pleasure having her as a client.

She never responded.

I guess when you were busy throwing bombs into your marriage, you wouldn't have time for therapy anymore. I just wanted to make sure that our ties were cut, and I didn't get dragged into this mess between her and Bray.

"You need to speak with her," I encouraged.

"I hear you, Doc. I'm trying to do my part and she's playing duck, duck, goose with me."

"You'll find a way to get it handled."

"Always do... call me when you're done with the appointment."

"Will do."

My doctor came back in and took my blood pressure herself this time, and it was lower than before, still higher than normal, so she prescribed me medicine to take and demanded I get it under control before my next visit. I was determined to rid myself of all the drama and bullshit that had been going on.

Jace was literally going to kill me if I continued to go down this road with him. I needed to cut him out of my life before I ended up in the hospital over this man. All of the stress I had been carrying because of him wasn't worth my life. Meanwhile he was as happy as could be after busting up my life and savings with his reckless decisions.

I picked the girls up and decided to have dinner at our favorite restaurant in town – *Grub*. Demi loved eating here because the food was a funky spin on classic comfort foods that we all loved. The restaurant was the perfect spot for a girl's brunch or dinner with its posh and girly atmosphere. There were beautiful pictures of black women in golden frames, along with velvet poufy chairs that matched the booths.

"I'm going to do the sweet potatoes Shepard's pie," Demi licked her lips and did a little dance in her seat. She was for sure my child because I used to do the same little dance when I was about to have something good to eat.

"That does sound good," Enzo countered while still studying her menu.

I opted for the grilled chicken Caesar salad since I was on thin ice with my doctor. We placed our orders and then quickly checked our phones before putting them away. It didn't matter if we were home or we were out to eat, I've always made a rule to remove devices from the table and encourage conversation with everyone surrounding the table. With two teens that were always glued to their phones, it was always a challenge and argument.

"How was your day at school? Anything exciting happen?" I looked to both of them, as they stored their phones into their pockets.

"School is school. We do the same things every day." Enzo shrugged.

"Same here. Was Enzo able to be excused to come with us to Orlando?"

"Yes. Her teacher emailed me earlier to let me know it was approved."

Enzo clapped her hands. "I know we're going for your dance recita—"

"Competition," Demi corrected.

"Anyway, can we do something fun like go to Disney or go to Universal Studios or something?"

To Demi, this was about her dance competition, and that was all. Enzo looked at this as a little getaway since it was going to be over the weekend, and the dance competition was just for one day. I wanted to make sure I was giving my girls equal attention on things that they wanted to do or become a part of. I never wanted them to feel like I cared about one, more than the other.

"We can add that into our plans. I know Demi will be busy with all of her dance friends, so maybe we can sneak away and do some of those things." I rubbed her hand from across the table.

"Yeah, we're having a big sleepover at the hotel, so I won't have much time to spend with you two."

"Oh, wow, what would we ever do without Demi being with us," Enzo sarcastically replied.

"Whatever, you two would be lost without me."

"That is very true," I agreed.

"Maybe for you... I wouldn't be lost at all." Enzo waved her sister off, clearly getting annoyed with her.

My girls were very different and similar at the same time. Some days, they wanted to rip each other's heads off, and then the others, they were like best friends. They were much closer in age than me and Harlym, so I knew the relationship between them would only become stronger.

"I wanted to talk to the two of you about something very important." I drew a breath and looked into both of their beautiful brown eyes.

Demi had her hair pulled up into a high bun with a few pieces of loose hair framing her face, while Enzo kept her hair straight and hanging down her back.

Their cinnamon-colored hair was always my favorite. I

wasn't a hater or ashamed to say that was something they had gotten from their father. Jace had the same color hair.

Enzo favored me, while Demi was her father's twin. Demi's perfectly sculpted cheekbones was created inside my body, but I often questioned if a sculptor had chiseled them himself because I had a hard time believing my body could create such beauty.

"Is it about the divorce?" Enzo blurted before I could finish.

"Who told you that we were getting a divorce?" Demi looked away. "Did you tell your sister that?"

"I mentioned it... didn't say it was written in stone or anything."

It was time for me to be a straight shooter and be honest with them. Before seeing those messages, I was going to give Jace a heads up so we could get our story together before breaking the news to the girls. Now, all I wanted was for my girls to know what was going on before things happened. I could give a fuck about that man, and how he felt about my decision after I served his ass those papers.

"Yes. I am going to file for divorce from Daddy. You both know that me and your father haven't been happy for a while, Demi let me in on that." I looked at Demi. "I wanted to sit and talk to you guys about it first."

"Do I want you to get divorced? No. Is it needed? Yes. I hate seeing Dad stomping around angry, and you silently allowing it because you feel the same way." Enzo shrugged. "That's double the birthday gifts and Christmas gifts, so I'm not tripping."

"You already know how I feel."

I felt weird asking them how they felt about me dating because I wasn't even divorced from their father yet. I was still married and living under the same roof with this man. Not that it stopped his ass from doing his dirt with Tonya.

"And how would it make you feel when I start dating?"

"Mom, as long as you are happy, it doesn't matter what we think. With Dad, we're probably going to have to get used to him dating too. We just want the both of you happy and as far away from each other as possible."

"Facts," Enzo concurred.

"Um, excuse me?" I laughed.

"Of course, me and Daddy will have to sit and talk about how things are going to work out and who will get the house and you guys."

"No offense to Dad, but I would rather live with you Mom. Seeing him on the weekends or after school is cool, but the man doesn't cook."

Enzo giggled. "I'm with sis on this one. He doesn't cook, and his laundry folding skills are horrid."

Jace didn't have any skill in any of those things because I had always been the one who handled it. Everything in the house was handled because of me, including raising our daughters. I wanted to make it so easy for my husband that all he had to do was come home and be present with his family, and this man couldn't even appreciate that.

"We'll talk about that."

"What if we have to sell the house?" Demi asked.

"Let's not think of that right now." I smiled at her. "Since you both know about Bray, do you have any questions?"

"Does he seriously own a shit load of hotels and resorts?" Enzo was the first to shoot her question off.

"First, watch your mouth. And yes, he does."

"He's loaded... I wouldn't mind having a loaded stepfather. We can do our TikTok's using drunk elephant products."

"Here we go with the drunk elephant products," I whistled.

Demi was obsessed with any and everything her aunt did, and since her aunt had been sent PR packages with this partic-ular brand, she always handed them off to Demi. The products were expensive, and nothing that I could afford to get two teenagers every month when they ran out, so she was holding a grudge.

"Those products are amazing. Auntie been holding her PR hostage from us." This time Enzo agreed with her sister.

"Why?"

"We refused to help her clean out her closet."

"To get something you have to be willing to do something in return. Anyway... He's a great guy and I do like him," I admitted to them.

I liked Bray more than a lot. Whenever he wasn't with me, I was always counting down the hours, minutes, and seconds until I was able to see him again. He made me feel womanlier than I had ever felt in the past, and I felt seen. He saw me and didn't just brush past the emotions I was feeling. These were things that I was feeling for him, and I never wanted the feelings to fade away.

That was what scared me the most about jumping into something so blindly. We both were about to be going through our own divorces, what if things changed between us? We found solace in each other because of the disfunction of our own marriages. What if all these feelings and emotions faded when we're officially out of those marriages?

"When can we meet him?"

I narrowed my eyes at both of them. "So, you're both are cool with meeting another man that's not your father? You do both know we're still married."

Enzo rolled her eyes. "Legally, yeah. Emotionally, you haven't been married for a long time... where's your ring, mom?"

I hadn't put my ring on since I slipped it off in the Maldives. It sat on the jewelry dish on my dresser. Jace didn't care to notice, so I kept it off. Kyle made a comment about me not wearing it once, and I brushed him off about it.

I enjoyed not wearing that piece of jewelry that showcased how much of a fool I was to stay married to a man that didn't appreciate me. That ring used to mean something to me and as the years passed by, I stopped caring about it, or the meaning behind it. It wasn't like my husband gave a fuck what that ring meant to our marriage when he was fucking other women.

It felt toxic to wear that ring while pretending not to see the infidelity, and lack of effort on his part. He never tried or fought as hard as I did for *us*.

"I forgot to put it on this morning."

"I better not be punished for telling a story, 'cause you are sitting here storytelling," Demi called me out.

"Are you both alright? I won't do this if you don't want me to do it." I meant every word I said.

If my girls told me they wanted their parents together, my stupid ass would pull up my sleeves and work hard to keep us together. I'd do anything for my girls.

"Stay with a man you're not in love with? We love you, Mom, but please don't do that. When I broke up with Scott last year, you told me that I should focus on going where I'm celebrated, not tolerated. Now, I'm telling you the same thing. If Bray makes you happy, then screw social norms. Who cares? The world is dying anyway." I brushed away the tears that fell from my eyes.

How did I raise such beautiful and smart girls? They were so gracious and understanding when they could have been the opposite. I sat with plenty of clients and listened to horror stories on how their children started acting out the moment they decided on divorce. It was honestly one of the reasons I never followed through with the papers.

My daughters were my main priority, and I never wanted them to feel like I put myself before them and never considered their feelings. There were plenty of times that my own mother had done that to me, and I refused to do it to them. I wanted them to always look at me and be proud, not sit in therapy for the next ten years of their lives pointing out all the things I've done that have ruined or triggered them as adults.

FOURTEEN
BRAY WILLSHIRE

"WELCOME, MR. WILLSHIRE. HOW ARE YOU DOING?" SECURITY greeted me as I breezed by to head up to the studio where Kami was.

"Morning, Stew... hope you and the kids good." I quickly turned and started walking backwards to acknowledge him.

This afternoon, I was on a mission to talk to Kami and get over this situation quick. She had been hiding out in the city and hadn't been to the house since she leaked our marriage on social media. Whenever I called, she would ignore the calls or send me one of those automated text messages letting me know she couldn't talk right now. Everything about her lately had been inconsistent or a secret. The only thing that remained consistent was her voice on the radio every morning.

Kami was big on keeping her private business away from work, so I was giving her the respect of not coming up to the studio to have the conversation. She continued to play these little ass games, so she was about to have to handle this shit in her place of work.

Soon as the elevator opened, her assistant was standing there. "Front desk called to let us know you were on your way up. Kami is still on the air, so you can take a se—"

"Yeah, I'm not about to do that." I stepped around her and headed straight to where I knew my future ex-wife was.

Like expected, she was sitting up on her chair talking to the mic and laughing like all was swell in her life. When I knocked on the glass, all the air left her body. That smile had quickly faded, and worry settled into her eyes.

"She's on the air, Bray," One of the producers told me.

I stepped inside and smirked. "What's good, Wifey?"

She didn't respond because she was still in shock. I took a seat opposite of her, grabbed the headphones, and pulled the second mic close to my lips.

"Good morning, New York and the whole tri-state area!" I put my best announcer voice on.

"Hey, hey, I have my husband on the air with me today. This is a surprise, Bray."

"Same here. I haven't seen you since you announced our marriage to all these people. Where you been hiding? Where you been?" I mocked Big Boi from the movie ATL.

While her voice seemed pleasant and excited, her eyes spoke a different story. Kami was shooting daggers while pleading with me to leave the studio.

Her producers got the cue and came in to take us off the air. Kami rushed out of her chair and out the room down to her office.

I coolly walked behind her, clearly channeling Ashton's chaotic ass behavior. This was some shit that he would end up doing if he had a wife.

"What the fuck do you think you are doing?" She slammed her hand on the desk she stood behind. "My fucking job, Bray? This is my career, and you're playing around like I can't lose it."

"When you playing hide and seek, you left me no other choice."

"You could have waited in my fucking office until I was done. This is my fucking career. I had to work hard to get here. My name isn't on the fucking side of the building!" she continued to scream while I sat down in one of the chairs and popped a piece of chocolate into my mouth.

"My name being on the side of *buildings* has nothing to do with what I did. You could have extended the same grace you're asking for when you decided to leak our marriage on your social media pages."

"I don't know what you're talking about." She crossed her arms and turned her back toward me.

"I could play dirty too, Kam. Do I want to do it? Nah. You know that I have the time and resources to play this game like you. Would the industry like to know you fuck the rappers you interview?"

She turned around so fast that she almost lost her footing. "That is not true, Bray," she whispered while pointing her freshly manicured nail at me. "It happened one fucking time, and you know it. I built my name by my hard work and hard-hitting interviews."

I shrugged. "The difference between us is that I considered your feelings before doing some whack shit like that. You didn't even think to talk to me before announcing that. Did you think it would stop me from moving forward with the divorce?"

"Is this blackmail, Bray? 'Cause I have some way darker shit that I can come back with. Your little friend is in a world of trouble."

"Little friend? What the hell are you talking about, Kam? You know as good as anybody I don't do the riddle and second-guessing shit."

"Dr. Astoria Jacobs. Do you know she's married, or did you purposely seek out to fuck my therapist?"

It was my turn to be thrown for a loop. Me and Astoria had been discreet with our relationship. Besides, when we were in the city, we held hands while shopping and going out to dinner. I was never worried because although I was known, I wasn't in the media unless one of our hotels were opening. It was probably one of the reasons that Kami fell in love with me. I was low-key with my life, and I preferred it that way. I'd rather have the money. The youngins could have the fame.

"I didn't know she was your therapist." Astoria never confirmed that Kami was her client, but I still put it together that she was. Why else would she be freaking out over a stranger she supposedly never met before?

"Her being your therapist isn't relevant to what we're going through. We met out the country, so it's not related."

"It's still a conflict of interest. Wonder what the board would think about her entanglement with a client's husband while also being married herself." Kami grew confident because she had something over my head. "She sent me over an email referring me back to her colleague with the quickness."

If she thought this was the way to get me to change my mind about the divorce, she was dead ass wrong. It made me not only not want to be around her, but to take her hand and force her to sign the papers.

"What you trying to say, Kam? Say the shit with your chest instead of talking in circles," I encouraged.

If we were putting everything on the table, then we needed to do it and stop talking in circles. I no longer wanted to be married or have anything to do with her. Today we were coming to an agreement before I left out of this office.

"I hired a private investigator to keep tabs on you. We haven't been intimate, and I refused to believe you weren't getting it from somewhere else, and you proved me wrong. That was until my guy sent me pictures of you in the city with her. Shopping, laughing and being affectionate... things that you never do with me. I went down a rabbit hole and compared both of your social media pages and saw that you both met out the country."

THE WORST THING you could do to someone is to invade their privacy. I was just as private as Kami was, and she betrayed me twice by doing some lame shit like that. If betraying me once wasn't enough, she decided to double that shit.

"Not that it matters." I leaned forward and cleared my throat. "I had no clue who she was when we met in the Maldives. Now that I do know who she is, I'm very much in love with her. When I love someone, I go hard for them, and they're taken care of always. You know... you remember what that feels like, right?"

"Bray, we've both done foul shi—"

"Foul shit? What did I ever do to you but love you, Kam? I'm not perfect, and I may have put work before you more times than I can count, but I always made up for it in other ways. The only thing we can both agree on is that our careers took priority over the marriage. It's time to get the fuck off this wheel and move on."

"I'm not ready to get off this wheel, and I refuse to sign those papers."

"Then it's going to hurt to watch your husband move on with someone else." I stood up, shoved my hands into my pockets and made it to the door. "Oh, and before something accidentally gets leaked, make sure you remember what I got on you. I would hate for your pettiness to throw your career away. And, yeah, that wasn't blackmail. It was a threat."

"How can we fix this?" She pleaded.

"Sign the papers. Why the fuck do you want to stay married to someone who you're not happy with?"

I always questioned why she held onto this marriage when I hadn't been acting like a husband to her in years. We didn't do date nights, cuddle at night or none of the shit you did as a married couple. If she didn't make the plans to move to Lennox Hills, we probably wouldn't have been sharing one roof.

Kami thought she would be able to fix things by moving, and shit was beyond repair. Living under one roof did nothing but convince me of all the reasons I wanted to divorce this woman. I wanted a woman that opened her mouth and communicated when things got tough, not her legs. So much could have been fixed if she had communicated what she needed from me.

"I don't want to fail at this. You know what my family said when we got married. They just knew we wouldn't last because we were so private about everything."

Had she not been so petty and kept things private between us, we could have divorced and moved on without anyone knowing that we were even married in the first place. As far as her family, that was a battle she would have to face on her own. She allowed her emotions to get in the way, and now she was going to have to announce that she was getting divorced in front of the very audience she kept me hidden from.

"You've failed, Kami. I hate to be the one to tell you, but you did fail. Can you say that you gave marriage a try? Hell yeah. We had a great run when it was good. Count that as your win and move on. Find someone that gives you all the things you require."

The producer knocking on the glass door forced us both to give him our attention. "Are we all good in there? There's only so many songs that we can play for your three-hour slot."

"Robert, give me a few more minutes to wrap this up."

"Will do."

He closed the door behind him, and Kami pulled out her compact mirror and started to fix her makeup. "What's next?

It was amazing how she went from tears to down to business in a snap of a finger. Had she operated like this in the first place, I wouldn't have had to come up here and act a fool.

"Simple. Sign the papers."

Kami scoffed. "It's not as simple as you're making it seem. This isn't a business contract of yours. It's our marriage, and it would be nice if you treated it like that."

I had checked out from this marriage so long ago that it felt like a bad business arrangement that I was desperately trying to separate from. When I came home from the Maldives, I had never been so determined to end our marriage than at that moment. Stori was it for me, and I didn't need a bunch of useless dates to know that. We completed one another and fit so perfectly in each other's lives.

"I get that. For me, this has been something I've wanted."

"What about the house? We just bought that house, and we're not even completely moved in. I have boxes in the garage that haven't been brought up to the bedroom."

"Do you plan on staying in Lennox Hills?"

She screwed her face up like she smelled something foul. "God, no. I only moved there because I thought it was what we needed."

Her idea to move away from the city wasn't a bad one. It was just a little too late for our relationship. "I want the house."

"Of course, you do." She used that little sponge shit to apply more makeup under her eyes. "So, you keep the house?"

"I will give you half of what it's worth. We can have a clean break and move on with our lives. Why put each other down and make this nasty when it doesn't have to be? I want to be on your virtual Christmas card list... feel me?"

She smiled. "Do you?"

"I don't hate you, Kami. I don't particularly trust you, but I don't wish bad for you. We don't have to be best friends, but I want to know that we can speak on each other without dogging the other out. People grow apart, and that's what happened to us."

"We grew apart because of me."

"True." I wasn't going to deny that fact.

"We set ourselves up for failure by trying to keep our lives the same as they were before we were married."

She should have corrected herself because *she* was the one that didn't want to follow the social norm for marriage. Kami wanted us to have our own rulebook when it came to our marriage, and I went along with it because it was what she wanted.

I enjoyed having my own space like the next person.

However, having my wife in my home every day was something I craved our entire marriage. It was nice to come home to a warm body that was just as excited to see you as you were to see them.

"It's a lesson for our next relationships."

"Do you love her?" Her voice cracked when she asked the question. I knew she heard me when I mentioned that I was in love with Stori. Maybe she needed to hear it again to finally let go and sign those damn papers.

"Are you prepared for that answer?"

She shook her head no and put her makeup away. "I'm not. Can you give me some time to sign the papers?"

"Yeah. I can do that." I folded my arms and leaned back on the wall. "Why do you need time though?"

"I just do."

"Okay." I respected her choice.

Kami stood up and straightened the dress she wore today. I could appreciate my wife's beauty, even if I wasn't the biggest fan of her. The short chocolate brown bob she wore today complimented her chestnut complexion. Kami had the cutest nose and thick, pouty lips that I used to obsess over. Looking down and seeing those lips wrapped around my dick always drove me crazy. She had the whole girl next door plain jane look down, which is why she was so popular. To New York, she was the everyday girl next door who knew music and gossip. When shit was right between us, I was in love with my wife.

It was when shit wasn't right that led us to this moment.

"Now if you don't mind, I have to go and fix the mess you created for me." She playfully rolled her eyes at me.

I headed out behind her and went straight to the elevators. We may have not had those papers signed yet, but we came to an agreement that I prayed she would stick to. It was time for the both of us to get the fuck off this rollercoaster.

※

"YOU MEETING HER DAUGHTERS? This shit is getting serious?" Ashton brought me back to reality as I tossed more shit into my carryon.

I didn't need much because we were just going away for the weekend. If I needed anything else, I could always buy it or have the concierge at the hotel fetch it for me.

"Yeah. I'm nervous as shit too."

"You sit in board meetings with stuffy ass older white men, and you nervous about meeting teenagers?"

"Have you met teenagers lately? They're not how we were as teens. Shit, these kids be having they own damn TikTok careers and shit."

"You right. They might hate yo' ass 'cause you taking they mommy away from their daddy." He broke out into laughter like the shit couldn't be a possibility.

"I'm mad that I even wasted my time calling you."

"Yeah, right."

"Um, are you going to be on the phone the entire time? I thought this session was about me?" I heard a woman snap on Ashton in the background.

"And I thought you said your thighs matched your ass? I guess we both walking around here lying."

It still amazed me that women went crazy for his rude ass. He didn't give a damn about having a filter and said whatever came to his mind. "You wrong as hell."

"Fuck her. She walking around my studio looking like she holding up balloons with pretzel sticks. How the fuck I'm supposed to fix that? Editing only does so fucking much."

"Bro, I'm gonna hit you when I'm back from Florida."

"Good luck. Tell my future sis in-law that I said what up."

"Got you."

When we ended the call, I rolled my suitcase to the elevator and waited for Stori and the girls to arrive. I didn't take meeting Stori's daughters lightly. She felt comfortable enough to intro-duce them to me, so I was determined to make the best impression. Teens were hard to please because they often saw through the bullshit.

I jumped when I heard the elevator chime, which meant she was on her way up. Why did I feel the need to clean up like the housekeepers didn't just leave yesterday? I tried to sit on the edge of the couch and be natural and ended up looking like a damn fool. Last minute, I jogged into the kitchen and pretended to be getting something to drink. Her daughters had the power to make or break this relationship and that shit terrified the hell out of me.

"Bray, are you here?" I heard my baby's voice and rounded the corner with an unopened water bottle in my hand.

"I'm here, Doc." I smiled, taking in my woman.

She wore a long, formfitting short sleeve maxi dress that touched the floor, a bomber jacket, and a pair of sneakers. Her braids were taken out, and she wore her natural curls, which was my favorite style on her yet. Her curls were healthy and bouncy as she walked over to me with a smile. I noticed she hesitated on kissing me and just hugged me instead.

With the way Stori spoke about her girls, I expected little girls to be standing behind her, not two girls that were equally her height. The shorter of the two was Stori's twin with her matching curls and smile. The taller of the two more than likely favored her father, still, you could see she belonged to Stori from her eyes.

Both girls stood there with smiles on their face. "Girls, this is Mr. Willshire."

"Not us having to call this man Mr. Willshire," the taller of the two spoke first, and it broke the silence because we all laughed.

"Don't call me that... just call me Bray."

They both looked to their mother. "It's fine," she assured them, and then the smiles returned to their faces.

"Hey, Bray, I'm Demi."

"And I'm Enzo."

Her daughter's names were so unique and different, especially Enzo. "Nice to meet the two of you." I leaned on the edge of the couch. "I appreciate you both allowing me to tag along."

"Mom says you saved the day, so I guess you earned your place on this trip," Demi said and folded her arms.

"We left our bags downstairs with the doorman... is that okay?"

"Yeah, my stuff would have been down there too if I had packed last night."

"Oh, Mom, he's a last-minute packer like you?" Enzo teased.

I chuckled because they had personalities, and I could see small pieces of Astoria in them. "Alright, now you telling my business."

"It's alright... we can be last minute packers together." I pulled her close, forgetting about the girls that quickly.

I peeped Enzo discreetly shove her sister, and they shared a smirk between the two of them. "Alright, so the truck is downstairs and ready. If you two want to use the bathrooms, you're free to."

Enzo had already abandoned the foyer and was staring out at that million-dollar view. "How could you live here? I wouldn't get anything done if I lived here."

"Trust me, it's hard."

"I also feel like you're sticking it to the man too," she said.

"How so?" I stood beside her, taking in the view I wouldn't see for a few days.

"You know the history behind Central Park, right?"

"I do."

"Rather you own this place with this view than somebody else." She narrowed her eyes at me, and I chuckled.

"I like you." I nudged her gently.

"Respect." She dapped me up and then went back to standing near her sister and mother.

"We're gonna go downstairs. Please don't take too long

kissing and stuff," Demi said and called the elevator that was already waiting.

Soon as the elevator doors closed, I pulled Stori over to me. "Fuck, I wanted to kiss you the minute you stepped off the elevator." I kissed her lips a few times.

"Me too. I'm just trying to be respectful and not do too much... you know?"

"I can respect that. But, before we get on that plane, I need you to take care of this real quick, Doc." I placed her hand on my rock-hard dick, and she smirked.

Pulling that extra-long ass dress up, she pulled her panties down and bent over the couch. "Come on, we need to be quick."

That was all I needed to hear because I was already pulling my sweats down and sliding right in. She must have been waiting for this because she was so damn wet when I slid in. We locked hands as I slammed my dick into her, and damn near bit my bottom lip off because the shit felt so good.

It felt so fucking right.

With my free hand, I slapped her ass before gripping my favorite side of her waist. We broke our hand embrace, and she gripped the back of the couch and threw that ass back onto me, causing the both of us to release our juices and collapse on the edge of the couch.

If time had been on my side, we would have made our way to my bedroom and finished. We had the girls waiting on us, so that didn't make for much time to continue, but I planned to make up for it soon as we checked into the hotel.

The ride over to the private airport was filled with traffic. I loved my city and hated it at the same time. If you needed to be somewhere, you needed to leave an hour earlier just to make it on time. Luckily, the jet wasn't taking off unless we were on board, so we didn't have to worry about missing it. When they let us through the security gates and the car drove near the jet, both Demi and Enzo started squealing.

"We're getting on a jet. Oh, baby, my TikTok is about to be lit as hell!" Demi squealed.

"Language," Stori corrected.

"Sorry, Mom."

"Can you take my picture first? I already know you're gonna make me take a bunch for you," Enzo reasoned with her big sister.

"I got you, Zo," Demi assured her.

Demi and Enzo had me and their moms taking a bunch of pictures of them in front of the jet. When we got on the jet, they both sat across from each other and took pictures of one another. Me and Stori sat up toward the front next to each other. I had my laptop with me and needed to get some work done on the flight down to Florida. Stori had pulled out her Kindle and was preparing herself to read.

"You chartered a jet? Really, Bray?"

"Didn't charter anything... I own this muthafucka." I shrugged.

"We could have driven or even flew commercial."

"Turn around and look at your girls. They happy as shit and excited to experience this... let them get accustomed to princess treatment. Stop trying to make things simple for me, Doc. You're not a simple woman, so everything I do needs to be above and beyond. Same treatment for the girls. I want you to learn to say thank you and not question it."

She reached over and kissed me on the lips. "Thank you."

The three-hour ride down to Orlando was a breeze. While I worked, the girls listened to their music and continued to take pictures all over the jet. Stori was cuddled up beside me with her book until she eventually dozed off.

When Stori called and told me that Demi sprung this trip on her last minute, I jumped in and planned everything for the weekend, so she didn't have to worry about anything. This weekend would be the first of many for us, and I wanted shit to be perfect for us.

"So umm, are we taking the jet back home?" Demi asked on the ride from the airport to the hotel.

"Demi!" Stori scolded.

"What? I need to know these things."

"Girl, be grateful we are even in Orlando for this damn competition." Stori turned in her seat and looked her in the face.

"Yes, Mom," Demi muttered.

Willshire Orlando was prepared for us the minute the black Navigator pulled around the circular fountains. The doors opened, and the manager of the hotel welcomed us.

"Mr. Willshire, what an honor to have you staying with us this weekend." He extended his hand for me to shake.

"Thank you, Taj. This is my lady, Dr. Astoria Jacobs, and her daughters."

"Welcome, Dr. Jacobs. Hi ladies," he acknowledged my baby and her babies. "We're so excited to have you this weekend. Anything that any of you may need, please don't hesitate to reach out to my personal line in my office."

Soon as Taj opened the double doors to the presidential suite, Demi and Enzo rushed in filming on their phones. I never knew how much teens stayed on their phones until meeting the two of them. Stori held my hand as we both walked in. I instructed the bellman to put the bags in the separate bedrooms. This was one of those moments I was thankful that the master suite was on the other side of the suite.

"This suite is lit! Do you know how fire it would be if we had the dance sleepover here?" Demi did a cartwheel and then started running around the living room.

"Calm down, Dem," Stori told her.

"Can we have the sleepover here?"

"No."

"Let her have it here." I tried to convince her.

What was any of this for if I couldn't let her flex for her friends? "Seriously, Bray?"

I held my hands up. "I'm not trying to overstep."

"But you are," she snapped.

"Come here," I grabbed her hand and pulled her out onto the balcony that showcased downtown Orlando. "I'm not trying to step on your toes when it comes to your daughters."

"And yet you are. A whole suite for a sleepover is nuts."

"Is this how you're going to be the entire weekend with the girls? Uptight about everything? Let them live their best lives."

"I don't know." She hesitated and put her hand on her hips.

I rubbed her shoulders. "I told you to let me handle the weekend, right? We can get a regular suite for the night and let them do them. I could finish showing you how much I missed you," I whispered into her ears, and she blushed.

"Alright, alright." She finally agreed.

How many times could they really say they spent the weekend in a presidential suite with their friends? I wanted the girls to have a good experience, and maybe I was trying to win a few brownie points in the process. Stori needed to let go and allow me to lead her this weekend. When it came to the kids, I never wanted to overstep, which is why I pulled her outside to talk to her. This weekend was about Demi, and she had fully stressed all week leading up to this weekend, and I made it happen for her. Now that we were here, all she needed to do was chill and allow the girls to have fun.

Stori had gone to the other side of the suite to help the girls get settled and make sure they were getting ready for dinner. The dance competition was tomorrow and from what Stori was telling me, it could be all day. She said she usually watched Demi's competitions and then sat in her car while Demi supported her other dance friends. I could really see me waking up on the weekends and going to support Demi at her dance competitions.

"You would have thought I have never taken them anywhere with the way they were fighting over the rooms." Stori walked into the room and kicked her shoes off.

"They just excited."

"I know. It's nice to see them having fun after I had to have the divorce conversation with them."

"Oh, you, had it?" She told me she wanted to talk to the girls, I didn't think that meant discussing that she was going to file for divorce. "How did the conversation go?" I walked over to her, and sat down on the bed, pulling her down onto my lap.

"I'm surprised because it went better than I expected. They had already been anticipating it, and actually encouraged it because they know neither of us are happy with one another."

"Why are you surprised? You and your ex-husband raised some pretty dope kids together. They know what's best for their parents, and only want to see the both of you thrive."

"I'd be lying if I said our new reality doesn't scare me a little bit."

"If a new start doesn't scare you a bit, is it even considered a fresh start?" I kissed her cheek.

"You say all the perfect things to me. I look at you and can't believe that you're real and even in my life."

Squeezing her tightly, I kissed her lips. "You better get used to the shit because I'm not going anywhere."

"I sure hope not."

As much as I wanted to fuck the shit out of her, I knew we had dinner reservations, and that would set us back some time. I made reservations at one of the best spots in Orlando. I needed to show Stori that I didn't just speak of wanting her to live the princess life. I was going to actively show her too. She deserved vacations, shopping sprees and fancy dinners.

Why?

Because she constantly put everyone in her life before herself, and those were the kind of people that made it into heaven with first class tickets. Stori reminded me a lot of my mother, and I think that was why I found her spirit and personality so comforting. My mother was the rock of our family, and there was nothing that she wouldn't do for any of us. When it came to herself, she never put herself first. My father died, making me promise that my mother would take care of herself and worry about her since he was no longer around. I wanted Stori to do the same thing. She needed to become comfortable being selfish.

"Oh, my goodness, this yellow tail is immaculate," Enzo complimented the chef when he came to put down the rest of our food.

"Why thank you, ma'am. Have you had a chance to try our squid seaweed salad... it's a favorite." He gently pushed the small plate with the seaweed drenched in squid dressing.

Enzo eloquently took a sample size onto her plate and tasted it. "Oh, wow. The flavors are amazing... is that nutmeg I taste?"

"This one has a good palate... not many people catch that hint of nutmeg that I add." He smiled, grateful that someone as young as Enzo appreciated his food.

We were at a very popular sushi restaurant in downtown Orlando. The place had a Michelin star, and the reviews were amazing. Last I came here, it was a smaller restaurant with about eight tables and bar seating. The owners had taken over the next-door store, knocked out the wall and extended the restaurant. Despite them expanding the restaurant, it still held that quaint, cozy atmosphere that it always had.

"Enjoy your food. It's a pleasure as always, Mr. Willshire." He bowed and excused himself.

"Watching all of your cooking shows is paying off." Stori winked at her daughter, who was proud of herself.

"I think I want to focus on culinary next semester," she informed her mother. "There's a culinary course that I can apply to, and they have off campus classes too."

"We can look into that, if that's what you want to do." Stori was the kind of mother that would support her girls no matter what they wanted to do.

She'd break her leg chasing beside her daughters so they could follow their dreams. I admired the kind of mother that she was, and if God blessed us, I wanted her to be that kind of mother to our child too.

"Mom, so after my dance set is over, I was going to hang out with Kendra and the rest of the girls at the competition all day. Then we can have the sleepover at the suite. Is that cool?" she looked from her mother to me to confirm.

"Sounds fine with me," Stori said.

I had already spoken with the concierge, and they were going to set everything up for the girls. Enzo decided last minute that she wanted to do the sleepover, so it was going to be me and Stori for the night, which I never minded.

"Do you have kids, Bray?" Enzo questioned.

"I don't."

"Do you want any?" Demi chimed in.

"If God sees fit for me to be a father, then I will be."

"Sir, don't talk around the question."

Me and Stori both broke out into laughter. "Demi, I'm going to pop you in the mouth."

"I'm just saying. If you want my mama to have your baby, say that. I'd rather know now before I get that *we* need to talk text from Mom down the line." Demi continued while Enzo nodded her head in agreement.

"I guess I should ask you this, do you want another sibling?"

"Hmm, I'm not against it. A little sister would be cute."

"Or a little brother," Enzo added.

"Can I ask how you guys feel about me and your mom?"

Demi popped a piece of sashimi into her mouth before she responded. "I enjoy seeing Mom smile more. She doesn't do it often, so the fact that you're able to make her smile means you're special. Plus, she doesn't just openly trust anyone, so I'm guessing you're the real deal."

"Just don't hurt her. She deserves to be happy because she goes out her way to make us all happy." It was Enzo's turn to speak her peace.

I looked both of them in the eyes. "You both have my word that I would never hurt your mother or you guys. As much as

I'm having fun getting to know your mom, I want to do the same with the both of you."

Stori gave my knee a light squeeze and smiled at me. The girls were satisfied with how our conversation was going, so they started back up recording their meal.

Me and Stori continued to eat and talk while the girls were in their own worlds. I was excited about the future with her and the girls. They were so outspoken and smart. It didn't surprise me in the least, because they were being raised by a smart and outspoken woman.

FIFTEEN
DR. ASTORIA JACOBS

DEMI'S DANCE COMPETITION WENT WELL, AND THE LENNOX DOLLS won the competition, which never surprised me. Those girls worked hard, and their coach worked harder. With all the money I spent on dance, it felt good seeing my daughter kill the competition every time.

Her coach went above and beyond for the girls, including having merch made for them to sell at each competition. Each girl had her own graphic T-shirt, and the money went back into the studio. There w.ere a few moms that were upset that the individual child didn't get to keep the money since it was their face on the shirt.

"You are so extra," I laughed at Bray, who was wearing a Demi doll dance T-shirt. "Did you really have to buy six shirts?"

"Hell yeah. They were the last six shirts. Nobody 'bout to outdo my girl. What she get if all her merch sells out?"

"I think they get to lead the team on the next competition. Dem is always leader though, and her merch never sells out." We walked over toward the concession stand where Enzo was waiting for us.

Enzo hated everything that had to do with dance. When she was younger, I put both she and Demi into ballet. While Demi loved it, Enzo hated every part of it. They were both girly girls, Enzo just wasn't into dance the same way that Demi was. This was Demi's passion, and she couldn't see herself doing anything but dance.

"So, Enzo, I was thinking we can go to Disney while Demi is staying at the competition all day."

Her face lit up because this had been something she wanted to do. I needed to make the time and space for both my daughters without one feeling neglected.

"Seriously?"

"Yep. I know you wanted to go, and Bray got us tickets. We can jump from each park."

Bray tried to get us that VIP tour that allowed us to skip lines and get insider information about the ins and outs of Disney World. He was slick about not letting me see how much it cost. All I had to do was google, and I put a stop to it. I truly appreciated how he just wanted us to have a good time and didn't care how much it cost. Still, I didn't want him trying to do everything to win the girls over. If things grew more serious than they already were, he couldn't always buy their love.

"Why are we still waiting here? Let's get the hell out of here."

I gently tug at my daughter's ponytail. "Language, Enzo."

"Sorry, Mom."

Bray was on a call as he trailed behind us to the car. Enzo was skipping and all smiles because we were finally doing something that she wanted to do. It had been so long since me and the girls had been on a vacation. Whenever Demi had dance competitions out the state, I drove to support, and we were usually heading home that same day.

We never went on vacations because Jace was always complaining about money. He complained when it came to taking a family trip. Yet, he went on vacations with his friends plenty of times and never uttered one complaint.

There was so many new traditions that I wanted to set for me and the girls. I no longer wanted to work so much that I didn't get to spend time with them. Our lives had become work, school, and any after school activities they had. Things were about to shift so much that I wanted to keep our bond tight and connected.

"You on speaker," Bray said when we got into the rental.

"What's up, Sis?" Ashton's voice came across the car's speaker.

"Hey, Ash. How have you been?"

"Chilling, doing my thing."

"You on speaker and there's a child in the car," Bray quickly reminded him. Even I knew Ashton had a wild mouth and needed a disclaimer before he said some off the wall shit.

"I wasn't even going to get crazy."

"You're always crazy."

"I saw that picture you posted on your Instagram... I want one of those shirts... shit is tough."

"I gotta few. You gotta buy them though. Money goes to Demi."

"You acting like I'm some broke as... some broke man," he corrected himself.

"I got you." Bray chuckled.

"What you getting into now?"

"We're going to Disney. Enzo wanted to go while we were here," I explained.

"What's good, Zo-Zo?" Ashton greeted like he had known Enzo her entire life.

"Um, hey?" Enzo was amused clearly.

"Damn, why she... never mind. I'll hit you later. Moms is already on me for Thanksgiving dinner. It's at your house or what?"

"Yeah, at the apartment."

"I've seen many apartments, and your shit ain't no apartment. Call it for what it is, a damn penthouse."

"I agree," Enzo added.

"See, Zo-Zo knows what it is. Have fun at Disney... I'm gonna hit y'all later."

"Bet."

Enzo put her headphones on and enjoyed the ride in the back. I looked over at Bray, and we made eye contact. I was the type that would usually turn away whenever our eyes met, and today I didn't.

"Thank you for all of this."

"You don't gotta keep thanking me, Doc. I'm having the most fun I've had in a while."

"Are you? This isn't too much."

"Not at all."

Astoria, call me whenever you get the chance - mom.

For the life of me, I could never understand why my mother ended her messages like I didn't know it was her who sent me the text in the first place? Me and my mother didn't have the best relationship when I was growing up. I was the second mother to Harlym before I had babies of my own. I was the one who got her from school and helped with homework and bath times. My mom would come in from work so tired that the last thing I wanted was for her to have to worry about us.

I knew now as an adult, that my childhood wasn't healthy. I was a child raising a child. Who was taking care of me when I needed it the most? That seemed to be my problem with all my relationships in my life. I often gave too much to the wrong people, and I was the one who almost always ended up with nothing in return. My mother expected me to do my part within the house while remaining damn near perfect. I was supposed to get good grades and still do everything.

I always wished I had that close knit relationship with my mom. Someone I could go and talk to when I needed advice. She was always at work or emotionally unavailable to me. It was my aunt that picked up the pieces and was there for me. She was the one who poured into me after I was empty from being every-thing to everyone.

Okay. I'll call you when I'm back at the hotel.

That's right, Dem's competition. Tell her I said good luck.

Okay.

I could be angry and downright bitter with my mother. However, I learned that she did the best she could with what she had been offered. Her own mother wasn't the best mom, so she didn't know any better. My relationship with her and the girl's relationship with her was night and day.

She loved her granddaughters and would do whatever she had to for them. Whenever she was off, she would drive up to spend time with them. They loved going shopping with their grandmother and spending time with her. She may not have been the best mother growing up, but she was a damn good grandmother. Even if she had gotten off to a rocky start when she first became a grandmother.

I couldn't say the same about Jace's mother. The thought of that woman caused my blood pressure to rise more even more than it already was. The girls respected her because she was their grandmother. Even though they preferred not to spend too much time with her. Jace didn't even spend much time with her for the same reason as his daughters. So, he never gave the girls shit because they didn't want to spend time with their grandmother. He knew his mother was a handful and would probably die being one too.

The one thing I was excited about was not having to spend future holidays pretending and trying to keep the peace for the sake of the kids. If I never saw that woman again, it would have been way too soon.

BRAY WOULD MAKE the perfect girl dad. He allowed Enzo to swindle him into buying her a bunch of stuff from the different shops throughout Disney. By the time we were done and walking to the parking lot, we had a bunch of bags filled with shit she didn't need. I had to admit the smile on my girl's face was priceless.

She had been wanting to go to Disney for some time and I always promised her that we would go. Something would come up, like a broken water heater, or maintenance on the car, so that promise kept getting broken every year. I was happy that she had been able to go, and we had a great time. It was even more special because it a memory that just me and her shared together. A memory that she didn't have to share with her sister.

Enzo was a thrill seeker, so she wanted to ride all the bigger rides, and Bray was game. While I waited with my iced coffee, they rode every ride that I was too scared to ride.

Demi's coach dropped her back to the hotel with the other girls. By the time we arrived back to the hotel, all the girls were in our suite. Enzo couldn't wait to tell them about the day we had at Disney. The one thing I enjoyed about my girls was that they were always genuinely happy for each other. Demi didn't want to go to Disney because of dance, however, that didn't stop her from being excited for her sister.

Bray had moved some of our stuff down the hall to another suite. It was smaller in size with the same view from the balcony and bedroom. If the girls needed anything, they would be right down the hall from us. He had instructed them to order whatever they wanted from room service and not to hesitate to come get us if they needed anything, or there was an emergency. The balcony was off-limits since there would be no adult present in the suite.

After washing the parks and the day off my body, I pulled on a pair of my favorite pajama pants from Target and headed out onto the balcony to cuddle on the couch. My mom had probably been waiting for me to call her back all day, so I pressed her contact's name.

"Hey, Astoria. How did today go?"

"Hey, mommy. It well, she won."

"As always. That's my girl."

The line grew quiet. We didn't have much to talk about and it showed. "She does her thing. What's going on, Ma?"

"It's Shericka."

My heartbeat sped up. "Please don't tell me."

"I'm sorry, Stori. The cancer has returned." She poured more salt into a wound that had never completely healed.

"Oh God." I held my chest.

My aunt was diagnosed with breast cancer three years ago. As a family, we wrapped our arms around her and helped her fight it. When she went into remission, we thanked God. My aunt was my entire world, the right to my wrong and my voice of reason. We used to be so close, and I was the one who pulled away because she didn't approve of Jace. Shericka had never steered me wrong, and I still couldn't bring myself to trust that she knew what she was talking about when it came to Jace.

I allowed my love for my husband to drive my aunt away and put a strain on our relationship. Had I listened to her, I probably wouldn't have been going through all I had during the course of my marriage. We still found time to catch up, but it was never the same. She eventually moved out of New York and down to Virginia because her husband had gotten a better job with the police force there.

When he was killed in the line of duty, I drove all the way to Virginia to be with her. A few months after, she found out that she had breast cancer. We wanted her to move back and be around family, and she refused, so we all took turns being there for her. Harlym took it the hardest because she and my aunt were so close.

"When is she going to catch a break," my mother sighed.

"Does Har know?"

"I called her earlier. She's flying down to Virginia and bringing your aunt to stay with her."

"And she wants that?"

"Shericka knows she can't beat this alone in Virginia. She and Harlym have always had that close relationship, kind of like what y'all used to have before you fucked it up over Jace's dumb ass."

There she goes.

I knew it was only a matter of time before she poked at Jace. My mother didn't like Jace before he was my husband, and she damn sure didn't like him after. Mama was the first person to call me a damn fool when I found out about Tyler. She told me I was as dumb as rocks to stick around for a man that wasn't worth it.

Her delivery wasn't always the best and often came out harsh, which is what I hated. Still, she told no lies and had predicted the future more than a few times. I thought I could change that man, and he ended up making a fool out of me.

"Not now, Mama," I whispered.

My heart hadn't stopped beating since she relayed the news to me. This wasn't about Jace or the strained relationship between me and my aunt.

"All I'm saying is that you and Shericka ain't been right since you cut her off for telling you about Jace and that baby mama of his."

"I know."

Shericka had saw Jace out with Tonya, and she called me. I was hormonal with a new baby, and I lashed out on her. I was so overwhelmed with being a mother to two babies, no help and pursuing a degree. My anger was with her because I knew I couldn't direct it to Jace. It wasn't like I was going to do anything or end things with him.

Back then, I *needed* him. Who was going to want a girl with not one, but two damn babies? I felt like my back was against the wall and he was all I had. Whenever he spoke about us as his *family*, I felt like we were going to make it. I was so foolish back then that I cringed when I thought about all the shit, I used to tell myself in order to make our relationship work.

My aunt moved, and I didn't bother to attend her going away party. I was so angry at her, and I couldn't figure out why. All she was doing was looking out for her niece, and I was mad like she had put both Jace and Tonya together. Years later, I realized that my anger wasn't with my aunt. It was with Jace for making me look stupid in front of her.

He knew how my family felt about him, and how they were banking on us not lasting. If you knew this, why the fuck would you go and prove them right? When we moved to Lennox Hills, it was easier to lie about our marriage and post pictures that told the perfect love story.

On the outside looking in, you saw a husband, wife and two beautiful girls living in a nice suburban neighborhood. On the inside, the walls of our home had so many cracks that I was running out of spackle trying to fix them. They didn't see the wife who sobbed in the shower because she was so miserable with life. Or the husband that didn't give a fuck about his wife's feelings. All they saw was the family that went to the pumpkin patch, or raked leaves in the front yard while joking around.

"We're going to get her through this one like we did the last time."

My mother didn't know it, but I needed that peek of hope right now. "Yeah, we are."

"I know you invited me over for Thanksgiving, and I appreciate the invitation."

"But you're not coming."

"I don't enjoy being around your damn husband, Astoria. What part of that have you not gotten through your head?"

"Okay, Mama."

"Plus, I have to work the next morning, so it's best if I just cook at home and rest for the one day I have off this week."

"We'll miss you."

"I'm so sure," she snickered. "Let me get off this phone... I love you."

"Love you too."

"Alright, bye-bye." She ended the call, and I leaned my head back while tears cascaded down my cheeks.

How much was too much? I know God gave his hardest battles to the strongest soldiers, and I would never question God. Yet, it was hard not to question him when he kept giving my aunt the same battle. She had already lost so much, and now she had to roll up her sleeves to battle this damn demon again.

All the memories of my aunt flooded my mind. Every time I needed her, she was there for me, she could never tell me no. Even when I would tell her no, she could never accept that. Demi and Enzo were her babies, and she didn't give a damn if she had work, she would help out with them so I could go to school.

"Mama, can you please watch Demi for me today? I can't miss this exam and Jace isn't answering his phone," I begged.

My mother stared me up and down as she refilled her cup with more Pepsi. I held my heavy one year old daughter on my hip, while holding my pregnant belly with the other. Last night I slept horribly with my daughter's foot in my back most of the night, then the baby inside of me kept doing somersaults. All I wanted was a deep tissue massage and a four-hour nap. However, that wasn't my reality right now.

Massages cost money, and that wasn't something that I had a lot of right now.

The silence from her was loud and had answered the question before she opened her mouth. I gave up waiting and turned to head back to my bedroom. "'Cause you know you played yourself. Asking me to watch Demi like I don't have my own shit going on. You know I love my grandbaby, but this is the first day I've had off in nearly two weeks, and you think I want to spend it with a teething baby? I told you about that stupid ass boy before you decided to get pregnant by him!" She hollered at my back.

For the sake of getting out the door without an argument, I choked down my words and sat Demi back on the bed while I packed her diaper bag and my book bag. I had two hours to drop my daughter across the city and make it to school to take this exam. The last few times that I couldn't make it, my professor was nice enough to let me take the exam during his office hours. This time, he stressed that he couldn't keep

*allowing me to miss important exams and making them up afterwards,
which was fair. My grades were so important to me, and so far, I had
managed to be pregnant once, deliver a baby and maintain my grades.*

*Having a child and getting good grades wasn't something I strug-
gled with. I was in labor with Demi when I took my final exam online
while going through contractions. When I got pregnant with Demi, my
mother swore I was going to be working at the airport with her. She had
always stressed college and getting a good career, but because I turned
up pregnant she didn't think that was a possibility for me any longer.
She even went as far as to bring me home an application from her job
after I found out I was pregnant. I had always been a straight A
student because that was what I could control. My home life was
unstable and always changing, and as a kid, I was never in control of it.*

*The one thing I could control was getting good grades and doing
the best that I could in school. I excelled in everything academic, and
that never seemed to be good enough for my mother. I was expected to
color inside the lines, get my alphabet correct, ace all my tests and take
care of my sister.*

*When I was younger, my mother would drop me off at my grand-
mother's house for weeks at a time and wouldn't care. Whenever she
got done running the streets and remembered she had a child, she
would pick me up and take me home. As a kid, I never knew where I
was going to sleep that night. I could sleep in my bed, or my mother
could wake me up out my sleep to bring me over to my grandmother or
aunt's house. Which is why it bothered me that she couldn't extend help
to me, when she used to be in the same shoes as me. The only difference
was that I needed help so I could finish college, and she wanted help so
she could hang out with different boyfriends.*

*I don't think I slept in my bed for a week straight during my entire
childhood. If anything, I lived out my overnight bag more than
anything. Even though I hated how my mother floated me around from
family member to family member, the one thing I could control was
school. I was in control of my grades and how good they were. It was
up to me to excel in every subject and grade I was put in.*

It didn't matter where I slept that night, I always made sure that I got my homework done. My mother never checked or cared about my homework. Half the time, I was at my grandmother or aunt's house, and they were the two who was keeping up with my schoolwork and tests.

There was no room for imperfections, so I put so much pressure on myself, so that I never had any.

I was perfect.

That was something that I could and would control.

I did everything as if my mother was cheering me on because I wanted to make her proud. Hearing her utter I'm so proud of you would have meant the world to me.

She never did.

It wasn't until she got pregnant with Harlym that things became more stabler for us. She got a new job and held that down for years, which meant it was up to me to make sure the house ran smoothly until she was able to get off and come home.

While Demi was distracted with her baby brush, I quickly rushed down the hall to the bathroom to brush my teeth and call my aunt.

She always watched Demi whenever I couldn't afford daycare or Jace was missing in action, like now. I could really use him right now, but he was nowhere to be found, and continued to click my calls to voicemail when I did call him.

My mother sat on the couch with her Pepsi watching Maury when I headed out the door. She didn't bother to ask if I needed a ride, or reconsider watching her granddaughter. I wasn't lost on the fact that she wanted to enjoy her day off, but why couldn't she help me out and do this solid for me this one time?

I pushed Demi down the block to the train while dialing my aunt's number. My aunt Shericka was my mother's younger sister by two years. She had a city job, her own apartment and was married to her college boyfriend. In my eyes, my aunt was goals, and she had the life that I desired for me and Demi.

"Hey, Stori... what's going on?" she answered on the fourth ring.

"Hey Ricka, are you working today?"

"Not today. I took today off to take mama to the doctor... I'm heading back home now. What's up?"

I thanked the lucky stars that she was off today. *"Everything alright with Grandma?"*

"Other than being hardheaded, everything with your grandmother is fine. She hates going to get her checkups, so I went to make sure she went."

"Good."

"Stori, what's going on?"

"I hate to spring this on you... can you watch Demi for me? I have an exa—"

"Bring my niece over to my house now. I'll keep her for the night so you can get some sleep too."

I blew a sigh of relief. *"Okay. I'm heading to your house now,"* I assured her and ended the call.

Demi was leaning back in her stroller eating a baby biscuit as I breezed down the block to the subway. The entire walk there I hated the fact that I would have to struggle with the stroller down the subway steps. Anytime I struggled with one stroller, I became nervous for when my second daughter got here.

How was I going to be able to do it?

I struggled to do it with one, and now I had two that were going to depend on me. Jace was around whenever it was convenient for him, which I hated. We could be good for a few months, and then he would randomly start acting weird and doing disappearing acts.

Today would have been the perfect time for him to be here to help with his daughter. Instead, I was breezing down the block while seven months pregnant with his daughter, and he couldn't even be bothered enough to answer the phone for me.

"Ma'am, let me help you out?" The white man snapped me out of my thoughts.

"Are you sure?"

"Yes. You're pregnant and shouldn't be lifting this stroller." I took the diaper bag off the back of the stroller, and with one lift, he had Demi and her stroller up in the air as he carefully walked down the steps.

When we made it down into the subway, he watched me swipe my metro card and opened the exit door for me. We were going our separate ways, but that didn't stop him from helping me down onto the platform and then jogging back up the stairs to make his train that happened to be pulling into the station.

"Have the best day!" He called from across the platform as he went to jump onto his train.

"You too, sir!" I called back and waved to him.

If he hadn't offered, I didn't know how I was going to manage all of this on my own. My doctor had already given me plenty of warnings about slowing down. How was I supposed to slow down when I had so much going on with little to no help?

Shericka never had a problem watching Demi for me. I always felt guilty dropping my daughter off because I didn't have anyone else to help. You would think because I lived with my mother that she would help me out. It was like living on my own because she never helped me out with Demi. There were so many times that I needed her to change a diaper or give Demi a bath and she refused. She claimed she was teaching me a lesson by not raising my baby for me.

The train ride over to my aunt's house wasn't too bad. Demi loved the train, so I didn't hear a fuss out of her. Not that she fussed much anyway. My baby was a good baby and had always been. Whenever I was studying, I would put Mickey Mouse Club House on, and she would sit and watch for hours without making a sound.

My aunt lived in a two story walk up on Atlantic Avenue. She was right in the middle of all the action in Brooklyn. When I turned onto her block, I spotted her standing out front talking to a neighbor. When she saw me, she smiled and met me halfway.

"You look tired, girl." She noted the huge bags of luggage that had accumulated under my eyes.

"School and life are kicking my ass," I admitted as she took control of the stroller, giving me a minute to stretch.

The subway at my aunt's stop had an elevator that came out onto the street, so I was saved from having to hike this stroller up two flights of stairs.

"What yo' mama was doing?"

I rolled my eyes. *"Watching her shows and chugging Pepsi."*

She shook her head and pulled the stroller up the four steps in front of her building. I was thankful that she lived on the first-floor apartment because I didn't think I could make it up any more steps.

"I don't know why she insists on making your life harder." She held the front door open for me.

Desmond, Shericka's husband, was packing his work bag at the kitchen table. *"Hey, Stori... you brought our girl over, so you can go on and leave now,"* he joked.

"Whatever, Des. We're a packaged deal." I smiled and gave him a quick side hug before plopping down onto the couch.

"You need to take it easy, Stori...you what now? Six months pregnant?"

"Seven," I corrected.

"Even more reason why you need to be sitting your ass down," my aunt chimed in as she sat Demi in the walker I kept at her house.

"Exactly."

"Trust me... I would sit still if I could. I don't have that luxury right now, and I don't want to keep putting that on you both."

"Why do you think we're here? We want to help you out as much as we're able." My aunt handed me a bottle of water.

I always felt ashamed when I had to accept the help that was offered to me. Mostly because I was the one who put myself in this situation, and now I needed the help. After I had Demi, I should have broken things off with Jace. Instead, I allowed him to sweet talk his way back into my panties and now I was pregnant for the second time with no help from him - again.

I was stupid.

"I just don't want to take over your life with my bullshit. It's not fair to keep dumping her on you both when she has a father."

"Your mama got your mind so messed up, Stori." Desmond shook his head. *"This is what family does for each other, and you are family."*

Shericka looked over at her husband with love and admiration. This was the first healthy relationship I had ever witnessed in my life. It *always made me crave the same thing for myself. I wanted to raise my daughters in love, not destruction.*

When it came to her father, I felt like we were water and oil. No matter how much we tried to mix and get it right, it never worked out for us. We were both toxic for each other, and it didn't matter how much we knew this, we were still attracted together like magnets.

"You're nineteen years old with a lot on your plate. It's not like you're sitting around having babies with no goals."

I wanted to become a therapist since I was a child pretending my stuffed animals were my clients. This was something that I had always dreamed of, and I was determined to make it happen. I had two daughters that were going to be looking up to me, and I couldn't let them down.

I wanted them to know they could do whatever their hearts desired.

"Thanks." I sipped my water and leaned my head back.

"Going to college and working a part time job with a damn one year old is tough. Me and your aunt don't even have kids and having full-time jobs is hard." Desmond closed up his work bag. "Alright, I'm gone. I'll call you later on, Love."

Shericka walked over toward her husband and kissed him on the lips. "Please be safe out there... I love you, Des."

"Love you more." He held her around the waist and kissed her lips a few times before releasing her. "Be good, Stori."

I smiled. "I'm never good... but I'll try."

"As long as we try... that's all we can ask, right?"

"Yup."

"Later, Munchie." He pinched Demi's cheeks, and then headed out the door. Demi and Desmond were like one person. Whenever she saw him, her entire face lit up.

He always allowed her to have her way.

"Now, you need to call a cab to school. I'm not letting you take the subway into school today."

"I don't have any money for a cab," I groaned.

"Don't think I asked if you had money or not."

My aunt and my mother were like night and day. They were so different that it was hard to believe that they were even sisters. My aunt Pam, their older sister had moved out of the city years ago and barely kept in touch. Me and Shericka were the closest, and I often looked at her like my big sister rather than my aunt.

"Shericka, you need to stop spending your money on me. You work hard for that, and I don't need you blowing it all on me."

"I can and will spend my money on whatever I want. What is going on with Jace?" she sat down at the counter and looked over at me.

I had been sitting for a little while now, and I still couldn't catch my breath. "I don't know. Whenever I call, he clicks the phone."

Whenever Jace was in the mood to be a family man, that's when he would come over and be present. It was when he wanted to do him, that's when I never heard from him and couldn't get him on the phone.

Despite all the shit he put me through, whenever he did called, I would be right there, ready to welcome him in with open arms. I hated how stupidly in love I was with his ass. My brain knew I deserved better, and even knowing better, my heart always won the battle with him.

"You're going to have a second mouth to feed soon. Jace needs to get his shit together and start helping you out, Astoria," she sternly warned me.

My aunt disliked Jace and told me that I shouldn't have gotten involved with him. The heart wants what it wanted, so I ignored all the warnings and red flags that were being waved in my face. I desperately wanted this man to want to be a family with me and his daughters.

"We're going to get it together, Shericka… I promise," I told her, not knowing if we were ever truly going to get our life in order.

I prayed that we did.

I sniffled and wiped my face with the inside of my shirt. It was hard trying to do right by everyone and feeling like you've failed. I tried to do right by Jace, and that ended up straining the relationship I did have with my aunt. I was jealous of her and Harlym's relationship that they had. As much as Harlym loved Cam, she never let him come between her family. Whenever I disapproved, she simply stopped talking about him around me.

I jumped when my phone started ringing. Picking my phone up, I cut my eyes at the picture of me and Jace kissing. I had set that as his contact photo years ago and here Apple went showing me how delusional I had been.

"Hey," I sniffled.

"Where the fuck you at, and who the fuck are you with?"

"What?"

"I know I didn't fucking stutter," Jace snarled.

"What the hell are you talking about? You know exactly where we are." I wasn't in the mood for his stupid ass questions.

"With who?"

"Your girls."

His ominous laughter sent chills down my spine. "Check your text messages."

The message notification popped up as soon as he said it. I exited out of the phone screen and went to my messages. I paused when I saw the screenshot from Demi's Instagram. It was a picture of her food. However, if you were a nosey person like me and peeped people's backgrounds, you could see a little of Bray's Rolex in the picture, and my hand was rested on top of his.

"You ain't got shit to say, do you? Who the fuck do you have around my daughters, Astoria?"

"A friend. Why the fuck are you stalking our daughter's social media account?"

"I don't even have her as a fucking friend on social media. Tyler sent me this shit, and you foul as fuck. Who bought that new truck and that diamond necklace you been wearing?"

So, he had been paying attention, he just wasn't saying anything about it. "He's a friend."

"Now I'm stupid," he muttered more to himself than to me. "Why haven't I met this friend?"

Something inside of me snapped. I didn't care to spare his feelings and make things better for him. "He's fucking me, Jace.

Is that what you wanted to hear? I'm sucking his dick, he's fucking me, and he's been for a little while now."

When the line went silent, I became scared. Did I cause this man to have a stroke?

"Fucking bitch," he snarled.

"Oh, your chest hurting because somebody else is fucking me? How do you think I felt all these years?"

Fuck being cordial and mature. I had been that person this entire marriage, and all he had ever done was walk all over me. He didn't respect me because I was so quick to wave the white flag and let him declare victory. I was so busy trying to keep the peace while slowly destroying my own.

Fuck that.

Jace didn't deserve the nice side of me anymore. He had the nerve to fix his mouth to call me a bitch and had been fucking Tonya this whole time. That was his problem. He never saw an issue with the pain he inflicted on others, only what others did to him.

"I'll be that."

"You brought my kids around another man…showing them how to be little whores?"

"Watch your fucking mouth when it comes to my daughters, Jace. I've allowed whatever when it came to me, but I'll knock your head off behind Demi and Enzo."

"What fucking example are you showing them?"

"I'm finally showing them to do whatever makes them happy. You have a lot of nerve when you've been fucking Tonya again." He went quiet again, probably shocked that I knew about him and his baby mama. "You shouldn't take your medicine and leave your phone unlocked."

"I ain't fucking nobody," he continued to lie when I already knew the truth.

Tonya was usually a full headache and made her presence known. Other than the car trouble, she had been real quiet and accepting of whatever Jace did for her. That should have been the first sign that they started back messing around with each other.

"You can lie to yourself all you want. I know the truth and have known for a while."

"You just love talking so you can hear yourself speak. If you so-called knew about me cheating, why did you continue to let me fuck?"

It was my turn to laugh, except I was laughing at myself. "I was a fool for you. Stupid behind a man that didn't give a fuck about me. That was my fault because I accepted the bullshit you continued to bring to me. Not anymore."

"What does that mean?"

"I'm filing for divorce when we're back home. I want you out of my house, and we can work out a schedule with the girls."

"Get the fuck outta here. I'm not leaving my house... you gonna have to remove me yourself if you want me to leave."

"Don't make this harder than it needs to be, Jace."

"I'm not making shit hard. You're my wife, and this is our home... I'm not leaving shit!"

I could picture the spit flying from his mouth as he yelled on his phone. There was no need to sit and try to convince him why he needed to leave. He just needed to leave, and if I had to get the cops to remove him, I would.

"Bye, Jace."

"Don't fucking han—" I ended the call.

I leaned back on the chair and closed my eyes. The balcony door opened, and Bray came and sat beside me. "My bad. The call ran longer than I expected."

"You're good. I know you have to work."

He paused and examined my face. "What's wrong?"

I let out a low chuckle. "Why are you assuming there's something wrong?"

"Doc, your eyes are red. You don't need to pretend to be fine around me... I'm the one person that should know that you're not fine, so I can fix it."

"There's so much." I tilted my head back because I was so tired of crying. "My aunt's cancer came back, and Jace just called because he saw your arm on Demi's Instagram story."

"Damn. What kind of cancer does she have?"

"Breast cancer."

"I'm sorry." He took my hand into his and kissed the back of it. "I know the best oncologist. We can see if we ca—"

"Stop, please," I pleaded.

"Doc, you can get her in to se—"

"Money can't buy every fucking thing, Bray!" I hollered. "My aunt has fucking cancer for the second time... money didn't save your father, did it? Everything isn't about *your* money."

Fuck.

I felt guilty as soon as the words left my mouth. If I could, I wouldn't have said that to him. "I hear you... I'm big on giving people space, and you seem like you need that. I ordered that beet root tea that helps with blood pressure. It's on the counter in the kitchen."

"Bra—"

"We're good, Doc. I'm gonna give you the space you need." He excused himself and went back inside the suite.

I started punching the pillows before collapsing back onto the couch while crying. Why the fuck would I say such a horrible thing to him? I cried so much that I eventually fell asleep with the pillow over my head.

My phone chiming pulled me from my sleep. I leaned up and scooped my phone up. I had slept out here for the past four hours. The blanket that I was under told me that Bray came out here and covered me up while I slept peacefully. It was a quarter past three in the morning, so I folded the blanket up and headed inside.

Pulling my pants and cami off, I climbed into bed and wrapped my arms around Bray. He stirred from his sleep and stared me in the eyes. "You all good?"

"I'm so sorry. I was wrong for saying that to you, and the second that the words left my mouth, I regretted them."

"It's cool."

"No, it's not." I kissed his lips.

He turned over fully and noticed that I was naked. "I could think of a few ways that you can make it up to me." He got on his back and pulled his pajama pants down.

We didn't need to exchange words to know what he wanted. I climbed on top of him and lowered myself down onto his dick. He held my waist as I rode him slowly. Our eyes remained locked on one another the entire time. I tossed my head back, breaking our eye contact and held onto his chest while I bounced up and down on his dick.

His small grunts told me that he was enjoying the ride, and that I was making up for the hateful shit that I allowed to fly out my mouth earlier. I leaned forward and kissed him on the lips.

"I love you, Astoria," he admitted.

I believed him because I felt the same way about him. "I love you too, Bray."

When he got the confirmation that I felt the same way about him, he flipped me over on the bed, and I allowed him to take control. I lived my entire life in the driver's seat, so having him take control turned me on more than he ever knew.

SIXTEEN
BRAY WILLSHIRE

THANKSGIVING WAS IN TWO DAYS AND WORK HADN'T SLOWED DOWN. With all the shit I had going on and the few properties that were lined up for us to purchase, I hadn't been sleeping the best either. I had meetings in all different time zones, and the little sleep I did get wasn't much because I was always being pulled from my sleep by a new meeting alarm.

Me and Stori had been able to squeeze a few dates here and there. Between her work schedule and mine, we couldn't make the time to spend together. Our daily text and FaceTime's were what kept us locked in. I could have allowed our little argument in Orlando ruin us, instead I didn't match her emotion with even more emotion. What she said hurt because it was true. No amount of money could save my father or bring him back.

"Since you're eating lunch, I figured this is the best time to schedule this."

"What?"

"Paris? Did you forget?"

I motioned for Kimberly to take a seat. "I didn't."

"Actually, I have two things to run past you this morning." She pulled up her iPad and crossed her legs.

"Go ahead."

"So, your cousin Woody is actually in town with his girl-friend. He called to arrange dinner between the both of you. So, tomorrow night, I was thinking I could make a reservation at Carbone's... does that work for you?"

"Yeah, can you make sure to send a sexy pair of heels for Astoria?"

She quickly wrote it down. "Of course. I will call the personal shopper and have something sent to her."

There were a few things that I loved about Astoria. Her feet were one of those things. The French pedicure always did it for me. I could get off on just her feet alone. Whenever she slipped on a pair of heels, that shit had me ready to lose my shit every time.

She also mentioned wanting to start her heel collection, and I wanted to contribute to it. "The next thing?"

"Paris. I have everything arranged with hotel and the jet. I just need to confirm the dates with you."

"I have the day after Christmas into New Year. I figured it could be a work trip and time to spend time with your mother too."

"Add Astoria and her daughters too."

"Oh?" Kimberly was shocked.

I wanted to surprise the girls with a trip to Paris. "There a problem?"

"She must be very special." Kimberly winked and rose to her feet. "If those days work, then I will go on and confirm every-thing. I'll also let Woody's assistant know that dinner is tomorrow."

"Appreciate it, Kimberly."

"Don't mention it." she closed the door behind her, then doubled back. "I meant to ask, about Paris—"

"Yes, you're coming on that trip."

I could see the excitement in her eyes. This was a work trip and I had work that needed to be done, so Kimberly would be needed. After we handled all of our shit, we could enjoy the trip and be tourist in the city of love.

"Okay. Thanks."

I continued to eat lunch while texting Stori between her sessions. Orlando was a success with the girls. They had so much fun, and I felt like they truly got to know me and see their mother happy. I knew it would take some convincing on Stori's part to get their father to agree to let them go to Paris. I wanted to at least extend the offer.

As a man, I knew that no matter how I felt about him, there had to be respect there for him as their father. I couldn't come into their life and start doing shit for them without their father having a say in it. Things were still new, so I wasn't trying to create tension between us when it didn't need to be there.

I witnessed my mother and Laurent's mom tension for years. Though they never treated us kids different, we could always tell shit wasn't sweet between them. My mother showed all of her damn teeth in a smile whenever we dropped Laurent off, and I could tell she was faking the shit. It was funny to see years later, that they both could be cordial and put their differences aside for Luna.

Hey, mind if I come over to the house later? The message from Kami popped up on my desktop monitor.

Come through.

We hadn't had any conversation since I pulled up on her at work. She asked for more time before she signed the divorce papers, and I was giving it to her. Other than packing a few things, she hadn't been back to the house. I wasn't concerned with where she was staying because it wasn't my concern anymore.

With the holiday approaching, I had given everyone a half day to kick off their holiday vacation time. Laurent was working from home this week since Alice decided she was going to spend the holidays with them. I wished she would disappear and stop playing with his heart. He was trying to hold onto something that was meant to be let go.

On the way out, I called Stori. "Hey, baby," she greeted.

"What's good, Doc? What you doing?"

"Finished my last client of the day. What about you?"

"Heading home."

"You have two homes... which one?"

"The one where I have a chance to see you."

She giggled. "Oh, you wanna see me?"

"I do."

Out of respect for Kami, I didn't bring Astoria over to our house in Lennox Hills. While her stuff was still there, it was still her home, and I refused to disrespect her by bringing Astoria there.

"What are you doing tomorrow night?"

"Well, Jace's mother is going to be in town. I plan to hide in my room all night."

"My cousin is in town. Come out to dinner with me."

"Food and you? How could I turn an offer like that down?"

"Miss you."

"I miss you too. The girls asked about you this morning."

I smiled. "Sounds like I'm becoming a favorite."

"The favorite with the jet... yeah."

"Damn, Doc. I never thought you were a hater... shit, it doesn't sound good on you."

"Shut up." She giggled.

"How's homeboy been since the argument the other day?"

"Bitter. I'm not paying him any mind. He wants to argue about shit that doesn't even matter anymore. If he refuses to leave the house, then I will move out. I refuse to stay in a house with his ass because he refuses to leave."

It took everything in me not to drive over to her house the night she called me with him hollering in the background. Stori begged me to stay and not make a terrible situation worse. I had become so used to fixing her problems that it didn't sit right with me that I couldn't fix this one problem.

"Did you file the papers?"

"Yep."

"Damn, it's official, huh?"

"And I feel free. I want to be done with him and move on with my life. It's been so long since I felt free, and now I'm about to be single."

"Chill out, you ain't about to be shit."

"Oh, please. Anyway, drive safe and text me when you make it here."

"I got you." I ended my call with Stori and hopped in my truck, hoping that I would be able to avoid the traffic.

I didn't have any plans on staying at the house in Lennox Hills since we were having Thanksgiving at the penthouse. My mother was there now getting everything together with the catering staff. Since Kami wanted to meet, I was going to make the drive so we could talk.

I prayed she came on some peaceful shit because I didn't have the patience to go back and forth with her today. The drive was smooth, and traffic was minimal. Usually, I listened to music and podcasts on long drives. Today, I was deep in thought about Astoria.

Some would say she came into my life at the wrong time. Mainly because we were both legally married with a host of marital insecurities and problems. That right there was a disaster waiting to happen for some. Not for us though. Our broken marriage propelled us into each other, and we haven't detached since.

To me, she couldn't have come at a more perfect time. I needed a woman like her in my life, and God sent her to me. He always gave us what we needed in the moment we started to question him. And man, I was questioning the hell out of him because of my situation at the time.

I often prayed about me and Kami's marriage for clarity. I was so unsure on what I was doing or supposed to be doing. Was I supposed to forgive her and grant her a second chance even when my heart was telling me not to? My spirit wouldn't allow me to give her a second chance to hurt me.

Whenever Stori slept over, I watched her sleep peacefully underneath me. It always felt like she had never experienced true peace. The small shit that I did as a man always surprised her, or she praised me for it. It told me a lot about her husband and what she allowed from him.

I didn't need to be praised for holding the door, or for making sure she ate for the day. As her man those were things that I was supposed to do for her. If a man wasn't doing those things, then you needed to cut that nigga loose.

By the time I made it to the house, Kami had let me know she was leaving the city. I took a quick shower and laid down on the couch in the guest room for a quick nap. By the time we were done here, I was going to be heading back to the city. The door chimed soon as I opened my eyes from my nap.

"Bray?"

"Up here," I cleared my throat and sat up.

Whenever the nap was good, you almost always woke up confused with one sock on. My sock was across the room while I had dried up drool caked up on the side of my mouth.

"You fell asleep?"

"These meetings been kicking my ass. I've been trying to keep up with three different time zones... Australia being the worst one."

"Damn. You look tired too." She leaned in the doorway.

"How you been?"

"Better. I brought some food. Want to share a meal together?"

"I could eat." I stood while rubbing my stomach.

We made our way to the dining room, and she had grabbed my favorite Chinese food from the hood. "I know this is your favorite."

"You drove all the way over there for this?"

"I had my intern grab it before I left the city. It's still warm too." she held the bag up.

Kami plated our food while I sat in the chair trying to get my thoughts together. I needed to prioritize sleep because I was groggy as shit and couldn't shake it.

"They egg foo young always bust."

"For real."

I cleared my throat and took a sip of my soda. "What's on your mind?"

Kami removed the hair from her face. "Our sister station in Miami offered me my own show."

"You have your own show here though... what's different from what you're doing up here?"

"More money and control. I'll have more control over the content that I produce, and I'll be executive producer of the show too."

"Oh shit, that sounds like an amazing opportunity. Did you accept it?"

"I told them I would think about it."

"Why?"

"I wanted your opinion."

"We're going through a divorce, Kam... it don't matter what I think."

She heaved a sigh and pushed her plate away. "I want you opinion as my friend, not my ex-husband. Do you think this is a smart decision? To move away from all that I know, the fanbase I already have here... you know?"

She was scared and second guessing herself. Kami was known as the voice of New York. However, her influence extended way past that. She had fans all over the country.

"I think you're scared. Because it's more comfortable here, it's easier for you to make a million excuses why you shouldn't go."

She smirked. "God, I hate how you're able to see right through me."

"It's true, though. You've accomplished so much here, and that could never be taken away from you. It's time for you to make some new goals and crush them shits like you did here."

"Sounds like you just wanting to pack me up and ship me out."

"Nah, not even. I just know you have a gift, and you need to stop trying to put it in a box because you're afraid. Spread those wings and live your best life in Miami."

"Thanks, Bray...for everything."

"You never have to thank me, you know that."

She grabbed her bag and pulled out the papers. "I signed the papers. It was the hardest thing signing them, knowing I was the cause of our marriage ending."

"We both did and said shit that landed us here."

"You are just being nice. I know the reason we ended up here was because of me. There's so much that I tried to control, and so much that I tried to hide, and you never truly got to know the real me because I never opened up to let you in. I know I've apologized a million times, and you probably never thought any of them were genuine, but they were. I'm sorry, Bray. Sorry for my role in all of this."

I didn't know what she meant by there was so much she tried to hide from me, and I wasn't sure that I even wanted to know. I've always felt like she wasn't as transparent as I was in our marriage. Kami had built her walls so high that it was often hard to break them down, and at times it felt useless to try.

"I appreciate that."

She slid the paper over to me with the signature. "I could have just signed the electronic version, which would have been easier. I figured we could sign it together and mark the end of an era."

"And boy, was it an era." I smiled.

Our marriage wasn't all bad, and that was the part I wanted to remember. I didn't want to remember the hate and ill feelings I felt for her after she cheated. The arguments and petty bullshit we both did back and forth was something I wanted to put behind us. We both deserved to move forward and live happily ever after.

Couples seemed to forget that happily ever after could exist a part. You didn't need to stay with someone because you both promised each other forever when things were good. Everyone wanted to keep their marriage and fight for it. Some marriages weren't worth trying to save. You'll lose yourself trying to fix something that wasn't meant to be fixed.

She placed a long velvet box in front of me, along with the papers. "You know I'm extra, so I got you a little parting gift."

"Oh shit, you signed the papers, and I get a gift?"

"Aye don't look too damn excited." she nudged me.

I opened the box and gently took out the silver ballpoint pen. "You know I love a good pen."

"Read it."

I turned it around and laughed. She had it engraved with *I do, I did, I'm done.* "Yo, that's mad funny."

"I got a matching one and used mine to sign."

I twisted the cap. "Guess that means it's my turn, huh?"

"It does."

I scribbled my signature on the signature line and then turned the paper to repeat the process. When I was done, I closed the pen and fixed the papers.

"Guess that means we're official, huh?"

"I'm afraid so." She stood with her arms folded.

I stood up and reached for a hug. She stepped into my embrace and hugged me tighter. "Take care of yourself, Kam. I already know if you decide to go to Miami, you gonna go beast mode."

"You too, Bray. If it's worth anything, I never planned to say or do anything about Dr. Jacobs. She was helpful in helping me determined that our marriage wasn't going to work."

"She really had no clue we were married," I continued to

assure her, so she didn't part ways thinking Astoria sought me out.

"I believe that now."

Kami grabbed a few more things before she ended up leaving. She let me know her movers were going to come sometime next week to grab the rest of her things. I truly wished her the best and prayed she found someone that made her happy. I felt relief knowing that we were able to do this and remain cordial. Hell, she may even get a Christmas present from me this year. I just knew she was going to make this a big deal and drag it out in court. Kami surprised me by being mature and knowing when to walk away with your dignity intact.

For that, I had nothing but respect for her.

"I LOVE how you love these shoes on my feet, Pa." Stori paused as she fixed the straps on her heel. "However, they feel like a torture device."

"Don't all heels feel like that though?"

"Some more than others," she muttered as she sat down on the lobby bench to fully fix the shoe.

"I can carry you... you know I could."

"Into the restaurant? Sir, don't be outrageous."

"Bet I carry your ass to that bed when we back to the crib." I kissed her on the neck.

"I am not spending the night tonight. Your mom is there, and she won't look at me like some kind of whore." She stood and adjusted the brown and beige sweater dress she wore. Her hair was straightened and pinned up out of her face, except for a few stubborn pieces. The gold Tom Ford heels I had sent to her office yesterday set the outfit off.

If we didn't have this dinner with my cousin and his girlfriend, I probably would have canceled and took her ass back upstairs. The truck pulled around and I held her hand.

"Did I tell you how beautiful you look tonight?"

"Only about a million times. Thank you, baby." She reached up and kissed me on the lips.

I held her hand as she climbed into the back of the truck, and I climbed in behind her. Woody was probably going to be confused when I showed up with Astoria instead of Kami. We hadn't got on the phone since I got back from the Maldives, so I wasn't able to update him on what was new with me.

"How are the girls?" I hadn't seen the girls since Orlando, and I couldn't act like I didn't miss them.

"They're good. I've been trying to figure out what we're going to do for Christmas break. Me and Jace are supposed to sit down and toss everything on the table. I'm asking for all major holidays, and I don't care how he feels about it."

He had brought the savage out of her. I could tell she was ready to fight until she saw blood, and it wasn't shit he could do about it.

"Speaking of Christmas break."

"What are you about to ask me?" she smirked.

"I want to take you and the girls to Paris with me and my mom. I have to go and check out one of our new hotels that we're buying, and I wanted to make it a work trip, and have some fun too."

"Paris, Bray?"

"Yeah, you ever been?"

"Is that a trick question? No, I've never been, and my girls damn sure haven't either. The only countries they have visited were those on the cruise line."

I snorted. "I've never been on a cruise."

She turned fully in her seat. "Are you kidding me?"

"The thought of being on a boat for seven days doesn't sound appealing."

"And being on a yacht isn't the same thing?"

"I spend a few hours on yachts at most… the sea life ain't for me," I explained.

Laurent and Ashton were known for chartering a yacht for days at a time and hanging in the middle of the sea. It was cool for them. As for me, I needed to be on land when I closed my eyes at night. The wavering of the boat never sat right with me.

"We're going on a cruise next year... maybe we can do one to celebrate our divorces being finalized."

"I'm down for celebrating, Doc. You not getting me on no damn cruise ship," I told her.

She had this cute smirk fixed on her face. "Fine, whatever."

Stori was about to say something else, and her phone disrupted her. "Handle that."

She answered, putting her phone on speaker. "Hello?"

"Hey Astoria, I was trying to get Jace and couldn't get through to him. He left a message with the after-service care team. I was just calling to let you know his new script has been called in, and it should be ready tomorrow."

"Is his medicine changing?" Stori seemed confused by the whole conversation.

"Jace told me that he knocked all his pills in the kitchen sink this morning. Said he was trying to make coffee and take his medicine at the same time, and it ended horribly," the doctor chuckled.

"Thank you. I will let Jace know." Astoria kept it short and quickly ended the conversation.

She remained quiet for a while. "Everything good?"

"I felt like he was becoming too addicted to those damn pain meds. He would ask me to pick up his prescription when it wasn't due yet. He never waits the amount of time before each dosage, and now he's lying to the doctor to get more."

"How do you know he's lying?"

"Jace's medicine was nice and full when I left to go to the grocery store this morning. He's mobile now with the help of the walker, so he's not as unstable as he's making it seem."

"Those pain meds do more harm than good."

"And I warned him about them before he started taking them. He was in so much pain though."

"Doc, if you need to go home, we can cancel the dinner."

"Absolutely not. We have dinner reservations, and we're going to have a good time tonight. I will deal with him when I go home. I've put him first for too long. I'm not about to focus on him tonight."

I reached across and caressed her leg, inching my hand higher and higher up her leg. She kept looking at the driver and then back at me. Eventually, my hand had made it inside her panties, and I dipped my fingers into her honeypot. Pulling my fingers out, I sucked my fingers and looked at her.

"Needed a little taste until later."

"You gonna get yourself in trouble, Mr. Willshire."

"Only if it's with you." I reached over and kissed her on the lips.

We arrived at Carbone's and were seated right away. If you knew anything about Carbone's, you weren't getting reservations unless you were lucky, or putting money down for one. As we walked over to our table, I noticed my cousin.

"About time this knucklehead made his way back home." I slapped him in the back of the neck.

He stood up and smiled. "Put your hands on me one more time. I'm gonna bust yo' ass."

"I hear a little southern twang now?"

"Never that...I just live there... that's all."

I turned my attention to his girlfriend. "I'm finally meeting the beautiful Dr. Saanu Nathans. How are you doing, Love?"

She stood up and hugged me. "It feels good to finally meet you. I feel like we already know each other with how much you and Wood talk."

"For real." I stepped back and admired her beauty.

Much like me, Woody had a thing for curvier women, and I wasn't mad at it. "Nice to meet you. My rude ass cousin ain't introduce us. I'm Woody Willshire." Woody extended his hand and kissed both Astoria's cheeks.

"Hey, Woody. I'm Astoria Jacobs."

"Dr. Astoria Jacobs," I added.

Saanu smiled and greeted Astoria. "Hey, Dr. Jacobs. I love to meet other black women doing their thing."

"Girl, I could say the same thing about you."

We all sat down and ordered drinks and appetizers for the table while talking. This is why I fucked with my cousin so much. It was always good vibes when we got together. Neither of us spoke about work or dumb shit going on within the family.

Our main concern was spending quality time while we were in each other's cities. Woody was in town to visit his mother for the holidays. My uncle never married his mother, so our family never dealt with her. After she tried to run my uncle over, he left her crazy ass alone, and they just raised Woody together.

"So, what profession are you in, Astoria?" Woody asked before popping calamari into his mouth.

"I'm a therapist."

"Oh, alright... I see how you met. You were trying to help this looney nigga?"

Astoria grinned. "I specialize in marital therapy."

"I love that. We need more people who look like us helping our marriages. The divorce rate is seriously so damn high." Saanu joined in the conversation.

"Girl, and we're both about to add to it." She quickly looked at me before returning her focus back to Woody and Saanu.

"Been there and done that. So, no judgement here." She held her glass up and they both cheers to it.

"You're divorced?"

"Girl, yes. I couldn't wait for it to happen too."

"That's the same way I'm feeling about mine. I just want to be free from him, and then he can take a long walk off a short pier." Astoria snickered to herself.

"You and Kami decided to announce the marriage and then break up?"

"I didn't decide shit. She did that shit being petty because I asked for a divorce."

I spared Kami by not telling the truth about what really happened between us. "What happened?"

"We grew apart. She was focused on her career, and I was too focused on mine," I told half the truth.

"What makes Astoria different?" Saanu asked.

"She just is. I feel different with her, and I want her with me all the time. The urge to work all the time is subsiding because I'm rushing to spend time with her."

"Awe, Pa." She squeezed my cheeks.

"You know I want you to be happy in anything that you chose to do, and whoever you're with."

"For sure… I want the same for you."

"My baby is it for me." He pulled Saanu closer to him.

Woody and Saanu had been dating for a few years. I hadn't actually formally met her because our schedules were so different, and she was a doctor. Whenever Woody did travel back to New York, she was never with him because of her schedule. This was the first time we were able to meet and share a meal together.

"Do you plan on getting married again?"

"Girl, no," Saanu answered that question all too quickly. "I've done the marriage thing, and it ruins things in the end. Me and Wood are happy doing our own thing."

I wasn't so sure my cousin was feeling the same way as his girlfriend. Woody had a daughter from a previous relationship. He was engaged to his daughter's mother, and she called the wedding off. If it was one man that believed in commitment, it was his ass.

"Do whatever works for you. Some of the happiest couples out there aren't even married."

"Exactly. I love Woody, and he loves me... that is all that matters."

"You guys are so cute together."

"Love will give you what you need, but also take what you don't appreciate," I added.

"Deep, my brother," Woody reached out and dapped my hands.

"Very." Saanu smiled.

Astoria held my hand under the table while I ordered for the both of us. She enjoyed having me take control whenever we were together. She could be blindfolded walking through Times Square, and she knew that as long as she was with me, she was going to end up at her destination without a scratch or a scuff of the shoes.

Whenever she was with me, she didn't have to use her brain. I would handle everything for us. Astoria was used to having to make every decision in her life, and I didn't want that for her whenever she was with me. As my woman, she was going to live that soft life that she deserved.

"Dinner was amazing." Astoria leaned on me while we took the elevator up. "Let me use the bathroom, and then you can get me a car."

"Doc, I told you that you're not going home."

She folded her arms. "Well, you damn sure can't hold me captive here."

I lightly bit her on the neck, letting out a low growl. "Want to try me?"

"Tomorrow is Thanksgiving. Jace's mom is at the house, and I'm sure she's going to wonder why I'm doing the walk of shame in the morning."

"You got clothes here, so ain't no shame about you going home in the morning."

"Everything is always so planned out, huh?"

"When it comes to you... yes."

The elevator doors opened, and I spotted that the TV off to

the side was on. My mom was cuddled on the couch with popcorn watching her favorite series on Netflix.

"Hey, I was wondering what time you were going to get back."

When Astoria first came, she refused to come upstairs, even though she had met my mother already.

"Ma, you know how it is when me and Woody get to chatting."

Her eyes wandered over toward Astoria. "Hello, gorgeous. Are you staying with us tonight?"

"It's so nice to meet you again, Mrs. Willshire."

"Likewise."

"I'm actually going to head home after I use the bathroom."

My mother tossed the blanket off her body. "Nonsense. It's too late for you to take a car service home. I'll put some tea on for all of us." She smiled, grateful that she had someone to share her nightly tea with.

"Um, okay. Can I quickly go change?"

"Yep."

Astoria quickly headed to the bedroom and grabbed some of my clothes. While she stood naked in the closet, I pulled her into me and kissed her lips. "I love everything about this body."

"This body has been through a lot," she snorted.

"It birthed two amazing girls." I gripped a handful of her ass. "And God willing, it will give me some more."

"You really want kids?"

"I'm not against it."

"What happens if we never have children?"

"As long as I have you, I'm fine with that. Children aren't a deal breaker for me, Doc."

She relaxed and kissed me back, then tossed on my old college T-shirt and a pair of sweatpants. "You coming for tea?"

"Hell no. That tea is her beauty tea, and it tastes like poison. She been drinking that shit since I was eight."

"So, leave me to suffer alone?"

"Yup." I looked at my watch. "Actually, I need to shower and call Laurent real quick to bring liquor tomorrow."

"You real foul." She narrowed her eyes at me and left the bedroom to have tea with my mother.

I showered and called my brother to remind him to bring the good shit. We had a liquor store out in Long Island that carried the foreign good shit that would knock you on your ass.

When I was done, I went into the kitchen and found my mother and Stori laughing and talking.

"You like that nasty tea?"

"Oh, be quiet, Bray." My mother mushed me.

"It's not good, but she told me that's what she drinks, and she doesn't look a day over forty... so I'll sip it and mind Mrs. Carol's business."

"She's smart." My mother chugged the rest of her tea.

"You never did give me an answer."

"About what?" She asked confused.

"Paris."

My mother's eyes became wide with excitement. "Are you going to Paris?"

"I haven't decided yet."

"I invited her and both her daughters."

"The more the merrier. I'll have some company to take shopping... It's settled. You and your girls are coming." My mom clapped her hands, grabbed her empty cup, and went to refill it. "Goodnight. I need to be up to let the catering staff in."

"Night Mrs. Carol."

"Night, Mama."

My mother shuffled out the kitchen and I took her seat. "You are so slick."

"Nobody tells my mama no, so I guess you and the girls are coming with us."

"Oh goodness, they are going to lose their minds."

"You ready to give me some pussy?"

Astoria's eyes bucked out her head as she covered her face. "Bray! Your mom just left out the kitchen."

I stood up and pulled her out the kitchen chair. "Yeah, you ready." I picked her up and tossed her over my shoulder with ease.

While she kicked her feet and had a fit of giggles, I carried her to the room so we could do what did best.

SEVENTEEN
DR. ASTORIA JACOBS

THANKSGIVING WAS USUALLY MY FAVORITE HOLIDAY WHEN I WASN'T spending it with Verlonda, Jace's mother. She made me wish I had never met her damn son with the way she treated me. For years I put up with her shit to keep the peace in our home. I could always count on getting into multiple arguments when Verlonda was over. Me and Jace always ended the holiday arguing because me and his mother got into it.

For the sake of my peace and the peace of this home, I bit my tongue more than I should have. Thanksgiving was my holiday to prep all of my favorite meals and spend time with the girls. We would listen to music, cook, and then cuddle up on the couch while everything baked in the kitchen. Then, Jace started the tradition of going over to his mother's house so my peaceful holidays went out the window.

With my mind being everywhere with this divorce, I didn't feel like slaving away in the hot kitchen, and I damn sure didn't want to share my kitchen with Verlonda. She was more than welcome to cook the whole meal alone. She probably would have preferred that anyway.

Bray sent a car service to pick me up the night before. Luckily for me, the traffic wasn't thick on the ride back home. He tried to drive me himself and I refused. This was a time for us to spend with our families, and he wasn't about to miss out on that time because of me.

Harlym was in Virginia with our aunt. So, it wasn't like she was even home. Ember decided to take a solo trip out the country for the holiday. I didn't blame her though. The holidays since her divorce were hard on her. I made sure to check in on her every so often to see where her head was.

This holiday was going to be spent with Jace, the girls, his mom and me. His own sister wasn't coming this year. I celebrated when I heard she wasn't going to come. With the way her children tore my house up last year for Christmas, that was the last time they had been invited over. She didn't have any control over her kids, and never taught them any home training, so she wouldn't be missed.

"You usually spend the night out?" Verlonda asked when I came into the kitchen to make coffee.

Bray had me up all night in many different positions, and I was feeling it this morning. Sex with that man was amazing. He always made me feel like the most beautiful woman he's been with. In his eyes, I was the star.

"Now I do."

"Is that really appropriate being a married woman?"

I took a deep breath and popped the pod into my Nespresso. "Me and Jace are getting a divorce, so it doesn't matter what is appropriate."

"He told me about that. I thought you would have been smarter and reconsidered."

"Reconsider? I would be a fool to stay married to your son. You may think he's an angel," I sucked my teeth. "Try being married to him while raising kids. I'm not perfect, but your son is something else."

"I told Jace the minute you got that little degree that you would switch up. You've always felt like you were better than him because you went to college and got all those damn degrees."

"You've always hated me because I'm educated. I don't think I'm better than Jace; I know I am. And that has nothing to do with degrees. I treat people better than he does, and I'm not selfish or self-centered. So, yeah, I'm better."

"Morning, Mom... Did you tell Bray we said hi?" Enzo asked, and I kissed her on the head.

"Always do." I winked at Verlonda. If you looked close enough, you probably saw the steam coming from her ears. "Where's Demi?"

"In the shower."

I took my coffee into the living room and sat on the couch. This was where I planned to spend my day while stuffing my face. There was a small part of me that was unsure if I even wanted to eat the food she prepared. Her ass seemed like the type that would poison me.

After Demi finished in the shower, me and the girls sat and watched movies all day while Verlonda cooked in the kitchen. Enzo offered to help a few times and she shooed her out the kitchen. Demi kept reminding me that fighting with her wasn't worth it. Had she not continued to remind me of that, I was on my way in that kitchen to start World War Three with her mean ass.

Between dozing off and snacking on the desserts I had bought from the grocery store, I was ready for real food. The purpose of Thanksgiving was to eat all day until the main meal. That was how my family normally did things.

It was after five, and we were no close to eating because she was just now frying the chicken. "I'm starving, Mom," Demi complained.

"Me too," I agreed.

I made a mental promise that our holiday next year wouldn't look like this. Jace hadn't come out that back room yet, and

Verlonda only stayed in that kitchen. A few times she came out with her hands on her hip looking at what we were watching.

The one time she could have spent time with her grand-daughter, she shooed her out the kitchen. "I'm here!"

We looked over the couch, and Tyler came through the front door. "Hey, Ty," Demi greeted her brother.

"What's up, Ty?" Enzo followed up.

"Hey, Ty… I didn't know you were coming over."

"Grandma invited me and my mom over for Thanksgiving dinner."

All the hair on my body stood up when he mentioned what his bald-headed ass grandmother had done. "Ty, tell your mama not to even get out the car. She's not stepping foot in my house."

"Grandma said you were alright with it."

"Your grandmother is a liar."

"Tyler, I didn't know you were here. Come here, baby… look at you." Tyler was her favorite. Maybe because she preferred Tonya over me. Either way, Verlonda had crossed a line she couldn't gaslight her ass back over.

"Why the fuck did you tell her that she could come *in* my house?"

"Last I checked, this is your stepson, and this is my son's house too."

"Ty is always welcome here. His mother on the other hand isn't welcome, and you thought I was about to sit and break bread with this woman? Verlonda, use your fucking brain."

"What the hell?" Jace made his way into the front room with his cane. "What is going on? I'm trying to watch the game."

"Why did your mother invite Tonya for Thanksgiving dinner?" I looked over and noticed that he had changed out of his pajamas and was now fully dressed.

"You did what?" Even Jace was confused as to why his mother would do some wild shit like that.

Tonya wasn't an ex-wife, or even a ex-girlfriend that Jace had before we met. She was the other woman who knew about me and my daughters and proceeded to still sleep with him and have a baby by him. Jace was very much to blame because his loyalty was supposed to be toward me, however, I wasn't going to sit and accept this woman into my home.

"She's family." Verlonda doubled down on her actions without feeling any guilt. "We can sit and have a meal together. It's been years."

"Jace, you need to ask your mother to leave."

"What?"

"She has always disrespected me and my role as your wife, and you have never done anything about it. You allow her to get fly out the mouth and then fight with me when I match her energy. I don't care if she slaved in the kitchen all day, she needs to leave."

"Calm down. Ty, tell your mother that she can leave… you're going to stay." He turned his attention to his son, then to his mother. "You were dead wrong inviting her into our home. I don't care how you feel about Astoria. This is her house too and you need to respect that."

"You've always been a damn fool over her." She turned on her heels and went back into the kitchen. Verlonda didn't have an ounce of respect for anybody other than herself. It made sense why her son was the same way.

I crossed my arms and looked at Jace, who was stuck on what to do next. "She has to go."

"It's Thanksgiving. I'm not trying to hear all this damn drama, Astoria."

There he goes.

Whenever he felt cornered by a situation with his mother, he lashed out at me like I was the problem. "I'm supposed to sit here while she disrespects me?"

"Messiah is on his way to scoop me. I haven't been to the bar since the accident, and I need to get out this house."

The irony that not even a holiday on a Thursday could stop him from going out. "Wow."

"What now?"

"Nothing at all."

I had been done with Jace; however, this was the nail in the coffin. The iceberg that sank the ship. His mother just tried to invite his side bitch into our home, and all he could think about was going out with his friends.

"Speak your mind. You been running around here doing whatever you want anyway... You've already been done, huh?"

"You've been done way before I ever was."

The girls went up to their rooms, and Ty went to his, even though it was cluttered with all his father's shit. "Maybe I was. Tired of you always controlling everything and making me feel like less than a man."

"Really? I made you feel like less than a man? You've punished me every day of our marriage because I've made more than you or work harder than you. I've never made it a big deal because it wasn't a big deal to me."

"Sending me the mortgage so I can pay it like some bum on the street."

"Bitch, if the fucking tent fits, get inside it."

This wasn't my finest hour, and I was fine with that. I had been quiet, understandable, and all that other shit. That Astoria was gone, and she wasn't coming back anytime soon.

"I'm a bum now?"

"You have bum tendencies."

"Then why you still married to me?"

"Baby, that is a question for me and my future therapist. I tried to be the woman you wanted me to be, and I could never measure up. There was always some other woman that had your eye other than me. I gained weight carrying our children, and that was a problem for you. I joined the gym and did everything that I could to work the weight off, and that still wasn't enough. I'm done trying to please you. The quicker you sign those papers, the easier this will be."

"You been moving funny before mentioning divorce. I have

no problem signing the papers so you can head onto your new rich boyfriend."

"You are so childish."

"Got my daughters around that man, and I didn't even meet him."

"And do, will and can. I can bring my daughters around whoever I want. I know how to protect those girls and have been doing it since they were born."

He was trying to paint the picture like I brought a bunch of men around the girls. Bray was the first man they had met, and I had been dating him before exposing them to him. He wanted to be so protective of our daughters when it was convenient for him.

"You real low for turning my daughters against me."

"Jace, please respectfully go to hell. I have done nothing except encourage the relationship between you and the girls. You've been so occupied fucking Tonya that you don't see it."

"Why does Tonya bother you so bad? You seem triggered every time her name is mentioned." It was the smirk eased across his face that showed just how much he didn't give a fuck about me. My heart and feelings were just a game to him all these years, something that he never gave a fuck about.

That was what caused me to lose my shit.

"Do you fucking hate me that much? To open an old wound with the same knife you previously stabbed me with?"

After all the years I had given him, all he could give me was a shrug. Messiah honked his horn a few times, and he made his way toward the door. "Never hated you, Astoria."

"Yeah, well, you have a funny way of showing it. Your priorities had always been shit that you've wanted to do. Never about me or the girls."

"Yeah, believe that shit if you want to."

If you would have told me I would be having this argument in the middle of our living room on Thanksgiving, I would have laughed. Then again, I never imagined falling in love with another man while being married to Jace. I always believed that Jace was my soulmate mixed with a little piss. He wasn't perfect, and neither was I, so I stuck beside him.

If this marriage taught me one thing, it was to leave people where they had you fucked up at. Jace had me fucked up for a number of years and it was time for me to exit stage left. I couldn't sit here and pretend I was fine because I wasn't. This man disturbed my soul, bothered my spirt, and I needed to be away from him.

I headed upstairs, where I scared the girls who were listening in. "Um, girl, yeah, I was saying we can paint our bathroom," Demi tried to pretend they were talking about bathroom paint.

"You both are nosey." I bypassed them and went into my room.

"Are you okay, mom?" Enzo reached out and touched my shaking hand. "Breathe. You always tell me don't ever let another person have control over your emotions."

"You are so right, baby." I smiled as tears poured down my face.

Demi wiped my face. "Mom, can we go to Bray's? Grandma ruined the mood, and dad just left... He'll know how to fix things."

My heart jumped hearing my daughter mention that Bray would know how to fix it. She was right, he would know how to fix it and make it right. He told me that he wanted to always make everything right in my life, and he never wanted me to hesitate to ask for help.

"Pack some things... we're going to Bray's," I told them.

"All I needed to hear," Enzo dropped my damn hand so quickly and went into her room. Demi was right behind her. I shook my head, and at the same time felt blessed because the girls loved Bray. Now, did they actually love him or his penthouse and jet? Only time would tell.

Tyler had his mother come and pick him up, and Verlonda was still in the kitchen cooking when we left. I didn't bother to say shit to that hateful ass woman before we left. Since she thought her son was so damn perfect, she could sit across from his drunk ass whenever he returned from the bar with Messiah. Mrs. Carol was already sad that I wasn't staying for Thanksgiving dinner. I felt bad leaving, and now I realized I should have taken Bray's offer to pick the girls and spend it with his family. Bray's mother made me feel more welcomed than Verlonda ever did. She was the sweetest woman and had a lot of wisdom to offer. Me and my girls hopped on the freeway, and I headed straight to what felt right to me – *Pa*.

EIGHTEEN
BRAY WILLSHIRE

"PEOPLE GO ALL CRAZY FOR THIS TREE? IT LOOKS A LITTLE CRACK-ish to me." Demi shoved her hands into her pocket and leaned against Bray.

"You know what, I fuck with you." Ashton dapped Demi up.

She smirked. "We could be really cool if you shoot my dance pictures for free."

"Yo, this girl is a hustla... I respect the hustle." He looked at me, then at Astoria who was shaking her head.

The girls and Astoria were spending the weekend with me. We were leaving for Paris next week, and Astoria wanted to do all the corny tourist things with the girls. Neither of them was impressed by this tree or the funky ass lights.

"That's right... get those pictures," Astoria encouraged.

"Alright, I got you. Only if you bring your aunt with you." He winked.

Demi peeped game. "Oh, you feeling Auntie Har? Bro, I got you." They shook on the deal, and Ashton had a sly smirk on his face.

Harlym hadn't paid Ashton's ass any mind since the Maldives. She went as far as unfollowing him on social media. I've never seen Ashton so committed to trying to get on somebody's good side. His ass never gave a fuck about anyone's feelings except his own.

When Stori and the girls came to my house on Thanksgiving Day, I knew that was her way of telling me that she was all in. She didn't have to utter a word to me, I understood exactly what she meant. Since then, the girls had been coming back and forth with her to spend the weekends at my place.

I wanted the process for her divorce to be a simple one like me and Kami had. It took longer to chase her ass down to sign the papers than to get them finalized. Having a good lawyer also sped things along. My lawyer knew all the right people to get our divorce finalized before she moved to Miami.

Kami's moving men came and took all over her things, so she had nothing left in the house. Besides furniture and a few things that she didn't want, the house was pretty empty. It was a clean slate. We had a prenup, so she was technically supposed to leave with what she came in with. I wasn't cold-hearted, and it helped me sleep at night knowing she had that cushion to lean on. Not that she would need it. The promo for her new show was going crazy, and the station here had promo on all the trains and were supporting her switch.

Despite us not working out, I was proud of her and everything she did to bring her career where it was today. When she landed, she sent me what was her last text, and we haven't spoken since. I didn't need to reach out or speak to her all the time. What we had was over, and now we both needed to move on with our lives and be better people to the new people we decided to be with.

"Can I cook tonight?" Enzo questioned.

"Is it one of those TikTok recipes?"

"Yup. Found an orange chicken one that would be so good."

"I'm down."

Enzo was into cooking, and I wanted to encourage her. She was learning, and the food she had been making wasn't half bad. I couldn't wait to bring them to Paris so she could critique the food. In my opinion, the food in Paris wasn't the best. I hadn't had a meal there that made me want to fly out just for that one meal.

Astoria hadn't told them we were going to France because she wanted to surprise them. I think I was more excited than Stori. It was a struggle trying to hold this secret from them. Anytime I almost slipped, Stori would damn near tackle me to the floor to keep the secret in.

"It was cool kicking it with y'all today. I'm about to go be a grown man now, feel me?" Ashton dapped me up.

Ashton only tagged along with us because he thought Harlym would pop out. I was surprised when he stuck around after discovering that she wasn't coming with us.

"Later, Ash." Astoria hugged him.

We walked over to a small coffee shop near the tree that had a few free seats. While Astoria and the girls snagged seats, I grabbed us coffee and hot chocolate so we could warm up. I texted the driver to let him know our location and sat down beside Astoria.

"Thanks for today, Bray." Demi sipped her hot chocolate.

"This was all your mother's idea… I can't take credit for it."

"You didn't have to come with us, and you did. You even told us some fun facts that we didn't know. So, you can take a little credit," Enzo smiled at me.

"Appreciate that." I looked at Stori, who sipped her coffee slowly. "You alright, Doc?" I asked her.

"I'm tired. We've had a long day, and I really just need a nap."

"The car should be pulling up any minute. I hope you not getting sick before…" I allowed my voice to trail off, realizing I was about to spoil the surprise.

"Pa, just tell them," Astoria weakly chuckled.

"Tell us what?" Demi was the first to ask.

"I'm taking your mother and you girls to Paris next week."

Everyone in the crowded coffee shop jumped when the girls

jumped out of their seats squealing with joy. They didn't care who was watching them as they hugged each other.

"Are you shitting us?" Enzo shouted.

"I don't even have the energy to correct her ass." Astoria giggled.

"Yeah. We're gonna spend New Year's there too. This next surprise your moms don't know about."

"Oh lord, what are you about to say?"

The girls were on the edge of their seat waiting for me to tell them. "I set up private shopping so all three of y'all can get Paris ready. I have a meeting in Philly, so while I'm gone, you can spend time with the girls, Ember, and Harlym."

"Awe… that's so sweet."

I felt bad that I had to drive to Philly while they were staying at my place, so I set up a day of shopping for them to bond and have that time together.

"Bray, you really cool, bro. Now, are we taking the jet to Paris?"

I laughed. "Yeah, Dem."

"God bless you, brotha."

Demi and Enzo went to the movie room when we made it back to my place. I watched as Astoria stripped out of her clothes and took a quick shower. "Babe, you sure you're alright?"

"I've been feeling funny lately. With the way we've been on each other like bunnies, I wouldn't be surprised if you got me pregnant. I felt the same exact way when I was pregnant with Enzo."

"How do you feel about that?"

"Don't know yet. I do know I want to sleep and then wake up to finish that apple pie Enzo baked last night."

"Will you tell me when you figure out how you feel?"

"Yes, babe. I will let you know exactly how I feel." I sat down on the edge of the bed and kissed her on the lips. "You need to pack because you have an early morning."

"I love you, Astoria."

"I love you more. If I am pregnant, we will handle the situation when it happens."

"I want you and the girls to move into the house in Lennox Hills. Even if I don't move in, I want you and the girls to move in. I know your ex has been giving you shit about the house, and I don't want you to fight with him. Let him have it and move into that bigger one."

"Are you serious?"

"Dead serious. If he wants to fight over a house he can't afford, let that nigga have it. You said yourself that you're not emotionally attached to the house."

"I'm not."

"Then let him have it, as long as he signs the divorce papers and agrees on your terms for the custody of the girls."

"I want you to live in there with us, Bray," she told me.

"You sure?"

"Yes. We can talk to the girls about it, but I do want you to live there with us." She kissed me on the lips.

If her ex-husband wanted smoke, I was going to make his ass choke on the smoke he was causing. He wanted the house and was being stubborn about signing the papers until she allowed him to have it. Rather than drag out a whole divorce proceeding over a house she never liked, he could have that shit, and she could move into my house.

He shouldn't complain since the girls will remain in their same schools and within distance to split time between both houses. All I wanted was peace for Astoria, and that was what I planned to deliver. There were very few people in the world that deserved everything good, and she was one of them. If she was pregnant with my baby, she would never have to want for anything. Even if she wasn't pregnant, she would never want for anything because I was going to take care of her and the girls. Had she not been already married, I would have probably married her. All I had wanted was this feeling that I felt whenever she was near me. I spent my entire relationship with Kami chasing this feeling, and this woman had managed to pull those feelings out of me.

"I'm going to watch movies with the girls, and then I'll pack."

"Oh please, you're gonna wait until morning and then rush around trying to find stuff to pack," she called my bluff.

"Wanna place a bet?"

"Nope." She nuzzled her face into her pillow and closed her eyes. "Enjoy the movies."

"Love you, Doc."

"Love you too, Papa." She yawned and pulled the covers over her face.

NINETEEN
HARLYM 'HAR' JACOBS

"Yes!" I gasped. "I'm finally going to be able to see my man."
I danced in my chair while my sister and Ember stared at me.

"Don't you get to see him every other weekend?" Ember
nonchalantly asked while taking a picture of her food. I could
tell she wasn't interested in discussing my visitation schedule
with Cam.

"If you must know, he got into a fight, and he had his visits
taken away from him for the past month," I replied and
responded to the email the prison had just sent me.

Astoria rolled her eyes and put her phone on the table.
"When are you going to grow tired of this? Cam has been in
prison for the past two years, and you're still doing this back and
forth with him. When is enough ever going to be enough?"

"He's my man, Astoria." I stared at her like she had lost her
mind. "Am I supposed to end things because he's in prison?"

"What do you think is going to happen when he comes
home? You think he's going to want to start a family?"

"Um, yes. It's all we talk about when we're on the phone or
when I visit him. He wants the same things that I want, Stori." I
tried to convince her, like I always did whenever she decided to
pick apart my relationship.

She shook her head and took a sip of her orange juice. "All I want is for you to be happy. I don't want you wasting your life for a man that won't honor his word when he's on the outside. You're Harlym J. You can get any man you want and you're settling with this one."

"Why do you assume that he's not going to keep his word? Cam has always kept his word to me. Even with him being in prison, I still drive his cars and have money to make sure I'm well taken care of. Even my new content studio... he's the one who has been footing the bill for me to start it."

"You influencing does that. The car he provided, but you're the one who pays all the bills with the money you make from being an influencer and content creator. What money is he giving you?" Ember decided to chime in.

My sister has never been a fan of my relationship with Camren. Even my mother and aunt hated that I dedicated all these years to loving him. "Why do you both do this? Why can't anyone be happy for me? I get to see my man after not seeing him for a month. I'm always happy for anything that you both have going on, why can't either of you be happy for me?" I slapped my hand on the table, grabbed my purse, and stood up to leave.

"C'mon, Har... don't leave," Ember called behind me, but I was already up and heading out the door.

"Just let her leave. Whenever it comes to Cam, she either never tells us anything or pitches a fit when we're trying to tell her right from wrong." Astoria shook her head and finished her drink.

Astoria never failed to surprise me. It was bad enough I constantly had to defend my relationship to the world, but now I had to do it with her and Ember too. When Camren took the plea deal to do five years, we both knew what that meant for our relationship and future. We knew that meant we would have to wait to get married and have children. It wasn't an easy pill to swallow, but I knew that I wanted to be with Cam and eventually have a family one day. All I had to hold onto was our visits. Why couldn't my sister be happy for me instead of trying to lecture me on my relationship? It didn't matter if I didn't agree with their life decisions, I still supported them and never got into their business. Ember was so scared of being hurt again that she swore off men and tossed herself right into her work, and she was concerned about me and my man?

"Hello?" I answered my phone when I got into my car. I listened and waited for Cam's voice to come on after the automatic recording.

"Wassup, baby?" Cam's voice came through the line.

"Hey." I pulled away from valet and headed back to Lennox Hills. Today was supposed to be a beautiful shopping day filled with mimosas, gossip, and quality time with us girls. It went from that to me having to defend my actions and relationship to them.

"Aye, why you sound like that?" Cam could always tell when something was going on with me, and I hated it. I could never hide when I was having a bad day from him. I tried hard to hide my feelings from him because I knew he would end up stressing himself out over me. He was already locked up and needed to keep a clear head, so I didn't want to be another burden to him. I was supposed to be his light at the end of the tunnel, not the cloud.

"Nothing."

"Harlym, stop playing with me and tell me what's wrong."

"It's nothing, baby. Me and my Astoria got into a little argument over brunch."

"About us, again?"

"No."

"Stop flexing."

"Tell me about your day. Have you been keeping your head down and behaving yourself?"

"These niggas in here don't want no more smoke from me."

"Baby, if you keep fighting, then I'm never going to see you, and I miss you." I sulked. Seeing Cam every other week was the highlight of my life these days.

"You miss your nigga, huh?" I could picture him cheesing while holding the phone.

"Uh huh. I want you to give my booty a big squeeze."

"You already know I'm going to squeeze that big ass. I miss being out there with you and can't wait to get out."

"Three more years, baby. We can do this… I know we can." It was something that I constantly told myself so that I didn't drive myself crazy. Since me and Cam been together, we had never been away from each other. The past two years have been crazy, and I kept myself busy, so I didn't think about the fact that I was letting good years waste away while waiting on him. The fact remained that I desperately missed my man and wanted to be in his arms.

"Yeah," he paused. "How everything been going with your social media shit?"

"It's been busy."

"Busy is good."

I sighed. "I know. It helps keep my mind off us and everything we're facing."

"Stop stressing about it. You're the one who begged for me to take the plea deal, and now you want to stress about the shit." I hated whenever he snapped at me because he was frustrated with the situation we were in.

"It was better than the fifteen years you could have gotten if you went to trial," I argued. "Sometimes I don't know how or why I stuck by your side."

"Here we go with this shit again. Har, the shit happened two years ago, and you still on my ass about it."

Reed, Cam's cousin, baby mama, went into labor, so he couldn't take the usual drive from Virginia to New York. Instead of letting one of his other flunkies do the job, Cam decided he was going to be the one to go. He left for the weekend and was supposed to come back on that Monday. Little did I know he was fucking some Spanish bitch out there, and that trip was less about stepping in for his cousin, but more about killing two birds with one stone. Cam wanted to have his fun and handle business all in that one weekend. Meanwhile, I was home waiting on him to come back while he was out there playing me like a dummy.

When he crossed into New York, he was pulled over with that bitch in the car with him. Luckily for him, he had stopped at one of his stash houses in Jersey to unload before coming back to New York. So, all they ended up finding was a loaded gun and a couple pounds of weed. The cops arrested both of them. The only reason I found out about the woman was because I showed up to his court date, and there she was standing before the judge with him. Here I thought I was attending my man's court date, and I was really finding out the tea on what he had been up to.

My heart was shattered sitting in that courtroom with the media; meanwhile he was being arraigned with the bitch he was fucking. Cam didn't need to be in the street anymore because his rapping career was taking off, and now this had set him back even more. This whole time I thought what we had was real, and he was messing around with some out of town bitch. It wasn't like I had time to sit and forgive him. He was facing real time since this wasn't his first offense. Even with the best lawyers, he wasn't getting off without serving any time. Cam's head was so big from all the streets and music industry fame that he was willing to go to trial. He really thought that he was going to be able to walk out of the courthouse after hearing *not guilty*. As someone who used to want to be a criminal defense lawyer, I knew that wasn't going to be the outcome with his case, so I convinced him to take a plea deal.

Since Cam was caught with his pants down, he had no choice but to listen to me and his lawyer by taking the plea deal. I don't know how or why I forgave him for what he did. It took a lot for me to forgive Cam, and even now, I didn't know if he was truly forgiven. It wasn't like we had the chance to fix things because of his case and him being in jail the entire time. Just when I felt like I was on the verge of forgiving him, we got into stupid arguments like this one.

"Whatever, Cam," I dismissed him. Here I had spent time defending him to my sister, and he goes and proves everything she said about him right.

"Fuck you then, Harlym." He snarled.

"Yeah... thanks." I hung up the phone and tossed it into the passenger seat before heading home. I was so over this jail shit, and maybe I needed to stop being so stubborn and actually consider what Astoria was trying to tell me.

EPILOGUE

Dr. Astoria Jacobs

"Are you happy to be in Paris? Oui," Demi recited a famous TikTok sound as we walked back to our hotel from spending the day shopping with Carol.

Bray had been in and out of meetings the whole time we had been here, so we hadn't spent much time with him. He sent us out on different tours each day and made sure we weren't bored. I kept reminding him that it was hard to be bored while in Paris. It was still an adjustment accepting his credit card and not having any limit. This man didn't know what a budget was, and he expected the girls not to know what one was either. They were able to get any and everything they wanted, and he never told them no.

Whenever he did come back into our suite after a long day, they ran to tell him about our day. I thought they were so caught up in Bray's wealth that they didn't care about him as a person. They both proved me wrong. Enzo and Bray had reservations for this pastry-making class, and he and Demi were going to see a few shows while we were here.

The main reason I held onto my marriage with Jace was because of our girls. I worried what dating would look like after we were divorced. Would the girls hate or resent me because I divorced their father. That was something that I didn't want to happen, so I stayed with Jace as long as I did because of it. The girls and Bray had a great relationship without me, and that was all I wanted.

"Mama Carol, come on, you gotta say it with more attitude," Demi instructed Mrs. Carol on how to make her first TikTok.

"Who do you think invented attitude?"

"Alright, come on now," Enzo gassed her up.

Mrs. Carol loved spending time with the girls. When Bray did have time at night for a date, the girls would be in Mrs. Carol's room watching her do her skincare routine, which had many steps. I was enjoying my time here and couldn't have imagined being anywhere else with my girls and Bray.

"Welcome back, Mrs. Willshire and Dr. Jacobs," the doorman greeted us and quickly took our bags from us.

"I think I may go and take a nap before dinner. I'm not feeling all that good," I told Carol.

She leaned in next to me. "Take the test."

I let it slip on the jet that I was late and wasn't feeling too good. She didn't hesitate to send someone to scoop me a bunch of different pregnancy tests. "Will you wait in the bathroom with me?"

"Honey, if you want me to sit on the toilet with you, I will."

We both laughed because she was serious. "Okay."

The girls went to their rooms to decompress and upload all their videos while me and Carol went to the bathroom. I opened up the first box and was grateful it had English instructions included.

"How do you think the girls will feel?"

"Probably excited. At least I hope that they will be."

I went into the water closet and closed the door behind me. Peeing on the stick, I cleaned myself and went back into the main part of the bathroom. "We will all be excited for you. This is a new life you're bringing into this world. I know Bray will be the most excited."

I never pictured myself taking a pregnancy test in Paris with my boyfriend's mother. That was not what I had on my bingo card. For so long I had sacrificed my own happiness because I thought that was what I had to do. Every person I knew told me that marriage didn't mean flowers and rainbows every day. My marriage to Jace had never been flowers and rainbows. It was filled with so much regret, anger, and hurt. We were both emotionally immature when we got married, so our marriage never had the chance to mature.

Jace was hell bent on being bitter during this divorce. He was asking for shit that he never cared about or wanted. I told him he could have the house, and now he changed his mind and didn't want it. He tried asking for my truck, and I had to shut that down quick. Luckily, it was in Bray's name, so he had no claims to it. Jace was so angry that I had moved on, and he was taking it out on everyone else. It was his fault why he ended up losing me, and now he had to watch me be happy with someone else.

When it came to the girls, I wanted to make it as easy as possible. We can split holidays, and he can get them every weekend or every other weekend. The girls were old enough to have a say in how they wanted to spend their time. The only positive in this divorce was that we were all going to stay in the same area. We didn't need to pull the girls from their schools or commute between each other's houses.

I just wanted peace, so if I had to give up an ironing board, then he could have the shit. None of that shit in the house meant anything to me except my girl's pictures, awards, and trophies. Everything else, he could jump off a bridge with it, and it wouldn't mean shit to me. Bray hired me a good divorce lawyer that was certain that she would be able to get this divorce filed and closed without much back and forth.

If Jace was smart, he would accept the little bending I was doing in order to keep this peaceful. I wasn't even asking for child support, which I could have since our daughters were fifteen and fourteen years old. I wanted to be the bitch that busted up his life so bad, but what for? I was receiving blessings while he was still hobbling around on partial disability. His karma was already eating his ass up, so I didn't have to do anything more.

"Pregnant," Carol held the test up.

"Wow." No other words left my mouth. Even though deep down I knew I was pregnant, I still didn't believe it. Seeing that little positive sign on the test solidified that I was having Bray's baby.

With the way we been humping like bunnies, I shouldn't have been surprised. We started off using protection, and then somewhere along the line, the quickies were too quick for him to strap up. It was so soon in our relationship and that was the part that scared me. Babies changed everything, and I never wanted anything to change between the both of us.

"You're in shock," Carol wrapped her arms around me and kissed my cheeks. "I'm going to be a grammy again."

"Yes, you are."

"Are you alright?"

"Just shocked. I am happy, this is just unexpected." I hugged her back.

"You make my son so happy, and I can see he does the same for you. When love is involved, time never matters. I fell in love with Bray's father in one weekend. I knew when that weekend was over that I wanted to spend forever with that man, and I did until his last breath."

Now we were both wiping tears away. "I'm sorry."

"Don't be. I experienced the greatest love of my life. Was it perfect? No. Show me a love that is perfect, and I'll show you a liar. A love like the one you and Bray share only comes around once in a blue moon."

"Thank you, Mrs. Carol." I hugged her tightly.

She spoke so highly of her husband and the love they shared. Bray was a direct result of the love they shared, and if we could even have half of that, I would be satisfied.

"HAPPY NEW YEAR, AUNTIE!" I smiled into the phone, knowing there was a time difference. She would more than likely be asleep by the time the ball dropped back home.

Keeping my pregnancy a secret from Bray these past few days had been so hard. I wanted to reveal it to him in my own way, and tonight was perfect. Ember, Harlym, Ashton, and Laurent flew in to celebrate New Year's with us. My mom was staying at Harlym's house with my aunt while she was here in Paris.

"Thank you, baby. How is it there? Does it get crazy like here?"

"Girl, yes. Fireworks and everything. Look," I flipped the camera so she could see the Eiffel Tower. "You see it?"

"It's beautiful, Stori. I've always wanted to visit it."

"Auntie, we will come back here the day you're in remission. I promise you." I held back my tears as I watched her.

Harlym had tears in her eyes. "We will eat in the restaurant and pop the most expensive fucking bottle," she added.

Ashton was sitting next to her. I was waiting for him to say something slick, but instead, he handed her a napkin. "And that's on me." He said.

I smiled at him. "I'm holding all of you to it." She pointed her finger at me.

"Hey Auntie, how you feeling?" Bray came behind me and got into the camera.

"Better. Radiation is always so rough on me. I want to thank you for helping us with that oncologist."

"We're family."

"We never count favors," Ashton said.

When she yawned for the third time, I knew she was tired. "Alright, Auntie. I will call you tomorrow. I have some news to tell you."

"Okay. Love you, girls."

"Love you more." I handed Harlym back her phone.

Em was over near the bar on facetime. I waited patiently while she finished up her call and then hugged her. "Happy New Year, Em."

"Whew, we've had a tough year."

"We did." I held her closer to me and whispered. "I'm pregnant."

She pulled back with wide eyes. "Are you serious?"

"I wanted to tell you because I know how sens—"

"No. We're not doing that. I am happy for you, Astoria. Just because my blessing hasn't happened doesn't mean I'm not happy. Does Bray know?"

"I'm going to tell him later."

"You deserve this and everything that is happening for you and the girls." She hugged me tightly.

"Thank you, Em."

"See, it was worth going on that trip." She winked.

Everyone danced until the early hours of the morning. Me and Bray went out onto the patio, and the Eiffel Tower lights had been shut off. "Damn, they turn it off?"

"Apparently so." He wrapped his arms around me and kissed me on the neck. "I haven't been honest with you, Bray."

I could feel his body tense up behind me. "Doc, let's enjoy tonight."

"I have to get this off my chest." I turned around and stared up at him.

I dug into the wide leg trouser pants I wore and placed the pregnancy test into his hand. "You're pregnant?"

"Yes."

Bray swooped in and picked me up while spinning me around. "I knew it. I fucking knew I had knocked you up."

"How?"

"You've been tired all the time, and you started getting picky with the food you wanted. I felt like something was off with you."

"Well, now we know why."

"Do you know how you feel about it yet?"

"I'm happy. Excited that I get to go on this journey with you. I raised two babies in survival mode, and I never got to truly enjoy them because I was so busy trying to make sure we could afford to eat. I guess I'm excited to experience being a mother that has time to spend with her newborn."

"I know how much your career means to you, so I would never ask you to quit."

"Not quit. I am okay with taking some time away to focus on having a healthy baby." He was surprised by my response.

I had a man that wanted to take care of me, and I was going to allow him to do it. Bray had told me numerous times that I didn't have to work unless I wanted to. With me and the girls moving into the new house with him, I wanted to focus on this pregnancy and turning that house into *our* home.

Bray kissed me on the lips. "I love the shit out of you, Astoria."

"I love you so much more, Baby. Thank you." I kissed him on the lips and rested my head on his chest.

Whenever someone used to ask me if I was alright, my natural response was to say that I was fine and then thank them for their concern. The truth was that I was never actually fine and had been operating on autopilot. Masking my emotions because I knew that the person I was with didn't give a damn about them. Now, whenever someone asked if I was alright, I could say that I was fine and actually mean it.

The End

Made in the USA
Columbia, SC
03 November 2023

25279792R00195